D1607297

Table Talk: Essays on Men and Manners

by William Hazlitt

Copyright © 7/7/2015
Jefferson Publication

ISBN-13: 978-1514869260

Contents

VOLUME I

ESSAY I. ON THE PLEASURE OF PAINTING

'There is a pleasure in painting which none but painters know.' In writing, you have to contend with the world; in painting, you have only to carry on a friendly strife with Nature. You sit down to your task, and are happy. From the moment that you take up the pencil, and look Nature in the face, you are at peace with your own heart. No angry passions rise to disturb the silent progress of the work, to shake the hand, or dim the brow: no irritable humours are set afloat: you have no absurd opinions to combat, no point to strain, no adversary to crush, no fool to annoy—you are actuated by fear or favour to no man. There is 'no juggling here,' no sophistry, no intrigue, no tampering with the evidence, no attempt to make black white, or white black: but you resign yourself into the hands of a greater power, that of Nature, with the simplicity of a child, and the devotion of an enthusiast—'study with joy her manner, and with rapture taste her style.' The mind is calm, and full at the same time. The hand and eye are equally employed. In tracing the commonest object, a plant or the stump of a tree, you learn something every moment. You perceive unexpected differences, and discover likenesses where you looked for no such thing. You try to set down what you see—find out your error, and correct it. You need not play tricks, or purposely mistake: with all your pains, you are still far short of the mark. Patience grows out of the endless pursuit, and turns it into a luxury. A streak in a flower, a wrinkle in a leaf, a tinge in a cloud, a stain in an old wall or ruin grey, are seized with avidity as the *spolia opima* of this sort of mental warfare, and furnish out labour for another half-day. The hours pass away untold, without chagrin, and without weariness; nor would you ever wish to pass them otherwise. Innocence is joined with industry, pleasure with business; and the mind is satisfied, though it is not engaged in thinking or in doing any mischief.(1)

I have not much pleasure in writing these *Essays*, or in reading them afterwards; though I own I now and then meet with a phrase that I like, or a thought that strikes me as a true one. But after I begin them, I am only anxious to get to the end of them, which I am not sure I shall do, for I seldom see my way a page or even a sentence beforehand; and when I have as by a miracle escaped, I trouble myself little more about them. I sometimes have to write them twice over: then it is necessary to read the *proof*, to prevent mistakes by the printer; so that by the time they appear in a tangible shape, and one can con them over with a conscious, sidelong glance to the public approbation, they have lost their gloss and relish, and become 'more tedious than a twice-told tale.' For a person to read his own works over with any great delight, he ought first to forget that he ever wrote them. Familiarity naturally breeds contempt. It is, in fact, like poring fondly over a piece of blank paper; from repetition, the words convey no distinct meaning to the mind—are mere idle sounds, except that our vanity claims an interest and property in them. I have more satisfaction in my own thoughts than in dictating them to others: words are necessary to explain the impression of certain things upon me to the reader, but they rather weaken and draw a veil over than strengthen it to myself. However I might say with the poet, 'My mind to me a kingdom is,' yet I have little ambition 'to set a throne or chair of state in the understandings of other men.' The ideas we cherish most exist best in a kind of shadowy abstraction,

Pure in the last recesses of the mind,

and derive neither force nor interest from being exposed to public view. They are old familiar acquaintance, and any change in them, arising from the adventitious ornaments of style or dress, is little to their advantage. After I have once written on a subject, it goes out of my mind: my feelings about it have been melted down into words, and *then* I forget. I have, as it were, discharged my memory of its old habitual reckoning, and rubbed out the score of real sentiment. For the future it exists only for the sake of others. But I cannot say, from my own experience, that the same process takes place in transferring our ideas to canvas; they gain more than they lose in the mechanical transformation. One is never tired of painting, because you have to set down not what you knew already, but what you have just discovered. In the former case you translate feelings into words; in the latter, names into things. There is a continual creation out of nothing going on. With every stroke of the brush a new field of inquiry is laid open; new difficulties arise, and new triumphs are prepared over them. By comparing the imitation with the original, you see what you have done, and how much you have still to do. The test of the senses is severer than that of fancy, and an over-match even for the delusions of our self-love. One part of a picture shames another, and you determine to paint up to yourself, if you cannot come up to Nature. Every object becomes lustrous from the light thrown back upon it by the mirror of art: and by the aid of the pencil we may be said to touch and handle the objects of sight. The air-drawn visions that hover on the verge of existence have a bodily presence given them on the canvas: the form of beauty is changed into a substance: the dream and the glory of the universe is made 'palpable to feeling as well as sight.'—And see! a rainbow starts from the canvas, with its humid train of glory, as if it were drawn from its cloudy arch in heaven. The spangled landscape glitters with drops of dew after the shower. The 'fleecy fools' show their coats in the gleams of the setting sun. The shepherds pipe their farewell notes in the fresh evening air. And is this bright vision made from a dead, dull blank, like a bubble reflecting the mighty fabric of the universe? Who would think this miracle of Rubens' pencil possible to be performed? Who, having seen it, would not spend his life to do the like? See how the rich fallows, the bare stubble-field, the scanty harvest-home, drag in Rembrandt's landscapes! How often have I looked at them and nature, and tried to do the same, till the very 'light thickened,' and there was an earthiness in the feeling of the air! There is no end of the refinements of art and nature in this respect. One may look at the misty glimmering horizon till the eye dazzles and the imagination is lost, in hopes to transfer the whole interminable expanse at one blow upon the canvas. Wilson said, he used to try to paint the effect of the motes dancing in the setting sun. At another time, a friend, coming into his painting-room when he was sitting on the ground in a melancholy posture, observed that his picture looked like a landscape after a shower: he started up with the greatest delight, and said, 'That is the effect I intended to produce, but thought I had failed.' Wilson was neglected; and, by degrees, neglected his art to apply himself to brandy. His hand became unsteady, so that it was only by repeated attempts that he could reach the place or produce the effect he aimed at; and when he had done a little to a picture, he would say to any acquaintance who chanced to drop in, 'I have painted enough for one day: come, let us go somewhere.' It was not so Claude left his pictures, or his studies on the banks of the Tiber, to go in search of other enjoyments, or ceased to gaze upon the glittering sunny vales and distant hills; and while his eye drank in the clear sparkling hues and lovely forms of nature, his hand stamped them on the lucid canvas to last there for ever! One of the most delightful parts of my life was one fine summer, when I used to walk out of an evening to catch the last light of the sun, gemming the green slopes or russet lawns, and gilding tower or tree, while the blue sky, gradually turning to purple and gold, or skirted with dusky grey, hung its broad marble pavement over all, as we see it in the great master of Italian landscape. But to come to a more particular explanation of the subject:—

The first head I ever tried to paint was an old woman with the upper part of the face shaded by her bonnet, and I certainly laboured (at) it with great perseverance. It took me numberless sittings to do it. I have it by me still, and sometimes look at it with surprise, to think how much pains were thrown away to little purpose,—yet not altogether in vain if it taught me to see good in everything, and to know that there is nothing vulgar in Nature seen with the eye of science or of true art. Refinement creates beauty everywhere: it is the grossness of the spectator that discovers nothing but grossness in the object. Be this as it may, I spared no pains to do my best. If art was long, I thought that life was so too at that moment. I got in the general effect the first day; and pleased and surprised enough I was at my success. The rest was a work of time—of weeks and months (if need were), of patient toil and careful finishing. I had seen an old head by Rembrandt at Burleigh House, and if I could produce a head at all like Rembrandt in a year, in my lifetime, it would be glory and felicity and wealth and fame enough for me! The head I had seen at Burleigh was an exact and wonderful facsimile of nature, and I resolved to make mine (as nearly as I could) an exact facsimile of nature. I did not then, nor do I now believe, with Sir Joshua, that the perfection of art consists in giving general appearances without individual details, but in giving general appearances with individual details. Otherwise, I had done my work the first day. But I saw something more in nature than general effect, and I thought it worth my while to give it in the picture. There was a gorgeous effect of light and shade; but there was a delicacy as well as depth in the chiaroscuro which I was bound to follow into its dim and scarce perceptible variety of tone and shadow. Then I had to make the transition from a strong light to as dark a shade, preserving the masses, but gradually softening off the intermediate parts. It was so in nature; the difficulty was to make it so in the copy. I tried, and failed again and again; I strove harder, and succeeded as I thought. The wrinkles in Rembrandt were not hard lines, but broken and irregular. I saw the same appearance in nature, and strained every nerve to give it. If I could hit off this edgy appearance, and insert the reflected light in the furrows of old age in half a morning, I did not think I had lost a day. Beneath the shrivelled yellow parchment look of the skin, there was here and there a streak of the blood-colour tinging the face; this I made a point of conveying, and did not cease to compare what I saw with what I did (with jealous, lynx-eyed watchfulness) till I succeeded to the best of my ability and judgment. How many revisions were there! How many attempts to catch an expression which I had seen the day before! How often did we try to get the old position, and wait for the return of the same light! There was a puckering up of the lips, a cautious introversion of the eye under the shadow of the bonnet, indicative of the feebleness and suspicion of old age, which at last we managed, after many trials and some quarrels, to a tolerable nicety. The picture was never finished, and I might have gone on with it to the present hour.(2) I used to sit it on the ground when my day's work was done, and saw revealed to me with swimming eyes the birth of new hopes and of a new world of objects. The painter thus learns to look at Nature with different eyes. He before saw her 'as in a glass darkly, but now face to face.' He understands the texture and meaning of the visible universe, and 'sees into the life of things,' not by the help of mechanical instruments, but of the improved exercise of his faculties, and an intimate sympathy with Nature. The meanest thing is not lost upon him, for he looks at it with an eye to itself, not merely to his own vanity or interest, or the opinion of the world. Even where there is neither beauty nor use—if that ever were—still there is truth, and a sufficient source of gratification in the indulgence of curiosity and activity of mind. The humblest printer is a true scholar; and the best of scholars—the scholar of Nature. For myself, and for the real comfort and satisfaction of the thing, I had rather have been Jan Steen, or Gerard Dow, than the greatest casuist or philologer that ever lived. The painter does not view things in clouds or 'mist, the common gloss of theologians,' but applies the same standard of truth and disinterested spirit of inquiry, that influence his daily practice, to other subjects. He perceives form, he distinguishes character. He reads men and books with an intuitive eye. He is a critic as well as a connoisseur. The conclusions he draws are clear and convincing, because they are taken from the things themselves. He is not a fanatic, a dupe, or a slave; for the habit of seeing for himself also disposes him to judge for himself. The most sensible men I know (taken as a class) are painters; that is, they are the most lively observers of what passes in the world about them, and the closest observers of what passes in their own minds. From their profession they in general mix more with the world than authors; and if they have not the same fund of acquired knowledge, are obliged to rely more on individual sagacity. I might mention the names of Opie, Fuseli, Northcote, as persons distinguished for striking description and acquaintance with the subtle traits of character.(3) Painters in ordinary society, or in obscure situations where their value is not known, and they are treated with neglect and indifference, have sometimes a forward self-sufficiency of manner; but this is not so much their fault as that of others. Perhaps their want of regular education may also be in fault in such cases. Richardson, who is very tenacious of the respect in which the profession ought to be held, tells a story of Michael Angelo, that after a quarrel between him and Pope Julius II., 'upon account of a slight the artist conceived the pontiff had put upon him, Michael Angelo was introduced by a bishop, who, thinking to serve the artist by it, made it an argument that the Pope should be reconciled to him, because men of his profession were commonly ignorant, and of no consequence otherwise; his holiness, enraged at the bishop, struck him with his staff, and told him, it was he that was the blockhead, and affronted the man himself would not offend: the prelate was driven out of the chamber, and Michael Angelo had the Pope's benediction, accompanied with presents. This bishop had fallen into the vulgar error, and was rebuked accordingly.'

Besides the exercise of the mind, painting exercises the body. It is a mechanical as well as a liberal art. To do anything, to dig a hole in the ground, to plant a cabbage, to hit a mark, to move a shuttle, to work a pattern,—in a word, to attempt to produce any effect, and to *succeed,* has something in it that gratifies the love of power, and carries off the restless activity of the mind of man. Indolence is a delightful but distressing state; we must be doing something to be happy. Action is no less necessary than thought to the instinctive tendencies of the human frame; and painting combines them both incessantly.(4) The hand is furnished a practical test of the correctness of the eye; and the eye, thus admonished, imposes fresh tasks of skill and industry upon the hand. Every stroke tells as the verifying of a new truth; and every new observation, the instant it is made, passes into an act and emanation of the will. Every step is nearer what we wish, and yet there is always more to do. In spite of the facility, the fluttering grace, the evanescent hues, that play round the pencil of Rubens and Van-dyke, however I may admire, I do not envy them this power so much as I do the slow, patient, laborious execution of Correggio, Leonardo da Vinci, and Andrea del Sarto, where every touch appears conscious of its charge, emulous of truth, and where the painful artist has so distinctly wrought,

    That you might almost say his picture thought.

In the one case the colours seem breathed on the canvas as if by magic, the work and the wonder of a moment; in the other they seem inlaid in the body of the work, and as if it took the artist years of unremitting labour, and of delightful never-ending progress to perfection.(5) Who would wish ever to come to the close of such works,—not to dwell on them, to return to them, to be wedded to them to the last? Rubens, with his florid, rapid style, complains that when he had just learned his art, he should be forced to die. Leonardo, in the slow advances of his, had lived long enough!

Painting is not, like writing, what is properly understood by a sedentary employment. It requires not indeed a strong, but a continued and steady exertion of muscular power. The precision and delicacy of the manual operation, makes up for the want of vehemence,—as to balance himself for any time in the same position the rope-dancer must strain every nerve. Painting for a whole morning gives one as excellent an appetite for one's dinner as old Abraham Tucker acquired for his by riding over Banstead Downs. It is related of Sir Joshua Reynolds, that 'he took no other exercise than what he used in his painting-room,'—the writer means, in walking backwards and forwards to look at his picture; but the act of painting itself, of laying on the colours in the proper place and proper quantity, was a much harder exercise than this alternate receding from and returning to the picture. This last would be rather a relaxation and relief than an effort. It is not to be wondered at, that an artist like Sir Joshua, who delighted so much in the sensual and practical part of his art, should have found himself at a considerable loss when the decay of his sight precluded him, for the last year or two of his life, from the following up of his profession,—'the source,' according to his own remark, 'of thirty years' uninterrupted enjoyment and prosperity to him.' It is only those who never think at all, or else who have accustomed themselves to brood incessantly on abstract ideas, that never feel ennui.

To give one instance more, and then I will have done with this rambling discourse. One of my first attempts was a picture of my father, who was then in a green old age, with strong-marked features, and scarred with the smallpox. I drew it out with a broad light crossing the face, looking down, with spectacles on, reading. The book was Shaftesbury's *Characteristics*, in a fine old binding, with Gribelin's etchings. My father would as lieve it had been any other book; but for him to read was to be content, was 'riches fineless.' The sketch promised well; and I set to work to finish it, determined to spare no time nor pains. My father was willing to sit as long as I pleased; for there is a natural desire in the mind of man to sit for one's picture, to be the object of continued attention, to have one's likeness multiplied; and besides his satisfaction in the picture, he had some pride in the artist, though he would rather I should have written a sermon than painted like Rembrandt or like Raphael. Those winter days, with the gleams of sunshine coming through the chapel-windows, and cheered by the notes of the robin-redbreast in our garden (that 'ever in the haunch of winter sings'),—as my afternoon's work drew to a close,—were among the happiest of my life. When I gave the effect I intended to any part of the picture for which I had prepared my colours; when I imitated the roughness of the skin by a lucky stroke of the pencil; when I hit the clear, pearly tone of a vein; when I gave the ruddy complexion of health, the blood circulating under the broad shadows of one side of the face, I thought my fortune made; or rather it was already more than made, I might one day be able to say with Correggio, '*I also am a painter!*' It was an idle thought, a boy's conceit; but it did not make me less happy at the time. I used regularly to set my work in the chair to look at it through the long evenings; and many a time did I return to take leave of it before I could go to bed at night. I remember sending it with a throbbing heart to the Exhibition, and seeing it hung up there by the side of one of the Honourable Mr. Skeffington (now Sir George). There was nothing in common between them, but that they were the portraits of two very good-natured men. I think, but am not sure, that I finished this portrait (or another afterwards) on the same day that the news of the battle of Austerlitz came; I walked out in the afternoon, and, as I returned, saw the evening star set over a poor man's cottage with other thoughts and feelings than I shall ever have again. Oh for the revolution of the great Platonic year, that those times might come over again! I could sleep out the three hundred and sixty-five thousand intervening years very contentedly!—The picture is left: the table, the chair, the window where I learned to construe Livy, the chapel where my father preached, remain where they were; but he himself is gone to rest, full of years, of faith, of hope, and charity!

FN to ESSAY I

(1) There is a passage in Werter which contains a very pleasing illustration of this doctrine, and is as follows:—

'About a league from the town is a place called Walheim. It is very agreeably situated on the side of a hill: from one of the paths which leads out of the village, you have a view of the whole country; and there to a good old woman who sells wine, coffee, and tea there: but better than all this are two lime-trees before the church, which spread their branches over a little green, surrounded by barns and cottages. I have seen few places more retired and peaceful. I send for a chair and table from the old woman's, and there I drink my coffee and read Homer. It was by accident that I discovered this place one fine afternoon: all was perfect stillness; everybody was in the fields, except a little boy about four years old, who was sitting on the ground, and holding between his knees a child of about six months; he pressed it to his bosom with his little arms, which made a sort of great chair for it; and notwithstanding the vivacity which sparkled in his eyes, he sat perfectly still. Quite delighted with the scene, I sat down on a plough opposite, and had great pleasure in drawing this little picture of brotherly tenderness. I added a bit of the hedge, the barn-door, and some broken cart-wheels, without any order, just as they happened to lie; and in about an hour I found I had made a drawing of great expression and very correct design without having put in anything of my own. This confirmed me in the resolution I had made before, only to copy Nature for the future. Nature is inexhaustible, and alone forms the greatest masters. Say what you will of rules, they alter the true features and the natural expression.'

(2) It is at present covered with a thick slough of oil and varnish (the perishable vehicle of the English school), like an envelope of goldbeaters' skin, so as to be hardly visible.

(3) Men in business, who are answerable with their fortunes for the consequences of their opinions, and are therefore accustomed to ascertain pretty accurately the grounds on which they act, before they commit themselves on the event, are often men of remarkably quick and sound judgements. Artists in like manner must know tolerably well what they are about, before they can bring the result of their observations to the test of ocular demonstration.

(4) The famous Schiller used to say, that he found the great happiness of life, after all, to consist in the discharge of some mechanical duty.

(5) The rich *impasting* of Titian and Giorgione combines something of the advantages of both these styles, the felicity of the one with the carefulness of the other, and is perhaps to be preferred to either.

ESSAY II. THE SAME SUBJECT CONTINUED

The painter not only takes a delight in nature, he has a new and exquisite source of pleasure opened to him in the study and contemplation of works of art—

```
Whate'er Lorraine light touch'd with soft'ning hue,
Or savage Rosa dash'd, or learned Poussin drew.
```

He turns aside to view a country gentleman's seat with eager looks, thinking it may contain some of the rich products of art. There is an air round Lord Radnor's park, for there hang the two Claudes, the Morning and Evening of the Roman Empire—round Wilton House, for there is Vandyke's picture of the Pembroke family—round Blenheim, for there is his picture of the Duke of Buckingham's children, and the most magnificent collection of Rubenses in the world—at Knowsley, for there is Rembrandt's Handwriting on the Wall—and at Burleigh, for there are some of Guido's angelic heads. The young artist makes a pilgrimage to each of these places, eyes them wistfully at a distance, 'bosomed high in tufted trees,' and feels an interest in them of which the owner is scarce conscious: he enters the well-swept walks and echoing archways, passes the threshold, is led through wainscoted rooms, is shown the furniture, the rich hangings, the tapestry, the massy services of plate—and, at last, is ushered into the room where his treasure is, the idol of his vows—some speaking face or bright landscape! It is stamped on his brain, and lives there thenceforward, a tally for nature, and a test of art. He furnishes out the chambers of the mind from the spoils of time, picks and chooses which shall have the best places—nearest his heart. He goes away richer than he came, richer than the possessor; and thinks that he may one day return, when he perhaps shall have done something like them, or even from failure shall have learned to admire truth and genius more.

My first initiation in the mysteries of the art was at the Orleans Gallery: it was there I formed my taste, such as it is; so that I am irreclaimably of the old school in painting. I was staggered when I saw the works there collected, and looked at them with wondering and with longing eyes. A mist passed away from my sight: the scales fell off. A new sense came upon me, a new heaven and a new earth stood before me. I saw the soul speaking in the face—'hands that the rod of empire had swayed' in mighty ages past—'a forked mountain or blue promontory,'

```
—with trees upon't
That nod unto the world, and mock our eyes with air.
```

Old Time had unlocked his treasures, and Fame stood portress at the door. We had all heard of the names of Titian, Raphael, Guido, Domenichino, the Caracci—but to see them face to face, to be in the same room with their deathless productions, was like breaking some mighty spell—was almost an effect of necromancy! From that time I lived in a world of pictures. Battles, sieges, speeches in parliament seemed mere idle noise and fury, 'signifying nothing,' compared with those mighty works and dreaded names that spoke to me in the eternal silence of thought. This was the more remarkable, as it was but a short time before that I was not only totally ignorant of, but insensible to the beauties of art. As an instance, I remember that one afternoon I was reading *The Provoked Husband* with the highest relish, with a green woody landscape of Ruysdael or Hobbima just before me, at which I looked off the book now and then, and wondered what there could be in that sort of work to satisfy or delight the mind—at the same time asking myself, as a speculative question, whether I should ever feel an interest in it like what I took in reading Vanbrugh and Cibber?

I had made some progress in painting when I went to the Louvre to study, and I never did anything afterwards. I never shall forget conning over the Catalogue which a friend lent me just before I set out. The pictures, the names of the painters, seemed to relish in the mouth. There was one of Titian's Mistress at her toilette. Even the colours with which the painter had adorned her hair were not more golden, more amiable to sight, than those which played round and tantalised my fancy ere I saw the picture. There were two portraits by the same hand—'A young Nobleman with a glove'—Another, 'a companion to it.' I read the description over and over with fond expectancy, and filled up the imaginary outline with whatever I could conceive of grace, and dignity, and an antique gusto—all but equal to the original. There was the Transfiguration too. With what awe I saw it in my mind's eye, and was overshadowed with the spirit of the artist! Not to have been disappointed with these works afterwards, was the highest compliment I can pay to their transcendent merits. Indeed, it was from seeing other works of the same great masters that I had formed a vague, but no disparaging idea of these. The first day I got there, I was kept for some time in the French Exhibition Room, and thought I should not be able to get a sight of the old masters. I just caught a peep at them through the door (vile hindrance!) like looking out of purgatory into paradise—from Poussin's noble, mellow-looking landscapes to where Rubens hung out his gaudy banner, and down the glimmering vista to the rich jewels of Titian and the Italian school. At last, by much importunity, I was admitted, and lost not an instant in making use of my new privilege. It was *un beau jour* to me. I marched delighted through a quarter of a mile of the proudest efforts of the mind of man, a whole creation of genius, a universe of art! I ran the gauntlet of all the schools from the bottom to the top; and in the end got admitted into the inner room, where they had been repairing some of their greatest works. Here the Transfiguration, the St. Peter Martyr, and the St. Jerome of Domenichino stood on the floor, as if they had bent their knees, like camels stooping, to unlade their riches to the spectator. On one side, on an easel, stood Hippolito de Medici (a portrait by Titian), with a boar-spear in his hand, looking through those he saw, till you turned away from the keen glance; and thrown together in heaps were landscapes of the same hand, green pastoral hills and vales, and shepherds piping to their mild mistresses underneath the flowering shade. Reader, 'if thou hast not seen the Louvre thou art damned!'—for thou hast not seen the choicest remains of the works of art; or thou hast not seen all these together with their mutually reflected glories. I say nothing of the statues; for I know but little of sculpture, and never liked any till I saw the Elgin Marbles.... Here, for four months together, I strolled and studied, and daily heard the warning sound—'Quatres heures passees, il faut fermer, Citoyens'—(Ah! why did they ever change their style?) muttered in coarse provincial French; and brought away with me some loose draughts and fragments, which I have been forced to part with, like drops of life-blood, for 'hard money.' How often, thou tenantless mansion of godlike magnificence—how often has my heart since gone a pilgrimage to thee!

It has been made a question, whether the artist, or the mere man of taste and natural sensibility, receives most pleasure from the contemplation of works of art; and I think this question might be answered by another as a sort of *experimentum crucis*, namely, whether any one out of that 'number numberless' of mere gentlemen and amateurs, who visited Paris at the period here spoken of, felt as much interest, as much pride or pleasure in this display of the most striking monuments of art as the humblest student would? The first entrance into the Louvre would be only one of the events of his journey, not an event in his life, remembered ever after with thankfulness and regret. He would explore it with the same unmeaning curiosity and idle wonder as he would the Regalia in the Tower, or the Botanic Garden in the Tuileries, but not with the fond enthusiasm of an artist. How should he? His is 'casual fruition, joyless, unendeared.' But the painter is wedded to his art—the mistress, queen, and idol of his soul. He has embarked his all in it, fame, time, fortune, peace of mind—his hopes in youth, his consolation in age: and shall he not feel a more intense interest in whatever relates to it than the mere indolent trifler? Natural sensibility alone, without the entire application of the mind to that one object, will not enable the possessor to sympathise with all the degrees of beauty and power in the conceptions of a Titian or a Correggio; but it is he only who does this, who follows them into all their force and matchless race, that does or can feel their full value. Knowledge is pleasure as well as power. No one but the artist who has studied nature and contended with the difficulties of art, can be aware of the beauties, or intoxicated with a passion for painting. No one who has not devoted his life and soul to the pursuit of art can feel the same exultation in its brightest ornaments and loftiest triumphs which an artist does. Where the treasure is, there the heart is also. It is now seventeen years since I was studying in the Louvre (and I have on since given up all thoughts of the art as a profession), but long after I returned, and even still, I sometimes dream of being there again—of asking for the old pictures—and not finding them, or finding them changed or faded from what they were, I cry myself awake! What gentleman-amateur ever does this at such a distance of time,—that is, ever received pleasure or took interest enough in them to produce so lasting an impression?

But it is said that if a person had the same natural taste, and the same acquired knowledge as an artist, without the petty interests and technical notions, he would derive a purer pleasure from seeing a fine portrait, a fine landscape, and so on. This, however, is not so much begging the question as asking an impossibility: he cannot have the same insight into the end without having studied the means; nor the same love of art without the same habitual and exclusive attachment to it. Painters are, no doubt, often actuated by jealousy to that only which they find useful to themselves in painting. Wilson has been seen poring over the texture of a Dutch cabinet-picture, so that he could not see the picture itself. But this is the perversion and pedantry of the profession, not its true or genuine spirit. If Wilson had never looked at anything but megilps and handling, he never would have put the soul of life and manners into his pictures, as he has done. Another objection is, that the instrumental parts of the art, the means, the first rudiments, paints, oils, and brushes, are painful and disgusting; and that the consciousness of the difficulty and anxiety with which perfection has been attained must take away from the pleasure of the finest performance. This, however, is only an additional proof of the greater pleasure derived by the artist from his profession; for these things which are said to interfere with and destroy the common interest in works of art do not disturb him; he never once thinks of them, he is absorbed in the pursuit of a higher object; he is intent, not on the means, but the end; he is taken up, not with the difficulties, but with the triumph over them. As in the case of the anatomist, who overlooks many things in the eagerness of his search after abstract truth; or the alchemist who, while he is raking into his soot and furnaces, lives in a golden dream; a lesser gives way to a greater object. But it is pretended that the painter may be supposed to submit to the unpleasant part of the process only for the sake of the fame or profit in view. So far is this from being a true state of the case, that I will venture to say, in the instance of a friend of mine who has lately succeeded in an important undertaking in his art, that not all the fame he has acquired, not all the money he has received from thousands of admiring spectators, not all the newspaper puffs,—nor even the praise of the *Edinburgh Review*,—not all these put together ever gave him at any time the same genuine, undoubted satisfaction as any one half-hour employed in the ardent and propitious pursuit of his art—in finishing to his heart's content a foot, a hand, or even a piece of drapery. What is the state of mind of an artist while he is at work? He is then in the act of realising the highest idea he can form of beauty or grandeur: he conceives, he embodies that which he understands and loves best: that is, he is in full and perfect possession of that which is to him the source of the highest happiness and intellectual excitement which he can enjoy.

In short, as a conclusion to this argument, I will mention a circumstance which fell under my knowledge the other day. A friend had bought a print of Titian's Mistress, the same to which I have alluded above. He was anxious to show it me on this account. I told him it was a spirited engraving, but it had not the look of the original. I believe he thought this fastidious, till I offered to show him a rough sketch of it, which I had by me. Having seen this, he said he perceived exactly what I meant, and could not bear to look at the print afterwards. He had good sense enough to see the difference in the individual instance; but a person better acquainted with Titian's manner and with art in general—that is, of a more cultivated and refined taste—would know that it was a bad print, without having any immediate model to compare it with. He would perceive with a glance of the eye, with a sort of instinctive feeling, that it was hard, and without that bland, expansive, and nameless expression which always distinguished Titian's most famous works. Any one who is accustomed to a head in a picture can never reconcile himself to a print from it; but to the ignorant they are both the same. To a vulgar eye there is no difference between a Guido and a daub—between a penny print, or the vilest scrawl, and the most finished performance. In other words, all that excellence which lies between these two extremes,—all, at least, that marks the excess above mediocrity,—all that constitutes true beauty, harmony, refinement, grandeur, is lost upon the common observer. But it is from this point that the delight, the glowing raptures of the true adept commence. An uninformed spectator may like an ordinary drawing better than the ablest connoisseur; but for that very reason he cannot like the highest specimens of art so well. The refinements not only of execution but of truth and nature are inaccessible to unpractised eyes. The exquisite gradations in a sky of Claude's are not perceived by such persons, and consequently the harmony cannot be felt. Where there is no conscious apprehension, there can be no conscious pleasure. Wonder at the first sights of works of art may be the effect of ignorance and novelty; but real admiration and permanent delight in them are the growth of taste and knowledge. 'I would not wish to have your eyes,' said a good-natured man to a critic who was finding fault with a picture in which the other saw no blemish. Why so? The idea which prevented him from admiring this inferior production was a higher idea of truth and beauty which was ever present with him, and a continual source of pleasing and lofty contemplations. It may be different in a taste for outward luxuries and the privations of mere sense; but the idea of perfection, which acts as an intellectual foil, is always an addition, a support, and a proud consolation!

Richardson, in his *Essays*, which ought to be better known, has left some striking examples of the felicity and infelicity of artists, both as it relates to their external fortune and to the practice of their art. In speaking of *the knowledge of hands*, he exclaims: 'When one is considering a picture or a drawing, one at the same time thinks this was done by him(1) who had many extraordinary endowments of body and mind, but was withal very capricious; who was honoured in life and death, expiring in the arms of one of the greatest princes of that age, Francis I., King of France, who loved him as a friend. Another is of him(2) who lived a long and happy life, beloved of Charles V. emperor; and many others of the first princes of Europe. When one has another in hand, we think this was done by one(3) who so excelled in three arts as that any of them in that degree had rendered him worthy of immortality; and one moreover that durst contend with his sovereign (one of the haughtiest popes that ever was) upon a slight offered to him, and extricated himself with honour. Another is the work of him(4) who, without any one exterior advantage but mere strength of genius, had the most sublime imaginations, and executed them accordingly, yet lived and died obscurely. Another we shall consider as the work of him(5) who restored Painting when it had almost sunk; of him whom art made honourable, but who, neglecting and despising greatness with a sort of cynical pride, was treated suitably to the figure he gave himself, not his intrinsic worth; which, (he) not having philosophy enough to bear it, broke his heart. Another is done by one(6) who (on the contrary) was a fine gentleman and lived in great magnificence, and was much honoured by his own and foreign princes; who was a courtier, a statesman, and a painter; and so much all these, that when he acted in either character, *that* seemed to be his business, and the others his diversion. I say when one thus reflects, besides the pleasure arising from the beauties and excellences of the work, the fine ideas it gives us of natural things, the noble way of thinking it suggest to us, an additional pleasure results from the above considerations. But, oh! the pleasure, when a connoisseur and lover of art has before him a picture or drawing of which he can say this is the hand, these are the thoughts of him(7) who was one of the politest, best-natured gentlemen that ever was; and beloved and assisted by the greatest wits and the greatest men then in Rome: of him who lived in great fame, honour, and magnificence, and died extremely lamented; and missed a Cardinal's hat only by dying a few months too soon; but was particularly esteemed and favoured by two Popes, the only ones who filled the chair of St. Peter in his time, and as great men as ever sat there since that apostle, if at least he ever did: one, in short, who could have been a Leonardo, a Michael Angelo, a Titian, a Correggio, a Parmegiano, an Annibal, a Rubens, or any other whom he pleased, but none of them could ever have been a Raffaelle.'

The same writer speaks feelingly of the change in the style of different artists from their change of fortune, and as the circumstances are little known I will quote the passage relating to two of them:—

'Guido Reni, from a prince-like affluence of fortune (the just reward of his angelic works), fell to a condition like that of a hired servant to one who supplied him with money for what he did at a fixed rate; and that by his being bewitched by a passion for gaming, whereby he lost vast sums of money; and even what he got in his state of servitude by day, he commonly lost at night: nor could he ever be cured of this cursed madness. Those of his works, therefore, which he did in this unhappy part of his life may easily be conceived to be in a different style to what he did before, which in some things, that is, in the airs of his heads (in the gracious kind) had a delicacy in them peculiar to himself, and almost more than human. But I must not multiply instance variation, and all the degrees of goodness, from the lowest of the indifferent up to the sublime. I can produce evident proofs of this in so easy a gradation, that one cannot deny but that he that did this might do that, and very probably did so; and thus one may ascend and descend, like the angels on Jacob's ladder, whose foot was upon the earth, but its top reached to Heaven.

'And this great man had his unlucky circumstance. He became mad after the philosopher's stone, and did but very little in painting or drawing afterwards. Judge what that was, and whether there was not an alteration of style from what he had done before this devil possessed him. His creditors endeavoured to exorcise him, and did him some good, for he set himself to work again in his own way; but if a drawing I have of a Lucretia be that he made for his last picture, as it probably is (Vasari says that was the subject of it), it is an evident proof of his decay; it is good indeed, but it wants much of the delicacy which is commonly seen in his works; and so I always thought before I knew or imagined it to be done in this his ebb of genius.'

We have had two artists of our own country whose fate has been as singular as it was hard: Gandy was a portrait-painter in the beginning of the last century, whose heads were said to have come near to Rembrandt's, and he was the undoubted prototype of Sir Joshua Reynolds's style. Yet his name has scarcely been heard of; and his reputation, like his works, never extended beyond his own country. What did he think of himself and of a fame so bounded? Did he ever dream he was indeed an artist? Or how did this feeling in him differ from the vulgar conceit of the lowest pretender? The best known of his works is a portrait of an alderman of Exeter, in some public building in that city.

9

Poor Dan. Stringer! Forty years ago he had the finest hand and the clearest eye of any artist of his time, and produced heads and drawings that would not have disgraced a brighter period in the art. But he fell a martyr (like Burns) to the society of country gentlemen, and then of those whom they would consider as more his equals. I saw him many years ago when he treated the masterly sketches he had by him (one in particular of the group of citizens in Shakespeare 'swallowing the tailor's news') as 'bastards of his genius, not his children,' and seemed to have given up all thoughts of his art. Whether he is since dead, I cannot say; the world do not so much as know that he ever lived!

FN to ESSAY II

(1) Leonardo da Vinci.

(2) Titian.

(3) Michael Angelo.

(4) Correggio.

(5) Annibal Caracci.

(6) Rubens.

(7) Raffaelle.

ESSAY III. ON THE PAST AND FUTURE

I have naturally but little imagination, and am not of a very sanguine turn of mind. I have some desire to enjoy the present good, and some fondness for the past; but I am not at all given to build castles in the air, nor to look forward with much confidence or hope to the brilliant illusions held out by the future. Hence I have perhaps been led to form a theory, which is very contrary to the common notions and feelings on the subject, and which I will here try to explain as well as I can. When Sterne in the *Sentimental Journey* told the French Minister, that if the French people had a fault, it was that they were too serious, the latter replied that if that was his opinion, he must defend it with all his might, for he would have all the world against him; so I shall have enough to do to get well through the present argument.

I cannot see, then, any rational or logical ground for that mighty difference in the value which mankind generally set upon the past and future, as if the one was everything, and the other nothing—of no consequence whatever. On the other hand, I conceive that the past is as real and substantial a part of our being, that it is as much a *bona fide*, undeniable consideration in the estimate of human life, as the future can possibly be. To say that the past is of no importance, unworthy of a moment's regard, because it has gone by, and is no longer anything, is an argument that cannot be held to any purpose; for if the past has ceased to be, and is therefore to be accounted nothing in the scale of good or evil, the future is yet to come, and has never been anything. Should any one choose to assert that the present only is of any value in a strict and positive sense, because that alone has a real existence, that we should seize the instant good, and give all else to the winds, I can understand what he means (though perhaps he does not himself);(1) but I cannot comprehend how this distinction between that which has a downright and sensible, and that which has only a remote and airy existence, can be applied to establish the preference of the future over the past; for both are in this point of view equally ideal, absolutely nothing, except as they are conceived of by the mind's eye, and are thus rendered present to the thoughts and feelings. Nay, the one is even more imaginary, a more fantastic creature of the brain than the other, and the interest we take in it more shadowy and gratuitous; for the future, on which we lay so much stress, may never come to pass at all, that is, may never be embodied into actual existence in the whole course of events, whereas the past has certainly existed once, has received the stamp of truth, and left an image of itself behind. It is so far then placed beyond the possibility of doubt, or as the poet has it,

Those joys are lodg'd beyond the reach of fate.

It is not, however, attempted to be denied that though the future is nothing at present, and has no immediate interest while we are speaking, yet it is of the utmost consequence in itself, and of the utmost interest to the individual, because it will have a real existence, and we have an idea of it as existing in time to come. Well, then, the past also has no real existence; the actual sensation and the interest belonging to it are both fled; but it *has had* a real existence, and we can still call up a vivid recollection of it as having once been; and therefore, by parity of reasoning, it is not a thing perfectly insignificant in itself, nor wholly indifferent to the mind whether it ever was or not. Oh no! Far from it! Let us not rashly quit our hold upon the past, when perhaps there may be little else left to bind us to existence. Is it nothing to have been, and to have been happy or miserable? Or is it a matter of no moment to think whether I have been one or the other? Do I delude myself, do I build upon a shadow or a dream, do I dress up in the gaudy garb of idleness and folly a pure fiction, with nothing answering to it in the universe of things and the records of truth, when I look back with fond delight or with tender regret to that which was at one time to me my all, when I revive the glowing image of some bright reality,

The thoughts of which can never from my heart?

Do I then muse on nothing, do I bend my eyes on nothing, when I turn back in fancy to 'those suns and skies so pure' that lighted up my early path? Is it to think of nothing, to set an idle value upon nothing, to think of all that has happened to me, an of all that can ever interest me? Or, to use the language of a fine poet (who is himself among my earliest and not least painful recollections)—

What though the radiance which was once so bright

Be now for ever vanish'd from my sight,

Though nothing can bring back the hour

Of glory in the grass, of splendour in the flow'r—

yet am I mocked with a lie when I venture to think of it? Or do I not drink in and breathe again the air of heavenly truth when I but 'retrace its footsteps, and its skirts far off adore'? I cannot say with the same poet—

```
And see how dark the backward stream,
A little moment past so smiling—
```

for it is the past that gives me most delight and most assurance of reality. What to me constitutes the great charm of the *Confessions* of Rousseau is their turning so much upon this feeling. He seems to gather up the past moments of his being like drops of honey-dew to distil a precious liquor from them; his alternate pleasures and pains are the bead-roll that he tells over and piously worships; he makes a rosary of the flowers of hope and fancy that strewed his earliest years. When he begins the last of the *Reveries of a Solitary Walker*, 'Il y a aujourd'hui, jour des Paques Fleuris, cinquante ans depuis que j'ai premier vu Madame Warens,' what a yearning of the soul is implied in that short sentence! Was all that had happened to him, all that he had thought and felt in that sad interval of time, to be accounted nothing? Was that long, dim, faded retrospect of years happy or miserable—a blank that was not to make his eyes fail and his heart faint within him in trying to grasp all that had once filled it and that had since vanished, because it was not a prospect into futurity? Was he wrong in finding more to interest him in it than in the next fifty years—which he did not live to see? Or if he had, what then? Would they have been worth thinking of, compared with the times of his youth, of his first meeting with Madame Warens, with those times which he has traced with such truth and pure delight 'in our heart's tables'? When 'all the life of life was flown,' was he not to live the first and best part of it over again, and once more be all that he then was?—Ye woods that crown the clear lone brow of Norman Court, why do I revisit ye so oft, and feel a soothing consciousness of your presence, but that your high tops waving in the wind recall to me the hours and years that are for ever fled; that ye renew in ceaseless murmurs the story of long-cherished hopes and bitter disappointment; that in your solitudes and tangled wilds I can wander and lose myself as I wander on and am lost in the solitude of my own heart; and that as your rustling branches give the loud blast to the waste below—borne on the thoughts of other years, I can look down with patient anguish at the cheerless desolation which I feel within! Without that face pale as the primrose with hyacinthine locks, for ever shunning and for ever haunting me, mocking my waking thoughts as in a dream; without that smile which my heart could never turn to scorn; without those eyes dark with their own lustre, still bent on mine, and drawing the soul into their liquid mazes like a sea of love; without that name trembling in fancy's ear; without that form gliding before me like Oread or Dryad in fabled groves, what should I do? how pass away the listless, leaden-footed hours? Then wave, wave on, ye woods of Tuderley, and lift your high tops in the air; my sighs and vows uttered by our mystic voice breathe into me my former being, and enable me to bear the thing I am!—The objects that we have known in better days are the main props that sustain the weight of our affections, and give us strength to await our future lot. The future is like a dead wall or a thick mist hiding all objects from our view; the past is alive and stirring with objects, bright or solemn, and of unfading interest. What is it in fact that we recur to oftenest? What subjects do we think or talk of? Not the ignorant future, but the well-stored past. Othello, the Moor of Venice, amused himself and his hearers at the house of Signor Brabantio by 'running through the story of his life even from his boyish days'; and oft 'beguiled them of their tears, when he did speak of some disastrous stroke which his youth suffered.' This plan of ingratiating himself would not have answered if the past had been, like the contents of an old almanac, of no use but to be thrown aside and forgotten. What a blank, for instance, does the history of the world for the next six thousand years present to the mind, compared with that of the last! All that strikes the imagination or excites any interest in the mighty scene is *what has been*!(2)

***

Neither in itself, then, nor as a subject of general contemplation, has the future any advantage over the past. But with respect to our grosser passions and pursuits it has. As far as regards the appeal to the understanding or the imagination, the past is just as good, as real, of as much intrinsic and ostensible value as the future; but there is another principle in the human mind, the principle of action or will; and of this the past has no hold, the future engrosses it entirely to itself. It is this strong lever of the affections that gives so powerful a bias to our sentiments on this subject, and violently transposes the natural order of our associations. We regret the pleasures we have lost, and eagerly anticipate those which are to come: we dwell with satisfaction on the evils from which we have escaped (*Posthaec meminisse iuvabit*)—and dread future pain. The good that is past is in this sense like money that is spent, which is of no further use, and about which we give ourselves little concern. The good we expect is like a store yet untouched, and in the enjoyment of which we promise ourselves infinite gratification. What has happened to us we think of no consequence: what is to happen to us, of the greatest. Why so? Simply because the one is still in our power, and the other not—because the efforts of the will to bring any object to pass or to prevent it strengthen our attachment or aversion to that object—because the pains and attention bestowed upon anything add to our interest in it—and because the habitual and earnest pursuit of any end redoubles the ardour of our expectations, and converts the speculative and indolent satisfaction we might otherwise feel in it into real passion. Our regrets, anxiety, and wishes are thrown away upon the past; but the insisting on the importance of the future is of the utmost use in aiding our resolutions and stimulating our exertions. If the future were no more amenable to our wills than the past; if our precautions, our sanguine schemes, our hopes and fears were of as little avail in the one case as the other; if we could neither soften our minds to pleasure, nor steel our fortitude to the resistance of pain beforehand; if all objects drifted along by us like straws or pieces of wood in a river, the will being purely passive, and as little able to avert the future as to arrest the past, we should in that case be equally indifferent to both; that is, we should consider each as they affected the thoughts and imagination with certain sentiments of approbation or regret, but without the importunity of action, the irritation of the will, throwing the whole weight of passion and prejudice into one scale, and leaving the other quite empty. While the blow is coming, we prepare to meet it, we think to ward off or break its force, we arm ourselves with patience to endure what cannot be avoided, we agitate ourselves with fifty needless alarms about it; but when the blow is struck, the pang is over, the struggle is no longer necessary, and we cease to harass or torment ourselves about it more than we can help. It is not that the one belongs to the future and the other to time past; but that the one is a subject of action, of uneasy apprehension, of strong passion, and that the other has passed wholly out of the sphere of action into the region of

```
Calm contemplation and majestic pains.(3)
```

It would not give a man more concern to know that he should be put to the rack a year hence, than to recollect that he had been put to it a year ago, but that he hopes to avoid the one, whereas he must sit down patiently under the consciousness of the other. In this hope he wears himself out in vain struggles with fate, and puts himself to the rack of his imagination every day he has to live in the meanwhile. When the event is so remote or so independent of the will as to set aside the necessity of immediate action, or to baffle all attempts to defeat it, it gives us little more disturbance or emotion than if it had already taken place, or were something to happen in another state of being, or to an indifferent person. Criminals are observed to grow more anxious as their trial approaches; but after their sentence is passed, they become tolerably resigned, and generally sleep sound the night before its execution.

It in some measure confirms this theory, that men attach more or less importance to past and future events according as they are more or less engaged in action and the busy scenes of life. Those who have a fortune to make, or are in pursuit of rank and power, think little of the past, for it does not contribute greatly to their views: those who have nothing to do but to think, take nearly the same interest in the past as in the future. The contemplation of the one is as delightful and real as that of the other. The season of hope has an end; but the remembrance of it is left. The past still lives in the memory of those who have leisure to look back upon the way that they have trod, and can from it 'catch-glimpses that may make them less forlorn.' The turbulence of action, and uneasiness of desire, must point to the future: it is only in the quiet innocence of shepherds, in the simplicity of pastoral ages, that a tomb was found with this inscription—'I ALSO WAS AN ARCADIAN!'

Though I by no means think that our habitual attachment to life is in exact proportion to the value of the gift, yet I am not one of those splenetic persons who affect to think it of no value at all. *Que peu de chose est la vie humaine*, is an exclamation in the mouths of moralists and philosophers, to which I cannot agree. It is little, it is short, it is not worth having, if we take the last hour, and leave out all that has gone before, which has been one way of looking at the subject. Such calculators seem to say that life is nothing when it is over, and that may in their sense be true. If the old rule—*Respice finem*—were to be made absolute, and no one could be pronounced fortunate till the day of his death, there are few among us whose existence would, upon those conditions, be much to be envied. But this is not a fair view of the case. A man's life is his whole life, not the last glimmering snuff of the candle; and this, I say, is considerable, and not a *little matter*, whether we regard its pleasures or its pains. To draw a peevish conclus desires or forgetful indifference is about as reasonable as to say, a man never was young because he has grown old, or never lived because he is now dead. The length or agreeableness of a journey does not depend on the few last steps of it, nor is the size of a building to be judged of from the last stone that is added to it. It is neither the first nor last hour of our existence, but the space that parts these two—not our exit nor our entrance upon the stage, but what we do, feel, and think while there—that we are to attend to in pronouncing sentence upon it. Indeed it would be easy to show that it is the very extent of human life, the infinite number of things contained in it, its contradictory and fluctuating interests, the transition from one situation to another, the hours, months, years spent in one fond pursuit after another; that it is, in a word, the length of our common journey and the quantity of events crowded into it, that, baffling the grasp of our actual perception, make it slide from our memory, and dwindle into nothing in its own perspective. It is too mighty for us, and we say it is nothing! It is a speck in our fancy, and yet what canvas would be big enough to hold its striking groups, its endless subjects! It is light as vanity, and yet if all its weary moments, if all its head and heart aches were compressed into one, what fortitude would not be overwhelmed with the blow! What a huge heap, a 'huge, dumb heap,' of wishes, thoughts, feelings, anxious cares, soothing hopes, loves, joys, friendships, it is composed of! How many ideas and trains of sentiment, long and deep and intense, often pass through the mind in only one day's thinking or reading, for instance! How many such days are there in a year, how many years in a long life, still occupied with something interesting, still recalling some old impression, still recurring to some difficult question and making progress in it, every step accompanied with a sense of power, and every moment conscious of 'the high endeavour or the glad success'; for the mind seizes only on that which keeps it employed, and is wound up to a certain pitch of pleasurable excitement or lively solicitude, by the necessity of its own nature. The division of the map of life into its component parts is beautifully made by King Henry VI.:—

```
Oh God! methinks it were a happy life
To be no better than a homely swain,
To sit upon a hill as I do now,
To carve out dials quaintly, point by point,
Thereby to see the minutes how they run
How many make the hour full complete,
How many hours bring about the day,
How many days will finish up the year,
How many years a mortal man may live:
When this is known, then to divide the times;
So many hours must I tend my flock,
So many hours must I take my rest,
So many hours must I contemplate,
So many hours must I sport myself;
So many days my ewes have been with young,
So many weeks ere the poor fools will yean,
So many months ere I shall shear the fleece:
So many minutes, hours, weeks, months, and years
Past over to the end they were created,
Would bring grey hairs unto a quiet grave.
```

I myself am neither a king nor a shepherd: books have been my fleecy charge, and my thoughts have been my subjects. But these have found me sufficient employment at the time, and enough to think of for the time to come.

The passions contract and warp the natural progress of life. They paralyse all of it that is not devoted to their tyranny and caprice. This makes the difference between the laughing innocence of childhood, the pleasantness of youth, and the crabbedness of age. A load of cares lies like a weight of guilt upon the mind: so that a man of business often has all the air, the distraction and restlessness and hurry of feeling of a criminal. A knowledge of the world takes away the freedom and simplicity of thought as effectually as the contagion of its example. The artlessness and candour of our early years are open to all impressions alike, because the mind is not clogged and preoccupied with other objects. Our pleasures and our pains come single, make room for one another, and the spring of the mind is fresh and unbroken, its aspect clear and unsullied. Hence 'the tear forgot as soon as shed, the sunshine of the breast.' But as we advance farther, the will gets greater head. We form violent antipathies and indulge exclusive preferences. We make up our minds to some one thing, and if we cannot have that, will have nothing. We are wedded to opinion, to fancy, to prejudice; which destroys the soundness of our judgments, and the serenity and buoyancy of our feelings. The chain of habit coils itself round the heart, like a serpent, to gnaw and stifle it. It grows rigid and callous; and for the softness and elasticity of childhood, full of proud flesh and obstinate tumours. The violence and perversity of our passions come in more and more to overlay our natural sensibility and well-grounded affections; and we screw ourselves up to aim only at those things which are neither desirable nor practicable. Thus life passes away in the feverish irritation of pursuit and the certainty of disappointment. By degrees, nothing but this morbid state of feeling satisfies us: and all common pleasures and cheap amusements are sacrificed to the demon of ambition, avarice, or dissipation. The machine is overwrought: the parching heat of the veins dries up and withers the flowers of Love, Hope, and Joy; and any pause, any release from the rack of ecstasy on which we are stretched, seems more insupportable than the pangs which we endure. We are suspended between tormenting desires and the horrors of *ennui*. The impulse of the will, like the wheels of a carriage going down hill, becomes too strong for the driver, Reason, and cannot be stopped nor kept within bounds. Some idea, some fancy, takes possession of the brain; and however ridiculous, however distressing, however ruinous, haunts us by a sort of fascination through life.

Not only is this principle of excessive irritability to be seen at work in our more turbulent passions and pursuits, but even in the formal study of arts and sciences, the same thing takes place, and undermines the repose and happiness of life. The eagerness of pursuit overcomes the satisfaction to result from the accomplishment. The mind is overstrained to attain its purpose; and when it is attained, the ease and alacrity necessary to enjoy it are gone. The irritation of action does not cease and go down with the occasion for it; but we are first uneasy to get to the end of our work, and then uneasy for want of something to do. The ferment of the brain does not of itself subside into pleasure and soft repose. Hence the disposition to strong stimuli observable in persons of much intellectual exertion to allay and carry off the over-excitement. The *improvisatori* poets (it is recorded by Spence in his *Anecdotes of Pope*) cannot sleep after an evening's continued display of their singular and difficult art. The rhymes keep running in their head in spite of themselves, and will not let them rest. Mechanics and labouring people never know what to do with themselves on a Sunday, though they return to their work with greater spirit for the relief, and look forward to it with pleasure all the week. Sir Joshua Reynolds was never comfortable out of his painting-room, and died of chagrin and regret because he could not paint on to the last moment of his life. He used to say that he could go on retouching a picture for ever, as long as it stood on his easel; but as soon as it was once fairly out of the house, he never wished to see it again. An ingenious artist of our own time has been heard to declare, that if ever the Devil got him into his clutches, he would set him to copy his own pictures. Thus secure, self-complacent retrospect to what is done is nothing, while the anxious, uneasy looking forward to what is to come is everything. We are afraid to dwell upon the past, lest it should retard our future progress; the indulgence of ease is fatal to excellence; and to succeed in life, we lose the ends of being!

FN to ESSAY III

(1) If we take away from the *present* the moment that Is just by and the moment that is next to come, how much of it will be left for this plain, practical theory to rest upon? Their solid basis of sense and reality will reduce itself to a pin's point, a hair line, on which our moral balance-masters will have some difficulty to maintain their footing without falling over on either side.

(2) A treatise on the Millennium is dull; but who was ever weary of reading the fables of the Golden Age? On my once observing I should like to have been Claude, a person said, 'they should not, for that then by this time it would have been all over with them.' As if it could possibly signify when we live (save and excepting the present minute), or as if the value of human life decreased or increased with successive centuries. At that rate, we had better have our life still to come at some future period, and so postpone our existence century after century *ad infinitum*.

(3) In like manner, though we know that an event must have taken place at a distance, long before we can hear the result, yet as long as we remain in Ignorance of it, we irritate ourselves about it, and suffer all the agonies of suspense, as if it was still to come; but as soon as our uncertainty is removed, our fretful impatience vanishes, we resign ourselves to fate, and make up our minds to what has happened as well as we can.

ESSAY IV. ON GENIUS AND COMMON SENSE

We hear it maintained by people of more gravity than understanding, that genius and taste are strictly reducible to rules, and that there is a rule for everything. So far is it from being true that the finest breath of fancy is a definable thing, that the plainest common sense is only what Mr. Locke would have called a *mixed mode*, subject to a particular sort of acquired and undefinable tact. It is asked, "If you do not know the rule by which a thing is done, how can you be sure of doing it a second time?" And the answer is, "If you do not know the muscles by the help of which you walk, how is it you do not fall down at every step you take?" In art, in taste, in life, in speech, you decide from feeling, and not from reason; that is, from the impression of a number of things on the mind, from which impression is true and well founded, though you may not be able to analyse or account for it in the several particulars. In a gesture you use, in a look you see, in a tone you hear, you judge of the expression, propriety, and meaning from habit, not from reason or rules; that is to say, from innumerable instances of like gestures, looks, and tones, in innumerable other circumstances, variously modified, which are too many and too refined to be all distinctly recollected, but which do not therefore operate the less powerfully upon the mind and eye of taste. Shall we say that these impressions (the immediate stamp of nature) do not operate in a given manner till they are classified and reduced to rules, or is not the rule itself grounded, upon the truth and certainty of that natural operation?

How then can the distinction of the understanding as to the manner in which they operate be necessary to their producing their due and uniform effect upon the mind? If certain effects did not regularly arise out of certain causes in mind as well as matter, there could be no rule given for them: nature does not follow the rule, but suggests it. Reason is the interpreter and critic of nature and genius, not their law-giver and judge. He must be a poor creature indeed whose practical convictions do not in almost all cases outrun his deliberate understanding, or who does not feel and know much more than he can give a reason for. Hence the distinction between eloquence and wisdom, between ingenuity and common sense. A man may be dexterous and able in explaining the grounds of his opinions, and yet may be a mere sophist, because he only sees one-half of a subject. Another may feel the whole weight of a question, nothing relating to it may be lost upon him, and yet he may be able to give no account of the manner in which it affects him, or to drag his reasons from their silent lurking-places. This last will be a wise man, though neither a logician nor rhetorician. Goldsmith was a fool to Dr. Johnson in argument; that is, in assigning the specific grounds of his opinions: Dr. Johnson was a fool to Goldsmith in the fine tact, the airy, intuitive faculty with which he skimmed the surfaces of things, and unconsciously formed his Opinions. Common sense is the just result of the sum total of such unconscious impressions in the ordinary occurrences of life, as they are treasured up in the memory, and called out by the occasion. Genius and taste depend much upon the same principle exercised on loftier ground and in more unusual combinations.

I am glad to shelter myself from the charge of affectation or singularity in this view of an often debated but ill-understood point, by quoting a passage from Sir Joshua Reynolds's *Discourses*, which is full, and, I think, conclusive to the purpose. He says:—

'I observe, as a fundamental ground common to all the Arts with which we have any concern in this Discourse, that they address themselves only to two faculties of the mind, its imagination and its sensibility.

'All theories which attempt to direct or to control the Art, upon any principles falsely called rational, which we form to ourselves upon a supposition of what ought in reason to be the end or means of Art, independent of the known first effect produced by objects on the imagination, must be false and delusive. For though it may appear bold to say it, the imagination is here the residence of truth. If the imagination be affected, the conclusion is fairly drawn; if it be not affected, the reasoning is erroneous, because the end is not obtained; the effect itself being the test, and the only test, of the truth and efficacy of the means.

'There is in the commerce of life, as in Art, a sagacity which is far from being contradictory to right reason, and is superior to any occasional exercise of that faculty which supersedes it and does not wait for the slow progress of deduction, but goes at once, by what appears a kind of intuition, to the conclusion. A man endowed with this faculty feels and acknowledges the truth, though it is not always in his power, perhaps, to give a reason for it; because he cannot recollect and bring before him all the materials that gave birth to his opinion; for very many and very intricate considerations may unite to form the principle, even of small and minute parts, involved in, or dependent on, a great many things:—though these in process of time are forgotten, the right impression still remains fixed in his mind.

'This impression is the result of the accumulated experience of our whole life, and has been collected, we do not always know how or when. But this mass of collective observation, however acquired, ought to prevail over that reason, which, however powerfully exerted on any particular occasion, will probably comprehend but a partial view of the subject; and our conduct in life, as well as in the arts, is or ought to be generally governed by this habitual reason: it is our happiness that we are enabled to draw on such funds. If we were obliged to enter into a theoretical deliberation on every occasion before we act, life would be at a stand, and Art would be impracticable.

'It appears to me therefore' (continues Sir Joshua) 'that our first thoughts, that is, the effect which any thing produces on our minds on its first appearance, is never to be forgotten; and it demands for that reason, because it is the first, to be laid up with care. If this be not done, the artist may happen to impose on himself by partial reasoning; by a cold consideration of those animated thoughts which proceed, not perhaps from caprice or rashness (as he may afterwards conceit), but from the fulness of his mind, enriched with the copious stores of all the various inventions which he had ever seen, or had ever passed in his mind. These ideas are infused into his design, without any conscious effort; but if he be not on his guard, he may reconsider and correct them, till the whole matter is reduced to a commonplace invention.

'This is sometimes the effect of what I mean to caution you against; that is to say, an unfounded distrust of the imagination and feeling, in favour of narrow, partial, confined, argumentative theories, and of principles that seem to apply to the design in hand, without considering those general impressions on the fancy in which real principles of *sound reason*, and of much more weight and importance, are involved, and, as it were, lie hid under the appearance of a sort of vulgar sentiment. Reason, without doubt, must ultimately determine everything; at this minute it is required to inform us when that very reason is to give way to feeling.'(1)

Mr. Burke, by whom the foregoing train of thinking was probably suggested, has insisted on the same thing, and made rather a perverse use of it in several parts of his *Reflections on the French Revolution*; and Windham in one of his *Speeches* has clenched it into an aphorism—'There is nothing so true as habit.' Once more I would say, common sense is tacit reason. Conscience is the same tacit sense of right and wrong, or the impression of our moral experience and moral apprehensions on the mind, which, because it works unseen, yet certainly, we suppose to be an instinct, implanted in the mind; as we sometimes attribute the violent operations of our passions, of which we can neither trace the source nor assign the reason, to the instigation of the Devil!

I shall here try to go more at large into this subject, and to give such instances and illustrations of it as occur to me.

One of the persons who had rendered themselves obnoxious to Government and been included in a charge for high treason in the year 1794, had retired soon after into Wales to write an epic poem and enjoy the luxuries of a rural life. In his peregrinations through that beautiful scenery, he had arrived one fine morning at the inn at Llangollen, in the romantic valley of that name. He had ordered his breakfast, and was sitting at the window in all the dalliance of expectation when a face passed, of which he took no notice at the instant—

but when his breakfast was brought in presently after, he found his appetite for it gone—the day had lost its freshness in his eye—he was uneasy and spiritless; and without any cause that he could discover, a total change had taken place in his feelings. While he was trying to account for this odd circumstance, the same face passed again—it was the face of Taylor the spy; and he was longer at a loss to explain the difficulty. He had before caught only a transient glimpse, a passing side-view of the face; but though this was not sufficient to awaken a distinct idea in his memory, his feelings, quicker and surer, had taken the alarm; a string had been touched that gave a jar to his whole frame, and would not let him rest, though he could not at all tell what was the matter with him. To the flitting, shadowy, half-distinguished profile that had glided by his window was linked unconsciously and mysteriously, but inseparably, the impression of the trains that had been laid for him by this person;—in this brief moment, in this dim, illegible short-hand of the mind he had just escaped the speeches of the Attorney and Solicitor-General over again; the gaunt figure of Mr. Pitt glared by him; the walls of a prison enclosed him; and he felt the hands of the executioner near him, without knowing it till the tremor and disorder of his nerves gave information to his reasoning faculties that all was not well within. That is, the same state of mind was recalled by one circumstance in the series of association that had been produced by the whole set of circumstances at the time, though the manner in which this was done was not immediately perceptible. In other words, the feeling of pleasure or pain, of good or evil, is revived, and acts instantaneously upon the mind, before we have time to recollect the precise objects which have originally given birth to it.(2) The incident here mentioned was merely, then, one case of what the learned understand by the *association of ideas*: but all that is meant by feeling or common sense is nothing but the different cases of the association of ideas, more or less true to the impression of the original circumstances, as reason begins with the more formal development of those circumstances, or pretends to account for the different cases of the association of ideas. But it does not follow that the dumb and silent pleading of the former (though sometimes, nay often, mistaken) is less true than that of its babbling interpreter, or that we are never to trust its dictates without consulting the express authority of reason. Both are imperfect, both are useful in their way, and therefore both are best together, to correct or to confirm one another. It does not appear that in the singular instance above mentioned, the sudden impression on the mind was superstition or fancy, though it might have been thought so, had it not been proved by the event to have a real physical and moral cause. Had not the same face returned again, the doubt would never have been properly cleared up, but would have remained a puzzle ever after, or perhaps have been soon forgot.—By the law of association as laid down by physiologists, any impression in a series can recall any other impression in that series without going through the whole in order; so that the mind drops the intermediate links, and passes on rapidly and by stealth to the more striking effects of pleasure or pain which have naturally taken the strongest hold of it. By doing this habitually and skillfully with respect to the various impressions and circumstances with which our experience makes us acquainted, it forms a series of unpremeditated conclusions on almost all subjects that can be brought before it, as just as they are of ready application to human life; and common sense is the name of this body of unassuming but practical wisdom. Common sense, however, is an impartial, instinctive result of truth and nature, and will therefore bear the test and abide the scrutiny of the most severe and patient reasoning. It is indeed incomplete without it. By ingrafting reason on feeling, we 'make assurance double sure.'

'Tis the last key-stone that makes up the arch...
Then stands it a triumphal mark! Then men
Observe the strength, the height, the why and when
It was erected; and still walking under,
Meet some new matter to look up, and wonder.

But reason, not employed to interpret nature, and to improve and perfect common sense and experience, is, for the most part, a building without a foundation. The criticism exercised by reason, then, on common sense may be as severe as it pleases, but it must be as patient as it is severe. Hasty, dogmatical, self-satisfied reason is worse than idle fancy or bigoted prejudice. It is systematic, ostentatious in error, closes up the avenues of knowledge, and 'shuts the gates of wisdom on mankind.' It is not enough to show that there is no reason for a thing that we do not see the reason of it: if the common feeling, if the involuntary prejudice sets in strong in favour of it, if, in spite of all we can do, there is a lurking suspicion on the side of our first impressions, we must try again, and believe that truth is mightier than we. So, in ordering a definition of any subject, if we feel a misgiving that there is any fact or circumstance emitted, but of which we have only a vague apprehension, like a name we cannot recollect, we must ask for more time, and not cut the matter short by an arrogant assumption of the point in dispute. Common sense thus acts as a check-weight on sophistry, and suspends our rash and superficial judgments. On the other hand, if not only no reason can be given for a thing, but every reason is clear against it, and we can account from ignorance, from authority, from interest, from different causes, for the prevalence of an opinion or sentiment, then we have a right to conclude that we have mistaken a prejudice for an instinct, or have confounded a false and partial impression with the fair and unavoidable inference from general observation. Mr. Burke said that we ought not to reject every prejudice, but should separate the husk of prejudice from the truth it encloses, and so try to get at the kernel within; and thus far he was right. But he was wrong in insisting that we are to cherish our prejudices 'because they are prejudices': for if all are well founded, there is no occasion to inquire into their origin or use; and he who sets out to philosophise upon them, or make the separation Mr. Burke talks of in this spirit and with this previous determination, will be very likely to mistake a maggot or a rotten canker for the precious kernel of truth, as was indeed the case with our Political sophist.

There is nothing more distinct than common sense and vulgar opinion. Common sense is only a judge of things that fall under common observation, or immediately come home to the business and bosoms of men. This is of the very essence of its principle, the basis of its pretensions. It rests upon the simple process of feeling,—it anchors in experience. It is not, nor it cannot be, the test of abstract, speculative opinions. But half the opinions and prejudices of mankind, those which they hold in the most unqualified approbation and which have been instilled into them under the strongest sanctions, are of this latter kind, that is, opinions not which they have ever thought, known, or felt one tittle about, but which they have taken up on trust from others, which have been palmed on their understandings by fraud or force, and which they continue to hold at the peril of life, limb, property, and character, with as little warrant from common sense in the first instance as appeal to reason in the last. The *ultima ratio regum* proceeds upon a very different plea. Common sense is neither priestcraft nor state-policy. Yet 'there's the rub that makes absurdity of so long life,' and, at the same time, gives the sceptical philosophers the advantage over us. Till nature has fair play allowed it, and is not adulterated by political and polemical quacks (as it so often has been), it is impossible to appeal to it as a defence against the errors and extravagances of mere reason. If we talk of common sense, we are twitted with vulgar prejudice, and asked how we distinguish the one from the other; but common and received opinion is indeed 'a compost heap' of crude notions, got together by the pride and passions of individuals, and reason is itself the thrall or manumitted slave of the same lordly and besotted masters, dragging its servile chain, or committing all sorts of Saturnalian licenses, the moment it feels itself freed from it.—If ten millions of Englishmen are furious in thinking themselves right in making war upon thirty millions of Frenchmen, and if the last are equally bent upon thinking the others always in the wrong, though it is a common and national prejudice, both opinions cannot be the dictate of good sense; but it may be the infatuated policy of one or both governments to keep their subjects always at variance. If a few centuries ago all Europe believed in the infallibility of the Pope, this was not an opinion derived from the proper exercise or erroneous direction of the common sense of the people; common sense had nothing to do with it—they believed whatever their priests told them. England at present is divided into Whigs and Tories, Churchmen and Dissenters; both parties have numbers on their side; but common sense and party spirit are two different things. Sects and heresies are upheld partly by sympathy, and partly by the love of contradiction; if there was nobody of a different way of thinking, they would fall to pieces of themselves. If a whole court say the same thing, this is no proof that they think it, but that the individual at the head of the court has said it; if a mob agree for a while in shouting the same watchword, this is not to me an example of the *sensus communis*, they only repeat what they have heard repeated by others. If indeed a large proportion of the people are in want of food, of clothing, of shelter—if they are sick, miserable, scorned, oppressed—an d if each feeling it in himself, they all say so with one voice and one heart, and lift up their hands to second their appeal, this I should say was but the dictate of common sense, the cry of nature. But to waive this part of the argument, which it is needless to push farther,—l believe that the best way to instruct mankind is not by pointing out to them their mutual errors, but by teaching them to think rightly on indifferent matters, where they will listen with patience in order to be amused, and where they do not consider a definition or a syllogism as the greatest injury you can offer them.

There is no rule for expression. It is got at solely by *feeling*, that is, on the principle of the association of ideas, and by transferring what has been found to hold good in one case (with the necessary modifications) to others. A certain look has been remarked strongly indicative of a certain passion or trait of character, and we attach the same meaning to it or are affected in the same pleasurable or painful manner by it, where it exists in a less degree, though we can define neither the look itself nor the modification of it. Having got the general clue, the exact result may be left to the imagination to vary, to extenuate or aggravate it according to circumstances. In the admirable profile of Oliver Cromwell after ——, the drooping eyelids, as if drawing a veil over the fixed, penetrating glance, the nostrils somewhat distended, and lips compressed so as hardly to let the breath escape him, denote the character of the man for high-reaching policy and deep designs as plainly as they can be written. How is it that we decipher this expression in the face? First, by feeling it. And how is it that we feel it? Not by re-established rules, but by the instinct of analogy, by the principle of association, which is subtle and sure in proportion as it is variable and indefinite. A circumstance, apparently of no value, shall alter the whole interpretation to be put upon an expression or action and it shall alter it thus powerfully because in proportion to its very insignificance it shows a strong general principle at work that extends in its ramifications to the smallest things. This in fact will make all the difference between minuteness and subtlety or refinement; for a small or trivial effect may in given circumstances imply the operation of a great power. Stillness may be the result of a blow too powerful to be resisted; silence may be imposed by feelings too agonising for utterance. The minute, the trifling and insipid is that which is little in itself, in its causes and its consequences; the subtle and refined is that which is slight and evanescent at first sight, but which mounts up to a mighty sum in the end, which is an essential part of an important whole, which has consequences greater than itself, and where more is meant than meets the eye or ear. We complain sometimes of littleness in a Dutch picture, where there are a vast number of distinct parts and objects, each small in itself, and leading to nothing else. A sky of Claude's cannot fall under this censure, where one imperceptible gradation is as it were the scale to another, where the broad arch of heaven is piled up of endlessly intermediate gold and azure tints, and where an infinite number of minute, scarce noticed particulars blend and melt into universal harmony. The subtlety in Shakespear, of which there is an immense deal scattered everywhere up and down, is always the instrument of passion, the vehicle of character. The action of a man pulling his hat over his forehead is indifferent enough in itself, and generally speaking, may mean anything or nothing; but in the circumstances in which Macduff is placed, it is neither insignificant nor equivocal.

What! man, ne'er pull your hat upon your brows, etc.

It admits but of one interpretation or inference, that which follows it:—

Give sorrow words: the grief that does not speak,

Whispers the o'er-fraught heart, and bids it break.

The passage in the same play, in which Duncan and his attendants are introduced, commenting on the beauty and situation of Macbeth's castle, though familiar in itself, has been often praised for the striking contrast it presents to the scenes which follow.—The same look in different circumstances may convey a totally different expression. Thus the eye turned round to look at you without turning the head indicates generally slyness or suspicion; but if this is combined with large expanded eyelids or fixed eyebrows, as we see it in Titian's pictures, it will denote calm contemplation or piercing sagacity, without anything of meanness or fear of being observed. In other cases it may imply merely indolent, enticing voluptuousness, as in Lely's portraits of women. The languor and weakness of the eyelids give the amorous turn to the expression. How should there be a rule for all this beforehand, seeing it depends on circumstances ever varying, and scarce discernible but by their effect on the mind? Rules are applicable to abstractions, but expression is concrete and individual. We know the meaning of certain looks, and we feel how they modify one another in conjunction. But we cannot have a separate rule to judge of all their combinations in different degrees and circumstances, without foreseeing all those combinations, which is impossible; or if we did foresee them, we should only be where we are, that is, we could only make the rule as we now judge without it, from imagination and the feeling of the moment. The absurdity of reducing expression to a preconcerted system was perhaps never more evidently shown than in a picture of the Judgment of Solomon by so great a man as N. Poussin, which I once heard admired for the skill and discrimination of the artist in making all the women, who are ranged on one side, in the greatest alarm at the sentence of the judge, while all the men on the opposite side see through the design of it. Nature does not go to work or cast things in a regular mould in this sort of way. I once heard a person remark of another, 'He has an eye like a vicious horse.' This was a fair analogy. We all, I believe, have noticed the look of a horse's eye just before he is going to bite or kick. But will any one, therefore, describe to me exactly what that look is? It was the same acute observer that said of a self-sufficient., prating music-master, 'He talks on all subjects *at sight*'—which expressed the man at once by an allusion to his profession, the coincidence was indeed perfect. Nothing else could compare with the easy assurance with which this gentleman would volunteer an explanation of things of which he was most ignorant, but the *nonchalance* with which a musician sits down to a harpsichord to play a piece he has never seen before. My physiognomical friend would not have hit on this mode of illustration without knowing the profession of the subject of his criticism; but having this hint given him, it instantly suggested itself to his 'sure trailing.' The manner of the speaker was evident; and the association of the music-master sitting down to play at sight, lurking in his mind, was immediately called out by the strength of his impression of the character. The feeling of character and the felicity of invention in explaining it were nearly allied to each other. The first was so wrought up and running over that the transition to the last was very easy and unavoidable. When Mr. Kean was so much praised for the action of Richard in his last struggle with his triumphant antagonist, where he stands, after his sword is wrested from him, with his hands stretched out, 'as if his will could not be disarmed, and the very phantoms of his despair had a withering power,' he said that he borrowed it from seeing the last efforts of Painter in his fight with Oliver. This assuredly did not lessen the merit of it. Thus it ever is with the man of real genius. He has the feeling of truth already shrined in his own breast, and his eye is still bent on Nature to see how she expresses herself. When we thoroughly understand the subject it is easy to translate from one language into another. Raphael, in muffling up the figure of Elymas the Sorcerer in his garments, appears to have extended the idea of blindness even to his clothes. Was this design? Probably not; but merely the feeling of analogy thoughtlessly suggesting this device, which being so suggested was retained and carried on, because it flattered or fell in with the original feeling. The tide of passion, when strong, overflows and gradually insinuates itself into all nooks and corners of the mind. Invention (of the best kind) I therefore do not think so distinct a thing from feeling as some are apt to imagine. The springs of pure feeling will rise and fill the moulds of fancy that are fit to receive it. There are some striking coincidences of colour in well-composed pictures, as in a straggling weed in the foreground streaked with blue or red to answer to a blue or red drapery, to the tone of the flesh or an opening in the sky:—not that this was intended, or done by the rule (for then it would presently become affected and ridiculous), but the eye, being imbued with a certain colour, repeats and varies it from a natural sense of harmony, a secret craving and appetite for beauty, which in the same manner soothes and gratifies the eye of taste, though the cause is not understood. *Tact, finesse*, is nothing but the being completely aware of the feeling belonging to certain situations, passions, etc., and the being consequently sensible to their slightest indications or movements in others. One of the most remarkable instances of this sort of faculty is the following story, told of Lord Shaftesbury, the grandfather of the author of the *Characteristics*. He had been to dine with Lady Clarendon and her daughter, who was at that time privately married to the Duke of York (afterwards James II.), and as he returned home with another nobleman who had accompanied him, he suddenly turned to him, and said, 'Depend upon it, the Duke has married Hyde's daughter.' His companion could not comprehend what he meant; but on explaining himself, he said, 'Her mother behaved to her with an attention and a marked respect that it is impossible to account for in any other way; and I am sure of it.' His conjecture shortly afterwards proved to be the truth. This was carrying the prophetic spirit of common sense as far as it could go.

FN to ESSAY IV

(1) Discourse XIII. vol. ii. pp. 113-117.

(2) Sentiment has the same source as that here pointed out. Thus the *Ranz des Vaches*, which has such an effect on the minds of the Swiss peasantry, when its well-known sound is heard, does not merely recall to them the idea of their country, but has associated with it a thousand nameless ideas, numberless touches of private affection, of early hope, romantic adventure and national pride, all which rush in (with mingled currents) to swell the tide of fond remembrance, and make them languish or die for home. What a fine instrument the human heart is! Who shall touch it? Who shall fathom it? Who shall 'sound it from Its lowest note to the top of its compass?' Who shall put his hand among the strings, and explain their wayward music? The heart alone, when touched by sympathy, trembles and responds to their hidden meaning!

ESSAY V. THE SAME SUBJECT CONTINUED

Genius or originality is, for the most part, *some strong quality in the mind, answering to and bringing out some new and striking quality in nature.*

Imagination is, more properly, the power of carrying on a given feeling into other situations, which must be done best according to the hold which the feeling itself has taken of the mind.(1) In new and unknown combinations the impression must act by sympathy, and not by rule, but there can be no sympathy where there is no passion, no original interest. The personal interest may in some cases oppress and circumscribe the imaginative faculty, as in the instance of Rousseau: but in general the strength and consistency of the imagination will be in proportion to the strength and depth of feeling; and it is rarely that a man even of lofty genius will be able to do more than carry on his own feelings and character, or some prominent and ruling passion, into fictitious and uncommon situations. Milton has by allusion embodied a great part of his political and personal history in the chief characters and incidents of *Paradise Lost*. He has, no doubt, wonderfully adapted and heightened them, but the elements are the same; you trace the bias and opinions of the man in the creations of the poe above the definition of genius. 'Born universal heir to all humanity,' he was 'as one, in suffering all who suffered nothing'; with a perfect sympathy with all things, yet alike indifferent to all: who did not tamper with Nature or warp her to his own purposes; who 'knew all qualities with a learned spirit,' instead of judging of them by his own predilections; and was rather 'a pipe for the Muse's finger to play what stop she pleasd,' than anxious to set up any character or pretensions of his own. His genius consisted in the faculty of transforming himself at will into whatever he chose: his originality was the power of seeing every object from the exact point of view in which others would see it. He was the Proteus of human intellect. Genius in ordinary is a more obstinate and less versatile thing. It is sufficiently exclusive and self-willed, quaint and peculiar. It docs some one thing by virtue of doing nothing else: it excels in some one pursuit by being blind to all excellence but its own. It is just the reverse of the cameleon; for it does not borrow, but lends its colour to all about it; or like the glow-worm, discloses a little circle of gorgeous light in the twilight of obscurity, in the night of intellect that surrounds it. So did Rembrandt. If ever there was a man of genius, he was one, in the proper sense of the term. He lived in and revealed to otters a world of his own, and might be said to have invented a new view of nature. He did not discover things *out of* nature, in fiction or fairy land, or make a voyage to the moon 'to descry new lands, rivers or mountains in her spotty globe,' but saw things *in* nature that every one had missed before him and gave others eyes to see them with. This is the test and triumph of originality, not to show us what has never been, and what we may therefore very easily never have dreamt of, but to point out to us what is before our eyes and under our feet, though we have had no suspicion of its existence, for want of sufficient strength of intuition, of determined grasp of mind, to seize and retain it. Rembrandt's conquests were not over the *ideal*, but the real. He did not contrive a new story or character, but we nearly owe to him a fifth part of painting, the knowledge of *chiaroscuro*—a distinct power and element in art and nature. He had a steadiness, a firm keeping of mind and eye, that first stood the shock of 'fierce extremes' in light and shade, or reconciled the greatest obscurity and the greatest brilliancy into perfect harmony; and he therefore was the first to hazard this appearance upon canvas, and give full effect to what he saw and delighted in. He was led to adopt this style of broad and startling contrast from its congeniality to his own feelings: his mind grappled with that which afforded the best exercise to its master-powers: he was bold in act, because he was urged on by a strong native impulse. Originality is then nothing but nature and feeling working in the mind. A man does not affect to be original: he is so, because he cannot help it, and often without knowing it. This extraordinary artist indeed might be said to have had a particular organ for colour. His eye seemed to come in contact with it as a feeling, to lay hold of it as a substance, rather than to contemplate it as a visual object. The texture of his landscapes is 'of the earth, earthy'—his clouds are humid, heavy, slow; his shadows are 'darkness that may be felt,' a 'palpable obscure'; his lights are lumps of liquid splendour! There is something more in this than can be accounted for from design or accident: Rembrandt was not a man made up of two or three rules and directions for acquiring genius.

I am afraid I shall hardly write so satisfactory a character of Mr. Wordsworth, though he too, like Rembrandt, has a faculty of making something out of nothing, that is, out of himself, by the medium through which he sees and with which he clothes the barrenest subject. Mr. Wordsworth is the last man to 'look abroad into universality,' if that alone constituted genius: he looks at home into himself, and is 'content with riches fineless.' He would in the other case be 'poor as winter,' if he had nothing but general capacity to trust to. He is the greatest, that is, the most original poet of the present day, only because he is the greatest egotist. He is 'self-involved, not dark.' He sits in the centre of his own being, and there 'enjoys bright day.' He does not waste a thought on others. Whatever does not relate exclusively and wholly to himself is foreign to his views. He contemplates a whole-length figure of himself, he looks along the unbroken line of his personal identity. He thrusts aside all other objects, all other interests, with scorn and impatience, that he may repose on his own being, that he may dig out the treasures of thought contained in it, that he may unfold the precious stores of a mind for ever brooding over itself. His genius is the effect of his individual character. He stamps that character, that deep individual interest, on whatever he meets. The object is nothing but as it furnishes food for internal meditation, for old associations. If there had been no other being in the universe, Mr. Wordsworth's poetry would have been just what it is. If there had been neither love nor friendship, neither ambition nor pleasure nor business in the World, the author of the *Lyrical Ballads* need not have been greatly changed from what he is—might still have 'kept the noiseless tenour of his way,' retired in the sanctuary of his own heart, hallowing the Sabbath of his own thoughts. With the passions, the pursuits, and imaginations of other men he does not profess to sympathise, but 'finds tongues in the trees, books in the running brooks, sermons in stones, and good in everything.' With a mind averse from outward objects, but ever intent upon its own workings, he hangs a weight of thought and feeling upon every trifling circumstance connected with his past history. The note of the cuckoo sounds in his ear like the voice of other years; the daisy spreads its leaves in the rays of boyish delight that stream from his thoughtful eyes; the rainbow lifts its proud arch in heaven but to mark his progress from infancy to manhood; an old thorn is buried, bowed down under the mass of associations he has wound about it; and to him, as he himself beautifully says,

```
    The meanest flow'r that blows can give
    Thoughts that do often lie too deep for tears.
```

It is this power of habitual sentiment, or of transferring the interest of our conscious existence to whatever gently solicits attention, and is a link in the chain of association without rousing our passions or hurting our pride, that is the striking feature in Mr. Wordsworth's mind and poetry. Others have left and shown this power before, as Wither, Burns, etc., but none have felt it so intensely and absolutely as to lend to it the voice of inspiration, as to make it the foundation of a new style and school in poetry. His strength, as it so often happens, arises from the excess of his weakness. But he has opened a new avenue to the human heart, has explored another secret haunt and nook of nature, 'sacred to verse, and sure of everlasting fame.' Compared with his lines, Lord Byron's stanzas are but exaggerated common-place, and Walter Scott's poetry (not his prose) old wives' fables.(2) There is no one in whom I have been more disappointed than in the writer here spoken of, nor with whom I am more disposed on certain points to quarrel; but the love of truth and justice which obliges me to do this, will not suffer me to blench his merits. Do what he can, he cannot help being an original-minded man. His poetry is not servile. While the cuckoo returns in the spring, while the daisy looks bright in the sun, while the rainbow lifts its head above the storm—

```
    Yet I'll remember thee, Glencairn,
    And all that thou hast done for me!
```

Sir Joshua Reynolds, in endeavouring to show that there is no such thing as proper originality, a spirit emanating from the mind of the artist and shining through his works, has traced Raphael through a number of figures which he has borrowed from Masaccio and others. This is a bad calculation. If Raphael had only borrowed those figures from others, would he, even in Sir Joshua's sense, have been entitled to the praise of originality? Plagiarism, in so far as it is plagiarism, is not originality. Salvator is considered by many as a great genius. He is what they call an irregular genius. My notion of genius is not exactly the same as theirs. It has also been made a question; whether there is not more genius in Rembrandt's Three Trees than in all Claude Lorraine's landscapes. I do not know how that may be; but it was enough for Claude to have been a perfect landscape-painter.

Capacity is not the same thing as genius. Capacity may be described to relate to the quantity of knowledge, however acquired; genius, to its quality and the mode of acquiring it. Capacity is power over given ideas combinations of ideas; genius is the power over those which are not given, and for which no obvious or precise rule can be laid down. Or capacity is power of any sort; genius is power of a different sort from what has yet been shown. A retentive memory, a clear understanding, is capacity, but it is not genius. The admirable Crichton was a person of prodigious capacity; but there is no proof (that I know) that he had an atom of genius. His verses that remain are dull and sterile. He could learn all that was known of any subject; he could do anything if others could show him the way to do it. This was very wonderful; but that is all you can say of it. It requires a good capacity to play well at chess; but, after all, it is a game of skill, and not of genius. Know what you will of it, the understanding still moves in certain tracks in which others have trod it before, quicker or slower, with more or less comprehension and presence of mind. The greatest skill strikes out nothing for itself, from its own peculiar resources; the nature of the game is a thing determinate and fixed: there is no royal or poetical road to checkmate your adversary. There is no place for genius but in the indefinite and unknown. The discovery of the binomial theorem was an effort of genius; but there was none shown in Jedediah Buxton's being able to multiply 9 figures by 9 in his head. If he could have multiplied 90 figures by 90 instead of 9, it would have been equally useless toil and trouble.(3) He is a man of capacity who possesses considerable intellectual riches: he is a man of genius who finds out a vein of new ore. Originality is the seeing nature differently from others, and yet as it is in itself. It is not singularity or affectation, but the discovery of new and valuable truth. All the world do not see the wh looking at. Habit blinds them to some things; short-sightedness to others. Every mind is not a gauge and measure of truth. Nature has her surface and her dark recesses. She is deep, obscure, and infinite. It is only minds on whom she makes her fullest impressions that can penetrate her shrine or unveil her *Holy of Holies*. It is only those whom she has filled with her spirit that have the boldness or the power to reveal her mysteries to others. But Nature has a thousand aspects, and one man can only draw out one of them. Whoever does this is a man of genius. One displays her force, another her refinement; one her power of harmony, another her suddenness of contrast; one her beauty of form, another her splendour of colour. Each does that for which he is bast fitted by his particular genius, that is to say, by some quality of mind into which the quality of the object sinks deepest, where it finds the most cordial welcome, is perceived to its utmost extent, and where again it forces its way out from the fulness with which it has taken possession of the mind of the student. The imagination gives out what it has first absorbed by congeniality of temperament, what it has attracted and moulded into itself by elective affinity, as the loadstone draws and impregnates iron. A little originality is more esteemed and sought for than the greatest acquired talent, because it throws a new light upon things, and is peculiar to the individual. The other is common; and may be had for the asking, to any amount.

The value of any work is to be judged of by the quantity of originality contained in it. A very little of this will go a great way. If Goldsmith had never written anything but the two or three first chapters of the *Vicar of Wakefield* or the character of a Village Schoolmaster, they would have stamped him a man of genius. The editors of Encyclopedias are not usually reckoned the first literary characters of the age. The works of which they have the management contain a great deal of knowledge, like chests or warehouses, but the goods are not their own. We should as soon think of admiring the shelves of a library; but the shelves of a library are useful and respectable. I was once applied to, in a delicate emergency, to write an article on a difficult subject for an Encyclopedia, and was advised to take time and give it a systematic and scientific form, to avail myself of all the knowledge that was to be obtained on the subject, and arrange it with clearness and method. I made answer that as to the first, I had taken time to do all that I ever pretended to do, as I had thought incessantly on different matters for twenty years of my life;(4) that I had no particular knowledge of the subject in question, and no head for arrangement; and that the utmost I could do in such a case would be, when a systematic and scientific article was prepared, to write marginal notes upon it, to insert a remark or illustration of my own (not to be found in former Encyclopedias), or to suggest a better definition than had been offered in the text. There are two sorts of writing. The first is compilation; and consists in collecting and stating all that is already known of any question in the best possible manner, for the benefit of the uninformed reader. An author of this class is a very learned amanuensis of other people's thoughts. The second sort proceeds on an entirely different principle: instead of bringing down the account of knowledge to the point at which it has already arrived, it professes to start from that point on the strength of the writer's individual reflections; and supposing the reader in possession of what is already known, supplies deficiencies, fills up certain blanks, and quits the beaten road in search of new tracts of observation or sources of feeling. It is in vain to object to this last style that it is disjointed, disproportioned, and irregular. It is merely a set of additions and corrections to other men's works, or to the common stock of human knowledge, printed separately. You might as well expect a continued chain of reasoning in the notes to a book. It skips all the trite, intermediate, level common-places of the subject, and only stops at the difficult passages of the human mind, or touches on some striking point that has been overlooked in previous editions. A view of a subject, to be connected and regular, cannot be all new. A writer will always be liable to be charged either with paradox or common-place, either with dulness or affectation. But we have no right to demand from any one more than he pretends to. There is indeed a medium in all things, but to unite opposite excellencies is a task ordinarily too hard for mortality. He who succeeds in what he aims at, or who takes the lead in any one mode or path of excellence, may think himself very well off. It would not be fair to complain of the style of an Encyclopedia as dull, as wanting volatile salt; nor of the style of an Essay because it is too light and sparkling, because it is not a *caput mortuum*. So it is rather an odd objection to a work that it is made up entirely of 'brilliant passages'—at least it is a fault that can be found with few works, and the book might be pardoned for its singularity. The censure might indeed seem like adroit flattery, if it were not passed on an author whom any objection is sufficient to render unpopular and ridiculous. I grant it is best to unite solidity with show, general information with particular ingenuity. This is the pattern of a perfect style; but I myself do not pretend to be a perfect writer. In fine, we do not banish light French wines from our tables, or refuse to taste sparkling Champagne when we can get it because it has not the body of Old Port. Besides, I do not know that dulness is strength, or that an observation is slight because it is striking. Mediocrity, insipidity, want of character is the great fault.

Mediocribus esse poetis
Non Dii, non homines, non concessere columnae.

Neither is this privilege allowed to prose-writers in our time any more than to poets formerly.

It is not then acuteness of organs or extent of capacity that constitutes rare genius or produces the most exquisite models of art, but an intense sympathy with some one beauty or distinguishing characteristic in nature. Irritability alone, or the interest taken in certain things, may supply the place of genius in weak and otherwise ordinary minds. As there are certain instruments fitted to perform certain kinds of labour, there are certain minds so framed as to produce certain *chef-d'oeuvres* in art and literature, which is surely the best use they can be put to. If a man had all sorts of instruments in his shop and wanted one, he would rather have that one than be supplied with a double set of all the others. If he had them twice over, he could only do what he can do as it is, whereas without that one he perhaps cannot finish any one work he has in hand. So if a man can do one thing better than anybody else, the value of this one thing is what he must stand or fall by, and his being able to do a hundred other things merely *as well* as anybody else would not alter the sentence or add to his respectability; on the contrary, his being able to do so many other things well would probably interfere with and encumber him in the execution of the only thing that others cannot do as well as he, and so far be a drawback and a disadvantage. More people, in fact, fail from a multiplicity of talents and pretensions than from an absolute poverty of resources. I have given instances of this elsewhere. Perhaps Shakespear's tragedies would in some respects have been better if he had never written comedies at all; and in that case his comedies might well have been spared, though they must have cost us some regret. Racine, it is said, might have rivalled Moliere in comedy; but he gave up the cultivation of his comic talents to devote himself wholly to the tragic Muse. If, as the French tell us, he in consequence attained to the perfection of tragic composition, this was better than writing comedies as well as Moliere and tragedies as well as Crebillon. Yet I count those persons fools who think it a pity Hogarth did not succeed better in serious subjects. The division of labour is an excellent principle in taste as well as in mechanics. Without this, I find from Adam Smith, we could not have a pin made to the degree of perfection it is. We do not, on any rational scheme of criticism, inquire into the variety of a man's excellences, or the number of his works, or his facility of production. *Venice Preserved* is sufficient for Otway's fame. I hate all those nonsensical stories about Lope de Vega and his writing a play in a morning before breakfast. He had time enough to do it after. If a man leaves behind him any work which is a model in its kind, we have no right to ask whether he could do anything else, or how he did it, or how long he was about it. All that talent which is not necessary to the actual quantity of excellence existing in the world, loses its object, is so much waste talent or *talent to let.* I heard a sensible man say he should like to do some one thing better than all the rest of the world, and in everything else to be like all the rest of the world. Why should a man do more than his part? The rest is vanity and vexation of spirit. We look with jealous and grudging eyes at all those qualifications which are not essential; first, because they are superfluous, and next, because we suspect they will be prejudicial. Why does Mr. Kean play all those harlequin tricks of singing, dancing, fencing, etc.? They say, 'It is for his benefit.' It is not for his reputation. Garrick indeed shone equally in comedy and tragedy. But he was first, not second-rate in both. There is not a greater impertinence than to ask, if a man is clever out of his profession. I have heard of people trying to cross-examine Mrs. Siddons. I would as soon try to entrap one of the Elgin Marbles into an argument. Good nature and common sense are required from all people; but one proud distinction is enough for any one individual to possess or to aspire to.

FN to ESSAY V

(1) I do not here speak of the figurative or fanciful exercise of the imagination, which consists in finding out some striking object or image to illustrate another.

(2) Mr. Wordsworth himself should not say this, and yet I am not sure he would not.

(3) The only good thing I have ever heard come of this man's singular faculty of memory was the following. A gentleman was mentioning his having been sent up to London from the place where he lived to see Garrick act. When he went back into the country he was asked what he thought of the player and the play. 'Oh!' he said, 'he did not know: he had only seen a little man strut about the stage and repeat 7956 words one hand to his forehead, and seeming mightily delighted, called out, 'Ay, indeed! And pray, was he found to be correct?' This was the supererogation of literal matter-of-fact curiosity. Jedediah Buxton's counting the number of words was idle enough; but here was a fellow who wanted some one to count them over again to see if he was correct.

    The force of *dulness* could no farther go!

(4) Sir Joshua Reynolds, being asked how long it had taken him to do a certain picture, made answer, 'All my life!.'

ESSAY VI. CHARACTER OF COBBETT

People have about as substantial an idea of Cobbett as they have of Cribb. His blows are as hard, and he himself is as impenetrable. One has no notion of him as making use of a fine pen, but a great mutton-fist; his style stuns his readers, and he 'fillips the ear of the public with a three-man beetle.' He is too much for any single newspaper antagonist; 'lays waste' a city orator or Member of Parliament, and bears hard upon the Government itself. He is a kind of *fourth estate* in the politics of the country. He is not only unquestionably the most powerful political writer of the present day, but one of the best writers in the language. He speaks and thinks plain, broad, downright English. He might be said to have the clearness of Swift, the naturalness of Defoe, and the picturesque satirical description of Mandeville; if all such comparisons were not impertinent. A really great and original write sense, Sterne was not a wit, nor Shakespear a poet. It is easy to describe second-rate talents, because they fall into a class and enlist under a standard; but first-rate powers defy calculation or comparison, and can be defined only by themselves. They are *sui generis*, and make the class to which they belong. I have tried half a dozen times to describe Burke's style without ever succeeding,—its severe extravagance; its literal boldness; its matter-of-fact hyperboles; its running away with a subject, and from it at the same time,—but there is no making it out, for there is no example of the same thing anywhere else. We have no common measure to refer to; and his qualities contradict even themselves.

Cobbett is not so difficult. He has been compared to Paine; and so far it is true there are no two writers who come more into juxtaposition from the nature of their subjects, from the internal resources on which they draw, and from the popular effect of their writings and their adaptation (though that is a bad word in the present case) to the capacity of every reader. But still if we turn to a volume of Paine's (his *Common Sense* or *Rights of Man*) we are struck (not to say somewhat refreshed) by the difference. Paine is a much more sententious writer than Cobbett. You cannot open a page in any of his best and earlier works without meeting with some maxim, some antithetical and memorable saying, which is a sort of starting-place for the argument, and the goal to which it returns. There is not a single *bon mot*, a single sentence in Cobbett that has ever been quoted again. If anything is ever quoted from him, it is an epithet of abuse or a nickname. He is an excellent hand at invention in that way, and has 'damnable iteration' in him. What could be better than his pestering Erskine year after year with his second title of Baron Clackmannan? He is rather too fond of *the Sons and Daughters of Corruption*. Paine affected to reduce things to first principles, to announce self-evident truths. Cobbett troubles himself about little but the details and local circumstances. The first appeared to have made up his mind beforehand to certain opinions, and to try to find the most compendious and pointed expressions for them: his successor appears to have no clue, no fixed or leading principles, nor ever to have thought on a question till he sits down to write about it; but then there seems no end of his matters of fact and raw materials, which are brought out in all their strength and sharpness from not having been squared or frittered down or vamped up to suit a theory—he goes on with his descriptions and illustrations as if he would never come to a stop; they have all the force of novelty with all the familiarity of old acquaintance; his knowledge grows out of the subject, and his style is that of a man who has an absolute intuition of what he is talking about, and never thinks of anything else. He deals in premises and speaks to evidence—the coming to a conclusion and summing up (which was Paine's *forte*) lies in a smaller compass. The one could not compose an elementary treatise on politics to become a manual for the popular reader, nor could the other in all probability have kept up a weekly journal for the same number of years with the same spirit, interest, and untired perseverance. Paine's writings are a sort of introduction to political arithmetic on a new plan: Cobbett keeps a day-book, and makes an entry at full of all the occurrences and troublesome questions that start up throughout the year. Cobbett, with vast industry, vast information, and the utmost power of making what he says intelligible, never seems to get at the beginning or come to the end of any question: Paine in a few short sentences seems by his peremptory manner 'to clear it from all controversy, past, present, and to come.' Paine takes a bird's-eye view of things. Cobbett sticks close to them, inspects the component parts, and keeps fast hold of the smallest advantages they afford him. Or, if I might here be indulged in a pastoral allusion, Paine tries to enclose his ideas in a fold for security and repose; Cobbett lets *his* pour out upon the plain like a flock of sheep to feed and batten. Cobbett is a pleasanter writer for those to read who do not agree with him; for he is less dogmatical, goes more into the common grounds of fact and argument to which all appeal, is more desultory and various, and appears less to be driving at a present conclusion than urged on by the force of present conviction. He is therefore tolerated by all parties, though he has made himself by turns obnoxious to all; and even those he abuses read him. The Reformers read him when he was a Tory, and the Tories read him now that he is a Reformer. He must, I think, however, be *caviare* to the Whigs.(1)

If he is less metaphysical and poetical than his celebrated prototype, he is more picturesque and dramatic. His episodes, which are numerous as they are pertinent, are striking, interesting, full of life and *naivete*, minute, double measure running over, but never tedious—*nunquam sufflaminandus erat*. He is one of those writers who can never tire us, not even of himself; and the reason is, he is always 'full of matter.' He never runs to lees, never gives us the vapid leavings of himself, is never 'weary, stale, and unprofitable,' but always setting out afresh on his journey, clearing away some old nuisance, and turning up new mould. His egotism is delightful, for there is no affectation in it. He does not talk of himself for lack of something to write about, but because some circumstance that has happened to himself is the best possible illustration of the subject, and he is not the man to shrink from giving the best possible illustration of the subject from a squeamish delicacy. He likes both himself and his subject too well. He does not put himself before it, and say, 'Admire me first,' but places us in the same situation with himself, and makes us see all that he does. There is no blindman's-buff, no conscious hints, no awkward ventriloquism, no testimonies of applause, no abstract, senseless self-complacency, no smuggled admiration of his own person by proxy: it is all plain and above-board. He writes himself plain William Cobbett, strips himself quite as naked as anybody would wish—in a word, his egotism is full of individuality, and has room for very little vanity in it. We feel delighted, rub our hands, and draw our chair to the fire, when we come to a passage of this sort: we know it will be something new and good, manly and simple, not the same insipid story of self over again. We sit down at table with the writer, but it is to a course of rich viands, flesh, fish, and wild-fowl, and not to a nominal entertainment, like that given by the Barmecide in the *Arabian Nights*, who put off his visitors with calling for a number of exquisite things that never appeared, and with the honour of his company. Mr. Cobbett is not a *make-believe* writer: his worst enemy cannot say that of him. Still less is he a vulgar one: he must be a puny, common-place critic indeed who thinks him so. How fine were the graphical descriptions he sent us from America: what a Transatlantic flavour, what a native gusto, what a fine *sauce piquante* of contempt they were seasoned with! If he had sat down to look at himself in the glass, instead of looking about him like Adam in Paradise, he would not have got up these articles in so capital a style. What a noble account of his first breakfast after his arrival in America! It might serve for a month. There is no scene on the stage more amusing. How well he paints the gold and scarlet plumage of the American birds, only to lament more pathetically the want of the wild wood-notes of his native land! The groves of the Ohio that had just fallen beneath the axe's stroke 'live in his description,' and the turnips that he transplanted from Botley 'look green' in prose! How well at another time he describes the poor sheep that had got the tick and had bled down in the agonies of death! It is a portrait in the manner of Bewick, with the strength, the simplicity, and feeling of that great naturalist. What havoc he makes, when he pleases, of the curls of Dr. Parr's wig and of the Whig consistency of Mr. (Coleridge?)! His *Grammar*, too, is as entertaining as a story-book. He is too hard upon the style of others, and not enough (sometimes) on his own.

As a political partisan no one can stand against him. With his brandished club, like Giant Despair in the *Pilgrim's Progress*, he knocks out their brains; and not only no individual but no corrupt system could hold out against his powerful and repeated attacks, but with the same weapon, swung round like a flail, that he levels his antagonists, he lays his friends low, and puts his own party *hors de combat*. This is a bad propensity., and a worse principle in political tactics, though a common one. If his blows were straightforward and steadily directed to the same object, no unpopular minister could live before him; instead of which he lays about right and left, impartially and remorselessly, makes a clear stage, has all the ring to himself, and then runs out of it, just when he should stand his ground. He throws his head into his adversary's stomach, and takes away from him all inclination for the fight, hits fair or foul, strikes at everything, and as you come up to his aid or stand ready to pursue his advantage, trips up your heels or lays you sprawling, and pummels you when down as much to his heart's content as ever the Yanguesian carriers belaboured Rosinante with their pack-staves. 'He has the back-trick simply the best of any man in Illyria.' He pays off both scores of old friendship and new-acquired enmity in a breath, in one perpetual volley, one raking fire of 'arrowy sleet' shot from his pen. However his own reputation or the cause may suffer in consequence, he cares not one pin about that, so that he disables all who oppose, or who pretend to help him. In fact, he cannot bear success of any kind, not even of his own views or party; and if any principle were likely to become popular, would turn round against it to show his power in shouldering it on one side. In short, wherever power is, there he is against it: he naturally butts at all obstacles, as unicorns are attracted to oak trees, and feels his own strength only by resistance to the opinions and wishes of the rest of the world. To sail with the stream, to agree with the company, is not his humour. If he could bring about a Reform in Parliament, the odds are that he would instantly fall foul of and try to mar his own handiwork; and he quarrels with his own creatures as soon as he has written them into a little vogue—and a prison. I do not think this is vanity or fickleness so much as a pugnacious disposition, that must have an antagonistic power to contend with, and only finds itself at ease in systematic opposition. If it were not for this, the high towers and rotten places of the world would fall before the battering-ram of his hard-headed reasoning; but if he once found them tottering, he would apply his strength to prop them up, and disappoint the expectations of his followers. He cannot agree to anything established, nor to set up anything else in its stead. While it is established, he presses hard against it, because it presses upon him, at least in imagination. Let it crumble under his grasp, and the motive to resistance is gone. He then requires some other grievance to set his face against. His principle is repulsion, his nature contradiction: he is made up of mere antipathies, an Ishmaelite indeed without a fellow. He is always playing at hunt-the-slipper in politics. He turns round upon whoever is next him. The way to wean him from any opinion, and make him conceive an intolerable hatred against it, would be to place somebody near him who was perpetually dinning it in his ears. When he is in England he does nothing but abuse the Boroughmongers and laugh at the whole system; when he is in America he grows impatient of freedom and a republic. If he had stayed there a little longer he would have become a loyal and a loving subject of His Majesty King George IV. He lampooned the French Revolution when it was hailed as the dawn of liberty by millions: by the time it was brought into almost universal ill-odour by some means or other (partly no doubt by himself), he had turned, with one or two or three others, staunch Buonapartist. He is always of the militant, not of the triumphant party: so far he bears a gallant show of magnanimity. But his gallantry is hardly of the right stamp. It wants principle; for though he is not servile or mercenary, he is the victim of self-will. He must pull down and pull in pieces: it is not in his disposition to do otherwise. It is a pity; for with his great talents he might do great things, if he would go right forward to any useful object, make thorough stitch-work of any question, or join hand and heart with any principle. He changes his opinions as he does his friends, and much on the same account. He has no comfort in fixed principles; as soon as anything is settled in his own mind, he quarrels with it. He has no satisfaction but the chase after truth, runs a question down, worries and kills it, then quits it like a vermin, and starts some new game, to lead him a new dance, and give him a fresh breathing through bog and brake, with the rabble yelping at his heels and the leaders perpetually at fault. This he calls sport-royal. He thinks it as good as cudgel-playing or single-stick, or anything else that has life in it. He likes the cut and thrust, the falls, bruises, and dry blows of an argument: as to any good or useful results that may come of the amicable settling of it, any one is welcome to them for him. The amusement is over when the matter is once fairly decided.

There is another point of view in which this may be put. I might say that Mr. Cobbett is a very honest man with a total want of principle, and I might explain this paradox thus:—I mean that he is, I think, in downright earnest in what he says, in the part he takes at the time; but in taking that part, he is led entirely by headstrong obstinacy, caprice, novelty 'pique, or personal motive of some sort, and not by a steadfast regard for truth or habitual anxiety for what is right uppermost in his mind. He is not a fee'd, time-serving, shuffling advocate (no man could write as he does who did not believe himself sincere); but his understanding is the dupe and slave of his momentary, violent, and irritable humours. He does not adopt an opinion 'deliberately or for money,' yet his conscience is at the mercy of the first provocation he receives, of the first whim he takes in his head: he sees things through the medium of heat and passion, not with reference to any general principles, and his whole system of thinking is deranged by the first object that strikes his fancy or sours his temper education. He is a self-taught man, and has the faults as well as excellences of that class of persons in their most striking and glaring excess. It must be acknowledged that the editor of the *Political Register* (the *twopenny trash*, as it was called, till a bill passed the House to raise the price to sixpence) is not 'the gentleman and scholar,' though he has qualities that, with a little better management, would be worth (to the public) both those titles. For want of knowing what has been discovered before him, he has not certain general landmarks to refer to, or a general standard of thought to apply to individual cases. He relies on his own acuteness and the immediate evidence, without being acquainted with the comparative anatomy or philosophical structure of opinion. He does not view things on a large scale or at the horizon (dim and airy enough, perhaps)—but as they affect himself, close, palpable, tangible. Whatever he finds out is his own, and he only knows what he finds out. He is in the constant hurry and fever of gestation; his brain teems incessantly with some fresh project. Every new light is the birth of a new system, the dawn of a new world outstripping and overreaching himself. The last opinion is the only true one. He is wiser to-day than he was yesterday. Why should he not be wiser to-morrow than he was to-day?—Men of a learned education are not so sharp-witted as clever men without it; but they know the balance of the human intellect better; if they are more stupid, they are more steady, and are less liable to be led astray by their own sagacity and the overweening petulance of hard-earned and late-acquired wisdom. They do not fall in love with every meretricious extravagance at first sight, or mistake an old battered hypothesis for a vestal, because they are new to the ways of this old world. They do not seize upon it as a prize, but are safe from gross imposition by being as wise and no wiser than those who went before them.

Paine said on some occasion, 'What I have written, I have written'—as rendering any further declaration of his principles unnecessary. Not so Mr. Cobbett. What he has written is no rule to him what he is to write maintain the opinions of the last six days against friend or foe. I doubt whether this outrageous inconsistency, this headstrong fickleness, this understood want of all rule and method, does not enable him to go on with the spirit, vigour, and variety that he does. He is not pledged to repeat himself. Every new *Register* is a kind of new Prospectus. He blesses himself from all ties and shackles on his understanding; he has no mortgages on his brain; his notions are free and unencumbered. If he was put in trammels, he might become a vile hack like so many more. But he gives himself 'ample scope and verge enough.' He takes both sides of a question, and maintains one as sturdily as the other. If nobody else can argue against him, he is a very good match for himself. He writes better in favour of Reform than anybody else; he used to write better against it. Wherever he is, there is the tug of war, the weight of the argument, the strength of abuse. He is not like a man in danger of being *bed-rid* in his faculties—he tosses and tumbles about his unwieldy bulk, and when he is tired of lying on one side, relieves himself by turning on the other. His shifting his point of view from time to time not merely adds variety and greater compass to his topics (so that the *Political Register* is an armoury and magazine for all the materials and weapons of political warfare), but it gives a greater zest and liveliness to his manner of treating them. Mr. Cobbett takes nothing for granted as what he has proved before; he does not write a book of reference. We see his ideas in their first concoction, fermenting and overflowing with the ebullitions of a lively conception. We look on at the actual process, and are put in immediate possession of the grounds and materials on which he forms his sanguine, unsettled conclusions. He does not give us samples of reasoning, but the whole solid mass, refuse and all.

> He pours out all as plain
> As downright Shippen or as old Montaigne.

This is one cause of the clearness and force of his writings. An argument does not stop to stagnate and muddle in his brain, but passes at once to his paper. His ideas are served up, like pancakes, hot and hot. Fresh theories give him fresh courage. He is like a young and lusty bridegroom that divorces a favourite speculation every morning, and marries a new one every night. He is not wedded to his notions, not he. He has not one Mrs. Cobbett among all his opinions. He makes the most of the last thought that has come in his way, seizes fast hold of it, rumbles it about in all directions with rough strong hands, has his wicked will of it, takes a surfeit, and throws it away.—Our author's changing his opinions for new ones is not so wonderful; what is more remarkable is his facility in forgetting his old ones. He does not pretend to consistency (like Mr. Coleridge); he frankly disavows all connection with himself. He feels no personal responsibility in this way, and cuts a friend or principle with the same decided indifference that Antipholis of Ephesus cuts AEgeon of Syracuse. It is a hollow thing. The only time he ever grew romantic was in bringing over the relics of Mr. Thomas Paine with him from America to go a progress with them through the disaffected districts. Scarce had he landed in Liverpool when he left the bones of a great man to shift for themselves; and no sooner did he arrive in London than he made a speech to disclaim all participation in the political and theological sentiments of his late idol, and to place the whole stock of his admiration and enthusiasm towards him to the account of his financial speculations, and of his having predicted the fate of paper-money. If he had erected a little gold statue to him, it might have proved the sincerity of this assertion; but to make a martyr and a patron saint of a man, and to dig up 'his canonised bones' in order to expose them as objects of devotion to the rabble's gaze, asks something that has more life and spirit in it, more mind and vivifying soul, than has to do with any calculation of pounds, shillings, and pence! The fact is, he *ratted* from his own project. He found the thing not so ripe as he had expected. His heart failed him; his enthusiasm fled, and he made his retractation. His admiration is short-lived; his contempt only is rooted, and his resentment lasting.—The above was only one instance of his building too much on practical *data*. He has an ill habit of prophesying, and goes on, though still decieved. The art of prophesying does not suit Mr. Cobbett's style. He has a knack of fixing names and times and places. According to him, the Reformed Parliament was to meet in March 1818—it did not, and we heard no more of the matter. When his predictions fail, he takes no further notice of them, but applies himself to new ones—like the country people who turn to see what weather there is in the almanac for the next week, though it has been out in its reckoning every day of the last.

Mr. Cobbett is great in attack, not in defence; he cannot fight an up-hill battle. He will not bear the least punishing. If any one turns upon him (which few people like to do) he immediately turns tail. Like an overgrown schoolboy, he is so used to have it all his own way, that he cannot submit to anything like competition or a struggle for the mastery; he must lay on all the blows, and take none. He is bullying and cowardly; a Big Ben in politics, who will fall upon others and crush them by his weight, but is not prepared for resistance, and is soon staggered by a few smart blows. Whenever he has been set upon, he has slunk out of the controversy. The *Edinburgh Review* made (what is called) a dead set at him some years ago, to which he only retorted by an eulogy on the superior neatness of an English kitchen-garden to a Scotch one. I remember going one day into a bookseller's shop in Fleet Street to ask for the *Review*, and on my expressing my opinion to a young Scotchman, who stood behind the counter, that Mr. Cobbett might hit as hard in his reply, the North Briton said with some alarm, 'But you don't think, sir, Mr. Cobbett will be able to injure the Scottish nation?' I said I could not speak to that point, but I thought he was very well able to defend himself. He, however, did not, but has borne a grudge to the *Edinburgh Review* ever since, which he hates worse than the *Quarterly*. I cannot say I do.(2)

FN to ESSAY VI

(1) The late Lord Thurlow used to say that Cobbett was the only writer that deserved the name of a political reasoner.

(2) Mr. Cobbett speaks almost as well as he writes. The only time I ever saw him he seemed to me a very pleasant man—easy of access, affable, clear-headed, simple and mild in his manner, deliberate and unruffled in his speech, though some of his expressions were not very qualified. His figure is tall and portly. He has a good, sensible face—rather full, with little grey eyes, a hard, square forehead, a ruddy complexion, with hair grey or powdered; and had on a scarlet broadcloth waistcoat with the flaps of the pockets hanging down, as was the custom for gentlemen-farmers in the last century, or as we see it in the pictures of Members of Parliament in the reign of George I. I certainly did not think less favourably of him for seeing him.

ESSAY VII. ON PEOPLE WITH ONE IDEA

There are people who have but one idea: at least, if they have more, they keep it a secret, for they never talk but of one subject.

There is Major Cartwright: he has but one idea or subject of discourse, Parliamentary Reform. Now Parliamentary Reform is (as far as I know) a very good subject to talk about; but why should it be the only one? To hear the worthy and gallant Major resume his favourite topic, is like law-business, or a person who has a suit in Chancery going on. Nothing can be attended to, nothing can be talked of but that. Now it is getting on, now again it is standing still; at one time the Master has promised to pass judgment by a certain day, at another he has put it off again and called for more papers, and both are equally reasons for speaking of it. Like the piece of packthread in the barrister's hands, he turns and twists it all ways, and cannot proceed a step without it. Some schoolboys cannot read but in their own book; and the man of one idea cannot converse out of his own subject. Conversation it is not; but a sort of recital of the preamble of a bill, or a collection of grave arguments for a man's being of opinion with himself. It would be well if there was anything of character, of eccentricity in all this; but that is not the case. It is a political homily personified, a walking common-place we have to encounter and listen to. It is just as if a man was to insist on your hearing him go through the fifth chapter of the Book of Judges every time you meet, or like the story of the Cosmogony in the *Vicar of Wakefield.* It is a tine played on a barrel-organ. It is a common vehicle of discourse into which they get and are set down when they please, without any pain or trouble to themselves. Neither is it professional pedantry or trading quackery: it has no excuse. The man has no more to do with the question which he saddles on all his hearers than you have. This is what makes the matter hopeless. If a farmer talks to you about his pigs or his poultry, or a physician about his patients, or a lawyer about his briefs, or a merchant about stock, or an author about himself, you know how to account for this, it is a common infirmity, you have a laugh at his expense and there is no more to be said. But here is a man who goes out of his way to be absurd, and is troublesome by a romantic effort of generosity. You cannot say to him, 'All this may be interesting to you, but I have no concern in it': you cannot put him off in that way. He retorts the Latin adage upon you-*Nihil humani a me alienum puto.* He has got possession of a subject which is of universal and paramount interest (not 'a fee-grief, due to some single breast'), and on that plea may hold you by the button as long as he chooses. His delight is to harangue on what nowise regards himself: how then can you refuse to listen to what as little amuses you? Time and tide wait for no man. The business of the state admits of no delay. The question of Universal Suffrage and Annual Parliaments stands first on the order of the day—takes precedence in its own right of every other question. Any other topic, grave or gay, is looked upon in the light of impertinence, and sent *to Coventry.* Business is an interruption; pleasure a digression from it. It is the question before every company where the Major comes, which immediately resolves itself into a committee of the whole upon it, is carried on by means of a perpetual virtual adjournment, and it is presumed that no other is entertained while this is pending—a determination which gives its persevering advocate a fair prospect of expatiating on it to his dying day. As Cicero says of study, it follows him into the country, it stays with him at home: it sits with him at breakfast, and goes out with him to dinner. It is like a part of his dress, of the costume of his person, without which he would be at a loss what to do. If he meets you in the street, he accosts you with it as a form of salutation: if you see him at his own house, it is supposed you come upon that. If you happen to remark, 'It is a fine day,' or 'The town is full,' it is considered as a temporary compromise of the question; you are suspected of not going the whole length of the principle. As Sancho, when reprimanded for mentioning his homely favourite in the Duke's kitchen, defended himself by saying, 'There I thought of Dapple, and there I spoke of him,' so the true stickler for Reform neglects no opportunity of introducing the subject wherever he is. Place its veteran champion under the frozen north, and he will celebrate sweet smiling Reform; place him under the mid-day Afric suns, and he will talk of nothing but Reform—Reform so sweetly smiling and so sweetly promising for the last forty years—

Dulce ridentem Lalagen,
Dulce loquentem!

A topic of this sort of which the person himself may be considered as almost sole proprietor and patentee is an estate for life, free from all encumbrance of wit, thought, or study, you live upon it as a settled income; and others might as well think to eject you out of a capital freehold house and estate as think to drive you out of it into the wide world of common sense and argument. Every man's house is his castle; and every man's common-place is his stronghold, from which he looks out and smiles at the dust and heat of controversy, raised by a number of frivolous and vexatious questions—'Rings the world with the vain stir!' A cure for this and every other evil would be a Parliamentary Reform; and so we return in a perpetual circle to the point from which we set out. Is not this a species of sober madness more provoking than the real? Has not the theoretical enthusiast his mind as much warped, as much enslaved by one idea as the acknowledged lunatic, only that the former has no lucid intervals? If you see a visionary of this class going along the street, you can tell as well what he is thinking of and will say next as the man that fancies himself a teapot or the Czar of Muscovy. The one is as inaccessible to reason as the other: if the one raves, the other dotes!

There are some who fancy the Corn Bill the root of all evil, and others who trace all the miseries of life to the practice of muffling up children in night-clothes when they sleep or travel. They will declaim by the hour together on the first, and argue themselves black in the face on the last. It is in vain that you give up the point. They persist in the debate, and begin again—'But don't you see—?' These sort of partial obliquities, as they are more entertaining and original, are also by their nature intermittent. They hold a man but for a season. He may have one a year or every two years; and though, while he is in the heat of any new discovery, he will let you hear of nothing else, he varies from himself, and is amusing undesignedly. He is not like the chimes at midnight.

People of the character here spoken of, that is, who tease you to death with some one idea, generally differ in their favourite notion from the rest of the world; and indeed it is the love of distinction which is mostly at the bottom of this peculiarity. Thus one person is remarkable for living on a vegetable diet, and never fails to entertain you all dinner-time with an invective against animal food. One of this self-denying class, who adds to the primitive simplicity of this sort of food the recommendation of having it in a raw state, lamenting the death of a patient whom he had augured to be in a good way as a convert to his system, at last accounted for his disappointment in a whisper—'But she ate meat privately, depend upon it.' It is not pleasant, though it is what one submits to willingly from some people, to be asked every time you meet, whether you have quite left off drinking wine, and to be complimented or condoled with on your looks according as you answer in the negative or affirmative. Abernethy thinks his pill an infallible cure for all disorders. A person once complaining to his physician that he thought his mode of treatment had not answered, he assured him it was the best in the world,—'and as a proof of it,' says he, 'I have had one gentleman, a patient with your disorder, under the same regimen for the last sixteen years!'—I have known persons whose minds were entirely taken up at all times and on all occasions with such questions as the Abolition of the Slave Trade, the Restoration of the Jews, or the progress of Unitarianism. I myself at one period took a pretty strong turn to inveighing against the doctrine of Divine Right, and am not yet cured of my prejudice on that subject. How many projectors have gone mad in good earnest from incessantly harping on one idea: the discovery of the philosopher's stone, the finding out the longitude, or paying off the national debt! The disorder at length comes to a fatal crisis; but long before this, and while they were walking about and talking as usual, the derangement of the fancy, the loss of all voluntary power to control or alienate their ideas from the single subject that occupied them, was gradually taking place, and overturning the fabric of the understanding by wrenching it all on one side. Alderman Wood has, I should suppose, talked of nothing but the Queen in all companies for the last six months. Happy Alderman Wood! Some persons have got a definition of the verb, others a system of short-hand, others a cure for typhus fever, others a method for preventing the counterfeiting of bank-notes, which they think the best possible, and indeed the only one. Others in leaving you to add a fourth. A man who has been in Germany will sometimes talk of nothing but what is German: a Scotchman always leads the discourse to his own country. Some descant on the Kantean philosophy. There is a conceited fellow about town who talks always and everywhere on this subject. He wears the Categories round his neck like a pearl-chain: he plays off the names of the primary and transcendental qualities like rings on his fingers. He talks of the Kantean system while he dances; he talks of it while he dines; he talks of it to his children, to his apprentices, to his customers. He called on me to convince me of it, and said I was only prevented from becoming a complete convert by one or two prejudices. He knows no more about it than a pikestaff. Why then does he make so much ridiculous fuss about it? It is not that he has got this one idea in his head, but that he has got no other. A dunce may talk on the subject of the Kantean philosophy with great impunity: if he opened his lips on any other he might be found out. A French lady who had married an Englishman who said little, excused him by saying, 'He is always thinking of Locke and Newton.' This is one way of passing muster by following in the suite of great names!—A friend of mine, whom I met one day in the street, accosted me with more than usual vivacity, and said, 'Well, we're selling, we're selling!' I thought he meant a house. 'No,' he said, 'haven't you seen the advertisement in the newspapers? I mean five and twenty copies of the Essay.' This work, a comely, capacious quarto on the most abstruse metaphysics, had occupied his sole thoughts for several years, and he concluded that I must be thinking of what he was. I believe, however, I may say I am nearly the only person that ever read, certainly that ever pretended to understand it. It is an original and most ingenious work, nearly as incomprehensible as it is original, and as quaint as it is ingenious. If the author is taken up with the ideas in his own head and no others, he has a right; for he has ideas there that are to be met with nowhere else, and which occasionally would not disgrace a Berkeley. A dextrous plagiarist might get himself an immense reputation by putting them in a popular dress. Oh! how little do they know, who have never done anything but repeat after others by rote, the pangs, the labour, the yearnings and misgivings of mind it costs to get at the germ of an original idea—to dig it out of the hidden recesses of thought and nature, and bring it half-ashamed, struggling, and deformed into the day—to give words and intelligible symbols to that which was never imagined or expressed before! It is as if the dumb should speak for the first time, as if things should stammer out their own meaning through the imperfect organs of mere sense. I wish that some of our fluent, plausible declaimers, who have such store of words to cover the want of ideas, could lend their art to this writer. If he, 'poor, unfledged' in this respect, 'who has scarce winged from view o' th' nest,' could find a language for his ideas, truth would find a language for some of her secrets. Mr. Fearn was buried in the woods of Indostan. In his leisure from business and from tiger-shooting, he took it into his head to look into his own mind. A whim or two, an odd fancy, like a film before the eye, now and then crossed it: it struck him as something curious, but the impression at first disappeared like breath upon glass. He thought no more of it; yet still the same conscious feelings returned, and what at first was chance or instinct became a habit. Several notions had taken possession of his brain relating to mental processes which he had never heard alluded to in conversation, but not being well versed in such matters, he did not know whether they were to be found in learned authors or not. He took a journey to the capital of the Peninsula on purpose, bout Locke, Reid, Stewart, and Berkeley, whom he consulted with eager curiosity when he got home, but did not find what he looked for. He set to work himself, and in a few weeks sketched out a rough draft of his thoughts and observations on bamboo paper. The eagerness of his new pursuit, together with the diseases of the climate, proved too much for his constitution, and he was forced to return to this country. He put his metaphysics, his bamboo manuscript, into the boat with him, and as he floated down the Ganges, said to himself, 'If I live, this will live; if I die, it will not be heard of.' What is fame to this feeling? The babbling of an idiot! He brought the work home with him and twice had it stereotyped. The first sketch he allowed was obscure, but the improved copy he thought could not fail to strike. It did not succeed. The world, as Goldsmith said of himself, made a point of taking no notice of it. Ever since he has had nothing but disappointment and vexation,—the greatest and most heart-breaking of all others—that of not being able to make yourself understood. Mr. Fearn tells me there is a sensible writer in the *Monthly Review* who sees the thing in its proper light, and says so. But I have heard of no other instance. There are, notwithstanding, ideas in this work, neglected and ill-treated as it has been, that lead to more curious and subtle speculations on some of the most disputed and difficult points of the philosophy of the human mind (such as *relation, abstraction*, etc.) than have been thrown out in any work for the last sixty years, I mean since Hume; for since his time there has been no metaphysician in this country worth the name. Yet his *Treatise on Human Nature*, he tells us, 'fell still-born from the press.' So it is that knowledge works its way, and reputation lingers far behind it. But truth is better than opinion, I maintain it; and as to the two stereotyped and unsold editions of the Essay on Consciousness, I say, *Honi soit qui mal y pense!*(1)—My Uncle Toby had one idea in his head, that of his bowling-green, and another, that of the Widow Wadman. Oh, spare them both! I will only add one more anecdote in illustration of this theory of the mind's being occupied with one idea, which is most frequently of a man's self. A celebrated lyrical writer happened to drop into a small party where they had just got the novel of *Rob Roy*, by the author of *Waverley*. The motto in the title-page was taken from a poem of his. This was a hint sufficient, a word to the wise. He instantly went to the book-shelf in the next room, took down the volume of his own poems, read the whole of that in question aloud with manifest complacency, replaced it on the shelf, and walked away, taking no more notice of Rob Roy than if there had been no such person, nor of the new novel than if it had not been written by its renowned author. There was no reciprocity in this. But the writer in question does not admit of any merit second to his own.(2)

Mr. Owen is a man remarkable for one idea. It is that of himself and the Lanark cotton-mills. He carries this idea backwards and forwards with him from Glasgow to London, without allowing anything for attrition, and expects to find it in the same state of purity and perfection in the latter place as at the former. He acquires a wonderful velocity and impenetrability in his undaunted transit. Resistance to him is vain, while the whirling motion of the mail-coach remains in his head.

      Nor Alps nor Apennines can keep him out,
        Nor fortified redoubt.

He even got possession, in the suddenness of his onset, of the steam-engine of the *Times* newspaper, and struck off ten thousand woodcuts of the Projected Villages, which afforded an ocular demonstration to all who saw them of the practicability of Mr. Owen's whole scheme. He comes into a room with one of these documents in his hand, with the air of a schoolmaster and a quack doctor mixed, asks very kindly how you do, and on hearing you are still in an indifferent state of health owing to bad digestion, instantly turns round and observes that 'All that will be remedied in his plan; that indeed he thinks too much attention has been paid to the mind, and not enough to the body; that in his system, which he has now perfected and which will shortly be generally adopted, he has provided effectually for both; that he has been long of opinion that the mind depends altogether on the physical organisation, and where the latter is neglected or disordered the former must languish and want its due vigour; that exercise is therefore a part of his system, with full liberty to develop every faculty of mind and body; that two Objections had been made to his *New View of Society*, viz. its want of relaxation from labour, and its want of variety; but the first of these, the too great restraint, he trusted he had already answered, for where the powers of mind and body were freely exercised and brought out, surely liberty must be allowed to exist in the highest degree; and as to the second, the monotony which would be produced by a regular and general plan of co-operation, he conceived he had proved in his *New View* and *Addresses to the Higher Classes*, that the co-operation he had recommended was necessarily conducive to the most extensive improvement of the ideas and faculties, and where this was the case there must be the greatest possible variety instead of a want of it.' And having said this, this expert and sweeping orator takes up his hat and walks downstairs after reading his lecture of truisms like a playbill or an apothecary's advertisement; and should you stop him at the door to say, by way of putting in a word in common, that Mr. Southey seems somewhat favourable to his plan in his late Letter to Mr. William Smith, he looks at you with a smile of pity at the futility of all opposition and the idleness of all encouragement. People who thus swell out some vapid scheme of their own into undue importance seem to me to labour under water in the head—to exhibit a huge hydrocephalus! They may be very worthy people for all that, but they are bad companions and very indifferent reasoners. Tom Moore says of some one somewhere, 'that he puts his hand in his breeches pocket like a crocodile.' The phrase is hieroglyphical; but Mr. Owen and others might be said to put their foot in the question of social improvement and reform much in the same unaccountable manner.

I hate to be surfeited with anything, however sweet. I do not want to be always tied to the same question, as if there were no other in the world. I like a mind more Catholic.

I love to talk with mariners,
That come from a far countree.

I am not for 'a collusion' but 'an exchange' of ideas. It is well to hear what other people have to say on a number of subjects. I do not wish to be always respiring the same confined atmosphere, but to vary the scene, and get a little relief and fresh air out of doors. Do all we can to shake it off, there is always enough pedantry, egotism, and self-conceit left lurking behind; we need not seal ourselves up hermetically in these precious qualities, so as to think of nothing but our own wonderful discoveries, and hear nothing but the sound of our own voice. Scholars, like princes, may learn something by being incognito. Yet we see those who cannot go into a bookseller's shop, or bear to be five minutes in a stage-coach, without letting you know who they are. They carry their reputation about with them as the snail does its shell, and sit under its canopy, like the lady in the lobster. I cannot understand this at all. What is the use of a man's always revolving round his own little circle? He must, one should think, be tired of it himself, as well as tire other people. A well-known writer says with much boldness, both in the thought and expression, that 'a Lord is imprisoned in the Bastille of a name, and cannot enlarge himself into man'; and I have known men of genius in the same predicament. Why must a man be for ever mouthing out his own poetry, comparing himself with Milton, passage by passage, and weighing every line in a balance of posthumous fame which he holds in his own hands? It argues a want of imagination as well as common sense. Has he no ideas but what he has put into verse; or none in common with his hearers? Why should he think it the only scholar-like thing, the only 'virtue extant,' to see the merit of his writings, and that 'men were brutes without them'? Why should he bear a grudge to all art, to all beauty, to all wisdom, that does not spring from his own brain? Or why should he fondly imagine that there is but one fine thing in the world, namely, poetry, and that he is the only poet in it? It will never do. Poetry is a very fine thing; but there are other things besides it. Everything must have its turn. Does a wise man think to enlarge his comprehension by turning his eyes only on himself, or hope to conciliate the admiration of others by scouting, proscribing, and loathing all that they delight in? He must either have a disproportionate idea of himself, or be ignorant of the world in which he lives. It is quite enough to have one class of people born to think the universe made for them!—It seems also to argue a want of repose, of confidence, and firm faith in a man's real pretensions, to be always dragging them forward into the foreground, as if the proverb held here—*Out of sight out of mind*. Does he, for instance, conceive that no one would ever think of his poetry unless he forced it upon them by repeating it himself? Does he believe all competition, all allowance of another's merit, fatal to him? Must he, like Moody in the *Country Girl*, lock up the faculties of his admirers in ignorance of all other fine things, painting, music, the antique, lest they should play truant to him? Methinks such a proceeding implies no good opinion of his own genius or their taste: it is deficient in dignity and in decorum. Surely if any one is convinced of the reality of an acquisition, he can bear not to have it spoken of every minute. If he knows he has an undoubted superiority in any respect, he will not be uneasy because every one he meets is not in the secret, nor staggered by the report of rival excellence. One of the first mathematicians and classical scholars of the day was mentioning it as a compliment to himself that a cousin of his, a girl from school, had said to him, 'You know (Manning) is a very plain good sort of a young man, but he is not anything at all out of the common.' Leigh Hunt once said to me, 'I wonder I never heard you speak upon this subject before, which you seem to have studied a good deal.' I answered, 'Why, we were not reduced to that, that I know of!'—

There are persons who, without being chargeable with the vice here spoken of, yet 'stand accountant for as great a sin'; though not dull and monotonous, they are vivacious mannerists in their conversation, and excessive egotists. Though they run over a thousand subjects in mere gaiety of heart, their delight still flows from one idea, namely, themselves. Open the book in what page you will, there is a frontispiece of themselves staring you in the face. They are a sort of Jacks o' the Green, with a sprig of laurel, a little tinsel, and a little smut, but still playing antics and keeping in incessant motion, to attract attention and extort your pittance of approbation. Whether they talk of the town or the country, poetry or politics, it comes to much the same thing. If they talk to you of the town, its diversions, 'its palaces, its ladies, and its streets,' they are the delight, the grace, and ornament of it. If they are describing the charms of the country, they give no account of any individual spot or object or source of pleasure but the circumstance of their being there. 'With them conversing, we forget all place, all seasons, and their change.' They perhaps pluck a leaf or a flower, patronise it, and hand it you to admire, but select no one feature of beauty or grandeur to dispute the palm of perfection with their own persons. Their rural descriptions are mere landscape backgrounds with their own portraits in an engaging attitude in front. They are not observing or enjoying the scene, but doing the honours as masters of the ceremonies to nature, and arbiters of elegance to all humanity. If they tell a love-tale of enamoured princesses, it is plain they fancy themselves the hero of the piece. If they discuss poetry, their encomiums still turn on something genial and unsophisticated, meaning their own style. If they enter into politics, it is understood that a hint from them to the potentates of Europe is sufficient. In short, as a lover (talk of what you will) brings in his mistress at every turn, so these persons contrive to divert your attention to the same darling object—they are, in fact, in love with themselves, and, like lovers, should be left to keep their own company.

FN to ESSAY VII.

(1) Quarto poetry, as well as quarto metaphysics, does not always sell. Going one day into a shop in Paternoster Row to see for some lines in Mr. Wordsworth's *Excursion* to interlard some prose with, I applied to the constituted authorities, and asked if I could look at a copy of the *Excursion?* The answer was, 'Into which country, sir?'

(2) These fantastic poets are like a foolish ringer at Plymouth that Northcote tells the story of. He was proud of his ringing, and the boys who made a jest of his foible used to get him in the belfry and ask him, 'Well now, John, how many good ringers are there in Plymouth?' 'Two,' he would say, without any hesitation. 'Ay, indeed! and who are they?' 'Why, first, there's myself, that's one; and— and—' 'Well, and who's the other?' 'Why, there's— there's— Ecod, I can't think of any other but myself.' *Talk we of one Master Launcelot.* The story is of ringers: it will do for any vain, shallow, self-satisfied egotist of them all.

ESSAY VIII. ON THE IGNORANCE OF THE LEARNED

```
For the more languages a man can speak,
His talent has but sprung the greater leak:
And, for the industry he has spent upon't,
Must full as much some other way discount.
The Hebrew, Chaldee, and the Syriac
Do, like their letters, set men's reason back,
And turn their wits that strive to understand It
(Like those that write the characters) left-handed.
Yet he that is but able to express
No sense at all in several languages
Will pass for learneder than he that's known
To speak the strongest reason in his own.
—BUTLER.
```

The description of persons who have the fewest ideas of all others are mere authors and readers. It is better to be able neither to read nor write than to be able to do nothing else. A lounger who is ordinarily seen with a book in his hand is (we may be almost sure) equally without the power or inclination to attend either to what passes around him or in his own mind. Such a one may be said to carry his understanding about with him in his pocket, or to leave it at home on his library shelves. He is afraid of venturing on any train of reasoning, or of striking out any observation that is not mechanically suggested to him by parsing his eyes over certain legible characters; shrinks from the fatigue of thought, which, for want of practice, becomes insupportable to him; and sits down contented with an endless, wearisome succession of words and half-formed images, which fill the void of the mind, and continually efface one another. Learning is, in too many cases, but a foil to common sense; a substitute for true knowledge. Books are less often made use of as 'spectacles' to look at nature with, than as blinds to keep out its strong light and shifting scenery from weak eyes and indolent dispositions. The book-worm wraps himself up in his web of verbal generalities, and sees only the glimmering shadows of things reflected from the minds of others. Nature *puts him out.* The impressions of real objects, stripped of the disguises of words and voluminous roundabout descriptions, are blows that stagger him; their variety distracts, their rapidity exhausts him; and he turns from the bustle, the noise, and glare, and whirling motion of the world about him (which he has not an eye to follow in its fantastic changes, nor an understanding to reduce to fixed principles), to the quiet monotony of the dead languages, and the less startling and more intelligible combinations of the letters of the alphabet. It is well, it is perfectly well. 'Leave me to my repose,' is the motto of the sleeping and the dead. You might as well ask the paralytic to leap from his chair and throw away his crutch, or, without a miracle, to 'take up his bed and walk,' as expect the learned reader to throw down his book and think for himself. He clings to it for his intellectual support; and his dread of being left to himself is like the horror of a vacuum. He can only breathe a learned atmosphere, as other men breathe common air. He is a borrower of sense. He has no ideas of his own, and must live on those of other people. The habit of supplying our ideas from foreign sources 'enfeebles all internal strength of thought,' as a course of dram-drinking destroys the tone of the stomach. The faculties of the mind, when not exerted, or when cramped by custom and authority, become listless, torpid, and unfit for the purposes of thought or action. Can we wonder at the languor and lassitude which is thus produced by a life of learned sloth and ignorance; by poring over lines and syllables that excite little more idea or interest than if they were the characters of an unknown tongue, till the eye closes on vacancy, and the book drops from the feeble hand! I would rather be a wood-cutter, or the meanest hind, that all day 'sweats in the eye of Phoebus, and at night sleeps in Elysium,' than wear out my life so, 'twixt dreaming and awake.' The learned author differs from the learned student in this, that the one transcribes what the other reads. The learned are mere literary drudges.

If you set them upon original composition, their heads turn, they don't know where they are. The indefatigable readers of books are like the everlasting copiers of pictures, who, when they attempt to do anything of their own, find they want an eye quick enough, a hand steady enough, and colours bright enough, to trace the living forms of nature.

Any one who has passed through the regular gradations of a classical education, and is not made a fool by it, may consider himself as having had a very narrow escape. It is an old remark, that boys who shine at school do not make the greatest figure when they grow up and come out into the world. The things, in fact, which a boy is set to learn at school, and on which his success depends, are things which do not require the exercise either of the highest or the most useful faculties of the mind. Memory (and that of the lowest kind) is the chief faculty called into play in conning over and repeating lessons by rote in grammar, in languages, in geography, arithmetic, etc., so that he who has the most of this technical memory, with the least turn for other things, which have a stronger and more natural claim upon his childish attention, will make the most forward school-boy. The jargon containing the definitions of the parts of speech, the rules for casting up an account, or the inflections of a Greek verb, can have no attraction to the tyro of ten years old, except as they are imposed as a task upon him by others, or from his feeling the want of sufficient relish of amusement in other things. A lad with a sickly constitution and no very active mind, who can just retain what is pointed out to him, and has neither sagacity to distinguish nor spirit to enjoy for himself, will generally be at the head of his form. An idler at school, on the other hand, is one who has high health and spirits, who has the free use of his limbs, with all his wits about him, who feels the circulation of his blood and the motion of his heart, who is ready to laugh and cry in a breath, and who had rather chase a ball or a butterfly, feel the open air in his face, look at the fields or the sky, follow a winding path, or enter with eagerness into all the little conflicts and interests of his acquaintances and friends, than doze over a musty spelling-book, repeat barbarous distichs after his master, sit so many hours pinioned to a writing-desk, and receive his reward for the loss of time and pleasure in paltry prize-medals at Christmas and Midsummer. There is indeed a degree of stupidity which prevents children from learning the usual lessons, or ever arriving at these puny academic honours. But what passes for stupidity is much oftener a want of interest, of a sufficient motive to fix the attention and force a reluctant application to the dry and unmeaning pursuits of school-learning. The best capacities are as much above this drudgery as the dullest are beneath it. Our men of the greatest genius have not been most distinguished for their acquirements at school or at the university.

Th' enthusiast Fancy was a truant ever.

Gray and Collins were among the instances of this wayward disposition. Such persons do not think so highly of the advantages, nor can they submit their imaginations so servilely to the trammels of strict scholastic discipline. There is a certain kind and degree of intellect in which words take root, but into which things have not power to penetrate. A mediocrity of talent, with a certain slenderness of moral constitution, is the soil that produces the most brilliant specimens of successful prize-essayists and Greek epigrammatists. It should not be forgotten that the least respectable character among modern politicians was the cleverest boy at Eton.

Learning is the knowledge of that which is not generally known to others, and which we can only derive at second-hand from books or other artificial sources. The knowledge of that which is before us, or about us, which appeals to our experience, passions, and pursuits, to the bosoms and businesses of men, is not learning. Learning is the knowledge of that which none but the learned know. He is the most learned man who knows the most of what is farthest removed from common life and actual observation, that is of the least practical utility, and least liable to be brought to the test of experience, and that, having been handed down through the greatest number of intermediate stages, is the most full of uncertainty, difficulties, and contradictions. It is seeing with the eyes of others, hearing with their ears, and pinning our faith on their understandings. The learned man prides himself in the knowledge of names and dates, not of men or things. He thinks and cares nothing about his next-door neighbours, but he is deeply read in the tribes and castes of the Hindoos and Calmue Tartars. He can hardly find his way into the next street, though he is acquainted with the exact dimensions of Constantinople and Pekin. He does not know whether his oldest acquaintance is a knave or a fool, but he can pronounce a pompous lecture on all the principal characters in history. He cannot tell whether an object is black or white, round or square, and yet he is a professed master of the laws of optics and the rules of perspective. He knows as much of what he talks about as a blind man does of colours. He cannot give a satisfactory answer to the plainest question, nor is he ever in the right in any one of his opinions upon any one matter of fact that really comes before him, and yet he gives himself out for an infallible judge on all these points, of which it is impossible that he or any other person living should know anything but by conjecture. He is expert in all the dead and in most of the living languages; but he can neither speak his own fluently, nor write it correctly. A person of this class, the second Greek scholar of his day, undertook to point out several solecisms in Milton's Latin style; and in his own performance there is hardly a sentence of common English. Such was Dr. ——. Such is Dr. ——. Such was not Porson. He was an exception that confirmed the general rule, a man that, by uniting talents and knowledge with learning, made the distinction between them more striking and palpable.

A mere scholar, who knows nothing but books, must be ignorant even of them. 'Books do not teach the use of books.' How should he know anything of a work who knows nothing of the subject of it? The learned pedant is conversant with books only as they are made of other books, and those again of others, without end. He parrots those who have parroted others. He can translate the same word into ten different languages, but he knows nothing of the *thing* which it means in any one of them. He stuffs his head with authorities built on authorities, with quotations quoted from quotations, while he locks up his senses, his understanding, and his heart. He is unacquainted with the maxims and manners of the world; he is to seek in the characters of individuals. He sees no beauty in the face of nature or of art. To him 'the mighty world of eye and ear' is hid; and 'knowledge,' except at one entrance, 'quite shut out.' His pride takes part with his ignorance; and his self-importance rises with the number of things of which he does not know the value, and which he therefore despises as unworthy of his notice. He knows nothing of pictures,—'Of the colouring of Titian, the grace of Raphael, the purity of Domenichino, the *corregioscity* of Correggio, the learning of Poussin, the airs of Guido, the taste of the Caracci, or the grand contour of Michael Angelo,'—of all those glories of the Italian and miracles of the Flemish school, which have filled the eyes of mankind with delight, and to the study and imitation of which thousands have in vain devoted their lives. These are to him as if they had never been, a mere dead letter, a by-word; and no wonder, for he neither sees nor understands their prototypes in nature. A print of Rubens' Watering-place or Claude's Enchanted Castle may be hanging on the walls of his room for months without his once perceiving them; and if you point them out to him he will turn away from them. The language of nature, or of art (which is another nature), is one that he does not understand. He repeats indeed the names of Apelles and Phidias, because they are to be found in classic authors, and boasts of their works as prodigies, because they no longer exist; or when he sees the finest remains of Grecian art actually before him in the Elgin Marbles, takes no other interest in them than as they lead to a learned dispute, and (which is the same thing) a quarrel about the meaning of a Greek particle. He is equally ignorant of music; he 'knows no touch of it,' from the strains of the all-accomplished Mozart to the shepherd's pipe upon the mountain. His ears are nailed to his books; and deadened with the sound of the Greek and Latin tongues, and the din and smithery of school-learning. Does he know anything more of poetry? He knows the number of feet in a verse, and of acts in a play; but of the soul or spirit he knows nothing. He can turn a Greek ode into English, or a Latin epigram into Greek verse; but whether either is worth the trouble he leaves to the critics. Does he understand 'the act and practique part of life' better than 'the theorique'? No. He knows no liberal or mechanic art, no trade or occupation, no game of skill or chance. Learning 'has no skill in surgery,' in agriculture, in building, in working in wood or in iron; it cannot make any instrument of labour, or use it when made; it cannot handle the plough or the spade, or the chisel or the hammer; it knows nothing of hunting or hawking, fishing or shooting, of horses or dogs, of fencing or dancing, or cudgel-playing, or bowls, or cards, or tennis, or anything else. The learned professor of all arts and sciences cannot reduce any one of them to practice, though he may contribute an account of them to an Encyclopedia. He has not the use of his hands nor of his feet; he can neither run, nor walk, nor swim; and he considers all those who actually understand and can exercise any of these arts of body or mind as vulgar and mechanical men,—though to know almost any one of them in perfection requires long time and practice, with powers originally fitted, and a turn of mind particularly devoted to them. It does not require more than this to enable the learned candidate to arrive, by painful study, at a doctor's degree and a fellowship, and to eat, drink, and sleep the rest of his life!

The thing is plain. All that men really understand is confined to a very small compass; to their daily affairs and experience; to what they have an opportunity to know, and motives to study or practise. The rest is affectation and imposture. The common people have the use of their limbs; for they live by their labour or skill. They understand their own business and the characters of those they have to deal with; for it is necessary that they should. They have eloquence to express their passions, and wit at will to express their contempt and provoke laughter. Their natural use of speech is not hung up in monumental mockery, in an obsolete language; nor is their sense of what is ludicrous, or readiness at finding out allusions to express it, buried in collections of *Anas*. You will hear more good things on the outside of a stage-coach from London to Oxford than if you were to pass a twelvemonth with the undergraduates, or heads of colleges, of that famous university; and more *home* truths are to be learnt from listening to a noisy debate in an alehouse than from attending a formal one in the House of Commons. An elderly country gentlewoman will often know more of character, and be able to illustrate it by more amusing anecdotes taken from the history of what has been said, done, and gossiped in a country town for the last fifty years, than the best bluestocking of the age will be able to glean from that sort of learning which consists in an acquaintance with all the novels and satirical poems published in the same period. People in towns, indeed, are woefully deficient in a knowledge of character, which they see only *in the bust*, not as a whole-length. People in the country not only know all that has happened to a man, but trace his virtues or vices, as they do his features, in their descent through several generations, and solve some contradiction in his behaviour by a cross in the breed half a century ago. The learned know nothing of the matter, either in town or country. Above all, the mass of society have common sense, which the learned in all ages want. The vulgar are in the right when they judge for themselves; they are wrong when they trust to their blind guides. The celebrated nonconformist divine, Baxter, was almost stoned to death by the good women of Kidderminster, for asserting from the pulpit that 'hell was paved with infants' skulls'; but, by the force of argument, and of learned quotations from the Fathers, the reverend preacher at length prevailed over the scruples of his congregation, and over reason and humanity.

Such is the use which has been made of human learning. The labourers in this vineyard seem as if it was their object to confound all common sense, and the distinctions of good and evil, by means of traditional maxims and preconceived notions taken upon trust, and increasing in absurdity with increase of age. They pile hypothesis on hypothesis, mountain high, till it is impossible to come at the plain truth on any question. They see things, not as they are, but as they find them in books, and 'wink and shut their apprehensions up,' in order that they may discover nothing to interfere with their prejudices or convince them of their absurdity. It might be supposed that the height of human wisdom consisted in maintaining contradictions and rendering nonsense sacred. There is no dogma, however fierce or foolish, to which these persons have not set their seals, and tried to impose on the understandings of their followers as the will of Heaven, clothed with all the terrors and sanctions of religion. How little has the human understanding been directed to find out the true and useful! How much ingenuity has been thrown away in the defence of creeds and systems! How much time and talents have been wasted in theological controversy, in law, in politics, in verbal criticism, in judicial astrology, and in finding out the art of making gold! What actual benefit do we reap from the writings of a Laud or a Whitgift, or of Bishop Bull or Bishop Waterland, or Prideaux' Connections, or Beausobre, or Calmet, or St. Augustine, or Puffendord, or Vattel, or from the more literal but equally learned and unprofitable labours of Scaliger, Cardan, and Scioppius? How many grains of sense are there in their thousand folio or quarto volumes? What would the world lose if they were committed to the flames to-morrow? Or are they not already 'gone to the vault of all the Capulets'? Yet all these were oracles in their time, and would have scoffed at you or me, at common sense and human nature, for differing with them. It is our turn to laugh now.

To conclude this subject. The most sensible people to be met with in society are men of business and of the world, who argue from what they see and know, instead of spinning cobweb distinctions of what things ought to be. Women have often more of what is called *good sense* than men. They have fewer pretensions; are less implicated in theories; and judge of objects more from their immediate and involuntary impression on the mind, and, therefore, more truly and naturally. They cannot reason wrong; for they do not reason at all. They do not think or speak by rule; and they have in general more eloquence and wit, as well as sense, on that account. By their wit, sense, and eloquence together, they generally contrive to govern their husbands. Their style, when they write to their friends (not for the booksellers), is better than that of most authors.—Uneducated people have most exuberance of invention and the greatest freedom from prejudice. Shakespear's was evidently an uneducated mind, both in the freshness of his imagination and in the variety of his views; as Milton's was scholastic, in the texture both of his thoughts and feelings. Shakespear had not been accustomed to write themes at school in favour of virtue or against vice. To this we owe the unaffected but healthy tone of his dramatic morality. If we wish to know the force of human genius we should read Shakespear. If we wish to see the insignificance of human learning we may study his commentators.

FN to ESSAY VIII

No notes for this essay.

ESSAY IX. THE INDIAN JUGGLERS

Coming forward and seating himself on the ground in his white dress and tightened turban, the chief of the Indian Jugglers begins with tossing up two brass balls, which is what any of us could do, and concludes with keeping up four at the same time, which is what none of us could do to save our lives, nor if we were to take our whole lives to do it in. Is it then a trifling power we see at work, or is it not something next to miraculous? It is the utmost stretch of human ingenuity, which nothing but the bending the faculties of body and mind to it from the tenderest infancy with incessant, ever anxious application up to manhood can accomplish or make even a slight approach to. Man, thou art a wonderful animal, and thy ways past finding out! Thou canst do strange things, but thou turnest them to little account!—To conceive of this effort of extraordinary dexterity distracts the imagination and makes admiration breathless. Yet it costs nothing to the performer, any more than if it were a mere mechanical deception with which he had nothing to do but to watch and laugh at the astonishment of the spectators. A single error of a hairsbreadth, of the smallest conceivable portion of time, would be fatal: the precision of the movements must be like a mathematical truth, their rapidity is like lightning. To catch four balls in succession in less than a second of time, and deliver them back so as to return with seeming consciousness to the hand again; to make them revolve round him at certain intervals like the planets in their spheres; to make them chase one another like sparkles of fire, or shoot up like flowers or meteors; to throw them behind his back and twine them round his neck like ribbons or like serpents; to do what appears an impossibility, and to do if with all the ease, the grace, the carelessness imaginable; to laugh at, to play with the glittering mockeries; to follow them with his eye as if he could fascinate them with its lambent fire, or as if he had only to see that they kept time with the music on the stage,—there is something in all this which he who does not admire may be quite sure he never really admired anything in the whole course of his life. It is skill surmounting difficulty, and beauty triumphing over skill. It seems as if the difficulty once mastered naturally resolved itself into ease and grace, and as if to be overcome at all, it must be overcome without an effort. The smallest awkwardness or want of pliancy or self-possession would stop the whole process. It is the work of witchcraft, and yet sport for children. Some of the other feats are quite as curious and wonderful, such as the balancing the artificial tree and shooting a bird from each branch through a quill; though none of them have the elegance or facility of the keeping up of the brass balls. You are in pain for the result, and glad when the experiment is over; they are not accompanied with the same unmixed, unchecked delight as the former; and I would not give much to be merely astonished without being pleased at the game time. As to the swallowing of the sword, the police ought to interfere to prevent it. When I saw the Indian Juggler do the same things before, his feet were bare, and he had large rings on the toes, which kept turning round all the time of the performance, as if they moved of themselves.—The hearing a speech in Parliament drawled or stammered out by the Honourable Member or the Noble Lord; the ringing the changes on their common-places, which any one could repeat after them as well as they, stirs me not a jot, shakes not my good opinion of myself; but the seeing the Indian Jugglers does. It makes me ashamed of myself. I ask what there is that I can do as well as this? Nothing. What have I been doing all my life? Have I been idle, or have I nothing to show for all my labour and pains? Or have I passed my time in pouring words like water into empty sieves, rolling a stone up a hill and then down again, trying to prove an argument in the teeth of facts, and looking for causes in the dark and not finding them? Is there no one thing in which I can challenge competition, that I can bring as an instance of exact perfection in which others cannot find a flaw? The utmost I can pretend to is to write a description of what this fellow can do. I can write a book: so can many others who have not even learned to spell. What abortions are these Essays! What errors, what ill-pieced transitions, what crooked reasons, what lame conclusions! How little is made out, and that little how ill! Yet they are the best I can do. I endeavour to recollect all I have ever observed or thought upon a subject, and to express it as nearly as I can. Instead of writing on four subjects at a time, it is as much as I can manage to keep the thread of one discourse clear and unentangled. I have also time on my hands to correct my opinions, and polish my periods; but the one I cannot, and the other I will not do. I am fond of arguing: yet with a good deal of pains and practice it is often as much as I can do to beat my man; though he may be an indifferent hand. A common fencer would disarm his adversary in the twinkling of an eye, unless he were a professor like himself. A stroke of wit will sometimes produce this effect, but there is no such power or superiority in sense or reas hardly know the professor from the impudent pretender or the mere clown.(1)

I have always had this feeling of the inefficacy and slow progress of intellectual compared to mechanical excellence, and it has always made me somewhat dissatisfied. It is a great many years since I saw Richer, the famous rope-dancer, perform at Sadler's Wells. He was matchless in his art, and added to his extraordinary skill exquisite ease, and unaffected, natural grace. I was at that time employed in copying a half-length picture of Sir Joshua Reynolds's; and it put me out of conceit with it. How ill this part was made out in the drawing! How heavy, how slovenly this other was painted! I could not help saying to myself, 'If the rope-dancer had performed his task in this manner, leaving so many gaps and botches in his work, he would have broken his neck long ago; I should never have seen that vigorous elasticity of nerve and precision of movement!'—Is it, then, so easy an undertaking (comparatively) to dance on a tight-rope? Let any one who thinks so get up and try. There is the thing. It is that which at first we cannot do at all which in the end is done to such perfection. To account for this in some degree, I might observe that mechanical dexterity is confined to doing some one particular thing, which you can repeat as often as you please, in which you know whether you succeed or fail, and where the point of perfection consists in succeeding in a given undertaking.—In mechanical efforts you improve by perpetual practice, and you do so infallibly, because the object to be attained is not a matter of taste or fancy or opinion, but of actual experiment, in which you must either do the thing or not do it. If a man is put to aim at a mark with a bow and arrow, he must hit it or miss it, that's certain. He cannot deceive himself, and go on shooting wide or falling short, and still fancy that he is making progress. No distinction between right and wrong, between true and false, is here palpable; and he must either correct his aim or persevere in his error with his eyes open, for which there is neither excuse nor temptation. If a man is learning to dance on a rope, if he does not mind what he is about he will break his neck. After that it will be in vain for him to argue that he did not make a false step. His situation is not like that of Goldsmith's pedagogue:—

    In argument they own'd his wondrous skill,
    And e'en though vanquish'd, he could argue still.

Danger is a good teacher, and makes apt scholars. So are disgrace, defeat, exposure to immediate scorn and laughter. There is no opportunity in such cases for self-delusion, no idling time away, no being off your guard (or you must take the consequences)—neither is there any room for humour or caprice or prejudice. If the Indian Juggler were to play tricks in throwing up the three case-knives, which keep their positions like the leaves of a crocus in the air, he would cut his fingers. I can make a very bad antithesis without cutting my fingers. The tact of style is more ambiguous than that of double-edged instruments. If the Juggler were told that by flinging himself under the wheels of the Juggernaut, when the idol issues forth on a gaudy day, he would immediately be transported into Paradise, he might believe it, and nobody could disprove it. So the Brahmins may say what they please on that subject, may build up dogmas and mysteries without end, and not be detected; but their ingenious countryman cannot persuade the frequenters of the Olympic Theatre that he performs a number of astonishing feats without actually giving proofs of what he says.—There is, then, in this sort of manual dexterity, first a gradual aptitude acquired to a given exertion of muscular power, from constant repetition, and in the next place, an exact knowledge how much is still wanting and necessary to be supplied. The obvious test is to increase the effort or nicety of the operation, and still to find it come true. The muscles ply instinctively to the dictates of habit. Certain movements and impressions of the hand and eye, having been repeated together an infinite number of times, are unconsciously but unavoidable cemented into closer and closer union; the limbs require little more than to be put in motion for them to follow a regular track with ease and certainty; so that the mere intention of the will acts mathematically like touching the spring of a machine, and you come with Locksley in *Ivanhoe*, in shooting at a mark, 'to allow for the wind.'

Further, what is meant by perfection in mechanical exercises is the performing certain feats to a uniform nicety, that is, in fact, undertaking no more than you can perform. You task yourself, the limit you fix is optional, and no more than human industry and skill can attain to; but you have no abstract, independent standard of difficulty or excellence (other than the extent of your own powers). Thus he who can keep up four brass balls does this *to perfection*; but he cannot keep up five at the same instant, and would fail every time he attempted it. That is, the mechanical performer undertakes to emulate himself, not to equal another.(2) But the artist undertakes to imitate another, or to do what Nature has done, and this it appears is more difficult, viz. to copy what she has set before us in the face of nature or 'human face divine,' entire and without a blemish, than to keep up four brass balls at the same instant, for the one is done by the power of human skill and industry, and the other never was nor will be. Upon the whole, therefore, I have more respect for Reynolds than I have for Richer; for, happen how it will, there have been more people in the world who could dance on a rope like the one than who could paint like Sir Joshua. The latter was but a bungler in his profession to the other, it is true; but then he had a harder taskmaster to obey, whose will was more wayward and obscure, and whose instructions it was more difficult to practise. You can put a child apprentice to a tumbler or rope-dancer with a comfortable prospect of success, if they are but sound of wind and limb; but you cannot do the same thing in painting. The odds are a million to one. You may make indeed as many Haydons and H——s as you put into that sort of machine, but not one Reynolds amongst them all, with his grace, his grandeur, his blandness of gusto, 'in tones and gestures hit,' unless you could make the man over again. To snatch this grace beyond the reach of art is then the height of art—where fine art begins, and where mechanical skill ends. The soft suffusion of the soul, the speechless breathing eloquence, the looks 'commercing with the skies,' the ever-shifting forms of an eternal principle, that which is seen but for a moment, but dwells in the heart always, and is only seized as it passes by strong and secret sympathy, must be taught by nature and genius, not by rules or study. It is suggested by feeling, not by laborious microscopic inspection; in seeking for it without, we lose the harmonious clue to it within; and in aiming to grasp the substance, we let the very spirit of art evaporate. In a word, the objects of fine art are not the objects of sight, but as these last are the objects of taste and imagination, that is, as they appeal to the sense of beauty, of pleasure, and of power in the human breast, and are explained by that finer sense, and revealed in their inner structure to the eye in return. Nature is also a language. Objects, like words, have a meaning; and the true artist is the interpreter of this language, which he can only do by knowing its application to a thousand other objects in a thousand other situations. Thus the eye is too blind a guide of itself to distinguish between the warm or cold tone of a deep-blue sky; but another sense acts as a monitor to it and does not err. The colour of the leaves in autumn would be nothing without the feeling that accompanies it; but it is that feeling that stamps them on the canvas, faded, seared, blighted, shrinking from the winter's flaw, and makes the sight as true as touch—

    And visions, as poetic eyes avow,
    Cling to each leaf and hang on every bough.

The more ethereal, evanescent, more refined and sublime part of art is the seeing nature through the medium of sentiment and passion, as each object is a symbol of the affections and a link in the chain of our endless being. But the unravelling this mysterious web of thought and feeling is alone in the Muse's gift, namely, in the power of that trembling sensibility which is awake to every change and every modification of its ever-varying impressions, that

    Thrills in each nerve, and lives along the line.

This power is indifferently called genius, imagination, feeling, taste; but the manner in which it acts upon the mind can neither be defined by abstract rules, as is the case in science, nor verified by continual, unvarying experiments, as is the case in mechanical performances. The mechanical excellence of the Dutch painters in colouring and handling is that which comes the nearest in fine art to the perfection of certain manual exhibitions of skill. The truth of the effect and the facility with which it is produced are equally admirable. Up to a certain point everything is faultless. The hand and eye have done their part. There is only a want of taste and genius. It is after we enter upon that enchanted ground that the human mind begins to droop and flag as in a strange road, or in a thick mist, benighted and making little way with many attempts and many failures, and that the best of us only escape with half a triumph. The undefined and the imaginary are the regions that we must pass like Satan, difficult and doubtful, 'half flying, half on foot.' The object in sense is a positive thing, and execution comes with practice.

Cleverness is a certain *knack* or aptitude at doing certain things, which depend more on a particular adroitness and off-hand readiness than on force or perseverance, such as making puns, making epigrams, making extempore verses, mimicking the company, mimicking a style, etc. Cleverness is either liveliness and smartness, or something answering to *sleight of hand*, like letting a glass fall sideways off a table, or else a trick, like knowing the secret spring of a watch. Accomplishments are certain external graces, which are to be learned from others, and which are easily displayed to the admiration of the beholder, viz. dancing, riding, fencing, music, and so on. These ornamental acquirements are only proper to those who are at ease in mind and fortune. I know an individual who, if he had been born to an estate of five thousand a year, would have been the most accomplished gentleman of the age. He would have been the delight and envy of the circle in which he moved—would have graced by his manners the liberality flowing from the openness of his heart, would have laughed with the women, have argued with the men, have said good things and written agreeable ones, have taken a hand at piquet or the lead at the harpsichord, and have set and sung his own verses—nugae canorae—with tenderness and spirit; a Rochester without the vice, a modern Surrey! As it is, all these capabilities of excellence stand in his way. He is too versatile for a professional man, not dull enough for a political drudge, too gay to be happy, too thoughtless to be rich. He wants the enthusiasm of the poet, the severity of the prose-writer, and the application of the man of business. Talent differs from genius as voluntary differs from involuntary power. Ingenuity is genius in trifles; greatness is genius in undertakings of much pith and moment. A clever or ingenious man is one who can do anything well, whether it is worth doing or not; a great man is one who can do that which when done is of the highest importance make of a small city a great one. This gives one a pretty good idea of the distinction in question.

Greatness is great power, producing great effects. It is not enough that a man has great power in himself; he must show it to all the world in a way that cannot be hid or gainsaid. He must fill up a certain idea in the public mind. I have no other notion of greatness than this twofold definition, great results springing from great inherent energy. The great in visible objects has relation to that which extends over space; the great in mental ones has to do with space and time. No man is truly great who is great only in his lifetime. The test of greatness is the page of history. Nothing can be said to be great that has a distinct limit, or that borders on something evidently greater than itself. Besides, what is short-lived and pampered into mere notoriety is of a gross and vulgar quality in itself. A Lord Mayor is hardly a great man. A city orator or patriot of the day only show, by reaching the height of their wishes, the distance they are at from any true ambition. Popularity is neither fame nor greatness. A king (as such) is not a great man. He has great power, but it is not his own. He merely wields the lever of the state, which a child, an idiot, or a madman can do. It is the office, not the man we gaze at. Any one else in the same situation would be just as much an object of abject curiosity. We laugh at the country girl who having seen a king expressed her disappointment by saying, 'Why, he is only a man!' Yet, knowing this, we run to see a king as if he was something more than a man.—To display the greatest powers, unless they are applied to great purposes, makes nothing for the character of greatness. To throw a barleycorn through the eye of a needle, to multiply nine figures by nine in the memory, argues definite dexterity of body and capacity of mind, but nothing comes of either. There is a surprising power at work, but the effects are not proportionate, or such as take hold of the imagination. To impress the idea of power on others, they must be made in some way to feel it. It must be communicated to their understandings in the shape of an increase of knowledge, or it must subdue and overawe them by subjecting their wills. Admiration to be solid and lasting must be founded on proofs from which we have no means of escaping; it is neither a slight nor a voluntary gift. A mathematician who solves a profound problem, a poet who creates an image of beauty in the mind that was not there before, imparts knowledge and power to others, in which his greatness and his fame consists, and on which it reposes. Jedediah Buxton will be forgotten; but Napier's bones will live. Lawgivers, philosophers, founders of religion, conquerors and heroes, inventors and great geniuses in arts and sciences, are great men, for they are great public benefactors, or formidable scourges to mankind. Among ourselves, Shakespear, Newton, Bacon, Milton, Cromwell, were great men, for they showed great power by acts and thoughts, that have not yet been consigned to oblivion. They must needs be men of lofty stature, whose shadows lengthen out to remote posterity. A great farce-writer may be a great man; for Moliere was but a great farce-writer. In my mind, the author of *Don Quixote* was a great man. So have there been many others. A great chess-player is not a great man, for he leaves the world as he found it. No act terminating in itself constitutes greatness. This will apply to all displays of power or trials of skill which are confined to the momentary, individual effort, and construct no permanent image or trophy of themselves without them. Is not an actor then a great man, because 'he dies and leaves the world no copy'? I must make an exception for Mrs. Siddons, or else give up my definition of greatness for her sake. A man at the top of his profession is not therefore a great man. He is great in his way, but that is all, unless he shows the marks of a great moving intellect, so that we trace the master-mind, and can sympathise with the springs that urge him on. The rest is but a craft or *mystery*. John Hunter was a great man—*that* any one might see without the smallest skill in surgery. His style and manner showed the man. He would set about cutting up the carcass of a whale with the same greatness of gusto that Michael Angelo would have hewn a block of marble. Lord Nelson was a great naval commander; but for myself, I have not much opinion of a seafaring life. Sir Humphry Davy is a great chemist, but I am not sure that he is a great man. I am not a bit the wiser for any of his discoveries, nor I never met with any one that was. But it is in the nature of greatness to propagate an idea of itself, as wave impels wave, circle without circle. It is a contradiction in terms for a coxcomb to be a great man. A really great man has always an idea of something greater than himself. I have observed that certain sectaries and polemical writers have no higher compliment to pay their most shining lights than to say that "Such a one was a considerable man in his day." Some new elucidation of a text sets aside the authority of the old interpretation, and a "great scholar's memory outlives him half a century," at the utmost. A rich man is not a great man, except to his dependents and his steward. A lord is a great man in the idea we have of his ancestry, and probably of himself, if we know nothing of him but his title. I have heard a story of two bishops, one of whom said (speaking of St. Peter's at Rome) that when he first entered it, he was rather awe-struck, but that as he walked up it, his mind seemed to swell and dilate with it, and at last to fill the whole building: the other said that as he saw more of it, he appeared to himself to grow less and less every step he took, and in the end to dwindle into nothing. This was in some respects a striking picture of a great and little mind; for greatness sympathises with greatness, and littleness shrinks into itself. The one might have become a Wolsey; the other was only fit to become a Mendicant Friar—or there might have been court reasons for making him a bishop. The French have to me a character of littleness in all about them; but they have produced three great men that belong to every country, Moliere, Rabelais, and Montaigne.

To return from this digression, and conclude Essay. A singular instance of manual dexterity was shown in the person of the late John Cavanaugh, whom I have several times seen. His death was celebrated at the time in an article in the *Examiner* newspaper (Feb. 7, 1819), written apparently between jest and earnest; but as it is *pat* to our purpose, and falls in with my own way of considering such subjects, I shall here take leave to quote it:—

'Died at his house in Burbage Street, St. Giles's, John Cavanagh, the famous hand fives-player. When a person dies who does any one thing better than any one else in the world, which so many others are trying to do well, it leaves a gap in society. It is not likely that any one will now see the game of fives played in its perfection for many years to come—for Cavanagh is dead, and has not left his peer behind him. It may be said that there are things of more importance than striking a ball against a wall—there are things, indeed, that make more noise and do as little good, such as making war and peace, making speeches and answering them, making verses and blotting them, making money and throwing it away. But the game of fives is what no one despises who has ever played at it. It is the finest exercise for the body, and the best relaxation for the mind. The Roman poet said that "Care mounted behind the horseman and stuck to his skirts." But this remark would not have applied to the fives-player. He who takes to playing at fives is twice young. He feels neither the past nor future "in the instant." Debts, taxes, "domestic treason, foreign levy, nothing can touch him further." He has no other wish, no other thought, from the moment the game begins, but that of striking the ball, of placing it, of *making* it! This Cavanagh was sure to do. Whenever he touched the ball there was an end of the chase. His eye was certain, his hand fatal, his presence of mind complete. He could do what he pleased, and he always knew exactly what to do. He saw the whole game, and played it; took instant advantage of his adversary's weakness, and recovered balls, as if by a miracle and from sudden thought, that every one gave for lost. He had equal power and skill, quickness and judgment. He could either outwit his antagonist by finesse, or beat him by main strength. Sometimes, when he seemed preparing to send the ball with the full swing of his arm, he would by a slight turn of his wrist drop it within an inch of the line. In general, the ball came from his hand, as if from a racket, in a straight, horizontal line; so that it was in vain to attempt to overtake or stop it. As it was said of a great orator that he never was at a loss for a word, and for the properest word, so Cavanagh always could tell the degree of force necessary to be given to a ball, and the precise direction in which it should be sent. He did his work with the greatest ease; never took more pains than was necessary; and while others were fagging themselves to death, was as cool and collected as if he had just entered the court. His style of play was as remarkable as his power of execution. He had no affectation, no trifling. He did not throw away the game to show off an attitude or try an experiment. He was a fine, sensible, manly player, who did what he could, but that was more than any one else could even affect to do. His blows were not undecided and ineffectual—lumbering like Mr. Wordsworth's epic poetry, nor wavering like Mr. Coleridge's lyric prose, nor short of the mark like Mr. Brougham's speeches, nor wide of it like Mr. Canning's wit, nor foul like the *Quarterly*, nor *let* balls like the *Edinburgh Review*. Cobbett and Junius together would have made a Cavanagh. He was the best *up-hill* player in the world; even when his adversary was fourteen, he would play on the same or better, and as he never flung away the game through carelessness and conceit, he never gave it through laziness or want of heart. The only peculiarity of his play was that he never *volleyed*, but let the balls hop; but if they rose an inch from the ground he never missed having them. There was not only nobody equal, but nobody second to him. It is supposed that he could give any other player half the game, or beat him with his left hand. His service was tremendous. He once played Woodward and Meredith together (two of the best players in England) in the Fives-court, St. Martin's street, and made seven and twenty aces following by services alone—a thing unheard of. He another time played Peru, who was considered a first-rate fives-player, a match of the best out of five games, and in the three first games, which of course decided the match, Peru got only one ace. Cavanagh was an Irishman by birth, and a house-painter by profession. He had once laid aside his working-dress, and walked up, in his smartest clothes, to the Rosemary Branch to have an afternoon's pleasure. A person accosted him, and asked him if he would have a game. So they agreed to play for half a crown a game and a bottle of cider. The first game began—it was seven, eight, ten, thirteen, fourteen, all. Cavanagh won it. The next was the same. They played on, and each game was hardly contested. "There," said the unconscious fives-player, "there was a stroke that Cavanagh could not take: I never played better in my life, and yet I can't win a game. I don't know how it is!" However, they played on, Cavanagh winning every game, and the bystanders drinking the cider and laughing all the time. In the twelfth game, when Cavanagh was only four, and the stranger thirteen, a person came in and said, "What! are you here, Cavanagh?" The words were no sooner pronounced than the astonished player let the ball drop from his hand, and saying, "What! have I been breaking my heart all this time to beat Cavanagh?" refused to make another effort. "And yet, I give you my word," said Cavanagh, telling the story with some triumph, "I played all the while with my clenched fist."—He used frequently to play matches at Copenhagen House for wagers and dinners. The wall against which they play is the same that supports the kitchen-chimney, and when the wall resounded louder than usual, the cooks exclaimed, "Those are the Irishman's balls," and the joints trembled on the spit!—Goldsmith consoled himself that there were places where he too was admired: and Cavanagh was the admiration of all the fives-courts where he ever played. Mr. Powell, when he played matches in the Court in St. Martin's Street, used to fill his gallery at half a crown a head with amateurs and admirers of talent in whatever department it is shown. He could not have shown himself in any ground in England but he would have been immediately surrounded with inquisitive gazers, trying to find out in what part of his frame his unrivalled skill lay, as politicians wonder to see the balance of Europe suspended in Lord Castlereagh's face, and admire the trophies of the British Navy lurking under Mr. Croker's hanging brow. Now Cavanagh was as good-looking a man as the Noble Lord, and much better looking than the Right Hon. Secretary. He had a clear, open countenance, and did not look sideways or down, like Mr. Murray the bookseller. He was a young fellow of sense, humour, and courage. He once had a quarrel with a waterman at Hungerford Stairs, and, they say, served him out in great style. In a word, there are hundreds at this day who cannot mention his name without admiration, as the best fives-player that perhaps ever lived (the greatest excellence of which they have any notion); and the noisy shout of the ring happily stood him in stead of the unheard voice of posterity!—The only person who seems to have excelled as much in another way as Cavanagh did in his was the late John Davies, the racket-player. It was remarked of him that he did not seem to follow the ball, but the ball seemed to follow him. Give him a foot of wall, and he was sure to make the ball. The four best racket-players of that day were Jack Spines, Jem Harding, Armitage, and Church. Davies could give any one of these two hands a time, that is, half the game, and each of these, at their best, could give the best player now in London the same odds. Such are the gradations in all exertions of human skill and art. He once played four capital players together, and beat them. He was also a first-rate tennis-player and an excellent fives-player. In the Fleet or King's Bench he would have stood against Powell, who was reckoned the best open-ground player of his time. This last-mentioned player is at present the keeper of the Fives-court, and we might recommend to him for a motto over his door, "Who enters here, forgets himself, his country, and his friends." And the best of it is, that by the calculation of the odds, none of the three are worth remembering!—Cavanagh died from the bursting of a blood-vessel, which prevented him from playing for the last two or three years. This, he was often heard to say, he thought hard upon him. He was fast recovering, however, when he was suddenly carried off, to the regret of all who knew him. As Mr. Peel made it a qualification of the present Speaker, Mr. Manners Sutton, that he was an excellent moral character, so Jack Cavanagh was a zealous Catholic, and could not be persuaded to eat meat on a Friday, the day on which he died. We have paid this willing tribute to his memory.

```
Let no rude hand deface it,
And his forlorn "Hic Jacet."'
```

FN to ESSAY IX

(1) The celebrated Peter Pindar (Dr. Wolcot) first discovered and brought out the talents of the late Mr. Opie the painter. He was a poor Cornish boy, and was out at work in the fields when the poet went in search of him. 'Well, my lad, can you go and bring me your very best picture?' The other flew like lightning, and soon came back with what he considered as his masterpiece. The stranger looked at it, and the young artist, after waiting for some time without his giving any opinion, at length exclaimed eagerly, 'Well, what do you think of it?' 'Think of it?' said Wolcot; 'Why, I think you ought to be ashamed of it—that you, who might do so well, do no better!' The same answer would have applied to this artist's latest performances, that had been suggested by one of his earliest efforts.

(2) If two persons play against each other at any game, one of them necessarily fails.

ESSAY X. ON LIVING TO ONE'S-SELF(1)

```
Remote, unfriended, melancholy, slow,
Or by the lazy Scheldt or wandering Po.
```

I never was in a better place or humour than I am at present for writing on this subject. I have a partridge getting ready for my supper, my fire is blazing on the hearth, the air is mild for the season of the year, I have had but a slight fit of indigestion to-day (the only thing that makes me abhor myself), I have three hours good before me, and therefore I will attempt it. It is as well to do it at once as to have it to do for a week to come.

If the writing on this subject is no easy task, the thing itself is a harder one. It asks a troublesome effort to ensure the admiration of others: it is a still greater one to be satisfied with one's own thoughts. As I look from the window at the wide bare heath before me, and through the misty moonlight air see the woods that wave over the top of Winterslow,

```
While Heav'n's chancel-vault is blind with sleet,
```

my mind takes its flight through too long a series of years, supported only by the patience of thought and secret yearnings after truth and good, for me to be at a loss to understand the feeling I intend to write about; but I do not know that this will enable me to convey it more agreeably to the reader.

Lady Grandison, in a letter to Miss Harriet Byron, assures her that 'her brother Sir Charles lived to-himself'; and Lady L. soon after (for Richardson was never tired of a good thing) repeats the same observation; to which Miss Byron frequently returns in her answers to both sisters, 'For you know Sir Charles lives to himself,' till at length it passes into a proverb among the fair correspondents. This is not, however, an example of what I understand by *living to one's-self*, for Sir Charles Grandison was indeed always thinking of himself; but by this phrase I mean never thinking at all about one's-self, any more than if there was no such person in existence. The character I speak of is as little of an egotist as possible: Richardson's great favourite was as much of one as possible. Some satirical critic has represented him in Elysium 'bowing over the *faded* hand of Lady Grandison' (Miss Byron that was)—he ought to have been represented bowing over his own hand, for he never admired any one but himself, and was the God of his own idolatry.—Neither do I call it living to one's-self to retire into a desert (like the saints and martyrs of old) to be devoured by wild beasts nor to descend into a cave to be considered as a hermit, nor to got to the top of a pillar or rock to do fanatic penance and be seen of all men. What I mean by living to one's-self is living in the world, as in it, not of it: it is as if no one know there was such a person, and you wished no one to know it: it is to be a silent spectator of the mighty scene of things, not an object of attention or curiosity in it; to take a thoughtful, anxious interest in what is passing in the world, but not to feel the slightest inclination to make or meddle with it. It is such a life as a pure spirit might be supposed to lead, and such an interest as it might take in the affairs of men, calm, contemplative, passive, distant, touched with pity for their sorrows, smiling at their follies without bitterness, sharing their affections, but not troubled by their passions, not seeking their notice, nor once dreamt of by them. He who lives wisely to himself and to his own heart looks at the busy world through the loop-holes of retreat, and does not want to mingle in the fray. 'He hears the tumult, and is still.' He is not able to mend it, nor willing to mar it. He sees enough in the universe to interest him without putting himself forward to try what he can do to fix the eyes of the universe upon him. Vain the attempt! He reads the clouds, he looks at the stars, he watches the return of the seasons, the falling leaves of autumn, the perfumed breath of spring, starts with delight at the note of a thrush in a copse near him, sits by the fire, listens to the moaning of the wind, pores upon a book, or discourses the freezing hours away, or melts down hours to minutes in pleasing thought. All this while he is taken up with other things, forgetting himself. He relishes an author's style without thinking of turning author. He is fond of looking at a print from an old picture in the room, without teasing himself to copy it. He does not fret himself to death with trying to be what he is not, or to do what he cannot. He hardly knows what he is capable of, and is not in the least concerned whether he shall ever make a figure in the world. He feels the truth of the lines—

```
The man whose eye is ever on himself,
Doth look one, the least of nature's works;
```

34

```
One who might move the wise man to that scorn
Which wisdom holds unlawful ever.
```

He looks out of himself at the wide, extended prospect of nature, and takes an interest beyond his narrow pretensions in general humanity. He is free as air, and independent as the wind. Woe be to him when he first begins to think what others say of him. While a man is contented with himself and his own resources, all is well. When he undertakes to play a part on the stage, and to persuade the world to think more about him than they do about themselves, he is got into a track where he will find nothing but briars and thorns, vexation and disappointment. I can speak a little to this point. For many years of my life I did nothing but think. I had nothing else to do but solve some knotty point, or dip in some abstruse author, or look at the sky, or wander by the pebbled seaside—

```
To see the children sporting on the shore,
And hear the mighty waters rolling evermore
```

I cared for nothing, I wanted nothing. I took my time to consider whatever occurred to me, and was in no hurry to give a sophistical answer to a question—there was no printer's devil waiting for me. I used to write a page or two perhaps in half a year; and remember laughing heartily at the celebrated experimentalist Nicholson, who told me that in twenty years he had written as much as would make three hundred octavo volumes. If I was not a great author, I could read with ever fresh delight, 'never ending, still beginning,' and had no occasion to write a criticism when I had done. If I could not paint like Claude, I could admire 'the witchery of the soft blue sky' as I walked out, and was satisfied with the pleasure it gave me. If I was dull, it gave me little concern: if I was lively, I indulged my spirits. I wished well to the world, and believed as favourably of it as I could. I was like a stranger in a foreign land, at which I looked with wonder, curiosity, and delight, without expecting to be an object of attention in return. I had no relations to the state, no duty to perform, no ties to bind me to others: I had neither friend nor mistress, wife nor child. I lived in a world of contemplation, and not of action.

This sort of dreaming existence is the best. He who quits it to go in search of realities generally barters repose for repeated disappointments and vain regrets. His time, thoughts, and feelings are no longer at his own disposal. From that instant he does not survey the objects of nature as they are in themselves, but looks asquint at them to see whether he cannot make them the instruments of his ambition, interest, or pleasure; for a candid, undesigning, undisguised simplicity of character, his views become jaundiced, sinister, and double: he takes no farther interest in the great changes of the world but as he has a paltry share in producing them: instead of opening his senses, his understanding, and his heart to the resplendent fabric of the universe, he holds a crooked mirror before his face, in which he may admire his own person and pretensions, and just glance his eye aside to see whether others are not admiring him too. He no more exists in the impression which 'the fair variety of things' makes upon him, softened and subdued by habitual contemplation, but in the feverish sense of his own upstart self-importance. By aiming to fix, he is become the slave of opinion. He is a tool, a part of a machine that never stands still, and is sick and giddy with the ceaseless motion. He has no satisfaction but in the reflection of his own image in the public gaze—but in the repetition of his own name in the public ear. He himself is mixed up with and spoils everything. I wonder Buonaparte was not tired of the N. N.'s stuck all over the Louvre and throughout France. Goldsmith (as we all know) when in Holland went out into a balcony with some handsome Englishwomen, and on their being applauded by the spectators, turned round and said peevishly, 'There are places where I also am admired.' He could not give the craving appetite of an author's vanity one day's respite. I have seen a celebrated talker of our own time turn pale and go out of the room when a showy-looking girl has come into it who for a moment divided the attention of his hearers.— Infinite are the mortifications of the bare attempt to emerge from obscurity; numberless the failures; and greater and more galling still the vicissitudes and tormenting accompaniments of success—

```
Whose top to climb
Is certain falling, or so slippery, that
The fear's as bad as falling.
```

'Would to God,' exclaimed Oliver Cromwell, when he was at any time thwarted by the Parliament, 'that I had remained by my woodside to tend a flock of sheep, rather than have been thrust on such a government as this!' When Buonaparte got into his carriage to proceed on his Russian expedition, carelessly twirling his glove, and singing the air, 'Malbrook to the war is going,' he did not think of the tumble he has got since, the shock of which no one could have stood but himself. We see and hear chiefly of the favourites of Fortune and the Muse, of great generals, of first-rate actors, of celebrated poets. These are at the head; we are struck with the glittering eminence on which they stand, and long to set out on the same tempting career,—not thinking how many discontented half-pay lieutenants are in vain seeking promotion all their lives, and obliged to put up with 'the insolence of office, and the spurns which patient merit of the unworthy takes'; how many half-starved strolling players are doomed to penury and tattered robes in country places, dreaming to the last of a London engagement; how many wretched daubers shiver and shake in the ague-fit of alternate hopes and fears, waste and pine away in the atrophy of genius, or else turn drawing-masters, picture-cleaners, or newspaper-critics; how many hapless poets have sighed out their souls to the Muse in vain, without ever getting their effusions farther known than the Poet's Corner of a country newspaper, and looked and looked with grudging, wistful eyes at the envious horizon that bounded their provincial fame!—Suppose an actor, for instance, 'after the heart-aches and the thousand natural pangs that flesh is heir to,' *does* get at the top of his profession, he can no longer bear a rival near the throne: to be second or only equal to another is to be nothing: he starts at the prospect of a successor, and retains the mimic sceptre with a convulsive grasp: perhaps as he is about to seize the first place which he has long had in his eye, an unsuspected competitor steps in before him, and carries off the prize, leaving him to commence his irksome toil again. He is in a state of alarm at every appearance or rumour of the appearance of a new actor: 'a mouse that takes up its lodgings in a cat's ear'(2) has a mansion of peace to him: he dreads every hint of an objection, and least of all, can forgive praise mingled with censure: to doubt is to insult; to discriminate is to degrade: he dare hardly look into a criticism unless some one has tasted it for him, to see that there is no offence in it: if he does not draw crowded houses every night, he can neither eat nor sleep; or if all these terrible inflections are removed, and he can 'eat his meal in peace,' he then becomes surfeited with applause and dissatisfied with his profession: he wants to be something else, to be distinguished as an author, a collector, a classical scholar, a man of sense and information, and weighs every word he utters, and half retracts it before he utters it, lest if he were to make the smallest slip of the tongue it should get buzzed abroad that *Mr. —— was only clever as an actor!* If ever there was a man who did not derive more pain than pleasure from his vanity, that man, says Rousseau, was no other than a fool. A country gentleman near Taunton spent his whole life in making some hundreds of wretched copies of second-rate pictures, which were bought up at his death by a neighbouring baronet, to whom

> Some Demon whisper'd, L——, have a taste!

A little Wilson in an obscure corner escaped the man of *virtu*, and was carried off by a Bristol picture-dealer for three guineas, while the muddled copies of the owner of the mansion (with the frames) fetched thirty, forty, sixty, a hundred ducats a piece. A friend of mine found a very fine Canaletti in a state of strange disfigurement, with the upper part of the sky smeared over and fantastically variegated with English clouds; and on inquiring of the person to whom it belonged whether something had not been done to it, received for answer 'that a gentleman, a great artist in the neighbourhood, had retouched some parts of it.' What infatuation! Yet this candidate for the honours of the pencil might probably have made a jovial fox-hunter or respectable justice of the peace it he could only have stuck to what nature and fortune intended him for. Miss —— can by no means be persuaded to quit the boards of the theatre at ——, a little country town in the West of England. Her salary has been abridged, her person ridiculed, her acting laughed at; nothing will serve—she is determined to be an actress, and scorns to return to her former business as a milliner. Shall I go on? An actor in the same company was visited by the apothecary of the place in an ague-fit, who, on asking his landlady as to his way of life, was told that the poor gentleman was very quiet and gave little trouble, that he generally had a plate of mashed potatoes for his dinner, and lay in bed most of his time, repeating his part. A young couple, every way amiable and deserving, were to have been married, and a benefit-play was bespoke by the officers of the regiment quartered there, to defray the expense of a license and of the wedding-ring, but the profits of the night did not amount to the necessary sum, and they have, I fear, 'virgined it e'er since'! Oh, for the pencil of Hogarth or Wilkie to give a view of the comic strength of the company at ——, drawn up in battle-array in the *Clandestine Marriage,* with a *coup d'oeil* of the pit, boxes, and gallery, to cure for ever the love of the *ideal*, and the desire to shine and make holiday in the eyes of others, instead of retiring within ourselves and keeping our wishes and our thoughts at home!—Even in the common affairs of life, in love, friendship, and marriage, how little security have we when we trust our happiness in the hands of others! Most of the friends I have seen have turned out the bitterest enemies, or cold, uncomfortable acquaintance. Old companions are like meats served up too often, that lose their relish and their wholesomeness. He who looks at beauty to admire, to adore it, who reads of its wondrous power in novels, in poems, or in plays, is not unwise; but let no man fall in love, for from that moment he is 'the baby of a girl.' I like very well to repeat such lines as these in the play of *Mirandola*—

> With what a waving air she goes
> Along the corridor! How like a fawn!
> Yet statelier. Hark! No sound, however soft,
> Nor gentlest echo telleth when she treads,
> But every motion of her shape doth seem
> Hallowed by silence.

But however beautiful the description, defend me from meeting with the original!

> The fly that sips treacle
> Is lost in the sweets;
> So he that tastes woman
> Ruin meets.

The song is Gay's, not mine, and a bitter-sweet it is. How few out of the infinite number of those that marry and are given in marriage wed with those they would prefer to all the world! nay, how far the greater proportion are joined together by mere motives of convenience, accident, recommendation of friends, or indeed not unfrequently by the very fear of the event, by repugnance and a sort of fatal fascination! yet the tie is for life, not to be shaken off but with disgrace or death: a man no longer lives to himself, but is a body (as well as mind) chained to another, in spite of himself—

> Like life and death in disproportion met.

So Milton (perhaps from his own experience) makes Adam exclaim in the vehemence of his despair,

> For either
> He never shall find out fit mate, but such
> As some misfortune brings him or mistake
> Or whom he wishes most shall seldom gain
> Through her perverseness, but shall sea her gain'd
> By a far worse; or it she love, withheld
> By parents; or his happiest choice too late
> Shall meet, already link'd and wedlock-bound
> To a fell adversary, his hate and shame;
> Which infinite calamity shall cause
> To human life, and household peace confound.

If love at first sight were mutual, or to be conciliated by kind offices; if the fondest affection were not so often repaid and chilled by indifference and scorn; if so many lovers both before and since the madman in Don Quixote had not 'worshipped a statue, hunted the wind, cried aloud to the desert'; if friendship were lasting; if merit were renown, and renown were health, riches, and long life; or if the homage of the world were paid to conscious worth and the true aspirations after excellence, instead of its gaudy signs and outward trappings, then indeed I might be of opinion that it is better to live to others than one's-self; but as the case stands, I incline to the negative side of the question.(3)

```
I have not loved the world, nor the world me;
I have not flattered its rank breath, nor bow'd
To its idolatries a patient knee—
Nor coin'd my cheek to smiles—nor cried aloud
In worship of an echo; in the crowd
They could not deem me one of such; I stood
Among them, but not of them; in a shroud
Of thoughts which were not their thoughts, and still could,
Had I not filled my mind which thus itself subdued.


I have not loved the world,  nor the world me—
But let us part fair foes; I do believe,
Though I have found them not, that there may be
Words which are things—hopes which will not deceive,
And virtues which are merciful nor weave
Snares for the failing: I would also deem
O'er others' griefs that some sincerely grieve;
That two, or one, are almost what they seem—
That goodness is no name, and happiness no dream.
```

Sweet verse embalms the spirit of sour misanthropy; but woe betide the ignoble prose-writer who should thus dare to compare notes with the world, or tax it roundly with imposture.

If I had sufficient provocation to rail at the public, as Ben Jonson did at the audience in the Prologues to his plays, I think I should do it in good set terms, nearly as follows:—There is not a more mean, stupid, dastardly, pitiful, selfish, spiteful, envious, ungrateful animal than the Public. It is the greatest of cowards, for it is afraid of itself. From its unwieldy, overgrown dimensions, it dreads the least opposition to it, and shakes like isinglass at the touch of a finger. It starts at its own shadow, like the man in the Hartz mountains, and trembles at the mention of its own name. It has a lion's mouth, the heart of a hare, with ears erect and sleepless eyes. It stands 'listening its fears.' It is so in awe of its own opinion that it never dares to form any, but catches up the first idle rumour, lest it should be behindhand in its judgment, and echoes it till it is deafened with the sound of its own voice. The idea of what the public will think prevents the public from ever thinking at all, and acts as a spell on the exercise of private judgment, so that, in short, the public ear is at the mercy of the first impudent pretender who chooses to fill it with noisy assertions, or false surmises, or secret whispers. What is said by one is heard by all; the supposition that a thing is known to all the world makes all the world believe it, and the hollow repetition of a vague report drowns the 'still, small voice' of reason. We may believe or know that what is said is not true; but we know or fancy that others believe it,—we dare not contradict or are too indolent to dispute with them, and therefore give up our internal, and, as we think, our solitary conviction to a sound without substance, without proof, and often without meaning. Nay more, we may believe and know not only that a thing is false, but that others believe and know it to be so, that they are quite as much in the secret of the imposture as we are, that they see the puppets at work, the nature of the machinery, and yet if any one has the art or power to get the management of it, he shall keep possession of the public ear by virtue of a cant phrase or nickname, and by dint of effrontery and perseverance make all the world believe and repeat what all the world know to be false. The ear is quicker than the judgment. We know that certain things are said; by that circumstance alone, we know that they produce a certain effect on the imagination of others, and we conform to their prejudices by mechanical sympathy, and for want of sufficient spirit to differ with them. So far then is public opinion from resting on a broad and solid basis, as the aggregate of thought and feeling in a community, that it is slight and shallow and variable to the last degree—the bubble of the moment; so that we may safely say the public is the dupe of public opinion, not its parent. The public is pusillanimous and cowardly, because it is weak. It knows itself to be a great dunce, and that it has no opinions but upon suggestion. Yet it is unwilling to appear in leading-strings, and would have it thought that its decisions are as wise as they are weighty. It is hasty in taking up its favourites, more hasty in laying them aside, lest it should be supposed deficient in sagacity in either case. It is generally divided into two strong parties, each of which will allow neither common sense nor common honesty to the other side. It reads the *Edinburgh* and *Quarterly Reviews*, and believes them both—or if there is a doubt, malice turns the scale. Taylor and Hessey told me that they had sold nearly two editions of the *Characters of Shakespear's Plays* in about three months, but that after the *Quarterly Review* of them came out they never sold another copy. The public, enlightened as they are, must have known the meaning of that attack as well as those who made it. It was not ignorance then, but cowardice, that led them to give up their own opinion. A crew of mischievous critics at Edinburgh having affixed the epithet of the *Cockney School* to one or two writers born in the metropolis, all the people in London became afraid of looking into their works, lest they too should be convicted of cockneyism. Oh, brave public! This epithet proved too much for one of the writers in question, and stuck like a barbed arrow in his heart. Poor Keats! What was sport to the town was death to him. Young, sensitive, delicate, he was like

```
A bud bit by an envious worm,
Ere he could spread his sweet leaves to the air
Or dedicate his beauty to the sun;
```

37

and unable to endure the miscreant cry and idiot laugh, withdrew to sigh his last breath in foreign climes. The public is as envious and ungrateful as it is ignorant, stupid, and pigeon-livered—

> A huge-sized monster of ingratitudes.

It reads, it admires, it extols, only because it is the fashion, not from any love of the subject or the man. It cries you up or runs you down out of mere caprice and levity. If you have pleased it, it is jealous of its own involuntary acknowledgment of merit, and seizes the first opportunity, the first shabby pretext, to pick a quarrel with you and be quits once more. Every petty caviller is erected into a judge, every tale-bearer is implicitly believed. Every little, low, paltry creature that gaped and wondered, only because others did so, is glad to find you (as he thinks) on a level with himself. An author is not then, after all, a being of another order. Public admiration is forced, and goes against the grain. Public obloquy is cordial and sincere: every individual feels his own importance in it. They give you up bound hand and foot into the power of your accusers. To attempt to defend yourself is a high crime and misdemeanor, a contempt of court, an extreme piece of impertinence. Or if you prove every charge unfounded, they never think of retracing their error or making you amends. It would be a compromise of their dignity; they consider themselves as the party injured, and resent your innocence as an imputation on their judgment. The celebrated Bub Doddington, when out of favour at court, said 'he would not *justify* before his sovereign: it was for Majesty to be displeased, and for him to believe himself in the wrong!' The public are not quite so modest. People already begin to talk of the Scotch Novels as overrated. How then can common authors be supposed to keep their heads long above water? As a general rule, all those who live by the public starve, and are made a by-word and a standing jest into the bargain. Posterity is no better (not a bit more enlightened or more liberal), except that you are no longer in their power, and that the voice of common fame saves them the trouble of deciding on your claims. The public now are the posterity of Milton and Shakespear. Our posterity will be the living public of a future generation. When a man is dead, they put money in his coffin, erect monuments to his memory, and celebrate the anniversary of his birthday in set speeches. Would they take any notice of him if he were living? No!—I was complaining of this to a Scotchman who had been attending a dinner and a subscription to raise a monument to Burns. He replied he would sooner subscribe twenty pounds to his monument than have given it him while living; so that if the poet were to come to life again, he would treat him just as he was treated in fact. This was an honest Scotchman. What *he* said, the rest would do.

Enough: my soul, turn from them, and let me try to regain the obscurity and quiet that I love, 'far from the madding strife,' in some sequestered corner of my own, or in some far-distant land! In the latter case, I might carry with me as a consolation the passage in Bolinbroke's *Reflections on Exile,* in which he describes in glowing colours the resources which a man may always find within himself, and of which the world cannot deprive him:—

'Believe me, the providence of God has established such an order in the world, that of all which belongs to us the least valuable parts can alone fall under the will of others. Whatever is best is safest; lies out of the reach of human power; can neither be given nor taken away. Such is this great and beautiful work of nature, the world. Such is the mind of man, which contemplates and admires the world, whereof it makes the noblest part. These are inseparably ours, and as long as we remain in one we shall enjoy the other. Let us march therefore intrepidly wherever we are led by the course of human accidents. Wherever they lead us, on what coast soever we are thrown by them, we shall not find ourselves absolutely strangers. We shall feel the same revolution of seasons, and the same sun and moon(4) will guide the course of our year. The same azure vault, bespangled with stars, will be everywhere spread over our heads. There is no part of the world from whence we may not admire those planets which roll, like ours, in different orbits round the same central sun; from whence we may not discover an object still more stupendous, that army of fixed stars hung up in the immense space of the universe, innumerable suns whose beams enlighten and cherish the unknown worlds which roll around them: and whilst I am ravished by such contemplations as these, whilst my soul is thus raised up to heaven, it imports me little what ground I tread-upon.'

FN to ESSAY X

(1) Written at Winterslow Hut, January 18-19, 1821.

(2) Webster's *Duchess of Malfy.*

(3) Shenstone and Gray were two men, one of whom pretended live to himself, and the other really did so. Gray shrunk from the public gaze (he did not even like his portrait to be prefixed to his works) into his own thoughts and indolent musings; Shenstone affected privacy that he might be sought out by the world; the one courted retirement in order to enjoy leisure and repose, as the other coquetted with it merely to be interrupted with the importunity of visitors and the flatteries of absent friends.

(4) Plut. of Banishment. He compares those who cannot live out of their own country to the simple people who fancied the moon of Athens was a finer moon than that of Corinth,

> Labentem coelo quae ducitis annum.
> —VIRG. *Georg.*

ESSAY XI. ON THOUGHT AND ACTION

Those persons who are much accustomed to abstract contemplation are generally unfitted for active pursuits, and *vice versa*. I myself am sufficiently decided and dogmatical in my opinions, and yet in action I am as imbecile as a woman or a child. I cannot set about the most indifferent thing without twenty efforts, and had rather write one of these Essays than have to seal a letter. In trying to throw a hat or a book upon a table, I miss it; it just reaches the edge and falls back again, and instead of doing what I mean to perform, I do what I intend to avoid. Thought depends on the habitual exercise of the speculative faculties; action, on the determination of the will. The one assigns reasons for things, the other puts causes into act. Abraham Tucker relates of a friend of his, an old special pleader, that once coming out of his chambers in the Temple with him to take a walk, he hesitated at the bottom of the stairs which way to go—proposed different directions, to Charing Cross, to St. Paul's—found some objection to them all, and at last turned back for want of a casting motive to incline the scale. Tucker gives this as an instance of professional indecision, or of that temper of mind which having been long used to weigh the reasons for things with scrupulous exactness, could not come to any conclusion at all on the spur of the occasion, or without some grave distinction to justify its choice. Louvet in his Narrative tells us, that when several of the Brisotin party were collected at the house of Barbaroux (I think it was) ready to effect their escape from the power of Robespierre, one of them going to the window and finding a shower of rain coming on, seriously advised their stopping till the next morning, for that the emissaries of government would not think of coming in search of them in such bad weather. Some of them deliberated on this wise proposal, and were nearly taken. Such is the effeminacy of the speculative and philosophical temperament, compared with the promptness and vigour of the practical! It is on such unequal terms that the refined and romantic speculators on possible good and evil contend with their strong-nerved, remorseless adversaries, and we see the result. Reasoners in general are undecided, wavering, and sceptical, or yield at last to the weakest motive as most congenial to their feeble habit of soul.(1)

Some men are mere machines. They are put in a go-cart of business, and are harnessed to a profession—yoked to Fortune's wheels. They plod on, and succeed. Their affairs conduct them, not they their affairs. All they have to do is to let things take their course, and not go out of the beaten road. A man may carry on the business of farming on the same spot and principle that his ancestors have done for many generations before him without any extraordinary share of capacity: the proof is, it is done every day, in every county and parish in the kingdom. All that is necessary is that he should not pretend to be wiser than his neighbours. If he has a grain more wit or penetration than they, if his vanity gets the start of his avarice only half a neck, if he has ever thought or read anything upon the subject, it will most probably be the ruin of him. He will turn theoretical or experimental farmer, and no more need be said. Mr. Cobbett, who is a sufficiently shrewd and practical man, with an eye also to the main chance, had got some notions in his head (from Tull's *Husbandry*) about the method of sowing turnips, to which he would have sacrificed not only his estate at Botley, but his native county of Hampshire itself, sooner than give up an inch of his argument. 'Tut! will you baulk a man in the career of his humour?' Therefore, that a man may not be ruined by his humours, he should be too dull and phlegmatic to have any: he must have 'no figures nor no fantasies which busy thought draws in the brains of men.' The fact is, that the ingenuity or judgment of no one man is equal to that of the world at large, which is the fruit of the experience and ability of all mankind. Even where a man is right in a particular notion, he will be apt to overrate the importance of his discovery, to the detriment of his affairs. Action requires co-operation, but in general if you set your face against custom, people will set their faces against you. They cannot tell whether you are right or wrong, but they know that you are guilty of a pragmatical assumption of superiority over them which they do not like. There is no doubt that if a person two hundred years ago had foreseen and attempted to put in practice the most approved and successful methods of cultivation now in use, it would have been a death-blow to his credit and fortune. So that though the experiments and improvements of private individuals from time to time gradually go to enrich the public stock of information and reform the general practice, they are mostly the ruin of the person who makes them, because he takes a part for the whole, and lays more stress upon the single point in which he has found others in the wrong than on all the rest in which they are substantially and prescriptively in the right. The great requisite, it should appear, then, for the prosperous management of ordinary business is the want of imagination, or of any ideas but those of custom and interest on the narrowest scale; and as the affairs of the world are necessarily carried on by the common run of its inhabitants, it seems a wise dispensation of Providence that it should be so. If no one could rent a piece of glebe-land without a genius for mechanical inventions, or stand behind a counter without a large benevolence of soul, what would become of the commercial and agricultural interests of this great (and once flourishing) country?—I would not be understood as saying that there is not what may be called a genius for business, an extraordinary capacity for affairs, quickness and comprehension united, an insight into character, an acquaintance with a number of particular circumstances, a variety of expedients, a tact for finding out what will do: I grant all this (in Liverpool and Manchester they would persuade you that your merchant and manufacturer is your only gentleman and scholar)—but still, making every allowance for the difference between the liberal trader and the sneaking shopkeeper, I doubt whether the most surprising success is to be accounted for from any such unusual attainments, or whether a man's making half a million of money is a proof of his capacity for thought in general. It is much oftener owing to views and wishes bounded but constantly directed to one particular object. To succeed, a man should aim only at success. The child of Fortune should resign himself into the hands of Fortune. A plotting head frequently overreaches itself: a mind confident of its resources and calculating powers enters on critical speculations, which in a game depending so much on chance and unforeseen events, and not entirely on intellectual skill, turn the odds greatly against any one in the long run. The rule of business is to take what you can get, and keep what you have got; or an eagerness in seizing every opportunity that offers for promoting your own interest, and a plodding, persevering industry in making the most of the advantages you have already obtained, are the most effectual as well as the safest ingredients in the composition of the mercantile character. The world is a book in which the *Chapter of Accidents* is none of the least considerable; or it is a machine that must be left, in a great measure, to turn itself. The most that a worldly-minded man can do is to stand at the receipt of custom, and be constantly on the lookout for windfalls. The true devotee in this way waits for the revelations of Fortune as the poet waits for the inspiration of the Muse, and does not rashly anticipate her favours. He must be neither capricious nor wilful. I have known people untrammelled in the ways of business, but with so intense an apprehension of their own interest, that they would grasp at the slightest possibility of gain as a certainty, and were led into as many mistakes by an overgriping, usurious disposition as they could have been by the most thoughtless extravagance.—We hear a great outcry about the want of judgment in men of genius. It is not a want of judgment, but an excess of other things. They err knowingly, and are wilfully blind. The understanding is out of the question. The profound judgment which soberer people pique themselves upon is in truth a want of passion and imagination. Give them an interest in anything, a sudden fancy, a bait for their favourite foible, and who so besotted as they? Stir their feelings, and farewell to their prudence! The understanding operates as a motive to action only in the silence of the passions. I have heard people of a sanguine temperament reproached with betting according to their wishes, instead of their opinion who should win; and I have seen those who reproached them do the very same thing the instant their own vanity or prejudices are concerned. The most mechanical people, once thrown off their balance, are the most extravagant and fantastical. What passion is there so unmeaning and irrational as avarice itself? The Dutch went mad for tulips, and —— —— for love! To return to what was said a little way back, a question might be started, whether as thought relates to the whole circumference of things and interests, and business is confined to a very small part of them, viz. to a knowledge of a man's own affairs and the making of his own fortune, whether a talent for the latter will not generally exist in proportion to the narrowness and grossness of his ideas, nothing drawing his attention out of his own sphere, or giving him an interest except in those things which he can realise and bring home to himself in the most undoubted shape? To the man of business all the world is a fable but the Stock Exchange: to the money-getter nothing has a real existence that he cannot convert into a tangible feeling, that he does not recognise as property, that he cannot 'measure with a two-foot rule or count upon ten fingers.' The want of thought, of imagination, drives the practical man upon immediate realities: to the poet or philosopher all is real and interesting that is true or possible, that can reach in its consequences to others, or be made a subject of curious speculation to himself!

But is it right, then, to judge of action by the quantity of thought implied in it, any more than it would be to condemn a life of contemplation for being inactive? Or has not everything a source and principle of its own, to which we should refer it, and not to the principles of other things? He who succeeds in any pursuit in which others fail may be presumed to have qualities of some sort or other which they are without. If he has not brilliant wit, he may have solid sense; if he has not subtlety of understanding, he may have energy and firmness of purpose; if he has only a few advantages, he may have modesty and prudence to make the most of what he possesses. Propriety is one great matter in the conduct of life; which, though, like a graceful carriage of the body, it is neither definable nor striking at first sight, is the result of finely balanced feelings, and lends a secret strength and charm to the whole character.

> Quicquid agit, quoquo vestigia vertit,
> Componit furtim, subsequiturque decor.

There are more ways than one in which the various faculties of the mind may unfold themselves. Neither words nor ideas reducible to words constitute the utmost limit of human capacity. Man is not a merely talking nor a merely reasoning animal. Let us then take him as he is, instead of 'curtailing him of nature's fair proportions' to suit our previous notions. Doubtless, there are great characters both in active and contemplative life. There have been heroes as well as sages, legislators and founders of religion, historians and able statesmen and generals, inventors of useful arts and instruments and explorers of undiscovered countries, as well as writers and readers of books. It will not do to set all these aside under any fastidious or pedantic distinction. Comparisons are odious, because they are impertinent, and lead only to the discovery of defects by making one thing the standard of another which has no relation to it. If, as some one proposed, we were to institute an inquiry, 'Which was the greatest man, Milton or Cromwell, Buonaparte or Rubens?' we should have all the authors and artists on one side, and all the military men and the whole diplomatic body on the other, who would set to work with all their might to pull in pieces the idol of the other party, and the longer the dispute continued, the more would each grow dissatisfied with his favourite, though determined to allow no merit to any one else. The mind is not well competent to take in the full impression of more than one style of excellence or one extraordinary character at once; contradictory claims puzzle and stupefy it; and however admirable any individual may be in himself and unrivalled in his particular way, yet if we try him by others in a totally opposite class, that is, if we consider not what he was but what he was not, he will be found to be nothing. We do not reckon up the excellences on either side, for then these would satisfy the mind and put an end to the comparison: we have no way of exclusively setting up our favourite but by running down his supposed rival; and for the gorgeous hues of Rubens, the lofty conceptions of Milton, the deep policy and cautious daring of Cromwell, or the dazzling exploits and fatal ambition of the modern chieftain, the poet is transformed into a pedant, the artist sinks into a mechanic, the politician turns out no better than a knave, and the hero is exalted into a madman. It is as easy to get the start of our antagonist in argument by frivolous and vexatious objections to one side of the question as it is difficult to do full and heaped justice to the other. If I am asked which is the greatest of those who have been the greatest in different ways, I answer, the one that we happen to be thinking of at the time; for while that is the case, we can conceive of nothing higher. If there is a propensity in the vulgar to admire the achievements of personal prowess or instances of fortunate enterprise too much, it cannot be denied that those who have to weigh out and dispense the meed of fame in books have been too much disposed, by a natural bias, to confine all merit and talent to the productions of the pen, or at least to those works which, being artificial or abstract representations of things, are transmitted to posterity, and cried up as models in their kind. This, though unavoidable, is hardly just. Actions pass away and are forgotten, or are only discernible in their effects; conquerors, statesmen, and kings live but by their names stamped on the page of history. Hume says rightly that more people think about Virgil and Homer (and that continually) than ever trouble their heads about Caesar or Alexander. In fact, poets are a longer-lived race than heroes: they breathe more of the air of immortality. They survive more entire in their thoughts and acts. We have all that Virgil or Homer did, as much as if we had lived at the same time with them: we can hold their works in our hands, or lay them on our pillows, or put them to our lips. Scarcely a trace of what the others did is left upon the earth, so as to be visible to common eyes. The one, the dead authors, are living men, still breathing and moving in their writings. The others, the conquerors of the world, are but the ashes in an urn. The sympathy (so to speak) between thought and thought is more intimate and vital than that between thought and action. Though of admiration to the manes of departed heroism is like burning incense in a marble monument. Words, ideas, feelings, with the progress of time harden into substances: things, bodies, actions, moulder away, or melt into a sound, into thin air!—Yet though the Schoolmen in the Middle Ages disputed more about the texts of Aristotle than the battle of Arbela, perhaps Alexander's Generals in his lifetime admired his pupil as much and liked him better. For not only a man's actions are effaced and vanish with him; his virtues and generous qualities die with him also: his intellect only is immortal and bequeathed unimpaired to posterity. Words are the only things that last for ever.

If, however, the empire of words and general knowledge is more durable in proportion as it is abstracted and attenuated, it is less immediate and dazzling: if authors are as good after they are dead as when they were living, while living they might as well be dead: and moreover with respect to actual ability, to write a book is not the only proof of taste, sense, or spirit, as pedants would have us suppose. To do anything well, to paint a picture, to fight a battle, to make a plough or a threshing-machine, requires, one would think, as much skill and judgment as to talk about or write a description of it when done. Words are universal, intelligible signs, but they are not the only real, existing things. Did not Julius Caesar show himself as much of a man in conducting his campaigns as in composing his Commentaries? Or was the Retreat of the Ten Thousand under Xenophon, or his work of that name, the most consummate performance? Or would not Lovelace, supposing him to have existed and to have conceived and executed all his fine stratagems on the spur of the occasion, have been as clever a fellow as Richardson, who invented them in cold blood? If to conceive and describe an heroic character is the height of a literary ambition, we can hardly make it out that to be and to do all that the wit of man can feign is nothing. To use means to ends; to set causes in motion; to wield the machine of society; to subject the wills of others to your own; to manage abler men than yourself by means of that which is stronger in them than their wisdom, viz. their weakness and their folly; to calculate the resistance of ignorance and prejudice to your designs, and by obviating, to turn them to account; to foresee a long, obscure, and complicated train of events, of chances and openings of success; to unwind the web of others' policy and weave your own out of it; to judge of the effects of things, not in the abstract, but with reference to all their bearings, ramifications, and impediments; to understand character thoroughly; to see latent talent or lurking treachery; to know mankind for what they are, and use them as they deserve; to have a purpose steadily in view, and to effect it after removing every obstacle; to master others and be true to yourself,—asks power and knowledge, both nerves and brain.

Such is the sort of talent that that may be shown and that has been possessed by the great leaders on the stage of the world. To accomplish great things argues, I imagine, great resolution: to design great things implies no common mind. Ambition is in some sort genius. Though I would rather wear out my life in arguing a broad speculative question than in caballing for the election to a wardmote, or canvassing for votes in a rotten borough, yet I should think that the loftiest Epicurean philosopher might descend from his punctilio to identify himself with the support of a great principle, or to prop a falling state. This is what the legislators and founders of empire did of old; and the permanence of their institutions showed the depth of the principles from which they emanated. A tragic poem is not the worse for acting well: if it will not bear this test it savours of effeminacy. Well-digested schemes will stand the touchstone of experience. Great thoughts reduced to practice become great acts. Again, great acts grow out of great occasions, and great occasions spring from great principles, working changes in society, and tearing it up by the roots. But I still conceive that a genius for actions depends essentially on the strength of the will rather than on that of the understanding; that the long-headed calculation of causes and consequences arises from the energy of the first cause, which is the will setting others in motion and prepared to anticipate the results; that its sagacity is activity delighting in meeting difficulties and adventures more than half-way, and its wisdom courage not to shrink from danger, but to redouble its efforts with opposition. Its humanity, if it has much, is magnanimity to spare the vanquished, exulting in power but not prone to mischief, with good sense enough to be aware of the instability of fortune, and with some regard to reputation. What may serve as a criterion to try this question by is the following consideration, that we sometimes find as remarkable a deficiency of the speculative faculty coupled with great strength of will and consequent success in active life as we do a want of voluntary power and total incapacity for business frequently joined to the highest mental qualifications. In some cases it will happen that 'to be wise is to be obstinate.' If you are deaf to reason but stick to your own purposes, you will tire others out, and bring them over to your way of thinking. Self-will and blind prejudice are the best defence of actual power and exclusive advantages. The forehead of the late king was not remarkable for the character of intellect, but the lower part of his face was expressive of strong passions and fixed resolution. Charles Fox had an animated, intelligent eye, and brilliant, elastic forehead (with a nose indicating fine taste), but the lower features were weak, unsettled, fluctuating, and without *purchase*—it was in them the Whigs were defeated. What a fine iron binding Buonaparte had round his face, as if it had been cased in steel! What sensibility about the mouth! What watchful penetration in the eye! What a smooth, unruffled forehead! Mr. Pitt, with little sunken eyes, had a high, retreating forehead, and a nose expressing pride and aspiring self-opinion: it was on that (with submission) that he suspended the decisions of the House of Commons and dangled the Opposition as he pleased. Lord Castlereagh is a man rather deficient than redundant in words and topics. He is not (any more than St. Augustine was, in the opinion of La Fontaine) so great a wit as Rabelais, nor is he so great a philosopher as Aristotle; but he has that in him which is not to be trifled with. He has a noble mask of a face (not well filled up in the expression, which is relaxed and dormant) with a fine person and manner. On the strength of these he hazards his speeches in the House. He has also a knowledge of mankind, and of the composition of the House. He takes a thrust which he cannot parry on his shield—is 'all tranquillity and smiles' under a volley of abuse, sees when to pay a compliment to a wavering antagonist, soothes the melting mood of his hearers, or gets up a speech full of indignation, and knows how to bestow his attentions on that great public body, whether he wheedles or bullies, so as to bring it to compliance. With a long reach of undefined purposes (the result of a temper too indolent for thought, too violent for repose) he has equal perseverance and pliancy in bringing his objects to pass. I would rather be Lord Castlereagh, as far as a sense of power is concerned (principle is out of the question), than such a man as Mr. Canning, who is a mere fluent sophist, and never knows the limit of discretion, or the effect which will be produced by what he says, except as far as florid common-places may be depended on. Buonaparte is referred by Mr. Coleridge to the class of active rather than of intellectual characters; and Cowley has left an invidious but splendid eulogy on Oliver Cromwell, which sets out on much the same principle. 'What,' he says, 'can be more extraordinary than that a person of mean birth, no fortune, no eminent qualities of body, which have sometimes, or of mind, which have often, raised men to the highest dignities, should have the courage to attempt, and the happiness to succeed in, so improbable a design as the destruction of one of the most ancient and most solidly-founded monarchies upon the earth? That he should have the power or boldness to put his prince and master to an open and infamous death; to banish that numerous and strongly-allied family; to do all this under the name and wages of a Parliament; to trample upon them too as he pleased, and spurn them out of doors when he grow weary of them; to raise up a new and unheard-of monster out of their ashes; to stifle that in the very infancy, and set up himself above all things that ever were called sovereign in England; to oppress all his enemies by arms, and all his friends afterwards by artifice; to serve all parties patiently for a while, and to command them victoriously at last; to overrun each corner of the three nations, and overcome with equal facility both the riches of the south and the poverty of the north; to be feared and courted by all foreign princes, and adopted a brother to the Gods of the earth; to call together Parliaments with a word of his pen, and scatter them again with the breath of his mouth; to be humbly and daily petitioned that he would please to be hired, at the rate of two millions a year, to be the master of those who had hired him before to be their servant; to have the estates and lives of three kingdoms as much at his disposal as was the little inheritance of his father, and to be as noble and liberal in the spending of them; and lastly (for there is no end of all the particulars of his glory), to bequeath all this with one word to his posterity; to die with peace at home, and triumph abroad; to be buried among kings, and with more than regal solemnity; and to leave a name behind him, not to be extinguished but with the whole world; which as it is now too little for his praises, so might have been too for his conquests, if the short line of his human life could have been stretched out to the extent of his immortal designs!'

Cromwell was a bad speaker and a worse writer. Milton wrote his despatches for him in elegant and erudite Latin; and the pen of the one, like the sword of the other, was 'sharp and sweet.' We have not that union in modern times of the heroic and literary character which was common among the ancients. Julius Caesar and Xenophon recorded their own acts with equal clearness of style and modesty of temper.

41

The Duke of Wellington (worse off than Cromwell) is obliged to get Mr. Mudford to write the History of his Life. Sophocles, AEschylus, and Socrates were distinguished for their military prowess among their contemporaries, though now only remembered for what they did in poetry and philosophy. Cicero and Demosthenes, the two greatest orators of antiquity, appear to have been cowards: nor does Horace seem to give a very favourable picture of his martial achievements. But in general there was not that division in the labours of the mind and body among the Greeks and Romans that has been introduced among us either by the progress of civilisation or by a greater slowness and inaptitude of parts. The French, for instance, appear to unite a number of accomplishments, the literary character and the man of the world, better than we do. Among us, a scholar is almost another name for a pedant or a clown: it is not so with them. Their philosophers and wits went into the world and mingled in the society of the fair. Of this there needs no other proof than the spirited print of most of the great names in French literature, to whom Moliere is reading a comedy in the presence of the celebrated Ninon de l'Enclos. D'Alembert, one of the first mathematicians of his age, was a wit, a man of gallantry and letters. With us a learned man is absorbed in himself and some particular study, and minds nothing else. There is something ascetic and impracticable in his very constitution, and he answers to the description of the Monk in Spenser—

From every work he challenged essoin

For contemplation's sake.

Perhaps the superior importance attached to the institutions of religion, as well as the more abstracted and visionary nature of its objects, has led (as a general result) to a wider separation between thought and action in modern times.

Ambition is of a higher and more heroic strain than avarice. Its objects are nobler, and the means by which it attains its ends less mechanical.

Better be lord of them that riches have,

Than riches have myself, and be their servile slave.

The incentive to ambition is the love of power; the spur to avarice is either the fear of poverty or a strong desire of self-indulgence. The amassers of fortunes seem divided into two opposite classes—lean, penurious-looking mortals, or jolly fellows who are determined to get possession of, because they want to enjoy, the good things of the wo others, in the fulness of their persons and the robustness of their constitutions, seem to bespeak the reversion of a landed estate, rich acres, fat beeves, a substantial mansion, costly clothing, a chine and curkey, choice wines, and all other good things consonant to the wants and full-fed desires of their bodies. Such men charm fortune by the sleekness of their aspects and the goodly rotundity of their honest faces, as the others scare away poverty by their wan, meagre looks. The last starve themselves into riches by care and carking; the first eat, drink, and sleep their way into the good things of this life. The greatest number of *warm* men in the city are good, jolly follows. Look at Sir William ——. Callipash and callipee are written in his face: he rolls about his unwieldy bulk in a sea of turtle-soup. How many haunches of venison does he carry on his back! He is larded with jobs and contracts: he is stuffed and swelled out with layers of bank-notes and invitations to dinner! His face hangs out a flag of defiance to mischance: the roguish twinkle in his eye with which he lures half the city and beats Alderman ——- hollow, is a smile reflected from heaps of unsunned gold! Nature and Fortune are not so much at variance as to differ about this fellow. To enjoy the good the Gods provide us is to deserve it. Nature meant him for a Knight, Alderman, and City Member; and Fortune laughed to see the goodly person and prospects of the man!(2) I am not, from certain early prejudices, much to admire the ostentatious marks of wealth (there are persons enough to admire them without me)—but I confess, there is something in the look of the old banking-houses in Lombard Street, the posterns covered with mud, the doors opening sullenly and silently, the absence of all pretence, the darkness and the gloom within, the gleaming of lamps in the day-time,

Like a faint shadow of uncertain light,

that almost realises the poetical conception of the cave of Mammon in Spenser, where dust and cobwebs concealed the roofs and pillars of solid gold, and lifts the mind quite off its ordinary hinges. The account of the manner in which the founder of Guy's Hospital accumulated his immense wealth has always to me something romantic in it, from the same force of contrast. He was a little shop-keeper, and out of his savings bought Bibles and purchased seamen's tickets in Queen Anne's wars, by which he left a fortune of two hundred thousand pounds. The story suggests the idea of a magician; nor is there anything in the *Arabian Nights* that looks more like a fiction.

FN to ESSAY XI

(1) When Buonaparte left the Chamber of Deputies to go and fight his last fatal battle, he advised them not to be debating the forms of Constitutions when the enemy was at their gates. Benjamin Constant thought otherwise. He wanted to play a game at *cat's-cradle* between the Republicans and Royalists, and lost his match. He did not care, so that he hampered a more efficient man than himself.

(2) A thorough fitness for any end implies the means. Where there is a will, there is a way. A real passion, an entire devotion to any object, always succeeds. The strong sympathy with what we wish and imagine realises it, dissipates all obstacles, and removes all scruples. The disappointed lover may complain as much as he pleases. He was himself to blame. He was a half-witted, *wishy-washy* fellow. His love might be as great as he makes it out; but it was not his ruling passion. His fear, his pride, his vanity was greater. Let any one's whole soul be steeped in this passion; let him think and care for nothing else; let nothing divert, cool, or intimidate him; let the *ideal* feeling become an actual one and take possession of his whole faculties, looks, and manner; let the same voluptuous hopes and wishes govern his actions in the presence of his mistress that haunt his fancy in her absence, and I will answer for his success. But I will not answer for the success of 'a dish of skimmed milk' in such a case.—I could always get to see a fine collection of pictures myself. The fact is, I was set upon it. Neither the surliness of porters nor the impertinence of footmen could keep me back. I had a portrait of Titian in my eye, and nothing could put me out in my determination. If that had not (as it were) been looking on me all the time I was battling my way, I should have been irritated or disconcerted, and gone away. But my liking to the end conquered my scruples or aversion to the means. I never understood the Scotch character but on these occasions. I would not take 'No' for an answer. If I had wanted a place under government or a writership to India, I could have got it from the same importunity, and on the same terms.

ESSAY XII. ON WILL-MAKING

Few things show the human character in a more ridiculous light than the circumstance of will-making. It is the latest opportunity we have of exercising the natural perversity of the disposition, and we take care to make a good use of it. We husband it with jealousy, put it off as long as we can, and then use every precaution that the world shall be no gainer by our deaths. This last act of our lives seldom belies the former tenor of them for stupidity, caprice, and unmeaning spite. All that we seem to think of is to manage matters so (in settling accounts with those who are so unmannerly as to survive us) as to do as little good, and to plague and disappoint as many people, as possible.

Many persons have a superstition on the subject of making their last will and testament, and think that when everything is ready signed and sealed, there is nothing further left to delay their departure. I have heard of an instance of one person who, having a feeling of this kind on his mind, and being teased into making his will by those about him, actually fell ill with pure apprehension, and thought he was going to die in good earnest, but having executed the deed over-night, awoke, to his great surprise, the next morning, and found himself as well as ever he was.(1)

An elderly gentleman possessed of a good estate and the same idle notion, and who found himself in a dangerous way, was anxious to do this piece of justice to those who remained behind him, but when it came to the point, his heart failed him, and his nervous fancies returned in full force. Even on his death-bed he still held back and was averse to sign what he looked upon as his own death-warrant, and just at the last gasp, amidst the anxious looks and silent upbraidings of friends and relatives that surrounded him, he summoned resolution to hold out his feeble hand, which was guided by others, to trace his name, and he fell back—a corpse! If there is any pressing reason for it, that is, if any particular person would be relieved from a state of harassing uncertainty or materially benefited by their making a will, the old and infirm (who do not like to be put out of their way) generally make this an excuse to themselves for putting it off to the very last moment, probably till it is too late; or where this is sure to make the greatest number of blank faces, contrive to give their friends the slip, without signifying their final determination in their favour. Where some unfortunate individual has been kept long in suspense, who has been perhaps sought out for that very purpose, and who may be in a great measure dependent on this as a last resource, it is nearly a certainty that there will be no will to be found; no trace, no sign to discover whether the person dying thus intestate ever had any intention of the sort, or why they relinquished it. This is to bespeak the thoughts and imaginations of others for victims after we are dead, as well as their persons and expectations for hangers-on while we are living. A celebrated beauty of the middle of the last century, towards its close, sought out a female relative, the friend and companion of her youth, who had lived during the forty years of their separation in rather straitened circumstances, and in a situation which admitted of some alleviations. Twice they met after that long lapse of time—once her relation visited her in the splendour of a rich old family mansion, and once she crossed the country to become an inmate of the humble dwelling of her early and only remaining friend. What was this for? Was it to revive the image of her youth in the pale and careworn face of her friend? Or was it to display the decay of her charms and recall her long-forgotten triumphs to the memory of the only person who could bear witness to them? Was it to show the proud remains of herself to those who remembered or had often heard what she was—her skin like shrivelled alabaster, her emaciated features chiselled by Nature's finest hand, her eyes that, when a smile lighted them up, still shone like diamonds, the vermilion hues that still bloomed among wrinkles? Was it to talk of bone-lace, of the flounces and brocades of the last century, of race-balls in the year '62, and of the scores of lovers that had died at her feet, and to set whole counties in a flame again, only with a dream of faded beauty? Whether it was for this, or whether she meant to leave her friend anything (as was indeed expected, all things considered, not without reason), nobody knows—for she never breathed a syllable on the subject herself, and died without a will. The accomplished coquette of twenty, who had pampered hopes only to kill them, who had kindled rapture with a look and extinguished it with a breath, could find no better employment at seventy than to revive the fond recollections and raise up the drooping hopes of her kinswoman only to let them fall—to rise no more. Such is the delight we have in trifling with and tantalising the feelings of others by the exquisite refinements, the studied sleights of love or friendship!

Where a property is actually bequeathed, supposing the circumstances of the case and the usages of society to leave a practical discretion to the testator, it is most frequently in such portions as can be of the least service. Where there is much already, much is given; where much is wanted, little or nothing. Poverty invites a sort of pity, a miserable dole of assistance; necessity, neglect and scorn; wealth attracts and allures to itself more wealth by natural association of ideas or by that innate love of inequality and injustice which is the favourite principle of the imagination. Men like to collect money into large heaps in their lifetime: they like to leave it in large heaps after they are dead. They grasp it into their own hands, not to use it for their own good, but to hoard, to lock it up, to make an object, an idol, and a wonder of it. Do you expect them to distribute it so as to do others good; that they will like those who come after them better than themselves; that if they were willing to pinch and starve themselves, they will not deliberately defraud their sworn friends and nearest kindred of what would be of the utmost use to them? No, they will thrust their heaps of gold and silver into the hands of others (as their proxies) to keep for them untouched, still increasing, still of no use to any one, but to pamper pride and avarice, to glitter in the huge, watchful, insatiable eye of fancy, to be deposited as a new offering at the shrine of Mammon, their God,—this is with them to put it to its intelligible and proper use; this is fulfilling a sacred, indispensable duty; this cheers them in the solitude of the grave, and throws a gleam of satisfaction across the stony eye of death. But to think of frittering it down, of sinking it in charity, of throwing it away on the idle claims of humanity, where it would no longer peer in monumental pomp over their heads,—and that, too, when on the point of death themselves, *in articulo mortis,* oh! it would be madness, waste, extravagance, impiety!—Thus worldlings feel and argue without knowing it; and while they fancy they are studying their own interest or that of some booby successor, their *alter idem,* are but the dupes and puppets of a favourite idea, a phantom, a prejudice, that must be kept up somewhere (no matter where), if it still plays before and haunts their imagination, while they have sense or understanding left to cling to their darling follies.

There was a remarkable instance of this tendency *to the heap,* this desire to cultivate an abstract passion for wealth, in a will of one of the Thelussons some time back. This will went to keep the greater part of a large property from the use of the natural heirs and next-of-kin for a length of time, and to let it accumulate at compound interest in such a way and so long, that it would at last mount up in value to the purchase-money of a whole county. The interest accruing from the funded property or the rent of the lands at certain periods was to be employed to purchase other estates, other parks and manors in the neighbourhood or farther off, so that the prospect of the future demesne that was to devolve at some distant time to the unborn lord of acres swelled and enlarged itself, like a sea, circle without circle, vista beyond vista, till the imagination was staggered and the mind exhausted. Now here was a scheme for the accumulation of wealth and for laying the foundation of family aggrandisement purely imaginary, romantic—one might almost say, disinterested. The vagueness, the magnitude, the remoteness of the object, the resolute sacrifice of all immediate and gross advantages, clothe it with the privileges of an abstract idea, so that the project has the air of a fiction or of a story in a novel. It was an instance of what might be called posthumous avarice, like the love of posthumous fame. It had little more to do with selfishness than if the testator had appropriated the same sums in the same way to build a pyramid, to construct an aqueduct, to endow a hospital, or effect any other patriotic or merely fantastic purpose. He wished to heap up a pile of wealth (millions of acres) in the dim horizon of future years, that could be of no use to him or to those with whom he was connected by positive and personal ties, but as a crotchet of the brain, a gewgaw of the fancy.(2) Yet to enable himself to put this scheme in execution, he had perhaps toiled and watched all his life, denied himself rest, food, pleasure, liberty, society, and persevered with the patience and self-denial of a martyr. I have insisted on this point the more, to show how much of the imaginary and speculative there is interfused even in those passions and purposes which have not the good of others for their object, and how little reason this honest citizen and builder of castles in the air would have had to treat those who devoted themselves to the pursuit of fame, to obloquy and persecution for the sake of truth and liberty, or who sacrificed their lives for their country in a just cause, as visionaries and enthusiasts, who did not understand what was properly due to their own interest and the securing of the main chance. Man is not the creature of sense and selfishness, even in those pursuits which grow out of that origin, so much as of imagination, custom, passion, whim, and humour.

I have heard of a singular instance of a will made by a person who was addicted to a habit of lying. He was so notorious for this propensity (not out of spite or cunning, but as a gratuitous exercise of invention) that from a child no one could ever believe a syllable he uttered. From the want of any dependence to be placed on him, he became the jest and by-word of the school where he was brought up. The last act of his life did not disgrace him; for, having gone abroad, and falling into a dangerous decline, he was advised to return home. He paid all that he was worth for his passage, went on ship-board, and employed a few remaining days he had to live in making and executing his will; in which he bequeathed large estates in different parts of England, money in the funds, rich jewels, rings, and all kinds of valuables to his old friends and acquaintance, who, not knowing how far the force of nature could go, were not for some time convinced that all this fairy wealth had never had an existence anywhere but in the idle coinage of his brain, whose whims and projects were no more!—The extreme keeping in this character is only to be accounted for by supposing such an original constitutional levity as made truth entirely indifferent to him, and the serious importance attached to it by others an object of perpetual sport and ridicule!

The art of will-making chiefly consists in baffling the importunity of expectation. I do not so much find fault with this when it is done as a punishment and oblique satire on servility and selfishness. It is in that case *Diamond cut Diamond*—a trial of skill between the legacy-hunter and the legacy-maker, which shall fool the other. The cringing toad-eater, the officious tale-bearer, is perhaps well paid for years of obsequious attendance with a bare mention and a mourning-ring; nor can I think that Gil Blas' library was not quite as much as the coxcombry of his pretensions deserved. There are some admirable scenes in Ben Jonson's *Volpone,* showing the humours of a legacy-hunter, and the different ways of fobbing him off with excuses and assurances of not being forgotten. Yet it is hardly right, after all, to encourage this kind of pitiful, barefaced intercourse without meaning to pay for it, as the coquette has no right to jilt the lovers she has trifled with. Flattery and submission are marketable commodities like any other, have their price, and ought scarcely to be obtained under false pretences. If we see through and despise the wretched creature that attempts to impose on our credulity, we can at any time dispense with his services: if we are soothed by this mockery of respect and friendship, why not pay him like any other drudge, or as we satisfy the actor who performs a part in a play by our particular desire? But often these premeditated disappointments are as unjust as they are cruel, and are marked with circumstances of indignity, in proportion to the worth of the object. The suspecting, the taking it for granted that your name is down in the will, is sufficient provocation to have it struck out: the hinting at an obligation, the consciousness of it on the part of the testator, will make him determined to avoid the formal acknowledgment of it at any expense. The disinheriting of relations is mostly for venial offences, not for base actions: we punish out of pique, to revenge some case in which we been disappointed of our wills, some act of disobedience to what had no reasonable ground to go upon; and we are obstinate in adhering to our resolution, as it was sudden and rash, and doubly bent on asserting our authority in what we have least right to interfere in. It is the wound inflicted upon our self-love, not the stain upon the character of the thoughtless offender, that calls for condign punishment. Crimes, vices may go unchecked or unnoticed; but it is the laughing at our weaknesses, or thwarting our humours, that is never to be forgotten. It is not the errors of others, but our own miscalculations, on which we wreak our lasting vengeance. It is ourselves that we cannot forgive. In the will of Nicholas Gimcrack the virtuoso, recorded in the *Tatler,* we learn, among other items, that his eldest son is cut off with a single cockleshell for his undutiful behaviour in laughing at his little sister whom his father kept preserved in spirits of wine. Another of his relations has a collection of grasshoppers bequeathed him, as in the testator's opinion an adequate reward and acknowledgment due to his merit. The whole will of the said Nicholas Gimcrack, Esq., is a curious document and exact picture of the mind of the worthy virtuoso defunct, where his various follies, littlenesses, and quaint humours are set forth as orderly and distinct as his butterflies' wings and cockle-shells and skeletons of fleas in glass cases.(3) We often successfully try, in this way, to give the finishing stroke to our pictures, hang up our weaknesses in perpetuity, and embalm our mistakes in the memories of others.

> Even from the tomb the voice of nature cries,
> Even in our ashes live their wonted fires.

I shall not speak here of unwarrantable commands imposed upon survivors, by which they were to carry into effect the sullen and revengeful purposes of unprincipled men, after they had breathed their last; but we meet with continual examples of the desire to keep up the farce (if not the tragedy) of life after we, the performers in it, have quitted the stage, and to have our parts rehearsed by proxy. We thus make a caprice immortal, a peculiarity proverbial. Hence we see the number of legacies and fortunes left on condition that the legatee shall take the name and style of the testator, by which device we provide for the continuance of the sounds that formed our names, and endow them with an estate, that they may be repeated with proper respect. In the *Memoirs of an Heiress* all the difficulties of the plot turn on the necessity imposed by a clause in her uncle's will that her future husband should take the family name of Beverley. Poor Cecilia! What delicate perplexities she was thrown into by this improvident provision; and with what minute, endless, intricate distresses has the fair authoress been enabled to harrow up the reader on this account! There was a Sir Thomas Dyot in the reign of Charles II. who left the whole range of property which forms Dyot Street, in St. Giles's, and the neighbourhood, on the sole and express condition that it should be appropriated entirely to that sort of buildings, and to the reception of that sort of population, which still keeps undisputed, undivided possession of it. The name was changed the other day to George Street as a more genteel appellation, which, I should think, is an indirect forfeiture of the estate. This Sir Thomas Dyot I should be disposed to put upon the list of old English worthies—as humane, liberal, and no flincher from what he took in his head. He was no common-place man in his line. He was the best commentator on that old-fashioned text—'The foxes have holes, and the birds of the air have nests, but the Son of man hath not where to lay his head.' We find some that are curious in the mode in which they shall be buried, and others in the place. Lord Camelford had his remains buried under an ash tree that grew on one of the mountains in Switzerland; and Sir Francis Bourgeois had a little mausoleum built for him in the college at Dulwich, where he once spent a pleasant, jovial day with the masters and wardens.(4) It is, no doubt, proper to attend, except for strong reasons to the contrary, to these sort of requests; for by breaking faith with the dead we loosen the confidence of the living. Besides, there is a stronger argument: we sympathise with the dead as well as with the living, and are bound to them by the most sacred of all ties, our own involuntary follow-feeling with others!

Thieves, as a last donation, leave advice to their friends, physicians a nostrum, authors a manuscript work, rakes a confession of their faith in the virtue of the sex—all, the last drivellings of their egotism and impertinence. One might suppose that if anything could, the approach and contemplation of death might bring men to a sense of reason and self-knowledge. On the contrary, it seems only to deprive them of the little wit they had, and to make them even more the sport of their wilfulness and shortsightedness. Some men think that because they are going to be hanged, they are fully authorised to declare a future state of rewards and punishments. All either indulge their caprices or cling to their prejudices. They make a desperate attempt to escape from reflection by taking hold of any whim or fancy that crosses their minds, or by throwing themselves implicitly on old habits and attachments.

An old man is twice a child: the dying man becomes the property of his family. He has no choice left, and his voluntary power is merged in old saws and prescriptive usages. The property we have derived from our kindred reverts tacitly to them; and not to let it take its course is a sort of violence done to nature as well as custom. The idea of property, of something in common, does not mix cordially with friendship, but is inseparable from near relationship. We owe a return in kind, where we feel no obligation for a favour; and consign our possessions to our next-of-kin as mechanically as we lean our heads on the pillow, and go out of the world in the same state of stupid amazement that we came into it!...*Caetera desunt.*

FN to ESSAY XII

(1) A poor woman at Plymouth who did not like the formality, or could not afford the expense of a will, thought to leave what little property she had in wearing apparel and household moveables to her friends and relations, *viva voce*, and before Death stopped her breath. She gave and willed away (of her proper authority) her chair and table to one, her bed to another, an old cloak to a third, a night-cap and petticoat to a fourth, and so on. The old crones sat weeping round, and soon after carried off all they could lay their hands upon, and left their benefactress to her fate. They were no sooner gone than she unexpectedly recovered, and sent to have her things back again; but not one of them could she get, and she was left without a rag to her back, or a friend to condole with her.

(2) The law of primogeniture has its origin in the principle here stated, the desire of perpetuating some one palpable and prominent proof of wealth and power.

(3) It is as follows:

'The Will of a Virtuoso.

I, Nicholas Gimcrack, being in sound Health of Mind, but in great Weakness of Body, do by this my Last Will and Testament bequeath my worldly Goods and Chattels in Manner following:—

Imprimis, To my dear Wife, One Box of Butterflies, One Drawer of Shells, A Female Skeleton, A Dried Cockatrice.

Item, To my Daughter Elizabeth, My Receipt for preserving dead Caterpillars, As also my Preparations of Winter May-Dew, and Embrio Pickle.

Item, to my little Daughter Fanny, Three Crocodiles' Eggs.

And upon the Birth of her first Child, if she marries with her Mother's Consent, The Nest of a Humming Bird.

Item, To my eldest Brother, as an acknowledgment for the Lands he has vested in my Son Charles, I bequeath My last Year's Collection of Grasshoppers.

Item, To his Daughter Susanna, being his only Child, I bequeath my English Weeds pasted on Royal Paper, With my large Folio of Indian Cabbage.

Having fully provided for my Nephew Isaac, by making over to him some years since A horned Searaboeus, The Skin of a Rattle-Snake, and The Mummy of an Egyptian King, I make no further Provision for him in this my Will.

I My eldest Son John having spoken disrespectfully of his little Sister, whom I keep by me in Spirits of Wine, and in many other Instances behaved himself undutifully towards me, I do disinherit, and wholly cut off from any Part of this my Personal Estate, by giving him a single Cockle-Shell.

To my Second Son Charles, I give and bequeath all my Flowers, Plants, Minerals, Mosses, Shells, Pebbles, Fossils, Beetles, Butterflies, Caterpillars, Grasshoppers, and Vermin, not above specified: As also my Monsters, both wet and dry, making the said Charles whole and

45

sole Executor of this my Last Will and Testament, he paying or causing to be paid the aforesaid Legacies within the Space of Six Months after my Decease. And I do hereby revoke all other Wills whatsoever by me formerly made.'—*Tatler,* vol. iv. No. 216.

(4) Kellerman lately left his heart to be buried in the field of Valmy, where the first great battle was fought in the year 1792, in which the Allies were repulsed. Oh! might that heart prove the root from which the tree of Liberty may spring up and flourish once more, as the basil tree grew and grew from the cherished head of Isabella's lover!

ESSAY XIII. ON CERTAIN INCONSISTENCIES IN SIR JOSHUA REYNOLDS'S DISCOURSES

The two chief points which Sir Joshua aims at in his *Discourses* are to show that excellence in the Fine Arts is the result of pains and study rather than of genius, and that all beauty, grace, and grandeur are to be found, not in actual nature, but in an idea existing in the mind. On both these points he appears to have fallen into considerable inconsistencies or very great latitude of expression, so as to make it difficult to know what conclusion to draw from his various reasonings. I shall attempt little more in this Essay than to bring together several passages that, from their contradictory import, seem to imply some radical defect in Sir Joshua's theory, and a doubt as to the possibility of placing an implicit reliance on his authority.

To begin with the first of these subjects, the question of original genius. In the Second Discourse, 'On the Method of Study,' Sir Joshua observes towards the end:

'There is one precept, however, in which I shall only be opposed by the vain, the ignorant, and the idle. I am not afraid that I shall repeat it too often. You must have no dependence on your own genius. If you have great talents, industry will improve them: if you have but moderate abilities, industry will supply their deficiency. Nothing is denied to well-directed labour; nothing is to be obtained without it. Not to enter into metaphysical discussions on the nature or essence of genius, I will venture to assert that assiduity unabated by difficulty, and a disposition eagerly directed to the object of its pursuit, will produce effects similar to those which some call the result of *natural powers.'*

The only tendency of the maxim here laid down seems to be to lure those students on with the hopes of excellence who have no chance of succeeding, and to deter those who have from relying on the only prop and source of real excellence—the strong bent and impulse of their natural powers. Industry alone can only produce mediocrity; but mediocrity in art is not worth the trouble of industry. Genius, great natural powers, will give industry and ardour in the pursuit of their proper object, but not if you divert them from that object into the trammels of common-place mechanical labour. By this method you neutralise all distinction of character—make a pedant of the blockhead and a drudge of the man of genius. What, for instance, would have been the effect of persuading Hogarth or Rembrandt to place no dependence on their own genius, and to apply themselves to the general study of the different branches of the art and of every sort of excellence, with a confidence of success proportioned to their misguided efforts, but to destroy both those great artists? 'You take my house when you do take the prop that doth sustain my house!' You undermine the superstructure of art when you strike at its main pillar and support, confidence and faith in nature. We might as well advise a person who had discovered a silver or a lead mine on his estate to close it up, or the common farmer to plough up every acre he rents in the hope of discovering hidden treasure, as advise the man of original genius to neglect his particular vein for the study of rules and the imitation of others, or try to persuade the man of no strong natural powers that he can supply their deficiency by laborious application. Sir Joshua soon after, in the Third Discourse, alluding to the terms, *inspiration, genius, gusto,* applied by critics and orators to painting, proceeds:

'Such is the warmth with which both the Ancients and Moderns speak of this divine principle of the art; but, as I have formerly observed, enthusiastic admiration seldom promotes knowledge. Though a student by such praise may have his attention roused and a desire excited of running in this great career, yet it is possible that what has been said to excite may only serve to deter him. He examines his own mind, and perceives there nothing of that divine inspiration with which, he is told, so many others have been favoured. He never travelled to heaven to gather new ideas; and he finds himself possessed of no other qualifications than what mere common observation and a plain understanding can confer. Thus he becomes gloomy amidst the splendour of figurative declamation, and thinks it hopeless to pursue an object which he supposes out of the reach of human industry.'

Yet presently after he adds:

'It is not easy to define in what this great style consists; nor to describe by words the proper means of acquiring it, *if the mind of the student should be at all capable of such an acquisition.* Could we teach taste or genius by rules, they would be no longer taste and genius.'

Here, then, Sir Joshua admits that it is a question whether the student is likely *to be at all capable of such an acquisition* as the higher excellencies of art, though he had said in the passage just quoted above that it is within the reach of constant assiduity and of a disposition eagerly directed to the object of its pursuit to effect all that is usually considered as the result of natural powers. Is the theory which our author means to inculcate a mere delusion, a mere arbitrary assumption? At one moment Sir Joshua attributes the hopelessness of the student to attain perfection to the discouraging influence of certain figurative and overstrained expressions, and in the next doubts his capacity for such an acquisition under any circumstances. Would he have him hope against hope, then? If he 'examines his own mind and finds nothing there of that divine inspiration with which he is told so many others have been favoured,' but which he has never felt himself; if 'he finds himself possessed of no other qualifications' for the highest efforts of genius and imagination 'than what mere common observation and a plain understanding can confer,' he may as well desist at once from 'ascending the brightest heaven of invention':—if the very idea of the divinity of art deters instead of animating him, if the enthusiasm with which others speak of it damps the flame in his own breast, he had better not enter into a competition where he wants the first principle of success, the daring to aspire and the hope to excel. He may be assured he is not the man. Sir Joshua himself was not struck at first by the sight of the masterpieces of the great style of art, and he seems unconsciously to have adopted this theory to show that he might still have succeeded in it but for want of due application. His hypothesis goes to this—to make the common run of his readers fancy they can do all that can be done by genius, and to make the mail of genius believe he can only do what is to be done by mechanical rules and systematic industry. This is not a very feasible scheme; nor is Sir Joshua sufficiently clear and explicit in his reasoning in support of it.

In speaking of Carlo Maratti, he confesses the inefficiency of this doctrine in a very remarkable manner:—

'Carlo Maratti succeeded better than those I have first named, and I think owes his superiority to the extension of his views: besides his master Andrea Sacchi, he imitated Raffaelle, Guido, and the Caraccis. It is true, there is nothing very captivating in Carlo Maratti; but this proceeded from a want which cannot be completely supplied; that is, want of strength of parts. *In this certainly men are not equal;* and a man can bring home wares only in proportion with the capital with which he goes to market. Carlo, by diligence, made the most of what he had; but there was undoubtedly a heaviness about him, which extended itself uniformly to his invention, expression, his drawing, colouring, and the general effect of his pictures. The truth is, he never equalled any of his patterns in any one thing, and he added little of his own.'

Here, then, Reynolds, we see, fairly gives up the argument. Carlo, after all, was a heavy hand; nor could all his diligence and his making the most of what he had make up for the want of 'natural powers.' Sir Joshua's good sense pointed out to him the truth in the individual instance, though he might be led astray by a vague general theory. Such, however, is the effect of a false principle that there is an evident bias in the artist's mind to make genius lean upon others for support, instead of trusting to itself and developing its own incommunicable resources. So in treating in the Twelfth Discourse of the way in which great artists are formed, Sir Joshua reverts very nearly to his first position:

'The daily food and nourishment of the mind of an Artist is found in the great works of his predecessors. There is no other way for him to become great himself. *Serpens, nigi serpentem comederit, non fit draco.* Raffaelle, as appears from what has been said, had carefully studied the works of Masaccio, and indeed there was no other, if we except Michael Angelo (whom he likewise imitated),(1) so worthy of his attention; and though his manner was dry and hard, his compositions formal, and not enough diversified, according to the custom of Painters in that early period, yet his works possess that grandeur and simplicity which accompany, and even sometimes proceed from, regularity and hardness of manner. We must consider the barbarous state of the arts before his time, when skill in drawing was so little understood, that the best of the painters could not even foreshorten the foot, but every figure appeared to stand upon his toes, and what served for drapery had, from the hardness and smallness of the folds, too much the appearance of cords clinging round the body. He first introduced large drapery, flowing in an easy and natural manner; indeed, he appears to be the first who discovered the path that leads to every excellence to which the art afterwards arrived, and may therefore be justly considered as one of the Great Fathers of Modern Art.

'Though I have been led on to a longer digression respecting this great painter than I intended, yet I cannot avoid mentioning another excellence which he possessed in a very eminent degree: he was as much distinguished among his contemporaries for his diligence and industry *as he was for the natural faculties of his mind.* We are told that his whole attention was absorbed in the pursuit of his art, and that he acquired the name of Masaccio from his total disregard to his dress, his person, and all the common concerns of life. He is indeed *a signal instance of what well-directed diligence* will do in a short time: he lived but twenty-seven years, yet in that short space carried the art so far beyond what it had before reached, that he appears to stand alone as a model for his successors. Vasari gives a long catalogue of painters and sculptors who formed their taste and learned their art by studying his works; among those, he names Michael Angelo, Leonardo da Vinci, Pietro Perugino, Raffaelle, Bartholomeo, Andrea del Sarto, Il Rosso, and Pierino del Vaga.'

Sir Joshua here again halts between two opinions. He tells us the names of the painters who formed themselves upon Masaccio's style: he does not tell us on whom he formed himself. At one time the natural faculties of his mind were as remarkable as his industry; at another he was only a signal instance of what well-directed diligence will do in a short t that leads to every excellence to which the Art afterwards arrived,' though he is introduced in an argument to show that 'the daily food and nourishment of the mind of the Artist must be found in the works of his predecessors.' There is something surely very wavering and unsatisfactory in all this.

Sir Joshua, in another part of his work, endeavours to reconcile and prop up these contradictions by a paradoxical sophism which I think turns upon himself. He says: 'I am on the contrary persuaded, that by imitation only' (by which he has just explained himself to mean the study of other masters), 'variety, and even originality of invention is produced. I will go further: even genius, at least, what is so called, is the child of imitation. But as this appears to be contrary to the general opinion, I must explain my position before I enforce it.

'Genius is supposed to be a power of producing excellencies which are out of the reach of the rules of art: a power which no precepts can teach, and which no industry can acquire.

'This opinion of the impossibility of acquiring those beauties which stamp the work with the character of genius, supposes that it is something more fixed than in reality it is, and that we always do and ever did agree in opinion with respect to what should be considered as the characteristic of genius. But the truth is, that the *degree* of excellence which proclaims *Genius* is different in different times and different places; and what shows it to be so is, that mankind have often changed their opinion upon this matter.

'When the Arts were in their infancy, the power of merely drawing the likeness of any object was considered as one of its greatest efforts. The common people, ignorant of the principles of art, talk the same language even to this day. But when it was found that every man could be taught to do this, and a great deal more, merely by the observance of certain precepts, the name of Genius then shifted its application, and was given only to him who added the peculiar character of the object he represented—to him who had invention, expression, grace, or dignity; in short, those qualities or excellencies, the power of producing which could not *then* be taught by any known and promulgated rules.

'We are very sure that the beauty of form, the expression of the passions, the art of composition, even the power of giving a general air of grandeur to a work, is at present very much under the dominion of rules. These excellencies were heretofore considered merely as the effects of genius; and justly, if genius is not taken for inspiration, but as the effect of close observation and experience.'

Sir Joshua began with undertaking to show that 'genius was the child of the imitation of others, and now it turns out not to be inspiration indeed, but the effect of close observation and experience.' The whole drift of this argument appears to be contrary to what the writer intended, for the obvious inference is that the essence of genius consists entirely, both in kind and degree, in the single circumstance of originality. The very same things are or are not genius, according as they proceed from invention or from mere imitation. In so far as a thing is original, as it has never been done before, it acquires and it deserves the appellation of genius: in so far as it is not original, and is borrowed from others or taught by rule, it is not, neither is it called, genius. This does not make much for the supposition that genius is a traditional and second-hand quality. Because, for example, a man without much genius can copy a picture of Michael Angelo's, does it follow that there was no genius in the original design, or that the inventor and copyist are equal? If indeed, as Sir Joshua labours to prove, mere imitation of existing models and attention to established rules could produce results exactly similar to those of natural powers, if the progress of art as a learned profession were a gradual but continual accumulation of individual excellence, instead of being a sudden and almost miraculous start to the highest beauty and grandeur nearly at first, and a regular declension to mediocrity ever after, then indeed the distinction between genius and imitation would be little worth contending for; the causes might be different, the effects would be the same, or rather skill to avail ourselves of external advantages would be of more importance and efficacy than the most powerful internal resources. But as the case stands, all the great works of art have been the offspring of individual genius, either projecting itself before the general advances of society or striking out a separate path for itself; all the rest is but labour in vain. For every purpose of emulation or instruction we go back to the original inventors, not to those who imitated, and, as it is falsely pretended, improved upon their models: or if those who followed have at any time attained as high a rank or surpassed their predecessors, it was not from borrowing their excellencies, but by unfolding new and exquisite powers of their own, of which the moving principle lay in the individual mind, and not in the stimulus afforded by previous example and general knowledge. Great faults, it is true, may be avoided, but great excellencies can never be attained in this way. If Sir Joshua's hypothesis of progressive refinement in art was anything more than a verbal fallacy, why does he go back to Michael Angelo as the God of his idolatry? Why does he find fault with Carlo Maratti for being heavy? Or why does he declare as explicitly as truly, that 'the judgment, after it has been long passive, by degrees loses its power of becoming active when exertion is necessary'?—Once more to point out the fluctuation in Sir Joshua's notions on this subject of the advantages of natural genius and artificial study, he says, when recommending the proper objects of ambition to the young artist:

'My advice in a word is this: keep your principal attention fixed upon the higher excellencies. If you compass them, and compass nothing more, you are still in the first class. We may regret the innumerable beauties which you may want; you may be very imperfect, but still you are an imperfect artist of the highest order.'

This is the Fifth Discourse. In the Seventh our artist seems to waver, and flings a doubt on his former decision, whereby 'it loses some colour.'

'Indeed perfection in an inferior style may be reasonably preferred to mediocrity in the highest walks of art. A landscape of Claude Lorraine *may*(2) be preferred to a history by Luca Giordano: but hence appears the necessity of the connoisseur's knowing in what consists the excellency of each class, in order to judge how near it approaches to perfection.'

As he advances, however, he grows bolder, and altogether discards his theory of judging of the artist by the class to which he belongs— 'But we have the sanction of all mankind,' he says, 'in preferring genius in a lower rank of art to feebleness and insipidity in the highest.' This is in speaking of Gainsborough. The whole passage is excellent, and, I should think, conclusive against the general and factitious style of art on which he insists so much at other times.

'On this ground, however unsafe, I will venture to prophesy, that two of the last distinguished painters of that country, I mean Pompeio Battoni and Rafaelle Mengs, however great their names may at present sound in our ears,(3) will very soon fall into the rank of Imperiale, Sebastian Concha, Placido Constanza, Musaccio, and the rest of their immediate predecessors; whose names, though equally renowned in their lifetime, are now fallen into what is little short of total oblivion. I do not say that those painters were not superior to the artist I allude to,(4) and whose loss we lament, in a certain routine of practice, which, to the eyes of common observers, has the air of a learned composition, and bears a sort of superficial resemblance to the manner of the great men who went before them. I know this perfectly well; but I know likewise, that a man looking for real and lasting reputation must unlearn much of the common-place method so observable in the works of the artists whom I have named. For my own part, I confess, I take more interest in and am more captivated with the powerful impression of nature, which Gainsborough exhibited in his portraits and in his landscapes, and the interesting simplicity and elegance of his little ordinary beggar-children, than with any of the works of that school, since the time of Andrea Sacchi, or perhaps we may say Carlo Maratti: two painters who may truly be said to be ULTIMI ROMANORUM.

'I am well aware how much I lay myself open to the censure and ridicule of the academical professors of other nations in preferring the humble attempts of Gainsborough to the works of those regular graduates in the great historical style. *But we have the sanction of all mankind in preferring genius in a lower rank of art to feebleness and insipidity in the highest.'*

Yet this excellent artist and critic had said but a few pages before when working upon his theory—'For this reason I shall beg leave to lay before you a few thoughts on the subject; to throw out some hints that may lead your minds to an opinion (which I take to be the true one) that Painting is not only not to be considered as an imitation operating by deception, but that it is, and ought to be, in many points of view and strictly speaking, no imitation at all of external nature. Perhaps it ought to be as far removed from the vulgar idea of imitation as the refined, civilised state in which we live is removed from a gross state of nature; and those who have not cultivated their imaginations, which the majority of mankind certainly have not, may be said, in regard to arts, to continue in this state of nature. Such men will always prefer imitation' (the imitation of nature) 'to that excellence which is addressed to another faculty that they do not possess; but these are not the persons to whom a painter is to look, any more than a judge of morals and manners ought to refer controverted points upon those subjects to the opinions of people taken from the banks of the Ohio or from New Holland.'

In opposition to the sentiment here expressed that 'Painting is and ought to be, in many points of view and strictly speaking, no imitation at all of external nature,' it is emphatically said in another place: 'Nature is and must be the fountain which alone is inexhaustible, and from which all excellences must originally flow.'

I cannot undertake to reconcile so many contradictions, nor do I think it an easy task for the student to derive any simple or intelligible clue from these conflicting authorities and broken hints in the prosecution of his art. Sir Joshua appears to have imbibed from others (Burke or Johnson) a spurious metaphysical notion that art was to be preferred to nature, and learning to genius, with which his own good sense and practical observation were continually at war, but from which he only emancipates himself for a moment to relapse into the same error again shortly after.(5) The conclusion of the Twelfth Discourse is, I think, however, a triumphant and unanswerable denunciation of his own favourite paradox on the objects and study of art.

'Those artists' (he says with a strain of eloquent truth) 'who have quitted the service of nature (whose service, when well understood, is perfect freedom) and have put themselves under the direction of I know not what capricious fantastical mistress, who fascinates and overpowers their whole mind, and from whose dominion there are no hopes of their being ever reclaimed (since they appear perfectly satisfied, and not at all conscious of their forlorn situation), like the transformed followers of Comus,

        Not once perceive their foul disfigurement;
        But boast themselves more comely than before.

'Methinks such men who have found out so short a path have no reason to complain of the shortness of life and the extent of art; since life is so much longer than is wanted for their improvement, or is indeed necessary for the accomplishment of their idea of perfection.(6) On the contrary, he who recurs to nature, at every recurrence renews his strength. The rules of art he is never likely to forget; they are few and simple: but Nature is refined, subtle, and infinitely various, beyond the power and retention of memory; it is necessary therefore to have continual recourse to her. In this intercourse there is no end of his improvement: the longer he lives, the nearer he approaches to the true and perfect idea of Art.'

FN to ESSAY XIII

(1) How careful is Sir Joshua, even in a parenthesis, to insinuate the obligations of this great genius to others, as if he would have been nothing without them.

(2) If Sir Joshua had an offer to exchange a Luca Giordano in his collection for a Claude Lorraine, he would not have hesitated long about the preference.

(3) Written in 1788.

(4) Gainsborough.

(5) Sir Joshua himself wanted academic skill and patience In the details of his profession. From these defects he seems to have been alternately repelled by each theory and style of art, the simply natural and elaborately scientific, as it came before him; and in his impatience of each, to have been betrayed into a tissue of inconsistencies somewhat difficult to unravel.

(6) He had been before speaking of Boucher, Director of the French Academy, who told him that 'when he was young, studying his art, he found it necessary to use models, but that he had left them off for many years.'

ESSAY XIV. THE SAME SUBJECT CONTINUED

The first inquiry which runs through Sir Joshua Reynolds's Discourses is whether the student ought to look at nature with his own eyes or with the eyes of others, and on the whole, he apparently inclines to the latter. The second question is what is to be understood by nature; whether it is a general and abstract idea, or an aggregate of particulars; and he strenuously maintains the former of these positions. Yet it is not easy always to determine how far or with what precise limitations he does so.

The first germ of his speculations on this subject is to be found in two papers in the *Idler*. In the last paragraph of the second of these, he says:

'If it has been proved that the painter, by attending to the invariable and general ideas of nature, produces beauty, he must, by regarding minute particularities and accidental discrimination, deviate from the universal rule, and pollute his canvas with deformity.'

In answer to this, I would say that deformity is not the being varied in the particulars, in which all things differ (for on this principle all nature, which is made up of individuals, would be a heap of deformity), but in violating general rules, in which they all or almost all agree. Thus there are no two noses in the world exactly alike, or without a great variety of subordinate parts, which may still be handsome, but a face without any nose at all, or a nose (like that of a mask) without any particularity in the details, would be a great deformity in art or nature. Sir Joshua seems to have been led into his notions on this subject either by an ambiguity of terms, or by taking only one view of nature. He supposes grandeur, or the general effect of the whole, to consist in leaving out the particular details, because these details are sometimes found without any grandeur of effect, and he therefore conceives the two things to be irreconcilable and the alternatives of each other. This is very imperfect reasoning. If the mere leaving out the detail constituted grandeur, any one could do this: the greatest dauber would at that rate be the greatest artist. A house or sign painter might instantly enter the lists with Michael Angelo, and might look down on the little, dry, hard manner of Raphael. But grandeur depends on a distinct principle of its own, not on a negation of the parts; and as it does not arise from their omission, so neither is it incompatible with their insertion or the highest finishing. In fact, an artist may give the minute particulars of any object one by one and with the utmost care, and totally neglect the proportions, arrangement, and general masses, on which the effect of the whole more immediately depends; or he may give the latter, viz. the proportions and arrangement of the larger parts and the general masses of light and shade, and leave all the minuter parts of which those parts are composed a mere blotch, one general smear, like the first crude and hasty getting in of the groundwork of a picture: he may do either of these, or he may combine both, that is, finish the parts, but put them in their right places, and keep them in due subordination to the general effect and massing of the whole. If the exclusion of the parts were necessary to the grandeur of the whole composition, if the more entire this exclusion, if the more like a *tabula rasa*, a vague, undefined, shadowy and abstracted representation the picture was, the greater the grandeur, there could be no danger of pushing this principle too far, and going the full length of Sir Joshua's theory without any restrictions or mental reservations. But neither of these suppositions is true. The greatest grandeur may coexist with the most perfect, nay with a microscopic accuracy of detail, as we see it does often in nature: the greatest looseness and slovenliness of execution may be displayed without any grandeur at all either in the outline or distribution of the masses of colour. To explain more particularly what I mean. I have seen and copied portraits by Titian, in which the eyebrows were marked with a number of small strokes, like hairlines (indeed, the hairs of which they were composed were in a great measure given)—but did this destroy the grandeur of expression, the truth of outline, arising from the arrangement of these hair-lines in a given form? The grandeur, the character, the expression remained, for the general form or arched and expanded outline remained, just as much as if it had been daubed in with a blacking-brush: the introduction of the internal parts and texture only added delicacy and truth to the general and striking effect of the whole. Surely a number of small dots or lines may be arranged into the form of a square or a circle indiscriminately; the square or circle, that is, the larger figure, remains the same, whether the line of which it consists is broken or continuous; as we may see in prints where the outlines, features, and masses remain the same in all the varieties of mezzotinto, dotted and lined engraving. If Titian in marking the appearance of the hairs had deranged the general shape and contour of the eyebrows, he would have destroyed the look of nature; but as he did not, but kept both in view, he proportionably improved his copy of it. So, in what regards the masses of light and shade, the variety, the delicate transparency and broken transitions of the tints is not inconsistent with the greatest breadth or boldest contrasts. If the light, for instance, is thrown strongly on one side of a face, and the other is cast into deep shade, let the individual and various parts of the surface be finished with the most scrupulous exactness both in the drawing and in the colours, provided nature is not exceeded, this will not nor cannot destroy the force and harmony of the composition. One side of the face will still have that great and leading distinction of being seen in shadow, and the other of being seen in the light, let the subordinate differences be as many and as precise as they will. Suppose a panther is painted in the sun: will it be necessary to leave out the spots to produce breadth and the great style, or will not this be done more effectually by painting the spots of one side of his shaggy coat as they are seen in the light, and those of the other as they really appear in natural shadow? The two masses are thus preserved completely, and no offence is done to truth and nature. Otherwise we resolve the distribution of light and shade into *local colouring*. The masses, the grandeur exist equally in external nature with the local differences of different colours. Yet Sir Joshua seems to argue that the grandeur, the effect of the whole object, is confined to the general idea in the mind, and that all the littleness and individuality is in nature. This is an essentially false view of the subject. This grandeur, this general effect, is indeed always combined with the details, or what our theoretical reasoner would designate as *littleness* in nature: and so it ought to be in art, as far as art can follow nature with prudence and profit. What is the fault of Denner's style?—It is, that he does *not* give this combination of properties: that he gives only one view of nature; that he abstracts the details, the finishing, the curiosities of natural appearances from the general result, truth, and character of the whole, and in finishing every part with elaborate care, totally loses sight of the more important and striking appearance of the object as it presents itself to us in nature. He gives every part of a face; but the shape, the expression, the light and shade of the whole is wrong, and as far as can be from what is natural. He gives an infinite variety of tints of the human face, nor are they subjected to any principle of light and shade. He is different from Rembrandt or Titian. The English schools, formed on Sir Joshua's theory, give neither the finishing of the parts nor the effect of the whole, but an inexplicable dumb mass without distinction or meaning. They do not do as Denner did, and think that not to do as he did is to do as Titian and Rembrandt did; I do not know whether they would take it as a compliment to be supposed to imitate nature. Some few artists, it must be said, have 'of late reformed this indifferently among us! Oh! let them reform it altogether!' I have no doubt they would if they could; but I have some doubts whether they can or not.—Before I proceed to consider the question of beauty and grandeur as it relates to the selection of form, I will quote a few passages from Sir Joshua with reference to what has been said on the imitation of particular objects. In the Third Discourse he observes: 'I will now add that nature herself is not to be too closely copied.... A mere copier of nature *can never produce anything great; can never raise and enlarge the conceptions, or warm the heart of the spectator.* The wish of the genuine painter must be more extensive: instead of endeavouring to amuse mankind with the minute neatness of his imitations, he must endeavour to improve them by the grandeur of his ideas; instead of seeking praise by deceiving the superficial sense of the spectator, he must strive for fame by captivating the imagination.'

From this passage it would surely seem that there was nothing in nature but minute neatness and superficial effect: nothing great in *her* style, for an imitator of it can produce nothing great; nothing 'to enlarge the conceptions or warm the heart of the spectator.'

What word hath passed thy lips, Adam severe!

All that is truly grand or excellent is a figment of the imagination, a vapid creation out of nothing, a pure effect of overlooking and scorning the minute neatness of natural objects. This will not do. Again, Sir Joshua lays it down without any qualification that—

'The whole beauty and grandeur of the art consists in being able to get above all singular forms, local customs, peculiarities, and *details* of every kind.'

Yet we find him acknowledging a different opinion.

'I am very ready to allow' (he says, in speaking of history-painting) 'that *some* circumstances of minuteness and particularity *frequently* tend to give an air of truth to a piece, and *to interest the spectator in an extraordinary manner.* Such circumstances therefore cannot wholly be rejected; but if there be anything in the Art which requires peculiar nicety of discernment, it is the disposition of these minute, circumstantial parts, which, according to the judgment employed in the choice, become so useful to truth or so injurious to grandeur.'

That's true; but the sweeping clause against 'all particularities and details of every kind' is clearly got rid of. The undecided state of Sir Joshua's feelings on this subject of the incompatibility between the whole and the details is strikingly manifested in two short passages which follow each other in the space of two pages. Speaking of some pictures of Paul Veronese and Rubens as distinguished by the dexterity and the unity of style displayed in them, he adds:

'It is by this, and this alone, that the mechanical power is ennobled, and raised much above its natural rank. And it appears to me that with propriety it acquires this character, as an instance of that superiority with which mind predominates over matter, by contracting into one whole what nature has made multifarious.'

This would imply that the principle of unity and integrity is only in the mind, and that nature is a heap of disjointed, disconnected particulars, a chaos of points and atoms. In the very next page the following sentence occurs:

'As painting is an art, they' (the ignorant) 'think they ought to be pleased in proportion as they see that art ostentatiously displayed; they will from this supposition prefer neatness, high finishing, and gaudy corlouring, to the truth, simplicity, and unity of nature.'

Before, neatness and high finishing were supposed to belong exclusively to the littleness of nature, but here truth, simplicity, and unity are her characteristics. Soon after, Sir Joshua says: 'I should be sorry if what has been said should be understood to have any tendency to encourage that carelessness which leaves work in an unfinished state. I commend nothing for the want of exactness; I mean to point out that kind of exactness which is the best, and which is alone truly to be so esteemed.' This Sir Joshua has already told us consists in getting above 'all particularities and details of every kind.' Once more we find it stated that—

'It is in vain to attend to the variation of tints, if in that attention the general hue of flesh is lost; or to finish ever so minutely the parts, if the masses are not observed, or the whole not well put together.'

Nothing can be truer; but why always suppose the two things at variance with each other?

'Titian's manner was then new to the world, but that unshaken truth on which it is founded has fixed it as a model to all succeeding painters; and those who will examine into the artifice will find it to consist in the power of generalising, and in the shortness and simplicity of the means employed.'

Titian's real excellence consisted in the power of generalising and of *individualising* at the same time: if it wore merely the former, it would be difficult to account for the error immediately after pointed out by Sir Joshua. He says in the very next paragraph:

'Many artists, as Vasari likewise observes, have ignorantly imagined they are imitating the manner of Titian when they leave their colours rough and neglect the detail; but not possessing the principles on which he wrought, they have produced what he calls *goffe pitture*— absurd, foolish pictures.'

Many artists have also imagined they were following the directions of Sir Joshua when they did the same thing, that is, neglected the detail, and produced the same results—vapid generalities, absurd, foolish pictures.

I will only give two short passages more, and have done with this part of the subject. I am anxious to confront Sir Joshua with his own authority:

'The advantage of this method of considering objects (as a whole) is what I wish now more particularly to enforce. At the same time I do not forget that a painter must have the power of contracting as well as dilating his sight; because he that does not at all express particulars expresses nothing; yet it is certain that a nice discrimination of minute circumstances and a punctilious delineation of them, whatever excellence it may have (and I do not mean to detract from it), never did confer on the artist the character of Genius.'

At page 53 we find the following words:

'Whether it is the human figure, an animal, or even inanimate objects, there is nothing, however unpromising in appearance, but may be raised into dignity, convey sentiment, and produce emotion, in the hands of a Painter of genius. What was said of Virgil, that he threw even the dung about the ground with an air of dignity, may be applied to Titian; whatever he touched, however naturally mean, and habitually familiar, by a kind of magic he invested with grandeur and importance.'—No, not by magic, but by seeking and finding in individual nature, and combined with details of every kind, that grace and grandeur and unity of effect which Sir Joshua supposes to be a mere creation of the artist's brain! Titian's practice was, I conceive, to give general appearances with individual forms and circumstances: Sir Joshua's theory goes too often, and in its prevailing bias, to separate the two things as inconsistent with each other, and thereby to destroy or bring into question that union of striking effect with accuracy of resemblance in which the essence of sound art (as far as relates to imitation) consists.

Farther, as Sir Joshua is inclined to merge the details of individual objects in general effect, so he is resolved to reduce all beauty or grandeur in natural objects to a central form or abstract idea of a certain class, so as to exclude all peculiarities or deviations from this ideal standard as unfit subjects for the artist's pencil, and as polluting his canvas with deformity. As the former principle went to destroy all exactness and solidity in particular things, this goes to confound all variety, distinctness, and characteristic force in the broader scale of nature. There is a principle of conformity in nature or of something in common between a number of individuals of the same class, but there is also a principle of contrast, of discrimination and identity, which is equally essential in the system of the universe and in the structure of our ideas both of art and nature. Sir Joshua would hardly neutralise the tints of the rainbow to produce a dingy grey, as a medium or central colour; why, then, should he neutralise all features, forms, etc., to produce an insipid monotony? He does not indeed consider his theory of beauty as applicable to colour, which he well understood, but insists upon and literally enforces it as to form and ideal conceptions, of which he knew comparatively little, and where his authority is more questionable. I will not in this place undertake to show that his theory of a middle form (as the standard of taste and beauty) is not true of the outline of the human face and figure or other organic bodies, though I think that even there it is only one principle or condition of beauty; but I do say that it has little or nothing to do with those other capital parts of painting, colour, character, expression, and grandeur of conception. Sir Joshua himself contends that 'beauty in creatures of the same species is the medium or centre of all its various forms'; and he maintains that grandeur is the same abstraction of the species in the individual. Therefore beauty and grandeur must be the same thing, which they are not; so that this definition must be faulty. Grandeur I should suppose to imply something that elevates and expands the mind, which is chiefly power or magnitude. Beauty is that which soothes and melts it; and its source, I apprehend, is a certain harmony, softness, and gradation of form, within the limits of our customary associations, no doubt, or of what we expect of certain species, but not independent of every other consideration. Our critic himself confesses of Michael Angelo, whom he regards as the pattern of the great or sublime style, that 'his people are a superior order of beings: there is nothing about them, nothing in the air of their actions or their attitudes, or the style or cast of their

51

limbs or features, that reminds us of their belonging to our own species. Raffaelle's imagination is not so elevated; his figures are not so much disjoined from our own diminutive race of beings, though his ideas are chaste, noble, and of great conformity to their subjects. Michael Angelo's works have a strong, peculiar, and marked character: they seem to proceed from his own mind entirely, and that mind so rich and abundant that he never needed, or seemed to disdain to look abroad for foreign help. Raffaelle's materials are generally borrowed, though the noble structure is his own.(1) How does all this accord with the same writer's favourite theory that all beauty, all grandeur, and all excellence consist in an approximation to that central form or habitual idea of mediocrity, from which every deviation is so much deformity and littleness? Michael Angelo's figures are raised above our diminutive race of beings, yet they are confessedly the standard of sublimity in what regards the human form. Grandeur, then, admits of an exaggeration of our habitual impressions; and 'the strong, marked, and peculiar character which Michael Angelo has at the same time given to his works' does not take away from it. This is fact against argument. I would take Sir Joshua's word for the goodness of a picture, and for its distinguishing properties, sooner than I would for an abstract metaphysical theory. Our artist also speaks continually of high and low subjects. There can be no distinction of this kind upon his principle, that the standard of taste is the adhering to the central form of each species, and that every species is in itself equally beautiful. The painter of flowers, of shells, or of anything else, is equally elevated with Raphael or Michael, if he adheres to the generic or established form of what he paints: the rest, according to this definition, is a matter of indifference. There must therefore be something besides the central or customary form to account for the difference of dignity, for the high and low style in nature or in art. Michael Angelo's figures, we are told, are more than ordinarily grand; why, by the same rule, may not Raphael's be more than ordinarily beautiful, have more than ordinary softness, symmetry, and grace?—Character and expression are still less included in the present theory. All character is a departure from the common-place form; and Sir Joshua makes no scruple to declare that expression destroys beauty. Thus he says:

'If you mean to preserve the most perfect beauty *in its most perfect state,* you cannot express the passions, all of which produce distortion and deformity, more or less, in the most beautiful faces.'

He goes on: 'Guido, from want of choice in adapting his subject to his ideas and his powers, or from attempting to preserve beauty where it could not be preserved, has in this respect succeeded very ill. His figures are often engaged in subjects that required great expression; yet his Judith and Holofernes, the daughter of Herodias with the Baptist's head, the Andromeda, and some even of the Mothers of the Innocents, have little more expression than his Venus attired by the Graces.'

What a censure is this passed upon Guido, and what a condemnation of his own theory, which would reduce and level all that is truly great and praiseworthy in art to this insipid, tasteless standard, by setting aside as illegitimate all that does riot come within the middle, central form! Yet Sir Joshua judges of Hogarth as he deviates from this standard, not as he excels in individual character, which he says is only good or tolerable as it partakes of general nature; and he might accuse Michael Angelo and Raphael, the one for his grandeur of style, the other for his expression; for neither are what he sets up as the goal of perfection—I will just stop to remark here that Sir Joshua has committed himself very strangely in speaking of the character and expression to be found in the Greek statues. He says in one place:

'I cannot quit the Apollo without making one observation on the character of this figure. He is supposed to have just discharged his arrow at the Python; and by the head retreating a little towards the right shoulder, he appears attentive to its effect. What I would remark is the difference of this attention from that of the Discobolus, who is engaged in the same purpose, watching the effect of his Discus. The graceful, negligent, though animated air of the one, and the vulgar eagerness of the other, furnish an instance of the judgment of the ancient Sculptors *in their nice discrimination of character.* They are both equally true to nature, and equally admirable.' After a few observations on the limited means of the art of sculpture, and the inattention of the ancients to almost everything but form, we meet with the following passage:—

'Those who think Sculpture can express more than we have allowed may ask, by what means we discover, at the first glance, the character that is represented in a Bust, a Cameo, or Intaglio? I suspect it will be found, on close examination, by him who is resolved not to see more than he really does see, that the figures are distinguished by their *insignia* more than by any variety of form or beauty. Take from Apollo his Lyre, from Bacchus his Thyrsus and Vine-leaves, and Meleager the Boar's Head, and there will remain little or no difference in their characters. In a Juno, Minerva, or Flora, the idea of the artist seems to have gone no further than representing perfect beauty, and afterwards adding the proper attributes, with a total indifference to which they gave them.'

(What, then, becomes of that 'nice discrimination of character' for which our author has just before celebrated them?)

'Thus John De Bologna, after he had finished a group of a young man holding up a young woman in his arms, with an old man at his feet, called his friends together, to tell him what name he should give it, and it was agreed to call it The Rape of the Sabines; and this is the celebrated group which now stands before the old Palace at Florence. The figures have the same general expression which is to be found in most of the antique Sculpture; and yet it would be no wonder if future critics should find out delicacy of expression which was never intended, and go so far as to see, in the old man's countenance, the exact relation which he bore to the woman who appears to be taken from him.'

So it is that Sir Joshua's theory seems to rest on an inclined plane, and is always glad of an excuse to slide, from the severity of truth and nature, into the milder and more equable regions of insipidity and inanity; I am sorry to say so, but so it appears to me.

I confess, it strikes me as a self-evident truth that variety or contrast is as essential a principle in art and nature as uniformity, and as necessary to make up the harmony of the universe and the contentment of the mind. Who would destroy the shifting effects of light and shade, the sharp, lively opposition of colours in the same or in different objects, the streaks in a flower, the stains in a piece of marble, to reduce all to the same neutral, dead colouring, the same middle tint? Yet it is on this principle that Sir Joshua would get rid of all variety, character, expression, and picturesque effect in forms, or at least measure the worth or the spuriousness of all these according to their reference to or departure from a given or average standard. Surely, nature is more liberal, art is wider than Sir Joshua's theory. Allow (for the sake of argument) that all forms are in themselves indifferent, and that beauty or the sense of pleasure in forms can therefore only arise from customary association, or from that middle impression to which they all tend: yet this cannot by the same rule apply to other things. Suppose there is no capacity in form to affect the mind except from its corresponding to previous expectation, the same thing cannot be said of the idea of power or grandeur. No one can say that the idea of power does not affect the mind with the sense of awe and sublimity.

That is, power and weakness, grandeur and littleness, are not indifferent things, the perfection of which consists in a medium between both. Again, expression is not a thing indifferent in itself, which derives its value or its interest solely from its conformity to a neutral standard. Who would neutralise the expression of pleasure and pain? or say that the passions of the human mind—pity, love, joy, sorrow, etc.—are only interesting to the imagination and worth the attention of the artist, as he can reduce them to an equivocal state which is neither pleasant nor painful, neither one thing nor the other? Or who would stop short of the utmost refinement, precision, and force in the delineation of each? Ideal expression is not neutral expression, but extreme expression. Again, character is a thing of peculiarity, of striking contrast, of distinction, and not of uniformity. It is necessarily opposed to Sir Joshua's exclusive theory, and yet it is surely a curious and interesting field of speculation for the human mind. Lively, spirited discrimination of character is one source of gratification to the lover of nature and art, which it could not be if all truth and excellence consisted in rejecting individual traits. Ideal character is not common-place, but consistent character marked throughout, which may take place in history or portrait. Historical truth in a picture is the putting the different features of the face or muscles of the body into consistent action. The picturesque altogether depends on particular points or qualities of an object, projecting as it were beyond the middle line of beauty, and catching the eye of the spectator. It was less, however, my intention to hazard any speculations of my own than to confirm the common-sense feelings on the subject by Sir Joshua's own admissions in different places. In the Tenth Discourse, speaking of some objections to the Apollo, he has these remarkable words:—

'In regard to the last objection (viz. that the lower half of the figure is longer than just proportion allows) it must be remembered that Apollo is here in the exertion of *one of his peculiar powers,* which is swiftness; he has therefore that proportion which is best adapted to that character. This is no more incorrectness than when there is given to a Hercules an extraordinary swelling and strength of muscles.'

Strength and activity then do not depend on the middle form; and the middle form is to be sacrificed to the representation of these positive qualities. Character is thus allowed not only to be an integrant part of the antique and classical style of art, but even to take precedence of and set aside the abstract idea of beauty. Little more would be required to justify Hogarth in his Gothic resolution, that if he were to make a figure of Charon, he would give him bandy legs, because watermen are generally bandy-legged. It is very well to talk of the abstract idea of a man or of a God, but if you come to anything like an intelligible proposition, you must either individualise and define, or destroy the very idea you contemplate. Sir Joshua goes into this question at considerable length in the Third Discourse:

'To the principle I have laid down, that the idea of beauty in each species of beings is an invariable one, it may be objected,' he says, 'that in every particular species there are various central forms, which are separate and distinct from each other, and yet are undeniably beautiful; that in the human figure, for instance the beauty of Hercules is one, of the Gladiator another, of the Apollo another, which makes so many different ideas of beauty. It is true, indeed, that these figures are each perfect in their kind, though of different characters and proportions; but still none of them is the representation of an individual, but of a class. And as there is one general form, which, as I have said, belongs to the human kind at large, so in each of these classes there is one common idea which is the abstract of the various individual forms belonging to that class. Thus, though the forms of childhood and age differ exceedingly, there is a common form in childhood, and a common form in age, which is the more perfect as it is remote from all peculiarities. But I must add further, that though the most perfect forms of each of the general divisions of the human figure are ideal, and superior to any individual form of that class, yet the highest perfection of the human figure is not to be found in any of them. It is not in the Hercules, nor in the Gladiator, nor in the Apollo; but in that form which is taken from all, and which partakes equally of the activity of the Gladiator, of the delicacy of the Apollo, and of the muscular strength of the Hercules. For perfect beauty in any species must combine all the characters which are beautiful in that species. It cannot consist in any one to the exclusion of the rest: no one, therefore, must be predominant, that no one may be deficient.'

Sir Joshua here supposes the distinctions of classes and character to be necessarily combined with the general leading idea of a middle form. This middle form is not to confound age, sex, circumstance, under one sweeping abstraction; but we must limit the general ideas by certain specific differences and characteristic marks, belonging to the several subordinate divisions and ramifications of each class. This is enough to show that there is a principle of individuality as well as of abstraction inseparable from works of art as well as nature. We are to keep the human form distinct from that of other living beings, that of men from that of women; we are to distinguish between age and infancy, between thoughtfulness and gaiety, between strength and softness. Where is this to stop? But Sir Joshua turns round upon himself in this very passage, and says: 'No: we are to unite the strength of the Hercules with the delicacy of the Apollo; for perfect beauty in any species must combine all the characters which are beautiful in that species.' Now if these different characters are beautiful in themselves, why not give them for their own sakes and in their most striking appearances, instead of qualifying and softening them down in a neutral form; which must produce a compromise, not a union of different excellences. If all excess of beauty, if all character is deformity, then we must try to lose it as fast as possible in other qualities. But if strength is an excellence, if activity is an excellence, if delicacy is an excellence, then the perfection, i.e. the highest degree of each of these qualities, cannot be attained but by remaining satisfied with a less degree of the rest. But let us hear what Sir Joshua himself advances on this subject in another part of the *Discourses:*

'Some excellences bear to be united, and are improved by union: others are of a discordant nature, and the attempt to unite them only produces a harsh jarring of incongruent principles. The attempt to unite contrary excellences (of form, for instance(2)) in a single figure can never escape degenerating into the monstrous but by sinking into the insipid; by taking away its marked character, and weakening its expression.

'Obvious as these remarks appear, there are many writers on our art who, not being of the profession and consequently not knowing what can or cannot be done, have been very liberal of absurd praises in their description of favourite works. They always find in them what they are resolved to find. They praise excellences that can hardly exist together; and, above all things, are fond of describing with great exactness the expression of a mixed passion, which more particularly appears to me out of the reach of our art.(3)

'Such are many disquisitions which I have read on some of the Cartoons and other pictures of Raffaelle, where the critics have described their own imaginations; or indeed where the excellent master himself may have attempted this expression of passions above the powers of the art, and has, therefore, by an indistinct and imperfect marking, left room for every imagination with equal probability to find a passion of his own. What has been, and what can be done in the art, is sufficiently difficult: we need not be mortified or discouraged at not being able to execute the conceptions of a romantic imagination. Art has its boundaries, though imagination has none. We can easily, like the ancients, suppose a Jupiter to be possessed of all those powers and perfections which the subordinate Deities were endowed with

53

separately. Yet when they employed their art to represent him, they confined his character to majesty alone. Pliny, therefore, though we are under great obligations to him for the information he has given us in relation to the works of the ancient artists, is very frequently wrong when he speaks of them, which he does very often, in the style of many of our modern connoisseurs. He observes that in a statue of Paris, by Euphranor, you might discover at the same time three different characters: the dignity of a Judge of the Goddesses, the Lover of Helen, and the Conqueror of Achilles. A statue in which you endeavour to unite stately dignity, youthful elegance, and stern valour, must surely possess none of these to any eminent degree.

'From hence it appears that there is much difficulty as well as danger in an endeavour to concentrate in a single subject those various powers which, rising from various points, naturally move in different directions.'

What real clue to the art or sound principles of judging the student can derive from these contradictory statements, or in what manner it is possible to reconcile them one to the other, I confess I am at a loss to discover. As it appears to me, all the varieties of nature in the infinite number of its qualities, combinations, characters, expressions, incidents, etc., rise from distinct points or centres and must move in distinct directions, as the forms of different species are to be referred to a separate standard. It is the object of art to bring them out in all their force, clearness, and precision, and not to blend them into a vague, vapid, nondescript *ideal* conception, which pretends to unite, but in reality destroys. Sir Joshua's theory limits nature and paralyses art. According to him, the middle form or the average of our various impressions is the source from which all beauty, pleasure, interest, imagination springs. I contend, on the contrary, that this very variety is good in itself, nor do I agree with him that the whole of nature as it exists in fact is stark naught, and that there is nothing worthy of the contemplation of a wise man but that *ideal perfection* which never existed in the world nor even on canvas. There is something fastidious and sickly in Sir Joshua's system. His code of taste consists too much of negations, and not enough of positive, prominent qualities. It accounts for nothing but the beauty of the common Antique, and hardly for that. The merit of Hogarth, I grant, is different from that of the Greek statues; but I deny that Hogarth is to be measured by this standard or by Sir Joshua's middle forms: he has powers of instruction and amusement that, 'rising from a different point, naturally move in a different direction,' and completely attain their end. It would be just as reasonable to condemn a comedy for not having the pathos of a tragedy or the stateliness of an epic poem. If Sir Joshua Reynolds's theory were true, Dr. Johnson's *Irene* would be a better tragedy than any of Shakespear's.

The reasoning of the *Discourses* is, I think, then, deficient in the following particulars:

1. It seems to imply that general effect in a picture is produced by leaving out the details, whereas the largest masses and the grandest outline are consistent with the utmost delicacy of finishing in the parts.

2. It makes no distinction between beauty and grandeur, but refers both to an *ideal* or middle form, as the centre of the various forms of the species, and yet inconsistently attributes the grandeur of Michael Angelo's style to the superhuman appearance of his prophets and apostles.

3. It does not at any time make mention of power or magnitude in an object as a distinct source of the sublime (though this is acknowledged unintentionally in the case of Michael Angelo, etc.), nor of softness or symmetry of form as a distinct source of beauty, independently of, though still in connection with another source arising from what we are accustomed to expect from each individual species.

4. Sir Joshua's theory does not leave room for character, but rejects it as an anomaly.

5. It does not point out the source of expression, but considers it as hostile to beauty; and yet, lastly, he allows that the middle form, carried to the utmost theoretical extent, neither defined by character, nor impregnated by passion, would produce nothing but vague, insipid, unmeaning generality.

In a word, I cannot think that the theory here laid down is clear and satisfactory, that it is consistent with itself, that it accounts for the various excellences of art from a few simple principles, or that the method which Sir Joshua has pursued in treating the subject is, as he himself expresses it, 'a plain and honest method.' It is, I fear, more calculated to baffle and perplex the student in his progress than to give him clear lights as to the object he should have in view, or to furnish him with strong motives of emulation to attain it.

FN to ESSAY XIV

(1) The Fifth Discourse.

(2) These are Sir Joshua's words.

(3) I do not know that; but I do not think the two passions could be expressed by expressing neither or something between both.

ESSAY XV. ON PARADOX AND COMMON-PLACE

I have been sometimes accused of a fondness for paradoxes, but I cannot in my own mind plead guilty to the charge. I do not indeed swear by an opinion because it is old; but neither do I fall in love with every extravagance at first sight because it is new. I conceive that a thing may have been repeated a thousand times without being a bit more reasonable than it was the first time: and I also conceive that an argument or an observation may be very just, though it may so happen that it was never stated before: but I do not take it for granted that every prejudice is ill-founded; nor that every paradox is self-evident, merely because it contradicts the vulgar opinion. Sheridan once said of some speech in his acute, sarcastic way, that 'it contained a great deal both of what was new and what was true: but that unfortunately what was new was not true, and what was true was not new.' This appears to me to express the whole sense of the question. I do not see much use in dwelling on a common-place, however fashionable or well established: nor am I very ambitious of starting the most specious novelty, unless I imagine I have reason on my side. Originality implies independence of opinion; but differs as widely from mere singularity as from the tritest truism. It consists in seeing and thinking for one's-self: whereas singularity is only the affectation of saying something to contradict other people, without having any real opinion of one's own upon the matter. Mr. Burke was an original, though an extravagant writer: Mr. Windham was a regular manufacturer of paradoxes.

The greatest number of minds seem utterly incapable of fixing on any conclusion, except from the pressure of custom and authority: opposed to these there is another class less numerous but pretty formidable, who in all their opinions are equally under the influence of novelty and restless vanity. The prejudices of the one are counterbalanced by the paradoxes of the other; and folly, 'putting in one scale a weight of ignorance, in that of pride,' might be said to 'smile delighted with the eternal poise.' A sincere and manly spirit of inquiry is neither blinded by example nor dazzled by sudden flashes of light. Nature is always the same, the storehouse of lasting truth, and teeming with inexhaustible variety; and he who looks at her with steady and well-practised eyes will find enough to employ all his sagacity, whether it has or has not been seen by others before him. Strange as it may seem, to learn what an object is, the true philosopher looks at the object itself, instead of turning to others to know what they think or say or have heard of it, or instead of consulting the dictates of his vanity, petulance, and ingenuity to see what can be said against their opinion, and to prove himself wiser than all the rest of the world. For want of this the real powers and resources of the mind are lost and dissipated in a conflict of opinions and passions, of obstinacy against levity, of bigotry against self-conceit, of notorious abuses against rash innovations, of dull, plodding, old-fashioned stupidity against new-fangled folly, of worldly interest against headstrong egotism, of the incorrigible prejudices of the old and the unmanageable humours of the young; while truth lies in the middle, and is overlooked by both parties. Or as Luther complained long ago, 'human reason is like a drunken man on horseback: set it up on one side, and it tumbles over on the other.'—With one sort, example, authority, fashion, ease, interest, rule all: with the other, singularity, the love of distinction, mere whim, the throwing off all restraint and showing an heroic disregard of consequences, an impatient and unsettled turn of mind, the want of sudden and strong excitement, of some new play-thing for the imagination, are equally 'lords of the ascendant,' and are at every step getting the start of reason, truth, nature, common sense, and feeling. With one party, whatever is, is right: with their antagonists, whatever is, is wrong. These swallow every antiquated absurdity: those catch at every new, unfledged project—and are alike enchanted with the velocipedes or the French Revolution. One set, wrapped up in impenetrable forms and technical traditions, are deaf to everything that has not been dinned in their ears, and in those of their forefathers, from time immemorial: their hearing is *thick* with the same old saws, the same unmeaning form of words, everlastingly repeated: the others pique themselves on a jargon of their own, a Babylonish dialect, crude, unconcocted, harsh, discordant, to which it is impossible for any one else to attach either meaning or respect. These last turn away at the mention of all usages, creeds, institutions of more than a day's standing as a mass of bigotry, superstition, and barbarous ignorance, whose leaden touch would petrify and benumb their quick, mercurial, 'apprehensive, forgetive' faculties. The opinion of to-day supersedes that of yesterday: that of to-morrow supersedes, by anticipation, that of to-day. The wisdom of the ancients, the doctrines of the learned, the laws of nations, the common sentiments of morality, are to them like a bundle of old almanacs. As the modern politician always asks for this day's paper, the modern sciolist always inquires after the latest paradox. With him instinct is a dotard, nature a changeling, and common sense a discarded by-word. As with the man of the world, what everybody says must be true, the citizen of the world has quite a different notion of the matter. With the one, the majority; 'the powers that be' have always been in the right in all ages and places, though they have been cutting one another's throats and turning the world upside down with their quarrels and disputes from the beginning of time: with the other, what any two people have ever agreed in is an error on the face of it. The credulous bigot shudders at the idea of altering anything in 'time-hallowed' institutions; and under this cant phrase can bring himself to tolerate any knavery or any folly, the Inquisition, Holy Oil, the Right Divine, etc.;—the more refined sceptic will laugh in your face at the idea of retaining anything which has the damning stamp of custom upon it, and is for abating all former precedents, 'all trivial, fond records,' the whole frame and fabric of society as a nuisance in the lump. Is not this a pair of wiseacres well matched? The one stickles through thick and thin for his own religion and government: the other scouts all religions and all governments with a smile of ineffable disdain. The one will not move for any consideration out of the broad and beaten path: the other is continually turning off at right angles, and losing himself in the labyrinths of his own ignorance and presumption. The one will not go along with any party: the other always joins the strongest side. The one will not conform to any common practice: the other will subscribe to any thriving system. The one is the slave of habit: the other is the sport of caprice. The first is like a man obstinately bed-rid: the last is troubled with St. Vitus's dance. He cannot stand still, he cannot rest upon any conclusion. 'He never is—but always to be *right.*'

The author of the Prometheus Unbound (to take an individual instance of the last character) has a fire in his eye, a fever in his blood, a maggot in his brain, a hectic flutter in his speech, which mark out the philosophic fanatic. He is sanguine-complexioned and shrill-voiced. As is often observable in the case of religious enthusiasts, there is a slenderness of constitutional stamina, which renders the flesh no match for the spirit. His bending, flexible form appears to take no strong hold of things, does not grapple with the world about him, but slides from it like a river—

    And in its liquid texture mortal wound
    Receives no more than can the fluid air.

The shock of accident, the weight of authority make no impression on his opinions, which retire like a feather, or rise from the encounter unhurt through their own buoyancy. He is clogged by no dull system of realities, no earth-bound feelings, no rooted prejudices, by nothing that belongs to the mighty trunk and hard husk of nature and habit, but is drawn up by irresistible levity to the regions of mere speculation and fancy, to the sphere of air and fire, where his delighted spirit floats in 'seas of pearl and clouds of amber.' There is no *caput mortuum* of worn-out, threadbare experience to serve as ballast to his mind; it is all volatile intellectual salt of tartar, that refuses to combine its evanescent, inflammable essence with anything solid or anything lasting. Bubbles are to him the only realities:—touch them, and they vanish. Curiosity is the only proper category of his mind, and though a man in knowledge, he is a child in feeling. Hence he puts everything into a metaphysical crucible to judge of it himself and exhibit it to others as a subject of interesting experiment, without first making it over to the ordeal of his common sense or trying it on his heart. This faculty of speculating at random on all questions may in its overgrown and uninformed state do much mischief without intending it, like an overgrown child with the power of a man. Mr. Shelley has been accused of vanity—I think he is chargeable with extreme levity; but this levity is so great that I do not believe he is sensible of its consequences. He strives to overturn all established creeds and systems; but this is in him an effect of constitution. He runs before the most extravagant opinions; but this is because he is held back by none of the merely mechanical checks of sympathy and habit. He tampers with all sorts of obnoxious subjects; but it is less because he is gratified with the rankness of the taint than captivated with the intellectual phosphoric light they emit. It would seem that he wished not so much to convince or inform as to shock the public by the tenor of his productions; but I suspect he is more intent upon startling himself with his electrical experiments in morals and philosophy; and though they may scorch other people, they are to him harmless amusements, the coruscations of an Aurora Borealis, that 'play round the head, but do not reach the heart.' Still I could wish that he would put a stop to the incessant, alarming whirl of his voltaic battery. With his zeal, his talent, and his fancy, he would do more good and less harm if he were to give, up his wilder theories, and if he took less pleasure in feeling his heart flutter in unison with the panic-struck apprehensions of his readers. Persons of this class, instead of consolidating useful and acknowledged truths, and thus advancing the cause of science and virtue, are never easy but in raising doubtful and disagreeable questions, which bring the former into disgrace and discredit. They are not contented to lead the minds of men to an eminence overlooking the prospect of social amelioration, unless, by forcing them up slippery paths and to the utmost verge of possibility, they can dash them down the precipice the instant they reach the promised Pisgah. They think it nothing to hang up a beacon to guide or warn, if they do not at the same time frighten the community like a comet. They do not mind making their principles odious, provided they can make themselves notorious. To win over the public opinion by fair means is to them an insipid, common-place mode of popularity: they would either force it by harsh methods, or seduce it by intoxicating potions. Egotism, petulance, licentiousness, levity of principle (whatever be the source) is a bad thing in any one, and most of all in a philosophical reformer. Their humanity, their wisdom, is always 'at the horizon.' Anything new, anything remote, anything questionable, comes to them in a shape that is sure of a cordial welcome—a welcome cordial in proportion as the object is new, as it is apparently impracticable, as it is a doubt whether it is at all desirable. Just after the final failure, the completion of the last act of the French Revolution, when the legitimate wits were crying out, 'The farce is over, now let us go to supper,' these provoking reasoners got up a lively hypothesis about introducing the domestic government of the Nayrs into this country as a feasible set-off against the success of the Borough-mongers. The practical is with them always the antipodes of the ideal; and like other visionaries of a different stamp, they date the Millennium or New Order of Things from the Restoration of the Bourbons. 'Fine words butter no parsnips,' says the proverb. 'While you are talking of marrying, I am thinking of hanging,' says Captain Macheath. Of all people the most tormenting are those who bid you hope in the midst of despair, who, by never caring about anything but their own sanguine, hair-brained Utopian schemes, have at no time any particular cause for embarrassment and despondency because they have never the least chance of success, and who by including whatever does not hit their idle fancy, kings, priests, religion, government, public abuses or private morals, in the same sweeping clause of ban and anathema, do all they can to combine all parties in a common cause against them, and to prevent every one else from advancing one step farther in the career of practical improvement than they do in that of imaginary and unattainable perfection.

Besides, all this untoward heat and precocity often argues rottenness and a falling-off. I myself remember several instances of this sort of unrestrained license of opinion and violent effervescence of sentiment in the first period of the French Revolution. Extremes meet: and the most furious anarchists have since become the most barefaced apostates. Among the foremost of these I might mention the present poet-laureate and some of his friends. The prose-writers on that side of the question—Mr. Godwin, Mr. Bentham, etc.—have not turned round in this extraordinary manner: they seem to have felt their ground (however mistaken in some points), and have in general adhered to their first principles. But 'poets (as it has been said) have *such seething brains,* that they are disposed to meddle with everything, and mar all. They make bad philosophers and worse politicians.(1) They live, for the most part, in an ideal world of their own; and it would perhaps be as well if they were confined to it. Their flights and fancies are delightful to themselves and to everybody else: but they make strange work with matter of fact; and if they were allowed to act in public affairs, would soon turn the world the wrong side out. They indulge only their own flattering dreams or superstitious prejudices, and make idols or bugbears of whatever they please, caring as little for history or particular facts as for general reasoning. They are dangerous leaders and treacherous followers. Their inordinate vanity runs them into all sorts of extravagances; and their habitual effeminacy gets them out of them at any price. Always pampering their own appetite for excitement, and wishing to astonish others, their whole aim is to produce a dramatic effect, one way or other—to shock or delight the observers; and they are apparently as indifferent to the consequences of what they write as if the world were merely a stage for them to play their fantastic tricks on, and to make their admirers weep. Not less romantic in their servility than their independence, and equally importunate candidates for fame or infamy, they require only to be distinguished, and are not scrupulous as to the means of distinction. Jacobins or Anti-Jacobins—outrageous advocates for anarchy and licentiousness, or flaming apostles of political persecution—always violent and vulgar in their opinions, they oscillate, with a giddy and sickening motion, from one absurdity to another, and expiate the follies of youth by the heartless vices of advancing age. None so ready as they to carry every paradox to its most revolting and ridiculous excess—none so sure to caricature, in their own persons, every feature of the prevailing philosophy! In their days of blissful innovation, indeed, the philosophers crept at their heels like hounds, while they darted on their distant quarry like hawks; stooping always to the lowest game; eagerly snuffing up the most tainted and rankest scents; feeding their vanity with a notion of the strength of their digestion of poisons, and most ostentatiously avowing whatever would most effectually startle the prejudices of others.(2) Preposterously seeking for the stimulus of novelty in abstract truth, and the eclat of theatrical exhibition in pure reason, it is no wonder that these persons at last became disgusted with their own pursuits, and that, in consequence of the violence of the change, the most inveterate prejudices and uncharitable sentiments have rushed in to fill up the void produced by the previous annihilation of common sense, wisdom, and humanity!'

I have so far been a little hard on poets and reformers. Lest I should be thought to have taken a particular spite to them, I will try to make them the *amende honorable* by turning to a passage in the writings of one who neither is nor ever pretended to be a poet or a reformer, but the antithesis of both, an accomplished man of the world, a courtier, and a wit, and who has endeavoured to move the previous question on all schemes of fanciful improvement, and all plans of practical reform, by the following declaration. It is in itself a finished *common-place;* and may serve as a test whether that sort of smooth, verbal reasoning which passes current because it excites no one idea in the mind, is much freer from inherent absurdity than the wildest paradox.

'My lot,' says Mr. Canning in the conclusion of his Liverpool speech, 'is cast under the British Monarchy. Under that I have lived; under that I have seen my country flourish;(3) under that I have seen it enjoy as great a share of prosperity, of happiness, and of glory as I believe any modification of human society to be capable of bestowing; and I am not prepared to sacrifice or to hazard the fruit of centuries of experience, of centuries of struggles, and of more than one century of liberty, as perfect as ever blessed any country upon the earth, for visionary schemes of ideal perfectibility, for doubtful experiments even of possible improvement.'(4)

Such is Mr. Canning's common-place; and in giving the following answer to it, I do not think I can be accused of falling into that extravagant and unmitigated strain of paradoxical reasoning with which I have already found so much fault.

The passage, then, which the gentleman here throws down as an effectual bar to all change, to all innovation, to all improvement, contains at every step a refutation of his favourite creed. He is not 'prepared to sacrifice or to hazard the fruit of centuries of experience, of centuries of struggles, and of one century of liberty, for visionary schemes of ideal perfectibility.' So here are centuries of experience and centuries of struggles to arrive at one century of liberty; and yet, according to Mr. Canning's general advice, we are never to make any experiments or to engage in any struggles either with a view to future improvement, or to recover benefits which we have lost. Man (they repeat in our ears, line upon line, precept upon precept) is always to turn his back upon the future, and his face to the past. He is to believe that nothing is possible or desirable but what he finds already established to his hands in time-worn institutions or inveterate abuses. His unde to be made into a political automaton, a go-cart of superstition and prejudice, never stirring hand or foot but as he is pulled by the wires and strings of the state-conjurers, the legitimate managers and proprietors of the show. His powers of will, of thought, and action are to be paralysed in him, and he is to be told and to believe that whatever is, must be. Perhaps Mr. Canning will say that men were to make experiments and to resolve upon struggles formerly, but that now they are to surrender their understandings and their rights into his keeping. But at what period of the world was the system of political wisdom *stereotyped,* like Mr. Cobbett's *Gold against Paper,* so as to admit of no farther alterations or improvements, or correction of errors of the press? When did the experience of mankind become stationary or retrograde, so that we must act from the obsolete inferences of past periods, not from the living impulse of existing circumstances, and the consolidated force of the knowledge and reflection of ages up to the present instant, naturally projecting us forward into the future, and not driving us back upon the past? Did Mr. Canning never hear, did he never think, of Lord Bacon's axiom, 'That those times are the ancient times in which we live, and not those which, counting backwards from ourselves, *ordine retrogrado,* we call ancient'? The latest periods must necessarily have the advantage of the sum-total of the experience that has gone before them, and of the sum-total of human reason exerted upon that experience, or upon the solid foundation of nature and history, moving on in its majestic course, not fluttering in the empty air of fanciful speculation, nor leaving a gap of centuries between us and the long-mouldered grounds on which we are to think and act. Mr. Canning cannot plead with Mr. Burke that no discoveries, no improvements have been made in political science and institutions; for he says we have arrived through centuries of experience and of struggles at one century of liberty. Is the world, then, at a stand? Mr. Canning knows well enough that it is in ceaseless progress and everlasting change, but he would have it to be the change from liberty to slavery, the progress of corruption, not of regeneration and reform. Why, no longer ago than the present year, the two epochs of November and January last presented (he tells us in this very speech) as great a contrast in the state of the country as any two periods of its history the most opposite or most remote. Well then, are our experience and our struggles at an end? No, he says, 'the crisis is at hand for every man to take part for or against the institutions of the British Monarchy.' His part is taken: 'but of this be sure, to do aught good will never be his task!' He will guard carefully against all possible improvements, and maintain all possible abuses sacred, impassive, immortal. He will not give up the fruit of centuries of experience, of struggles, and of one century at least of liberty, since the Revolution of 1688, for any doubtful experiments whatever. We are arrived at the end of our experience, our struggles, and our liberty—and are to anchor through time and eternity in the harbour of passive obedience and non-resistance. We (the people of England) will tell Mr. Canning frankly what we think of his magnanimous and ulterior resolution. It is our own; and it has been the resolution of mankind in all ages of the world. No people, no age, ever threw away the fruits of past wisdom, or the enjoyment of present blessings, for visionary schemes of ideal perfection. It is the knowledge of the past, the actual infliction of the present, that has produced all changes, all innovations, and all improvements—not (as is pretended) the chimerical anticipation of possible advantages, but the intolerable pressure of long-established, notorious, aggravated, and growing abuses. It was the experience of the enormous and disgusting abuses and corruptions of the Papal power that produced the Reformation. It was the experience of the vexations and oppressions of the feudal system that produced its abolition after centuries of sufferings and of struggles. It was the experience of the caprice and tyranny of the Monarch that extorted *Magna Charta* at Runnymede. It was the experience of the arbitrary and insolent abuse of the prerogative in the reigns of the Tudors and the first Stuarts that produced the resistance to it in the reign of Charles I. and the Grand Rebellion. It was the experience of the incorrigible attachment of the same Stuarts to Popery and Slavery, with their many acts of cruelty, treachery, and bigotry, that produced the Revolution, and set the House of Brunswick on the Throne. It was the conviction of the incurable nature of the abuse, increasing with time and patience, and overcoming the obstinate attachment to old habits and prejudices,—an attachment not to be rooted out by fancy or theory, but only by repeated, lasting, and incontrovertible proofs,—that has abated every nuisance that ever was abated, and introduced every innovation and every example of revolution and reform. It was the experience of the abuses, licentiousness, and innumerable oppressions of the old Government in France that produced the French Revolution. It was the experience of the determination of the British Ministry to harass, insult, and plunder them, that produced the Revolution of the United States. Away then with this miserable cant against fanciful theories, and appeal to acknowledged experience! Men never act against their prejudices but from the spur of their feelings, the necessity of their situations—their theories are adapted to their practical convictions and their varying circumstances. Nature has ordered it so, and Mr. Canning, by showing off his rhetorical paces, by his 'ambling and lisping and nicknaming God's creatures,' cannot invert that order, efface the history of the past, or arrest the progress of the future.—Public opinion is the result of public events and public feelings; and government must be moulded by that opinion, or maintain itself in opposition to it by the sword. Mr. Canning indeed will not consent that the social machine should in any case receive a different direction from what it has had, 'lest it should be hurried over the precipice and dashed to pieces.' These warnings of national ruin and terrific accounts of political precipices put one in mind of Edgar's exaggerations to Gloster; they make one's hair stand on end in the perusal but the poor old man, like poor old England, could fall no lower than he was. Mr. Montgomery, the ingenious and amiable poet, after he had been shut up in solitary confinement for a year and a half for printing the Duke of Richmond's Letter on Reform, when he first walked out into the narrow path of the adjoining field, was seized with an apprehension that he should fall over it, as if he had trod on the brink of an abrupt declivity. The author of the loyal Speech at the Liverpool Dinner has been so long kept in the solitary confinement of his prejudices, and the dark cells of his interest and vanity, that he is afraid of being dashed to pieces if he makes a single false step, to the right or the left, from his dangerous and crooked policy. As to himself, his ears are no doubt closed to any advice that might here be offered him; and as to his country, he seems bent on its destruction. If, however, an example of the futility of all his projects and all his reasonings on a broader scale, 'to warn and scare, be wanting,' let him look at Spain, and take leisure to recover from his incredulity and his surprise. Spain, as Ferdinand, as the Monarchy, has fallen from its pernicious height, never to rise again: Spain, as Spain, as the Spanish people, has risen from the tomb of liberty, never (it is to be hoped) to sink again under the yoke of the bigot and the oppressor!

FN to ESSAY XV

(1) As for politics, I think poets are *tories* by nature, supposing them to be by nature poets. The love of an individual person or family, that has worn a crown for many successions, is an inclination greatly adapted to the fanciful tribe. On the other hand, mathematicians, abstract reasoners of no manner of attachment to persons, at least to the visible part of them, but prodigiously devoted to the ideas of virtue, liberty, and so forth, are generally *whigs.* It happens agreeably enough to this maxim, that the whigs are friends to that wise, plodding, unpoetical people, the Dutch.'—*Shenstone's Letters,* p. 105.

(2) To give the modern reader *un petit apercu* of the tone of literary conversation about five or six and twenty years ago, I remember being present in a large party composed of men, women, and children, in which two persons of remarkable candour and ingenuity were labouring (as hard as if they had been paid for it) to prove that all prayer was a mode of dictating to the Almighty, and an arrogant assumption of superiority. A gentleman present said, with great simplicity and *naivete,* that there was one prayer which did not strike him as coming exactly under this description, and being asked what that was made answer, 'The Samaritan's—"Lord, be merciful to me, a sinner!"' This appeal by no means settled the sceptical dogmatism of the two disputants, and soon after the proposer of the objection went away; on which one of them observed with great marks of satisfaction and triumph—'I am afraid we have shocked that gentleman's prejudices.' This did not appear to me at that time quite the thing and this happened in the year 1794.—Twice has the iron entered my soul. Twice have the dastard, vaunting, venal Crew gone over it: once as they went forth, conquering and to conquer, with reason by their side, glittering like a falchion, trampling on prejudices and marching fearlessly on in the work of regeneration; once again when they returned with retrograde steps, like Cacus's oxen dragged backward by the heels, to the den of Legitimacy, 'rout on rout, confusion worse confounded,' with places and pensions and the *Quarterly Review* dangling from their pockets, and shouting, 'Deliverance for mankind,' for 'the worst, the second fall of man.' Yet I have endured all this marching and countermarching of poets, philosophers, and politicians over my head as well as I could, like 'the camomile that thrives, the more 'tis trod upon.' By Heavens, I think, I'll endure it no longer!

(3) *Troja fuit.*

(4) *Mr. Canning's Speech at the Liverpool Dinner, given in celebration of his Re-election,* March 18, 1820. Fourth edition, revised and corrected.

ESSAY XVI. ON VULGARITY AND AFFECTATION

Few subjects are more nearly allied than these two—vulgarity and affectation. It may be said of them truly that 'thin partitions do their bounds divide.' There cannot be a surer proof of a low origin or of an innate meanness of disposition than to be always talking and thinking of being genteel. One must feel a strong tendency to that which one is always trying to avoid: whenever we pretend, on all occasions, a mighty contempt for anything, it is a pretty clear sign that we feel ourselves very nearly on a level with it. Of the two classes of people, I hardly know which is to be regarded with most distaste, the vulgar aping the genteel, or the genteel constantly sneering at and endeavouring to distinguish themselves from the vulgar. These two sets of persons are always thinking of one another; the lower of the higher with envy, the more fortunate of their less happy neighbours with contempt. They are habitually placed in opposition to each other; jostle in their pretensions at every turn; and the same objects and train of thought (only reversed by the relative situation of either party) occupy their whole time and attention. The one are straining every nerve, and outraging common sense, to be thought genteel; the others have no other object or idea in their heads than not to be thought vulgar. This is but poor spite; a very pitiful style of ambition. To be merely not that which one heartily despises is a very humble claim to superiority: to despise what one really is, is still worse. Most of the characters in Miss Burney's novels—the Branghtons, the Smiths, the Dubsters, the Cecilias, the Delvilles, etc.—are well met in this respect, and much of a piece: the one half are trying not to be taken for themselves, and the other half not to be taken for the first. They neither of them have any pretensions of their own, or real standard of worth. 'A feather will turn the scale of their avoirdupois'; though the fair authoress was not aware of the metaphysical identity of her principal and subordinate characters. Affectation is the master-key to both.

Gentility is only a more select and artificial kind of vulgarity. It cannot exist but by a sort of borrowed distinction. It plumes itself up and revels in the homely pretensions of the mass of mankind. It judges of the worth of everything by name, fashion, and opinion; and hence, from the conscious absence of real qualities or sincere satisfaction in itself, it builds its supercilious and fantastic conceit on the wretchedness and wants of others. Violent antipathies are always suspicious, and betray a secret affinity. The difference between the 'Great Vulgar and the Small' is mostly in outward circumstances. The coxcomb criticises the dress of the clown, as the pedant cavils at the bad grammar of the illiterate, or the prude is shocked at the backslidings of her frail acquaintance. Those who have the fewest resources in themselves naturally seek the food of their self-love elsewhere. The most ignorant people find most to laugh at in strangers: scandal and satire prevail most in country-places; and a propensity to ridicule every the slightest or most palpable deviation from what we happen to approve, ceases with the progress of common sense and decency.(1) True worth does not exult in the faults and deficiencies of others; as true refinement turns away from grossness and deformity, instead of being tempted to indulge in an unmanly triumph over it. Raphael would not faint away at the daubing of a signpost, nor Homer hold his head the higher for being in the company of a Grub Street bard. Real power, real excellence, does not seek for a foil in inferiority; nor fear contamination from coming in contact with that which is coarse and homely. It reposes on itself, and is equally free from spleen and affectation. But the spirit of gentility is the mere essence of spleen and affectation; of affected delight in its own would-be qualifications, and of ineffable disdain poured out upon the involuntary blunders or accidental disadvantages of those whom it chooses to treat as its inferiors. Thus a fashionable Miss titters till she is ready to burst her sides at the uncouth shape of a bonnet or the abrupt drop of a curtsey (such as Jeanie Deans would make) in a country-girl who comes to be hired by her Mamma as a servant; yet to show how little foundation there is for this hysterical expression of her extreme good opinion of herself and contempt for the untutored rustic, she would herself the next day be delighted with the very same shaped bonnet if brought her by a French milliner and told it was all the fashion, and in a week's time will become quite familiar with the maid, and chatter with her (upon equal terms) about caps and ribbons and lace by the hour together. There is no difference between them but that of situation in the kitchen or in the parlour: let circumstances bring them together, and they fit like hand and glove. It is like mistress, like maid. Their talk, their thoughts, their dreams, their likings and dislikes are the same. The mistress's head runs continually on dress and finery, so does the maid's: the young lady longs to ride in a coach and six, so does the maid, if she could; Miss forms a *beau-ideal* of a lover with black eyes and rosy cheeks, which does not differ from that of her attendant; both like a smart man, the one the footman and the other his master, for the same reason; both like handsome furniture and fine houses; both apply the terms shocking and disagreeable to the same things and persons; both have a great notion of balls, plays, treats, song-books, and love-tales; both like a wedding or a christening, and both would give their little fingers to see a coronation—with this difference, that the one has a chance of getting a seat at it, and the other is dying with envy that she has not. Indeed, this last is a ceremony that delights equally the greatest monarch and the meanest of his subjects—the vilest of the rabble. Yet this which is the height of gentility and consummation of external distinction and splendour, is, I should say, a vulgar ceremony. For what degree of refinement, of capacity, of virtue is required in the individual who is so distinguished, or is necessary to his enjoying this idle and imposing parade of his person? Is he delighted with the stage-coach and gilded panels? So is the poorest wretch that gazes at it. Is he struck with the spirit, the beauty, and symmetry of the eight cream-coloured horses? There is not one of the immense multitude who flock to see the sight from town or country, St. Giles's or Whitechapel, young or old, rich or poor, gentle or simple, who does not agree to admire the same object. Is he delighted with the yeomen of the guard, the military escort, the groups of ladies, the badges of sovereign power, the kingly crown, the marshal's truncheon and the judge's robe, the array that precedes and follows him, the crowded streets, the windows hung with eager looks? So are the mob, for they 'have eyes and see them!' There is no one faculty of mind or body, natural or acquired, essential to the principal figure in this procession more than is common to the meanest and most despised attendant on it. A waxwork figure would answer the same purpose: a Lord Mayor of London has as much tinsel to be proud of. I would rather have a king do something that no one else has the power or magnanimity to do, or say something that no one else has the wisdom to say, or look more handsome, more thoughtful, or benign than any one else in his dominions. But I see nothing to raise one's idea of him in his being made a show of: if the pageant would do as well without the man, the man would do as well without the pageant! Kings have been declared to be 'lovers of low company'; and this maxim, besides the reason sometimes assigned for it, viz. that they meet with less opposition to their wills from such persons, will I suspect be found to turn at last on the consideration I am here stating, that they also meet with more sympathy in their tastes. The most ignorant and thoughtless have the greatest admiration of the baubles, the outward symbols of pomp and power, the sound and show, which are the habitual delight and mighty prerogative of kings. The stupidest slave worships the gaudiest tyrant. The same gross motives appeal to the same gross capacities, flatter the pride of the superior and excite the servility of the dependant; whereas a higher reach of moral and intellectual refinement might seek in vain for higher proofs of internal worth and inherent majesty in the object of its idolatry, and not finding the divinity lodged within, the unreasonable expectation raised would probably end in mortification on both sides!—There is little to distinguish a king from his subjects but the rabble's shout—if he loses that and is reduced to the forlorn hope of gaining the suffrages of the wise and good, he is of all men the most miserable.—But enough of this.

'I like it,' says Miss Branghton(2) in *Evelina* (meaning the opera), 'because it is not vulgar.' That is, she likes it, not because there is anything to like in it, but because other people are prevented from liking or knowing anything about it. Janus Weathercock, Esq., laugheth to scorn and spitefully entreateth and hugely condemneth my dramatic criticisms in the *London,* for a like exquisite reason. I must therefore make an example of him *in terrorem* to all such hypercritics. He finds fault with me and calls my taste vulgar, because I go to Sadler's Wells ('a place he has heard of'—O Lord, sir!)—because I notice the Miss Dennetts, 'great favourites with the Whitechapel orders'—praise Miss Valancy, 'a bouncing Columbine at Ashley's and them there places, as his barber informs him' (has he no way of establishing himself in his own good opinion but by triumphing over his barber's bad English?)—and finally, because I recognised the existence of the Coburg and the Surrey theatres, at the names of which he cries 'Faugh' with great significance, as if he had some personal disgust at them, and yet he would be supposed never to have entered them. It is not his cue as a well-bred critic. *C'est beau ca.* Now this appears to me a very crude, unmeaning, indiscriminate, wholesale, and vulgar way of thinking. It is prejudicing things in the lump, by names and places and classes, instead of judging of them by what they are in themselves, by their real qualities and shades of distinction. There is no selection, truth, or delicacy in such a mode of proceeding. It is affecting ignorance, and making it a title to wisdom. It is a vapid assumption of superiority. It is exceeding impertinence. It is rank coxcombry. It is nothing in the world else. To condemn because the multitude admire is as essentially vulgar as to admire because they admire. There is no exercise of taste or judgment in either case: both are equally repugnant to good sense, and of the two I should prefer the good-natured side. I would as soon agree with my barber as differ from him; and why should I make a point of reversing the sentence of the Whitechapel orders? Or how can it affect my opinion of the merits of an actor at the Coburg or the Surrey theatres, that these theatres are in or out of the Bills of Mortality? This is an easy, short-hand way of judging, as gross as it is mechanical. It is not a difficult matter to settle questions of taste by consulting the map of London, or to prove your liberality by geographical distinctions. Janus jumbles things together strangely. If he had seen Mr. Kean in a provincial theatre, at Exeter or Taunton, he would have thought it vulgar to admire him; but when he had been stamped in London, Janus would no doubt show his discernment and the subtlety of his tact for the display of character and passion by not being behind the fashion. The Miss Dennetts are 'little unformed girls,' for no other reason than because they danced at one of the minor theatres: let them but come out on the opera boards, and let the beauty and fashion of the season greet them with a fairy shower of delighted applause, and they would outshine Milanie 'with the foot of fire.' His gorge rises at the mention of a certain quarter of the town: whatever passes current in another, he 'swallows total grist unsifted, husks and all.' This is not taste, but folly. At this rate, the hackney-coachman who drives him, or his horse Contributor whom he has introduced as a select personage to the vulgar reader, knows as much of the matter as he does.—In a word, the answer to all this in the first instance is to say what vulgarity is. Now its essence, I imagine, consists in taking manners, actions, words, opinions on trust from others, without examining one's own feelings or weighing the merits of the case. It is coarseness or shallowness of taste arising from want of individual refinement, together with the confidence and presumption inspired by example and numbers. It may be defined to be a prostitution of the mind or body to ape the more or less obvious defects of others, because by so doing we shall secure the suffrages of those we associate with. To affect a gesture, an opinion, a phrase, because it is the rage with a large number of persons, or to hold it in abhorrence because another set of persons very little, if at all, better informed cry it down to distinguish themselves from the former, is in either case equal vulgarity and absurdity. A thing is not vulgar merely because it is common. 'Tis common to breathe, to see, to feel, to live. Nothing is vulgar that is natural, spontaneous, unavoidable. Grossness is not vulgarity, ignorance is not vulgarity, awkwardness is not vulgarity; but all these become vulgar when they are affected and shown off on the authority of others, or to fall in with *the fashion* or the company we keep. Caliban is coarse enough, but surely he is not vulgar. We might as well spurn the clod under our feet and call it vulgar. Cobbett is coarse enough, but he is not vulgar. He does not belong to the herd. Nothing real, nothing original, can be vulgar; but I should think an imitator of Cobbett a vulgar man. Emery's Yorkshireman is vulgar, because he is a Yorkshireman. It is the cant and gibberish, the cunning and low life of a particular district; it has 'a stamp exclusive and provincial.' He might 'gabble most brutishly' and yet not fall under the letter of the definition; but 'his speech bewrayeth him,' his dialect (like the jargon of a Bond Street lounger) is the damning circumstance. If he were a mere blockhead, it would not signify; but he thinks himself a *knowing hand,* according to the notions and practices of those with whom he was brought up, and which he thinks *the go* everywhere. In a word, this character is not the offspring of untutored nature but of bad habits; it is made up of ignorance and conceit. It has a mixture of *slang* in it. All slang phrases are for the same reason vulgar; but there is nothing vulgar in the common English idiom. Simplicity is not vulgarity; but the looking to affectation of any sort for distinction is. A cockney is a vulgar character, whose imagination cannot wander beyond the suburbs of the metropolis; so is a fellow who is always thinking of the High Street, Edinburgh. We want a name for this last character. An opinion is vulgar that is stewed in the rank breath of the rabble; nor is it a bit purer or more refined for having passed through the well-cleansed teeth of a whole court. The inherent vulgarity is in having no other feeling on any subject than the crude, blind, headling, gregarious notion acquired by sympathy with the mixed multitude or with a fastidious minority, who are just as insensible to the real truth, and as indifferent to everything but their own frivolous and vexatious pretensions. The upper are not wiser than the lower orders because they resolve to differ from them. The fashionable have the advantage of the unfashionable in nothing but the fashion. The true vulgar are the *servum pecus imitatorum*—the herd of pretenders to what they do not feel and to what is not natural to them, whether in high or low life. To belong to any class, to move in any rank or sphere of life, is not a very exclusive distinction or test of refinement. Refinement will in all classes be the exception, not the rule; and the exception may fall out in one class as well as another. A king is but an hereditary title. A nobleman is only one of the House of Peers. To be a knight or alderman is confessedly a vulgar thing. The king the other day made Sir Walter Scott a baronet, but not all the power of the Three Estates could make another Author of *Waverley*. Princes, heroes, are often commonplace people: Hamlet was not a vulgar character, neither was Don Quixote. To be an author, to be a painter, is nothing. It is a trick, it is a trade.

> An author! 'tis a venerable name:
> How few deserve it, yet what numbers claim!

Nay, to be a Member of the Royal Academy or a Fellow of the Royal Society is but a vulgar distinction; but to be a Virgil, a Milton, a Raphael, a Claude, is what fell to the lot of humanity but once! I do not think they were vulgar people; though, for anything I know to the contrary, the first Lord of the Bedchamber may be a very vulgar man; for anything I know to the contrary, he may not be so.—Such are pretty much my notions of gentility and vulgarity.

There is a well-dressed and an ill-dressed mob, both which I hate. *Odi profanum vulgus, et arceo.* The vapid affectation of the one to me is even more intolerable than the gross insolence and brutality of the other. If a set of low-lived fellows are noisy, rude, and boisterous to show their disregard of the company, a set of fashionable coxcombs are, to a nauseous degree, finical and effeminate to show their thorough breeding. The one are governed by their feelings, however coarse and misguided, which is something; the others consult only appearances, which are nothing, either as a test of happiness or virtue. Hogarth in his prints has trimmed the balance of pretension between the downright blackguard and the *soi-disant* fine gentleman unanswerably. It does not appear in his moral demonstrations (whatever it may do in the genteel letter-writing of Lord Chesterfield or the chivalrous rhapsodies of Burke) that vice by losing all its grossness loses half its evil. It becomes more contemptible, not less disgusting. What is there in common, for instance, between his beaux and belles, his rakes and his coquettes, and the men and women, the true heroic and ideal characters in Raphael? But his people of fashion and quality are just upon a par with the low, the selfish, the *unideal* characters in the contrasted view of human life, and are often the very same characters, only changing places. If the lower ranks are actuated by envy and uncharitableness towards the upper, the latter have scarcely any feelings but of pride, contempt, and aversion to the lower. If the poor would pull down the rich to get at their good things, the rich would tread down the poor as in a wine-press, and squeeze the last shilling out of their pockets and the last drop of blood out of their veins. If the headstrong self-will and unruly turbulence of a common alehouse are shocking, what shall we say to the studied insincerity, the insipid want of common sense, the callous insensibility of the drawing-room and boudoir? I would rather see the feelings of our common nature (for they are the same at bottom) expressed in the most naked and unqualified way, than see every feeling of our nature suppressed, stifled, hermetically sealed under the smooth, cold, glittering varnish of pretended refinement and conventional politeness. The one may be corrected by being better informed; the other is incorrigible, wilful, heartless depravity. I cannot describe the contempt and disgust I have felt at the tone of what would be thought good company, when I have witnessed the sleek, smiling, glossy, gratuitous assumption of superiority to every feeling of humanity, honesty, or principle, as a part of the etiquette, the mental and moral *costume* of the table, and every profession of toleration or favour for the lower orders, that is, for the great mass of our fellow-creatures, treated as an indecorum and breach of the harmony of well-regulated society. In short, I prefer a bear-garden to the adder's den; or, to put this case in its extremest point of view, I have more patience with men in a rude state of nature outraging the human form than I have with apes 'making mops and mows' at the extravagances they have first provoked. I can endure the brutality (as it is termed) of mobs better than the inhumanity of courts. The violence of the one rages like a fire; the insidious policy of the other strikes like a pestilence, and is more fatal and inevitable. The slow poison of despotism is worse than the convulsive struggles of anarchy. 'Of all evils,' says Hume, 'anarchy is the shortest lived.' The one may 'break out like a wild overthrow'; but the other from its secret, sacred stand, operates unseen, and undermines the happiness of kingdoms for ages, lurks in the hollow cheek, and stares you in the face in the ghastly eye of want and agony and woe. It is dreadful to hear the noise and uproar of an infuriated multitude stung by the sense of wrong and maddened by sympathy; it is more appalling to think of the smile answered by other gracious smiles, of the whisper echoed by other assenting whispers, which doom them first to despair and then to destruction. Popular fury finds its counterpart in courtly servility. If every outrage is to be apprehended from the one, every iniquity is deliberately sanctioned by the other, without regard to justice or decency. The word of a king, 'Go thou and do likewise,' makes the stoutest heart dumb: truth and honesty shrink before it.(3) If there are watchwords for the rabble, have not the polite and fashionable their hackneyed phrases, their fulsome, unmeaning jargon as well? Both are to me anathema!

To return to the first question, as it regards individual and private manners. There is a fine illustration of the effects of preposterous and affected gentility in the character of Gertrude, in the old comedy of *Eastward Hoe,* written by Ben Jonson, Marston, and Chapman in conjunction. This play is supposed to have given rise to Hogarth's series of prints of the Idle and Industrious Apprentice; and there is something exceedingly Hogarthian in the view both of vulgar and of genteel life here displayed. The character of Gertrude, in particular, the heroine of the piece, is inimitably drawn. The mixture of vanity and meanness, the internal worthlessness and external pretence, the rustic ignorance and fine lady-like airs, the intoxication of novelty and infatuation of pride, appear like a dream or romance, rather than anything in real life. Cinderella and her glass slipper are common-place to it. She is not, like Millamant (a century afterwards), the accomplished fine lady, but a pretender to all the foppery and finery of the character. It is the honeymoon with her ladyship, and her folly is at the full. To be a wife, and the wife of a knight, are to her pleasures 'worn in their newest gloss,' and nothing can exceed her raptures in the contemplation of both parts of the dilemma. It is not familiarity, but novelty, that weds her to the court. She rises into the air of gentility from the ground of a city life, and flutters about there with all the fantastic delight of a butterfly that has just changed its caterpillar state. The sound of My Lady intoxicates her with delight, makes her giddy, and almost turns her brain. On the bare strength of it she is ready to turn her father and mother out of doors, and treats her brother and sister with infinite disdain and judicial hardness of heart. With some speculators the modern philosophy has deadened and distorted all the natural affections; and before abstract ideas and the mischievous refinements of literature were introduced, nothing was to be met with in the primeval state of society but simplicity and pastoral innocence of manners—

        And all was conscience and tender heart

This historical play gives the lie to the above theory pretty broadly, yet delicately. Our heroine is as vain as she is ignorant, and as unprincipled as she is both, and without an idea or wish of any kind but that of adorning her person in the glass, and being called and thought a lady, something superior to a citizen's wife.(4) She is so bent on finery that she believes in miracles to obtain it, and expects the fairies to bring it her.(5) She is quite above thinking of a settlement, jointure, or pin-money. She takes the will for the deed all through the piece, and is so besotted with this ignorant, vulgar notion of rank and title as a real thing that cannot be counterfeited that she is the dupe of her own fine stratagems, and marries a gull, a dolt, a broken adventurer for an accomplished and brave gentleman. Her meanness is equal to her folly and her pride (and nothing can be greater), yet she holds out on the strength of her original pretensions for a long time, and plays the upstart with decency and imposing consistency. Indeed, her infatuation and caprices are akin to the flighty perversity of a disordered imagination; and another turn of the wheel of good or evil fortune would have sent her to keep company with Hogarth's *Merveilleuses* in Bedlam, or with Decker's group of coquettes in the same place.—The other parts of the play are a dreary lee-shore, like Cuckold's Point on the coast of Essex, where the preconcerted shipwreck takes place that winds up the catastrophe of the piece. But this is also characteristic of the age, and serves as a contrast to the airy and factitious character which is the principal figure in the plot. We had made but little progress from that point till Hogarth's time, if Hogarth is to be believed in his description of city manners. How wonderfully we have distanced it since!

Without going into this at length, there is one circumstance I would mention in which I think there has been a striking improvement in the family economy of modern times—and that is in the relation of mistresses and servants. After visits and finery, a married woman of the old school had nothing to do but to attend to her housewifery. She had no other resource, no other sense of power, but to harangue and lord it over her domestics. Modern book-education supplies the place of the old-fashioned system of kitchen persecution and eloquence. A well-bred woman now seldom goes into the kitchen to look after the servants:—formerly what was called a good manager, an exemplary mistress of a family, did nothing but hunt them from morning to night, from one year's end to another, without leaving them a moment's rest, peace, or comfort. Now a servant is left to do her work without this suspicious and tormenting interference and fault-finding at every step, and she does it all the better. The proverbs about the mistress's eye, etc., are no longer held for current. A woman from this habit, which at last became an uncontrollable passion, would scold her maids for fifty years together, and nothing could stop her: now the temptation to read the last new poem or novel, and the necessity of talking of it in the next company she goes into, prevent her—and the benefit to all parties is incalculable.

FN to ESSAY XVI

(1) If a European, when he has cut off his beard and put false hair on his head, or bound up his own natural hair in regular hard knots, as unlike nature as he could possibly make it; and after having rendered them immovable by the help of the fat of hogs, has covered the whole with flour, laid on by a machine with the utmost regularity; if when thus attired he issues forth, and meets with a Cherokee Indian, who has bestowed as much time at his toilet, and laid on with equal care and attention his yellow and red oker on particular parts of his forehead or cheeks, as he judges most becoming; whoever of these two despises the other for this attention to the fashion of his country, whichever first feels himself provoked to laugh, is the barbarian.'—Sir Joshua Reynolds's *Discourses,* vol. i. pp. 231, 232.

(2) This name was originally spelt Braughton in the manuscript, and was altered to Branghton by a mistake of the printer. Branghton, however, was thought a good name for the occasion and was suffered to stand. 'Dip it in the ocean,' as Sterne's barber says of the buckle, 'and it will stand!'

(3) A lady of quality, in allusion to the gallantries of a reigning prince, being told, 'I suppose it will be your turn next?' said, 'No, I hope not; for you know it is impossible to refuse!'

(4) '*Gertrude.* For the passion of patience, look if Sir Petronel approach. That sweet, that fine, that delicate, that—for love's sake, tell me if he come. Oh, sister Mill, though my father be a low-capt tradesman, yet I must be a lady, and I praise God my mother must call me madam. Does he come? Off with this gown for shame's sake, off with this gown! Let not my knight take me in the city cut, in any hand! Tear't! Pox on't (does he come?), tear't off! *Thus while she sleeps, I sorrow for her sake.* (Sings.)

Mildred. Lord, sister, with what an immodest impatiency and disgraceful scorn do you put off your city-tire! I am sorry to think you imagine to right yourself in wronging that which hath made both you and us.

Ger. I tell you, I cannot endure it: I must be a lady: do you wear your quoiff with a London licket! your stamel petticoat with two guards! the buffin gown with the tuftafitty cap and the velvet lace! I must be a lady, and I will be a lady. I like some humours of the city dames well; to eat cherries only at an angel a pound; good: to dye rich scarlet black; pretty: to line a grogram gown clean through with velvet; tolerable: their pure linen, their smocks of three pound a smock, are to be borne withal: but your mincing niceries, taffity pipkins, durance petticoats, and silver bodkins—God's my life! as I shall be a lady, I cannot endure it.

Mil. Well, sister, those that scorn their nest oft fly with a sick wing.

Ger. Bow-bell! Alas! poor Mill, when I am a lady, I'll pray for thee yet i'faith; nay, and I'll vouchsafe to call thee sister Mill still; for thou art not like to be a lady as I am, yet surely thou art a creature of God's making, and may'st peradventure be saved as soon as I (does he come?). *And ever and anon she doubled in her song.*

Mil. Now (lady's my comfort), what a profane ape's here!

Enter SIR PETRONEL FLASH, MR. TOUCHSTONE, and MRS. TOUCHSTONE.

Ger. Is my knight come? 0 the lord, my band! Sister, do my cheeks look well? Give me a little box o' the ear, that I may seem to blush. Now, now! so, there, there! here he is! 0 my dearest delight! Lord, lord! and how does my knight?

Touchstone. Fie, with more modesty.

Ger. Modesty! why, I am no citizen now. Modesty! am I not to be married? You're best to keep me modest, now I am to be a lady.

Sir Petronel. Boldness is a good fashion and court-like.

Ger. Aye, in, a country lady I hope it is, as I shall be. And how chance ye came no sooner, knight?

Sir Pet. Faith, I was so entertained in the progress with one Count Epernoun, a Welch knight: we had a match at baloon too with my Lord Whackum for four crowns.

Ger. And when shall's be married, my knight?

Sir Pet. I am come now to consummate: and your father may call a poor knight son-in-law.

Mrs. Touchstone. Yes, that he is a knight: I know where he had money to pay the gentlemen ushers and heralds their fees. Aye, that he is a knight: and so might you have been too, if you had been aught else but an ass, as well as some of your neighbours. An I thought you would not ha' been knighted, as I am an honest woman, I would ha' dubbed you myself. I praise God, I have wherewithal. But as for you, daughter—

Ger. Aye, mother, I must be a lady to-morrow; and by your leave, mother (I speak it not without my duty, but only in the right of my husband), I must take place of you, mother.

Mrs. Touch. That you shall, lady-daughter; and have a coach as well as I.

Ger. Yes, mother; but my coach-horses must take the wall of your coach-horses.

Touch. Come, come, the day grows low; 'tis supper time: and, sir, respect my daughter; she has refused for you wealthy and honest matches, known good men.

Ger. Body o' truth, citizen, citizens! Sweet knight, as soon as ever we are married, take me to thy mercy, out of this miserable city. Presently: carry me out of the scent of Newcastle coal and the hearing of Bow-bell, I beseech thee; down with me, for God's sake.'-Act I. Scene i.

This dotage on sound and show seemed characteristic of that age (see *New Way to Pay Old Debts,* etc.)—as if in the grossness of sense, and the absence of all intellectual and abstract topics of thought and discourse (the thin, circulating medium of the present day) the mind was attracted without the power of resistance to the tinkling sound of its own name with a title added to it, and the image of its own person tricked out in old-fashioned finery. The effect, no doubt, was also more marked and striking from the contrast between the ordinary penury and poverty of the age and the first and more extravagant demonstrations of luxury and artificial refinement.

(5) '*Gertrude.* Good lord, that there are no fairies nowadays, Syn.

Syndefy. Why, Madam?

Ger. To do miracles, and bring ladies money. Sure, if we lay in a cleanly house, they would haunt it, Synne? I'll sweep the chamber soon at night, and set a dish of water o' the hearth. A fairy may come and bring a pearl or a diamond. We do not know, Synne: or there may be a pot of gold hid in the yard, if we had tools to dig for't. Why may not we two rise early i' the morning, Synne, afore anybody is up, and find a jewel i' the streets worth a hundred pounds? May not some great court-lady, as she comes from revels at midnight, look out of her coach, as 'tis running, and lose such a jewel, and we find it? ha!

Syn. They are pretty waking dreams, these.

Ger. Or may not some old usurer be drunk overnight with a bag of money, and leave it behind him on a stall? For God's sake, Syn, let's rise to-morrow by break of day, and see. I protest, la, if I had as much money as an alderman, I would scatter some on't i' the streets for poor ladies to find when their knights were laid up. And now I remember my song of the Golden Shower, why may not I have such a fortune? I'll sing it, and try what luck I shall have after it.'—Act V. Scene i.'

VOLUME II

ESSAY I. ON A LANDSCAPE OF NICOLAS POUSSIN

`And blind Orion hungry for the morn.`

Orion, the subject of this landscape, was the classical Nimrod; and is called by Homer, 'a hunter of shadows, himself a shade.' He was the son of Neptune; and having lost an eye in some affray between the Gods and men, was told that if he would go to meet the rising sun he would recover his sight. He is represented setting out on his journey, with men on his shoulders to guide him, a bow in his hand, and Diana in the clouds greeting him. He stalks along, a giant upon earth, and reels and falters in his gait, as if just awakened out of sleep, or uncertain of his way;—you see his blindness, though his back is turned. Mists rise around him, and veil the sides of the green forests; earth is dank and fresh with dews, the 'gray dawn and the Pleiades before him dance,' and in the distance are seen the blue hills and sullen ocean. Nothing was ever more finely conceived or done. It breathes the spirit of the morning; its moisture, its repose, its obscurity, waiting the miracle of light to kindle it into smiles; the whole is, like the principal figure in it, 'a forerunner of the dawn.' The same atmosphere tinges and imbues every object, the same dull light 'shadowy sets off' the face of nature: one feeling of vastness, of strangeness, and of primeval forms pervades the painter's canvas, and we are thrown back upon the first integrity of things. This great and learned man might be said to see nature through the glass of time; he alone has a right to be considered as the painter of classical antiquity. Sir Joshua has done him justice in this respect. He could give to the scenery of his heroic fables that unimpaired look of original nature, full, solid, large, luxuriant, teeming with life and power; or deck it with all the pomp of art, with tempyles and towers, and mythologic groves. His pictures 'denote a foregone conclusion.' He applies Nature to his purposes, works out her images according to the standard of his thoughts, embodies high fictions; and the first conception being given, all the rest seems to grow out of and be assimilated to it, by the unfailing process of a studious imagination. Like his own Orion, he overlooks the surrounding scene, appears to 'take up the isles as a very little thing, and to lay the earth in a balance.' With a laborious and mighty grasp, he puts nature into the mould of the ideal and antique; and was among painters (more than any one else) what Milton was among poets. There is in both something of the same pedantry, the same stiffness, the same elevation, the same grandeur, the same mixture of art and nature, the same richness of borrowed materials, the same unity of character. Neither the poet nor the painter lowered the subjects they treated, but filled up the outline in the fancy, and added strength and reality to it; and thus not only satisfied, but surpassed the expectations of the spectator and the reader. This is held for the triumph and the perfection of works of art. To give us nature, such as we see it, is well and deserving of praise; to give us nature, such as we have never seen, but have often wished to see it, is better, and deserving of higher praise. He who can show the world in its first naked glory, with the hues of fancy spread over it, or in its high and palmy state, with the gravity of history stamped on the proud monuments of vanished empire,—who, by his 'so potent art,' can recall time past, transport us to distant places, and join the regions of imagination (a new conquest) to those of reality,—who shows us not only what Nature is, but what she has been, and is capable of,—he who does this, and does it with simplicity, with truth, and grandeur, is lord of Nature and her powers; and his mind is universal, and his art the master-art!

There is nothing in this 'more than natural,' if criticism could be persuaded to think so. The historic painter does not neglect or contravene Nature, but follows her more closely up into her fantastic heights or hidden recesses. He demonstrates what she would be in conceivable circumstances and under implied conditions. He 'gives to airy nothing a local habitation,' not 'a name.' At his touch, words start up into images, thoughts become things. He clothes a dream, a phantom, with form and colour, and the wholesome attributes of reality. *His* art is a second nature; not a different one. There are those, indeed, who think that not to copy nature is the rule for attaining perfection. Because they cannot paint the objects which they have they have, they fancy themselves qualified to paint the ideas which they have not seen. But it is possible to fail in this latter and more difficult style of imitation, as well as in the former humbler one. The detection, it is true, is not so easy, because the objects are not so nigh at hand to compare, and therefore there is more room both for false pretension and for self-deceit. They take an epic motto or subject, and conclude that the spirit is implied as a thing of course. They paint inferior portraits, maudlin lifeless faces, without ordinary expression, or one look, feature, or particle of nature in them, and think that this is to rise to the truth of history. They vulgarise and degrade whatever is interesting or sacred to the mind, and suppose that they thus add to the dignity of their profession. They represent a face that seems as if no thought or feeling of any kind had ever passed through it, and would have you believe that this is the very sublime of expression, such as it would appear in heroes, or demigods of old, when rapture or agony was raised to its height. They show you a landscape that looks as if the sun never shone upon it, and tell you that it is not modern—that so earth looked when Titan first kissed it with his rays. This is not the true ideal. It is not to fill the moulds of the imagination, but to deface and injure them; it is not to come up to, but to fall short of the poorest conception in the public mind. Such pictures should not be hung in the same room with that of Orion.(1)

Poussin was, of all painters, the most poetical. He was the painter of ideas. No one ever told a story half so well, nor so well knew what was capable of being told by the pencil. He seized on, and struck off with grace and precision, just that point of view which would be likely to catch the reader's fancy. There is a significance, a consciousness in whatever he does (sometimes a vice, but oftener a virtue) beyond any other painter. His Giants sitting on the tops of craggy mountains, as huge themselves, and playing idly on their Pan's-pipes, seem to have been seated there these three thousand years, and to know the beginning and the end of their own story. An infant Bacchus or Jupiter is big with his future destiny. Even inanimate and dumb things speak a language of their own. His snakes, the messengers of fate, are inspired with human intellect. His trees grow and expand their leaves in the air, glad of the rain, proud of the sun, awake to the winds of heaven. In his Plague of Athens, the very buildings seem stiff with horror. His picture of the Deluge is, perhaps, the finest historical landscape in the world. You see a waste of waters, wide, interminable the sun is labouring, wan and weary, up the sky the clouds, dull and leaden, lie like a load upon the eye, and heaven and earth seem commingling into one confused mass! His human figures are sometimes 'o'erinformed' with this kind of feeling. Their actions have too much gesticulation, and the set expression of the features borders too much on the mechanical and caricatured style. In this respect they form a contrast to Raphael's, whose figures never appear to be sitting for their pictures, or to be conscious of a spectator, or to have come from the painter's hand. In Nicolas Poussin, on the contrary, everything seems to have a distinct understanding with the artist; 'the very stones prate of their whereabout'; each object has its part and place assigned, and is in a sort of compact with the rest of the picture. It is this conscious keeping, and, as it were, *internal* design, that gives their peculiar character to the works of this artist. There was a picture of Aurora in the British Gallery a year or two ago. It was a suffusion of golden light. The Goddess wore her saffron-coloured robes, and appeared just risen from the gloomy bed of old Tithonus. Her very steeds, milk-white, were tinged with the yellow dawn. It was a personification of the morning. Poussin succeeded better in classic than in sacred subjects. The latter are comparatively heavy, forced, full of violent contrasts of colour, of red, blue, and black, and without the true prophetic inspiration of the characters. But in his pagan allegories and fables he was quite at home. The native gravity and native levity of the Frenchman were combined with Italian scenery and an antique gusto, and gave even to his colouring an air of learned indifference. He wants, in one respect, grace, form, expression; but he has everywhere sense and meaning, perfect costume and propriety. His personages always belong to the class and time represented, and are strictly versed in the business in hand. His grotesque compositions in particular, his Nymphs and Fauns, are superior (at least, as far as style is concerned) even to those of Rubens. They are taken more immediately out of fabulous history. Rubens' Satyrs and Bacchantes have a more jovial and voluptuous aspect, are more drunk with pleasure, more full of animal spirits and riotous impulses; they laugh and bound along—

Leaping like wanton kids in pleasant spring:

but those of Poussin have more of the intellectual part of the character, and seem vicious on reflection, and of set purpose. Rubens' are noble specimens of a class; Poussin's are allegorical abstractions of the same class, with bodies less pampered, but with minds more secretly depraved. The Bacchanalian groups of the Flemish painter were, however, his masterpieces in composition. Witness those prodigies of colour, character, and expression at Blenheim. In the more chaste and refined delineation of classic fable, Poussin was without a rival. Rubens, who was a match for him in the wild and picturesque, could not pretend to vie with the elegance and purity of thought in his picture of Apollo giving a poet a cup of water to drink, nor with the gracefulness of design in the figure of a nymph squeezing the juice of a bunch of grapes from her fingers (a rosy wine-press) which falls into the mouth of a chubby infant below. But, above all, who shall celebrate, in terms of fit praise, his picture of the shepherds in the Vale of Tempe going out in a fine morning of the spring, and coming to a tomb with this inscription: ET EGO IN ARCADIA VIXI! The eager curiosity of some, the expression of others who start back with fear and surprise, the clear breeze playing with the branches of the shadowing trees, 'the valleys low, where the mild zephyrs use,' the distant, uninterrupted, sunny prospect speak (and for ever will speak on) of ages past to ages yet to come!(2)

Pictures are a set of chosen images, a stream of pleasant thoughts passing through the mind. It is a luxury to have the walls of our rooms hung round with them, and no less so to have such a gallery in the mind, to con over the relies of ancient art bound up 'within the book and volume of the brain, unmixed (if it were possible) with baser matter!' A life passed among pictures, in the study and the love of art, is a happy noiseless dream: or rather, it is to dream and to be awake at the same time; for it has all 'the sober certainty of waking bliss,' with the romantic voluptuousness of a visionary and abstracted being. They are the bright consummate essences of things, and 'he who knows of these delights to taste and interpose them oft, is not unwise!'—The Orion, which I have here taken occasion to descant upon, is one of a collection of excellent pictures, as this collection is itself one of a series from the old masters, which have for some years back embrowned the walls of the British Gallery, and enriched the public eye. What hues (those of nature mellowed by time) breathe around as we enter! What forms are there, woven into the memory! What looks, which only the answering looks of the spectator can express! What intellectual stores have been yearly poured forth from the shrine of ancient art! The works are various, but the names the same—heaps of Rembrandts frowning from the darkened walls, Rubens' glad gorgeous groups, Titians more rich and rare, Claudes always exquisite, sometimes beyond compare, Guido's endless cloying sweetness, the learning of Poussin and the Caracci, and Raphael's princely magnificence crowning all. We read certain letters and syllables in the Catalogue, and at the well-known magic sound a miracle of skill and beauty starts to view. One might think that one year's prodigal display of such perfection would exhaust the labours of one man's life; but the next year, and the next to that, we find another harvest reaped and gathered in to the great garner of art, by the same immortal hands—

Old GENIUS the porter of them was;

He letteth in, he letteth out to wend.—

Their works seem endless as their reputation—to be many as they are complete—to multiply with the desire of the mind to see more and more of them; as if there were a living power in the breath of Fame, and in the very names of the great heirs of glory 'there were propagation to year; to have one last, lingering look yet to come. Pictures are scattered like stray gifts through the world; and while they remain, earth has yet a little gilding left, not quite rubbed off, dishonoured, and defaced. There are plenty of standard works still to be found in this country, in the collections at Blenheim, at Burleigh, and in those belonging to Mr. Angerstein, Lord Grosvenor, the Marquis of Stafford, and others, to keep up this treat to the lovers of art for many years; and it is the more desirable to reserve a privileged sanctuary of this sort, where the eye may dote, and the heart take its fill of such pictures as Poussin's Orion, since the Louvre is stripped of its triumphant spoils, and since he who collected it, and wore it as a rich jewel in his Iron Crown, the hunter of greatness and of glory, is himself a shade!

FN to ESSAY I

(1) Everything tends to show the manner in which a great artist is formed. If any person could claim an exemption from the careful imitation of individual objects, it was Nicolas Poussin. He studied the antique, but he also studied nature. 'I have often admired,' says Vignuel do Marville, who knew him at a late period of his life, 'the love he had for his art. Old as he was, I frequently saw him among the ruins of ancient Rome, out in the Campagna, or along the banks of the Tyber, sketching a scene that had pleased him; and I often met him with his handkerchief full of stones, moss, or flowers, which he carried home, that he might copy them exactly from nature. One day I asked him how he had attained to such a degree of perfection as to have gained so high a rank among the great painters of Italy? He answered, "I HAVE NEGLECTED NOTHING."'—*See his Life lately published.* It appears from this account that he had not fallen Into a recent error, that Nature puts the man of genius out. As a contrast to the foregoing description, I might mention, that I remember an old gentleman once asking Mr. West In the British Gallery if he had ever been at Athens? To which the President made answer, No; nor did he feel any great desire to go; for that he thought he had as good an idea of the place from the Catalogue as he could get by living there for any number of years. What would he have said, if any one had told him he could get as good an idea of the subject of one of his great works from reading the Catalogue of it, as from seeing the picture itself? Yet the answer was characteristic of the genius of the painter.

(2) Poussin has repeated this subject more than once, and appears to have revelled in its witcheries. I have before alluded to it, and may again. It is hard that we should not be allowed to dwell as often as we please on what delights us, when things that are disagreeable recur so often against our will.

ESSAY II. ON MILTON'S SONNETS

The great object of the Sonnet seems to be, to express in musical numbers, and as it were with undivided breath, some occasional thought or personal feeling, 'some fee-grief due to the poet's breast.' It is a sigh uttered from the fulness of the heart, an involuntary aspiration born and dying in the same moment. I have always been fond of Milton's Sonnets for this reason, that they have more of this personal and internal character than any others; and they acquire a double value when we consider that they come from the pen of the loftiest of our poets. Compared with *Paradise* Lost, they are like tender flowers that adorn the base of some proud column or stately temple. The author in the one could work himself up with unabated fortitude 'to the height of his great argument'; but in the other he has shown that he could condescend to men of low estate, and after the lightning and the thunderbolt of his pen, lets fall some drops of natural pity over hapless infirmity, mingling strains with the nightingale's, 'most musical, most melancholy.' The immortal poet pours his mortal sorrows into our breasts, and a tear falls from his sightless orbs on the friendly hand he presses. The Sonnets are a kind of pensive record of past achievements, loves, and friendships, and a noble exhortation to himself to bear up with cheerful hope and confidence to the last. Some of them are of a more quaint and humorous character; but I speak of those only which are intended to be serious and pathetical.—I do not know indeed but they may be said to be almost the first effusions of this sort of natural and personal sentiment in the language. Drummond's ought perhaps to be excepted, were they formed less closely on the model of Petrarch's, so as to be often little more than translations of the Italian poet. But Milton's Sonnets are truly his own in allusion, thought, and versification. Those of Sir Philip Sydney, who was a great transgressor in his way, turn sufficiently on himself and his own adventures; but they are elaborately quaint and intricate, and more like riddles than sonnets. They are 'very tolerable and not to be endured.' Shakespear's, which some persons better informed in such matters than I can pretend to be, profess to cry up as 'the divine, the matchless, what you will,'—to say nothing of the want of point or a leading, prominent idea in most of them, are I think overcharged and monotonous, and as to their ultimate drift, as for myself, I can make neither head nor tail of it. Yet some of them, I own, are sweet even to a sense of faintness, luscious as the woodbine, and graceful and luxuriant like it. Here is one:

```
From you have I been absent in the spring,
When proud-pied April, dress'd in all his trim,
Hath put a spirit of youth in every thing;
That heavy Saturn laugh'd and leap'd with him.
Yet nor the lays of birds, nor the sweet smell
Of different flowers in odour and in hue,
Could make me any summer's story tell,
Or from their proud lap pluck them where they grew:
Nor did I wonder at the lilies white,
Nor praise the deep vermilion in the rose;
They were but sweet, but figures of delight,
Drawn after you, you pattern of all those.
Yet seem'd it winter still, and you away,
As with your shadow, I with these did play.
```

65

I am not aware of any writer of Sonnets worth mentioning here till long after Milton, that is, till the time of Warton and the revival of a taste for Italian and for our own early literature. During the rage for French models the Sonnet had not been much studied. It is a mode of composition that depends entirely on *expression,* and this the French and artificial style gladly dispenses with, as it lays no particular stress on anything—except vague, general common-places. Warton's Sonnets are undoubtedly exquisite, both in style and matter; they are poetical and philosophical effusions of very delightful sentiment; but the thoughts, though fine and deeply felt, are not, like Milton's subjects, identified completely with the writer, and so far want a more individual interest. Mr. Wordsworth's are also finely conceived and high-sounding Sonnets. They mouth it well, and are said to be sacred to Liberty. Brutus's exclamation, 'Oh Virtue, I thought thee a substance, but I find thee a shadow,' was not considered as a compliment, but as a bitter sarcasm. The beauty of Milton's Sonnets is their sincerity, the spirit of poetical patriotism which they breathe. Either Milton's or the living bard's are defective in this respect. There is no Sonnet of Milton's on the Restoration of Charles II. There is no Sonnet of Mr. Wordsworth's corresponding to that of 'the poet blind and bold' 'On the late Massacre in Piedmont.' It would be no niggard praise to Mr. Wordsworth to grant that he was either half the man or half the poet that Milton was. He has not his high and various imagination, nor his deep and fixed principle. Milton did not worship the rising sun, nor turn his back on a losing and fallen cause.

Such recantation had no charms for him!

Mr. Southey has thought proper to put the author of *Paradise Lost* into his late Heaven, on the understood condition that he is 'no longer to kings and to hierarchs hostile.' In his lifetime he gave no sign of such an alteration; and it is rather presumptuous in the poet-laureate to pursue the deceased antagonist of Salmasius into the other world to compliment him with his own infirmity of purpose. It is a wonder he did not add in a note that Milton called him aside to whisper in his ear that he preferred the new English hexameters to his own blank verse!

Our first of poets was one of our first of men. He was an eminent instance to prove that a poet is not another name for the slave of power and fashion, as is the case with painters and musicians—things without an opinion—and who merely aspire to make up the pageant and show of the day. There are persons in common life who have that eager curiosity and restless admiration of bustle and splendour, that sooner than not be admitted on great occasions of feasting and luxurious display, they will go in the character of livery-servants to stand behind the chairs of the great. There are others who can so little bear to be left for any length of time out of the grand carnival and masquerade of pride and folly, that they will gain admittance to it at the expense of their characters as well as of a change of dress. Milton was not one of these. He had too much of the *ideal* faculty in his composition, a lofty contemplative principle, and consciousness of inward power and worth, to be tempted by such idle baits. We have plenty of chanting and chiming in among some modern writers with the triumphs over their own views and principles; but none of a patient resignation to defeat, sustaining and nourishing itself with the thought of the justice of their cause, and with firm-fixed rectitude. I do not pretend to defend the tone of Milton's political writings (which was borrowed from the style of controversial divinity), or to say that he was right in the part he took,—I say that he was consistent in it, and did not convict himself of error: he was consistent in it in spite of danger and obloquy, 'on evil days though fallen, and evil tongues,' and therefore his character has the salt of honesty about it. It does not offend in the nostrils of posterity. He had taken his part boldly and stood to it manfully, and submitted to the change of times with pious fortitude, building his consolations on the resources of his own mind and the recollection of the past, instead of endeavouring to make himself a retreat for the time to come. As an instance of this we may take one of the best and most admired of these Sonnets, that addressed to Cyriac Skinner, on his own blindness:—

Cyriac, this three years' day, these eyes, though clear,
To outward view, of blemish or of spot,
Bereft of light their seeing have forgot,
Nor to their idle orbs doth sight appear
Of sun or moon or stars throughout the year,
Or man or woman. Yet I argue not
Against Heav'n's hand or will, nor bate a jot
Of heart or hope; but still bear up and steer
Right onward. What supports me, dost thou ask?
The conscience, Friend, to have lost them overply'd
In liberty's defence, my noble task,
Of which all Europe talks from side to side.
This thought might lead me through the world's vain mask,
Content though blind, had I no better guide.

Nothing can exceed the mild, subdued tone of this Sonnet, nor the striking grandeur of the concluding thought. It is curious to remark what seems to be a trait of character in the two first lines. From Milton's care to inform the reader that 'his eyes wore still clear, to outward view, of spot or blemish,' it would be thought that he had not yet given up all regard to personal appearance; a feeling to which his singular beauty at an earlier age might be supposed naturally enough to lead. Of the political or (what may be called) his *State-Sonnets,* those to Cromwell, to Fairfax, and to the younger Vane are full of exalted praise and dignified advice. They are neither familiar nor servile. The writer knows what is due to power and to fame. He feels the true, unassumed equality of greatness. He pays the full tribute of admiration for great acts achieved, and suggests becoming occasion to deserve higher praise. That to Cromwell is a proof how completely our poet maintained the erectness of his understanding and spirit in his intercourse with men in power. It is such a compliment as a poet might pay to a conqueror and head of the state without the possibility of self-degradation:

Cromwell, our chief of men, who through a cloud,
Not of war only, but detractions rude,
Guided by faith and matchless fortitude,

To peace and truth thy glorious way hast plough'd,
And on the neck of crowned fortune proud
Hast rear'd God's trophies and his work pursued
While Darwen stream with blood of Scots imbrued,
And Dunbar field resounds thy praises loud,
And Worcester's laureat wreath. Yet much remains
To conquer still; peace hath her victories
No less renown'd than war: new foes arise
Threatening to bind our souls with secular chains;
Help us to save free conscience from the paw
Of hireling wolves, whose gospel is their maw.

The most spirited and impassioned of them all, and the most inspired with a sort of prophetic fury, is the one entitled, 'On the late Massacre in Piedmont.'

Avenge, O Lord, thy slaughter'd saints, whose bones
Lie scatter'd on the Alpine mountains cold;
Even them who kept thy truth so pure of old,
When all our fathers worshipp'd stocks and stones,
Forgot not: in thy book record their groans
Who were thy sheep, and in their ancient fold
Slain by the bloody Piedmontese that roll'd
Mother with infant down the rocks. Their moans
The vales redoubled to the hills, and they
To Heav'n. Their martyr'd blood and ashes sow
O'er all the Italian fields, where still doth sway
The triple Tyrant; that from these may grow
A hundred fold, who having learn'd thy way
Early may fly the Babylonian woe.

In the Nineteenth Sonnet, which is also 'On his blindness,' we see the jealous watchfulness of his mind over the use of his high gifts, and the beautiful manner in which he satisfies himself that virtuous thoughts and intentions are not the least acceptable offering to the Almighty:

When I consider how my light is spent
Ere half my days, in this dark world and wide,
And that one talent which is death to hide,
Lodged with me useless, though my soul more bent,
To serve therewith my Maker, and present
My true account, lest he returning chide;
Doth God exact day-labour, light denied,
I fondly ask: But patience to prevent
That murmur, soon replies, God doth not need
Either man's work or his own gifts; who best
Bear his mild yoke, they serve him best; his state
Is kingly; thousands at his bidding speed,
And post o'er land and ocean without rest;
They also serve who only stand and wait.

Those to Mr. Henry Lawes *on his Airs,* and to Mr. Lawrence, can never be enough admired. They breathe the very soul of music and friendship. Both have a tender, thoughtful grace; and for their lightness, with a certain melancholy complaining intermixed, might be stolen from the harp of Aeolus. The last is the picture of a day spent in social retirement and elegant relaxation from severer studies. We sit with the poet at table and hear his familiar sentiments from his own lips afterwards:—

Lawrence, of virtuous father virtuous son,
Now that the fields are dank and ways are mire,
Where shall we sometimes meet, and by the fire
Help waste a sullen day, what may be won
From the hard season gaining? Time will run
On smoother, till Favonius re-inspire
The frozen earth, and clothe in fresh attire

```
The lily and rose, that neither sow'd nor spun.
What neat repast shall feast us, light and choice,
Of Attic taste, with wine, whence we may rise
To hear the lute well-touched, or artful voice
Warble immortal notes and Tuscan air?
He who of these delights can judge, and spare
To interpose them oft, is not unwise.
```

In the last, 'On his deceased Wife,' the allusion to Alcestis is beautiful, and shows how the poet's mind raised and refined his thoughts by exquisite classical conceptions, and how these again were enriched by a passionate reference to actual feelings and images. It is this rare union that gives such voluptuous dignity and touching purity to Milton's delineation of the female character:—

```
Methought I saw my late espoused saint
Brought to me like Alcestis from the grave,
Whom Jove's great son to her glad husband gave,
Rescued from death by force, though pale and faint.
Mine, as whom wash'd from spot of child-bed taint
Purification in the old law did save,
And such, as yet once more I trust to have
Full sight of her in Heav'n without restraint,
Came vested all in white, pure as her mind:
Her face was veil'd, yet to my fancied sight
Love, sweetness, goodness in her person shined
So clear, as in no face with more delight:
But O as to embrace me she inclined,
I waked, she fled, and day brought back my night.
```

There could not have been a greater mistake or a more unjust piece of criticism than to suppose that Milton only shone on great subjects, and that on ordinary occasions and in familiar life his mind was unwieldy, averse to the cultivation of grace and elegance, and unsusceptible of harmless pleasures. The whole tenor of his smaller compositions contradicts this opinion, which, however, they have been cited to confirm. The notion first got abroad from the bitterness (or vehemence) of his controversial writings, and has been kept up since with little meaning and with less truth. His Letters to Donatus and others are not more remarkable for the display of a scholastic enthusiasm than for that of the most amiable dispositions. They are 'severe in youthful virtue unreproved.' There is a passage in his prose-works (the Treatise on Education) which shows, I think, his extreme openness and proneness to pleasing outward impressions in a striking point of view. 'But to return to our own institute,' he says, 'besides these constant exercises at home, there is another opportunity of gaining experience to be won from pleasure itself abroad. *In those vernal seasons of the year, when the air is calm and pleasant, it were an injury and sullenness against Nature not to go out and see her riches, and partake in her rejoicing with Heaven and earth.* I should not therefore be a persuader to them of studying much then, but to ride out in companies with prudent and well-staid guides, to all quarters of the land,' etc. Many other passages might be quoted, in which the poet breaks through the groundwork of prose, as it were, by natural fecundity and a genial, unrestrained sense of delight. To suppose that a poet is not easily accessible to pleasure, or that he does not take an interest in individual objects and feelings, is to suppose that he is no poet; and proceeds on the false theory, which has been so often applied to poetry and the Fine Arts, that the whole is not made up of the particulars. If our author, according to Dr. Johnson s account of him, could only have treated epic, high-sounding subjects, he would not have been what he was, but another Sir Richard Blackmore.—I may conclude with observing, that I have often wished that Milton had lived to see the Revolution of 1688. This would have been a triumph worthy of him, and which he would have earned by faith and hope. He would then have been old, but would not have lived in vain to see it, and might have celebrated the event in one more undying strain!

FN to ESSAY II

No notes for this essay

ESSAY III. ON GOING A JOURNEY

One of the pleasantest things in the world is going a journey; but I like to go by myself. I can enjoy society in a room; but out of doors, nature is company enough for me. I am then never less alone than when alone.

```
The fields his study, nature was his book.
```

I cannot see the wit of walking and talking at the same time. When I am in the country I wish to vegetate like the country. I am not for criticising hedge-rows and black cattle. I go out of town in order to forget the town and all that is in it. There are those who for this purpose go to watering-places, and carry the metropolis with them. I like more elbow-room and fewer encumbrances. I like solitude, when I give myself up to it, for the sake of solitude; nor do I ask for

A friend in my retreat,
Whom I may whisper solitude is sweet.

The soul of a journey is liberty, perfect liberty, to think, feel, do, just as one pleases. We go a journey chiefly to be free of all impediments and of all inconveniences; to leave ourselves behind much more to get rid of others. It is because I want a little breathing-space to muse on indifferent matters, where Contemplation

May plume her feathers and let grow her wings,
That in the various bustle of resort
Were all too ruffled, and sometimes impair'd,

that I absent myself from the town for a while, without feeling at a loss the moment I am left by myself. Instead of a friend in a postchaise or in a Tilbury, to exchange good things with, and vary the same stale topics over again, for once let me have a truce with impertinence. Give me the clear blue sky over my head, and the green turf beneath my feet, a winding road before me, and a three hours' march to dinner—and then to thinking! It is hard if I cannot start some game on these lone heaths. I laugh, I run, I leap, I sing for joy. From the point of yonder rolling cloud I plunge into my past being, and revel there, as the sun-burnt Indian plunges headlong into the wave that wafts him to his native shore. Then long-forgotten things, like 'sunken wrack and sumless treasuries,' burst upon my eager sight, and I begin to feel, think, and be myself again. Instead of an awkward silence, broken by attempts at wit or dull common-places, mine is that undisturbed silence of the heart which alone is perfect eloquence. No one likes puns, alliterations, antitheses, argument, and analysis better than I do; but I sometimes had rather be without them. 'Leave, oh, leave me to my repose!' I have just now other business in hand, which would seem idle to you, but is with me 'very stuff o' the conscience.' Is not this wild rose sweet without a comment? Does not this daisy leap to my heart set in its coat of emerald? Yet if I were to explain to you the circumstance that has so endeared it to me, you would only smile. Had I not better then keep it to myself, and let it serve me to brood over, from here to yonder craggy point, and from thence onward to the far-distant horizon? I should be but bad company all that way, and therefore prefer being alone. I have heard it said that you may, when the moody fit comes on, walk or ride on by yourself, and indulge your reveries. But this looks like a breach of manners, a neglect of others, and you are thinking all the time that you ought to rejoin your party. 'Out upon such half-faced fellowship,' say I. I like to be either entirely to myself, or entirely at the disposal of others; to talk or be silent, to walk or sit still, to be sociable or solitary. I was pleased with an observation of Mr. Cobbett's, that 'he thought it a bad French custom to drink our wine with our meals, and that an Englishman ought to do only one thing at a time.' So I cannot talk and think, or indulge in melancholy musing and lively conversation by fits and starts. 'Let me have a companion of my way,' says Sterne, 'were it but to remark how the shadows lengthen as the sun declines.' It is beautifully said; but, in my opinion, this continual comparing of notes interferes with the involuntary impression of things upon the mind, and hurts the sentiment. If you only hint what you feel in a kind of dumb show, it is insipid: if you have to explain it, it is making a toil of a pleasure. You cannot read the book of nature without being perpetually put to the trouble of translating it for the benefit of others. I am for this synthetical method on a journey in preference to the analytical. I am content to lay in a stock of ideas then, and to examine and anatomise them afterwards. I want to see my vague notions float like the down of the thistle before the breeze, and not to have them entangled in the briars and thorns of controversy. For once, I like to have it all my own way; and this is impossible unless you are alone, or in such company as I do not covet. I have no objection to argue a point with any one for twenty miles of measured road, but not for pleasure. If you remark the scent of a bean-field crossing the road, perhaps your fellow-traveller has no smell. If you point to a distant object, perhaps he is short-sighted, and has to take out his glass to look at it. There is a feeling in the air, a tone in the colour of a cloud, which hits your fancy, but the effect of which you are unable to account for. There is then no sympathy, but an uneasy craving after it, and a dissatisfaction which pursues you on the way, and in the end probably produces ill-humour. Now I never quarrel with myself, and take all my own conclusions for granted till I find it necessary to defend them against objections. It is not merely that you may not be of accord on the objects and circumstances that present themselves before you— these may recall a number of objects, and lead to associations too delicate and refined to be possibly communicated to others. Yet these I love to cherish, and sometimes still fondly clutch them, when I can escape from the throng to do so. To give way to our feelings before company seems extravagance or affectation; and, on the other hand, to have to unravel this mystery of our being at every turn, and to make others take an equal interest in it (otherwise the end is not answered), is a task to which few are competent. We must 'give it an understanding, but no tongue.' My old friend Coleridge, however, could do both. He could go on in the most delightful explanatory way over hill and dale a summer's day, and convert a landscape into a didactic poem or a Pindaric ode. 'He talked far above singing.' If I could so clothe my ideas in sounding and flowing words, I might perhaps wish to have some one with me to admire the swelling theme; or I could be more content, were it possible for me still to hear his echoing voice in the woods of All-Foxden.(1) They had 'that fine madness in them which our first poets had'; and if they could have been caught by some rare instrument, would have breathed such strains as the following:—

Here be woods as green
As any, air likewise as fresh and sweet
As when smooth Zephyrus plays on the fleet
Face of the curled streams, with flow'rs as many
As the young spring gives, and as choice as any;
Here be all new delights, cool streams and wells,
Arbours o'ergrown with woodbines, caves and dells;
Choose where thou wilt, whilst I sit by and sing,
Or gather rushes to make many a ring
For thy long fingers; tell thee tales of love,

```
How the pale Phoebe, hunting in a grove,
First saw the boy Endymion, from whose eyes
She took eternal fire that never dies;
How she convey'd him softly in a sleep,
His temples bound with poppy, to the steep
Head of old Latmos, where she stoops each night,
Gilding the mountain with her brother's light,
To kiss her sweetest.(2)
```

Had I words and images at command like these, I would attempt to wake the thoughts that lie slumbering on golden ridges in the evening clouds: but at the sight of nature my fancy, poor as it is, droops and closes up its leaves, like flowers at sunset. I can make nothing out on the spot: I must have time to collect myself.

In general, a good thing spoils out-of-door prospects: it should be reserved for Table-talk. Lamb is for this reason, I take it, the worst company in the world out of doors; because he is the best within. I grant there is one subject on which it is pleasant to talk on a journey, and that is, what one shall have for supper when we get to our inn at night. The open air improves this sort of conversation or friendly altercation, by setting a keener edge on appetite. Every mile of the road heightens the flavour of the viands we expect at the end of it. How fine it is to enter some old town, walled and turreted, just at approach of nightfall, or to come to some straggling village, with the lights streaming through the surrounding gloom; and then, after inquiring for the best entertainment that the place affords, to 'take one's ease at one's inn'! These eventful moments in our lives' history are too precious, too full of solid, heartfelt happiness to be frittered and dribbled away in imperfect sympathy. I would have them all to myself, and drain them to the last drop: they will do to talk of or to write about afterwards. What a delicate speculation it is, after drinking whole goblets of tea—

```
The cups that cheer, but not inebriate—
```

and letting the fumes ascend into the brain, to sit considering what we shall have for supper—eggs and a rasher, a rabbit smothered in onions, or an excellent veal-cutlet! Sancho in such a situation once fixed on cow-heel; and his choice, though he could not help it, is not to be disparaged. Then, in the intervals of pictured scenery and Shandean contemplation, to catch the preparation and the stir in the kitchen (getting ready for the gentleman in the parlour). *Procul, O procul este profani!* These hours are sacred to silence and to musing, to be treasured up in the memory, and to feed the source of smiling thoughts hereafter. I would not waste them in idle talk; or if I must have the integrity of fancy broken in upon, I would rather it were by a stranger than a friend. A stranger takes his hue and character from the time and place; he is a part of the furniture and costume of an inn. If he is a Quaker, or from the West Riding of Yorkshire, so much the better. I do not even try to sympathise with him, and he breaks no squares. (How I love to see the camps of the gypsies, and to sigh my soul into that sort of life. If I express this feeling to another, he may qualify and spoil it with some objection.) I associate nothing with my travelling companion but present objects and passing events. In his ignorance of me and my affairs, I in a manner forget myself. But a friend reminds one of other things, rips up old grievances, and destroys the abstraction of the scene. He comes in ungraciously between us and our imaginary character. Something is dropped in the course of conversation that gives a hint of your profession and pursuits; or from having some one with you that knows the less sublime portions of your history, it seems that other people do. You are no longer a citizen of the world; but your 'unhoused free condition is put into circumspection and confine.' The incognito of an inn is one of its striking privileges— 'lord of one's self, uncumbered with a name.' Oh! it is great to shake off the trammels of the world and of public opinion—to lose our importunate, tormenting, everlasting personal identity in the elements of nature, and become the creature of the moment, clear of all ties— to hold to the universe only by a dish of sweetbreads, and to owe nothing but the score of the evening—and no longer seeking for applause and meeting with contempt, to be known by no other title than *the Gentleman in the parlour!* One may take one's choice of all characters in this romantic state of uncertainty as to one's real pretensions, and become indefinitely respectable and negatively right-worshipful. We baffle prejudice and disappoint conjecture; and from being so to others, begin to be objects of curiosity and wonder even to ourselves. We are no more those hackneyed common-places that we appear in the world; an inn restores us to the level of nature, and quits scores with society! I have certainly spent some enviable hours at inns—sometimes when I have been left entirely to myself, and have tried to solve some metaphysical problem, as once at Witham Common, where I found out the proof that likeness is not a case of the association of ideas—at other times, when there have been pictures in the room, as at St. Neot's (I think it was), where I first met with Gribelin's engravings of the Cartoons, into which I entered at once, and at a little inn on the borders of Wales, where there happened to be hanging some of Westall's drawings, which I compared triumphantly (for a theory that I had, not for the admired artist) with the figure of a girl who had ferried me over the Severn, standing up in a boat between me and the twilight—at other times I might mention luxuriating in books, with a peculiar interest in this way, as I remember sitting up half the night to read *Paul and Virginia,* which I picked up at an inn at Bridgewater, after being drenched in the rain all day; and at the same place I got through two volumes of Madame D'Arblay's *Camilla.* It was on the 10th of April 1798 that I sat down to a volume of the *New Eloise,* at the inn at Llangollen, over a bottle of sherry and a cold chicken. The letter I chose was that in which St. Preux describes his feelings as he first caught a glimpse from the heights of the Jura of the Pays de Vaud, which I had brought with me as a *bon bouche* to crown the evening with. It was my birthday, and I had for the first time come from a place in the neighbourhood to visit this delightful spot. The road to Llangollen turns off between Chirk and Wrexham; and on passing a certain point you come all at once upon the valley, which opens like an amphitheatre, broad, barren hills rising in majestic state on either side, with 'green upland swells that echo to the bleat of flocks' below, and the river Dee babbling over its stony bed in the midst of them. The valley at this time 'glittered green with sunny showers,' and a budding ash-tree dipped its tender branches in the chiding stream. How proud, how glad I was to walk along the high road that overlooks the delicious prospect, repeating the lines which I have just quoted from Mr. Coleridge's poems! But besides the prospect which opened beneath my feet, another also opened to my inward sight, a heavenly vision, on which were written, in letters large as Hope could make them, these four words, LIBERTY, GENIUS, LOVE, VIRTUE; which have since faded into the light of common day, or mock my idle gaze.

The beautiful is vanished, and returns not.

70

Still I would return some time or other to this enchanted spot; but I would return to it alone. What other self could I find to share that influx of thoughts, of regret, and delight, the fragments of which I could hardly conjure up to myself, so much have they been broken and defaced. I could stand on some tall rock, and overlook the precipice of years that separates me from what I then was. I was at that time going shortly to visit the poet whom I have above named. Where is he now? Not only I myself have changed; the world, which was then new to me, has become old and incorrigible. Yet will I turn to thee in thought, O sylvan Dee, in joy, in youth and gladness as thou then wert; and thou shalt always be to me the river of Paradise, where I will drink of the waters of life freely!

There is hardly anything that shows the short-sightedness or capriciousness of the imagination more than travelling does. With change of place we change our ideas; nay, our opinions and feelings. We can by an effort indeed transport ourselves to old and long-forgotten scenes, and then the picture of the mind revives again; but we forget those that we have just left. It seems that we can think but of one place at a time. The canvas of the fancy is but of a certain extent, and if we paint one set of objects upon it, they immediately efface every other. We cannot enlarge our conceptions, we only shift our point of view. The landscape bares its bosom to the enraptured eye, we take our fill of it, and seem as if we could form no other image of beauty or grandeur. We pass on, and think no more of it: the horizon that shuts it from our sight also blots it from our memory like a dream. In travelling through a wild barren country I can form no idea of a woody and cultivated one. It appears to me that all the world must be barren, like what I see of it. In the country we forget the town, and in town we despise the country. 'Beyond Hyde Park,' says Sir Topling Flutter, 'all is a desert.' All that part of the map that we do not see before us is blank. The world in our conceit of it is not much bigger than a nutshell. It is not one prospect expanded into another, county joined to county, kingdom to kingdom, land to seas, making an image voluminous and vast; the mind can form no larger idea of space than the eye can take in at a single glance. The rest is a name written in a map, a calculation of arithmetic. For instance, what is the true signification of that immense mass of territory and population known by the name of China to us? An inch of pasteboard on a wooden globe, of no more account than a China orange! Things near us are seen of the size of life: things at a distance are diminished to the size of the understanding. We measure the universe by ourselves, and even comprehend the texture of our being only piecemeal. In this way, however, we remember an infinity of things and places. The mind is like a mechanical instrument that plays a great variety of tunes, but it must play them in succession. One idea recalls another, but it at the same time excludes all others. In trying to renew old recollections, we cannot as it were unfold the whole web of our existence; we must pick out the single threads. So in coming to a place where we have formerly lived, and with which we have intimate associations, every one must have found that the feeling grows more vivid the nearer we approach the spot, from the mere anticipation of the actual impression: we remember circumstances, feelings, persons, faces, names that we had not thought of for years; but for the time all the rest of the world is forgotten!—To return to the question I have quitted above:

I have no objection to go to see ruins, aqueducts, pictures, in company with a friend or a party, but rather the contrary, for the former reason reversed. They are intelligible matters, and will bear talking about. The sentiment here is not tacit, but communicable and overt. Salisbury Plain is barren of criticism, but Stonehenge will bear a discussion antiquarian, picturesque, and philosophical. In setting out on a party of pleasure, the first consideration always is where we shall go to: in taking a solitary ramble, the question is what we shall meet with by the way. 'The mind is its own place'; nor are we anxious to arrive at the end of our journey. I can myself do the honours indifferently well to works of art and curiosity. I once took a party to Oxford with no mean eclat—showed them that seat of the Muses at a distance,

With glistering spires and pinnacles adorn'd—

descanted on the learned air that breathes from the grassy quadrangles and stone walls of halls and colleges—was at home in the Bodleian; and at Blenheim quite superseded the powdered Cicerone that attended us, and that pointed in vain with his wand to commonplace beauties in matchless pictures. As another exception to the above reasoning, I should not feel confident in venturing on a journey in a foreign country without a companion. I should want at intervals to hear the sound of my own language. There is an involuntary antipathy in the mind of an Englishman to foreign manners and notions that requires the assistance of social sympathy to carry it off. As the distance from home increases, this relief, which was at first a luxury, becomes a passion and an appetite. A person would almost feel stifled to find himself in the deserts of Arabia without friends and countrymen: there must be allowed to be something in the view of Athens or old Rome that claims the utterance of speech; and I own that the Pyramids are too mighty for any single contemplation. In such situations, so opposite to all one's ordinary train of ideas, one seems a species by one's-self, a limb torn off from society, unless one can meet with instant fellowship and support. Yet I did not feel this want or craving very pressing once, when I first set my foot on the laughing shores of France. Calais was peopled with novelty and delight. The confused, busy murmur of the place was like oil and wine poured into my ears; nor did the mariners' hymn, which was sung from the top of an old crazy vessel in the harbour, as the sun went down, send an alien sound into my soul. I only breathed the air of general humanity. I walked over 'the vine-covered hills and gay regions of France,' erect and satisfied; for the image of man was not cast down and chained to the foot of arbitrary thrones: I was at no loss for language, for that of all the great schools of painting was open to me. The whole is vanished like a shade. Pictures, heroes, glory, freedom, all are fled: nothing remains but the Bourbons and the French people!—There is undoubtedly a sensation in travelling into foreign parts that is to be had nowhere else; but it is more pleasing at the time than lasting. It is too remote from our habitual associations to be a common topic of discourse or reference, and, like a dream or another state of existence, does not piece into our daily modes of life. It is an animated but a momentary hallucination. It demands an effort to exchange our actual for our ideal identity; and to feel the pulse of our old transports revive very keenly, we must 'jump' all our present comforts and connections. Our romantic and itinerant character is not to be domesticated. Dr. Johnson remarked how little foreign travel added to the facilities of conversation in those who had been abroad. In fact, the time we have spent there is both delightful, and in one sense instructive; but it appears to be cut out of our substantial, downright existence, and never to join kindly on to it. We are not the same, but another, and perhaps more enviable individual, all the time we are out of our own country. We are lost to ourselves, as well as our friends. So the poet somewhat quaintly sings:

Out of my country and myself I go.

Those who wish to forget painful thoughts, do well to absent themselves for a while from the ties and objects that recall them; but we can be said only to fulfil our destiny in the place that gave us birth. I should on this account like well enough to spend the whole of my life in travelling abroad, if I could anywhere borrow another life to spend afterwards at home!

FN to ESSAY III

(1) Near Nether-Stowey, Somersetshire, where the author of this Essay visited Coleridge in 1798. He was there again in 1803.
(2) Fletcher's 'Faithful Shepherdess,' i. 3 (Dyce's *Beaumont and Fletcher,* ii. 38, 39).

ESSAY IV. ON COFFEE-HOUSE POLITICIANS

There is a set of people who fairly come under this denomination. They spend their time and their breath in coffee-houses and other places of public resort, hearing or repeating some new thing. They sit with a paper in their hands in the morning, and with a pipe in their mouths in the evening, discussing the contents of it. The *Times,* the *Morning Chronicle,* and the *Herald* are necessary to their existence: in them 'they live and move and have their being.' The Evening Paper is impatiently expected and called for at a certain critical minute: the news of the morning becomes stale and vapid by the dinner-hour. A fresher interest is required, an appetite for the latest-stirring information is excited with the return of their meals; and a glass of old port or humming ale hardly relishes as it ought without the infusion of some lively topic that had its birth with the day, and perishes before night. 'Then come in the sweets of the evening':—the Queen, the coronation, the last new play, the next fight, the insurrection of the Greeks or Neapolitans, the price of stocks, or death of kings, keep them on the alert till bedtime. No question comes amiss to them that is quite new—none is ever heard of that is at all old.

> That of an hour's age doth hiss the speaker.

The World before the Flood or the Intermediate State of the Soul are never once thought of—such is the quick succession of subjects, the suddenness and fugitiveness of the interest taken in them, that the *Twopenny Post Bag* would be at present looked upon as an old-fashioned publication; and the Battle of Waterloo, like the proverb, is somewhat musty. It is strange that people should take so much interest at one time in what they so soon forget;—the truth is, they feel no interest in it at any time, but it does for something to talk about. Their ideas are served up to them, like their bill of fare, for the day; and the whole creation, history, war, politics, morals, poetry, metaphysics, is to them like a file of antedated newspapers, of no use, not even for reference, except the one which lies on the table! You cannot take any of these persons at a greater disadvantage than before they are provided with their cue for the day. They ask with a face of dreary vacuity, 'Have you anything new?'—and on receiving an answer in the negative, have nothing further to say. (They are like an oyster at the ebb of the tide, gaping for fresh *tidings.*) Talk of the Westminster Election, the Bridge Street Association, or Mr. Cobbett's Letter to John Cropper of Liverpool, and they are alive again. Beyond the last twenty-four hours, or the narrow round in which they move, they are utterly to seek, without ideas, feelings, interests, apprehensions of any sort; so that if you betray any knowledge beyond the vulgar routine of SECOND EDITIONS and first-hand private intelligence, you pass with them for a dull fellow, not acquainted with what is going forward in the world, or with the practical value of things. I have known a person of this stamp censure John Cam Hobhouse for referring so often as he does to the affairs of the Greeks and Romans, as if the affairs of the nation were not sufficient for his hands: another asks you if a general in modern times cannot throw a bridge over a river without having studied Caesar's *Commentaries;* and a third cannot see the use of the learned languages, as he has observed that the greatest proficients in them are rather taciturn than otherwise, and hesitate in their speech more than other people. A dearth of general information is almost necessary to the thorough-paced coffee-house politician; in the absence of thought, imagination, sentiment, he is attracted immediately to the nearest commonplace, and floats through the chosen regions of noise and empty rumours without difficulty and without distraction. Meet 'any six of these men in buckram,' and they will accost you with the same question and the same answer: they have seen it somewhere in print, or had it from some city oracle, that morning; and the sooner they vent their opinions the better, for they will not keep. Like tickets of admission to the theatre for a particular evening, they must be used immediately, or they will be worth nothing: and the object is to find auditors for the one and customers for the other, neither of which is difficult; since people who have no ideas of their own are glad to hear what any one else has to say, as those who have not free admissions to the play will very obligingly take up with an occasional order. It sometimes gives one a melancholy but mixed sensation to see one of the better sort of this class of politicians, not without talents or learning, absorbed for fifty years together in the all-engrossing topic of the day: mounting on it for exercise and recreation of his faculties, like the great horse at a riding-school, and after his short, improgressive, untired career, dismounting just where he got up; flying abroad in continual consternation on the wings of all the newspapers; waving his arm like a pump-handle in sign of constant change, and spouting out torrents of puddled politics from his mouth; dead to all interests but those of the state; seemingly neither older nor wiser for age; unaccountably enthusiastic, stupidly romantic, and actuated by no other motive than the mechanical operations of the spirit of newsmongering.(1)

'What things,' exclaims Beaumont in his verses to Ben Jonson, 'have we not seen done at the Mermaid!

> 'Then when there hath been thrown
> Wit able enough to justify the town
> For three days past, wit that might warrant be
> For the whole city to talk foolishly!'

I cannot say the same of the Southampton, though it stands on classic ground, and is connected by vocal tradition with the great names of the Elizabethan age. What a falling off is here l Our ancestors of that period seem not only to be older by two hundred years, and proportionably wiser and wittier than we, but hardly a trace of them is left, not even the memory of what has been. How should I make my friend Mounsey stare, if I were to mention the name of my still better friend, old honest Signor Friscobaldo, the father of Bellafront;—yet his name was perhaps invented, and the scenes in which he figures unrivalled might for the first time have been read aloud to thrilling ears on this very spot! Who reads Decker now? Or if by chance any one awakes the strings of that ancient lyre, and starts with delight as they yield wild, broken music, is he not accused of envy to the living Muse? What would a linen-draper from Holborn think, if I were to ask him after the clerk of St. Andrew's, the immortal, the forgotten Webster? His name and his works are no more heard of: though *these* were written with a pen of adamant, 'within the red-leaved tables of the heart,' his fame was 'writ in water.' So perishable is genius, so swift is time, so fluctuating is knowledge, and so far is it from being true that men perpetually accumulate the means of improvement and refinement. On the contrary, living knowledge is the tomb of the dead, and while light and worthless materials float on the surface, the solid and sterling as often sink to the bottom, and are swallowed up for ever in weeds and quicksands!—A striking instance of the short-lived nature of popular reputation occurred one evening at the Southampton, when we got into a dispute, the most learned and recondite that over took place, on the comparative merits of Lord Byron and Gray. A country gentleman happened to drop in, and thinking to show off in London company, launched into a lofty panegyric on *The Bard* of Gray as the sublimest composition in the English language. This assertion presently appeared to be an anachronism, though it was probably the opinion in vogue thirty years ago, when the gentleman was last in town. After a little floundering, one of the party volunteered to express a more contemporary sentiment, by asking in a tone of mingled confidence and doubt—'But you don't think, sir, that Gray is to be mentioned as a poet in the same day with my Lord Byron?' The disputants were now at issue: all that resulted was that Gray was set aside as a poet who would not go down among readers of the present day, and his patron treated the works of the Noble Bard as mere ephemeral effusions, and spoke of poets that would be admired thirty years hence, which was the farthest stretch of his critical imagination. His antagonist's did not even reach so far. This was the most romantic digression we over had; and the subject was not afterwards resumed.—No one here (generally speaking) has the slightest notion of anything that has happened, that has been said, thought, or done out of his own recollection. It would be in vain to hearken after those 'wit-skirmishes,' those 'brave sublunary things' which were the employment and delight of the Beaumonts and Bens of former times: but we may happily repose on dulness, drift with the tide of nonsense, and gain an agreeable vertigo by lending an ear to endless controversies. The confusion, provided you do not mingle in the fray and try to disentangle it, is amusing and edifying enough. Every species of false wit and spurious argument may be learnt here by potent examples. Whatever observations you hear dropt have been picked up in the same place or in a kindred atmosphere. There is a kind of conversation made up entirely of scraps and hearsay, as there are a kind of books made up entirely of references to other books. This may account for the frequent contradictions which abound in the discourse of persons educated and disciplined wholly in coffee-houses. There is nothing stable or well-grounded in it: it is 'nothing but vanity, chaotic vanity.' They hear a remark at the Globe which they do not know what to make of; another at the Rainbow in direct opposition to it; and not having time to reconcile them, vent both at the Mitre. In the course of half an hour, if they are not more than ordinarily dull, you are sure to find them on opposite sides of the question. This is the sickening part of it. People do not seem to talk for the sake of expressing their opinions, but to maintain an opinion for the sake of talking. We meet neither with modest ignorance nor studious acquirement. Their knowledge has been taken in too much by snatches to digest properly. There is neither sincerity nor system in what they say. They hazard the first crude notion that comes to hand, and then defend it how they can; which is for the most part but ill. 'Don't you think,' says Mounsey, 'that Mr. ——— ——- is a very sensible, well-informed man?' 'Why, no,' I say, 'he seems to me to have no ideas of his own, and only to wait to see what others will say in order to set himself against it. I should not think that is the way to get at the truth. I do not desire to be driven out of my conclusions (such as they are) merely to make way for his upstart pretensions.'—'Then there is ———: what of him?' 'He might very well express all he has to say in half the time, and with half the trouble. Why should he beat about the bush as he does? He appears to be getting up a little speech and practising on a smaller scale for a Debating Society—the lowest ambition a man can have. Besides, by his manner of drawling out his words, and interlarding his periods with innuendos and formal reservations, he is evidently making up his mind all the time which side he shall take. He puts his sentences together as printers set up types, letter by letter. There is certainly no principle of short-hand in his mode of elocution. He goes round for a meaning, and the sense waits for him. It is not conversation, but rehearsing a part. Men of education and men of the world order this matter better. They know what they have to say on a subject, and come to the point at once. Your coffee-house politician balances between what he heard last and what he shall say next; and not seeing his way clearly, puts you off with circumstantial phrases, and tries to gain time for fear of making a false step. This gentleman has heard some one admired for precision and copiousness of language; and goes away, congratulating himself that he has not made a blunder in grammar or in rhetoric the whole evening. He is a theoretical *Quidnunc*—is tenacious in argument, though wary; carries his point thus and thus, bandies objections and answers with uneasy pleasantry, and when he has the worst of the dispute, puns very emphatically on his adversary's name, if it admits of that kind of misconstruction.' George Kirkpatrick is admired by the waiter, who is a sleek hand,(2) for his temper in managing an argument. Any one else would perceive that the latent cause is not patience with his antagonist, but satisfaction with himself. I think this unmoved self-complacency, this cavalier, smooth, simpering indifference is more annoying than the extremest violence or irritability. The one shows that your opponent does care something about you, and may be put out of his way by your remarks; the other seems to announce that nothing you say can shake his opinion a jot, that he has considered the whole of what you have to offer beforehand, and that he is in all respects much wiser and more accomplished than you. Such persons talk to grown people with the same air of patronage and condescension that they do to children. 'They will explain'—is a familiar expression with them, thinking you can only differ from them in consequence of misconceiving what they say. Or if you detect them in any error in point of fact (as to acknowledged deficiency in wit or argument, they would smile at the idea), they add some correction to your correction, and thus have the whip-hand of you again, being more correct than you who corrected them. If you hint some obvious oversight, they know what you are going to say, and were aware of the objection before you uttered it:—'So shall their anticipation prevent your discovery.' By being in the right you gain no advantage: by being in the wrong you are entitled to the benefit of their pity or scorn. It is sometimes curious to see a select group of our little Gotham getting about a knotty point that will bear a wager, as whether Dr. Johnson's Dictionary was originally published in quarto or folio. The confident assertions, the cautious overtures, the length of time demanded to ascertain the fact, the precise terms of the forfeit, the provisos for getting out of paying it at last, lead to a long and inextricable discussion. George Kirkpatrick was, however, so convinced in his own mind that the *Mourning Bride* was written by Shakespear, that he ran headlong into the snare: the bet was decided, and the punch was drunk. He has skill in numbers, and seldom exceeds his sevenpence.—He had a brother once, no Michael Cassio, no great arithmetician. Roger Kirkpatrick was a rare fellow, of the driest humour, and the nicest tact, of infinite sleights and evasions, of a picked phraseology, and the very soul of mimicry. I fancy I have some insight into physiognomy myself, but he could often expound to me at a single glance the characters of those of my acquaintance that I had been most at fault about. The account as it was cast up and balanced between us was not always very favourable. How finely, how truly, how gaily he took off the company at the Southampton! Poor and faint are my sketches

73

compared to his! It was like looking into a *camera obscura*—you saw faces shining and speaking—the smoke curled, the lights dazzled, the oak wainscotting took a higher polish—there was old Sarratt, tall and gaunt, with his couplet from Pope and case at Nisi Prius, Mounsey eyeing the ventilator and lying *perdu* for a moral, and Hume and Ayrton taking another friendly finishing glass!—These and many more windfalls of character he gave us in thought, word, and action. I remember his once describing three different persons together to myself and Martin Burney, viz. the manager of a country theatre, a tragic and a comic performer, till we were ready to tumble on the floor with laughing at the oddity of their humours, and at Roger's extraordinary powers of ventriloquism, bodily and mental; and Burney said (such was the vividness of the scene) that when he awoke the next morning, he wondered what three amusing characters he had been in company with the evening before. Oh! it was a rich treat to see him describe Mudford, him of the *Courier,* the Contemplative Man, who wrote an answer to Coelebs, coming into a room, folding up his greatcoat, taking out a little pocket volume, laying it down to think, rubbing the calf of his leg with grave self-complacency, and starting out of his reverie when spoken to with an inimitable vapid exclamation of 'Eh!' Mudford is like a man made of fleecy hosiery: Roger was lank and lean 'as is the ribbed sea-sand.' Yet he seemed the very man he represented, as fat, pert, and dull as it was possible to be. I have not seen him of late:—

For Kais is fled, and our tents are forlorn.

But I thought of him the other day, when the news of the death of Buonaparte came, whom we both loved for precisely contrary reasons, he for putting down the rabble of the people, and I because he had put down the rabble of kings. Perhaps this event may rouse him from his lurking-place, where he lies like Reynard, 'with head declined, in feigned slumbers!'(3)

I had almost forgotten the Southampton Tavern. We for some time took C—— for a lawyer, from a certain arguteness of voice and slenderness of neck, and from his having a quibble and a laugh at himself always ready. On inquiry, however, he was found to be a patent-medicine seller, and having leisure in his apprenticeship, and a forwardness of parts, he had taken to study Blackstone and the *Statutes at Large.* On appealing to Mounsey for his opinion on this matter, he observed pithily, 'I don't like so much law: the gentlemen here seem fond of law, but I have law enough at chambers.' One sees a great deal of the humours and tempers of men in a place of this sort, and may almost gather their opinions from their characters. There is C——, a fellow that is always in the wrong—who puts might for right on all occasions—a Tory in grain—who has no one idea but what has been instilled into him by custom and authority—an everlasting babbler on the stronger side of the question—querulous and dictatorial, and with a peevish whine in his voice like a beaten schoolboy. He is a great advocate for the Bourbons and for the National Debt. The former he affirms to be the choice of the French people, and the latter he insists is necessary to the salvation of these kingdoms. This last point a little inoffensive gentleman among us, of a saturnine aspect but simple conceptions, cannot comprehend. 'I will tell you, sir—I will make my propositions so clear that you will be convinced of the truth of my observation in a moment. Consider, sir, the number of trades that would be thrown out of employ if it were done away with: what would become of the porcelain manufacture without it?' Any stranger to overhear one of these debates would swear that the English as a nation are bad logicians. Mood and figure are unknown to them. They do not argue by the book. They arrive at conclusions through the force of prejudice, and on the principles of contradiction. Mr. C—— having thus triumphed in argument, offers a flower to the notice of the company as a specimen of his flower-garden, a curious exotic, nothing like it to be found in this kingdom; talks of his carnations, of his country-house, and old English hospitality, but never invites any of his friends to come down and take their Sunday's dinner with him. He is mean and ostentatious at the same time, insolent and servile, does not know whether to treat those he converses with as if they were his porters or his customers: the prentice-boy is not yet wiped out of him, and his imagination still hovers between his mansion at —— and the workhouse. Opposed to him and to every one else is B., a radical reformer and logician, who makes clear work of the taxes and National Debt, reconstructs the Government from the first principles of things, shatters the Holy Alliance at a blow, grinds out the future prospects of society with a machine, and is setting out afresh with the commencement of the French Revolution five and twenty years ago, as if on an untried experiment. He minds nothing but the formal agreement of his premises and his conclusions, and does not stick at obstacles in the way, nor consequences in the end. If there was but one side of a question, he would be always in the right. He casts up one column of the account to admiration, but totally forgets and rejects the other. His ideas lie like square pieces of wood in his brain, and may be said to be piled up on a stiff architectural principle, perpendicularly, and at right angles. There is no inflection, no modification, no graceful embellishment, no Corinthian capitals. I never heard him agree to two propositions together, or to more than half a one at a time. His rigid love of truth bends to nothing but his habitual love of disputation. He puts one in mind of one of those long-headed politicians and frequenters of coffee-houses mentioned in Berkeley's *Minute Philosopher,* who would make nothing of such old-fashioned fellows as Plato and Aristotle. He has the new light strong upon him, and he knocks other people down with its solid beams. He denies that he has got certain views out of Cobbett, though he allows that there are excellent ideas occasionally to be met with in that writer. It is a pity that this enthusiastic and unqualified regard to truth should be accompanied with an equal exactness of expenditure and unrelenting eye to the main chance. He brings a bunch of radishes with him for cheapness, and gives a band of musicians at the door a penny, observing that he likes their performance better than all the Opera squalling. This brings the severity of his political principles into question, if not into contempt. He would abolish the National Debt from motives of personal economy, and objects to Mr. Canning's pension because it perhaps takes a farthing a year out of his own pocket. A great deal of radical reasoning has its source in this feeling.—He bestows no small quantity of his tediousness upon Mounsey, on whose mind all these formulas and diagrams fall like seed on stony ground: 'while the manna is descending,' he shakes his ears, and, in the intervals of the debate, insinuates an objection, and calls for another half-pint. I have sometimes said to him, 'Any one to come in here without knowing you, would take you for the most disputatious man alive, for you are always engaged in an argument with somebody or other.' The truth is, that Mounsey is a good-natured, gentlemanly man, who notwithstanding, if appealed to, will not let an absurd or unjust proposition pass without expressing his dissent; and therefore he is a sort of mark for all those (and we have several of that stamp) who like to tease other people's understandings as wool-combers tease wool. He is certainly the flower of the flock. He is the oldest frequenter of the place, the latest sitter-up, well-informed, inobtrusive, and that sturdy old English character, a lover of truth and justice. I never knew Mounsey approve of anything unfair or illiberal. There is a candour and uprightness about his mind which can neither be wheedled nor browbeat into unjustifiable complaisance. He looks straight forward as he sits with his glass in his hand, turning neither to the right nor the left, and I will venture to say that he has never had a sinister object in view through life. Mrs. Battle (it is recorded in her Opinions on Whist) could not make up her mind to use the word *'Go.'* Mounsey, from long practice, has got over this difficulty, and uses it incessantly. It is no matter what adjunct follows in the train of this despised monosyllable,—whatever liquid comes after this prefix is welcome. Mounsey, without being the most communicative, is the most conversible man I know. The social principle is inseparable from his person. If he has nothing to say, he drinks your health; and when you cannot, from the rapidity and carelessness of his utterance, catch what he says, you assent to it with equal confidence: you know his meaning is good. His favourite phrase is, 'We have all of us something of the coxcomb'; and yet he has none of it himself. Before I had exchanged half a dozen sentences with Mounsey, I found that he knew several of my old acquaintance (an immediate introduction of itself, for the discussing the characters and foibles of common friends is a great sweetener and cement of friendship)—and had been intimate with most of the wits and men about town for the last twenty years. He knew Tobin, Wordsworth, Porson, Wilson, Paley, Erskine, and many others. He speaks of Paley's pleasantry and unassuming manners, and describes Porson's long potations and long quotations formerly at the Cider Cellar in a very lively way. He has doubts, however, as to that sort of learning. On my saying that I had never seen the Greek Professor but once, at the Library of the London Institution, when he was dressed in an old rusty black coat with cobwebs hanging to the skirts of it, and with a large patch of coarse brown paper covering the whole length of his nose, looking for all the world like a drunken carpenter, and talking to one of the proprietors with an air of suavity, approaching to condescension, Mounsey could not help expressing some little uneasiness for the credit of classical literature. 'I submit, sir, whether common sense is not the principal thing? What is the advantage of genius and learning if they are of no use in the conduct of life?'—Mounsey is one who loves the hours that usher in the morn, when a select few are left in twos and threes like stars before the break of day, and when the discourse and the ale are 'aye growing better and better.' Wells, Mounsey, and myself were all that remained one evening. We had sat together several hours without being tired of one another's company. The conversation turned on the Beauties of Charles the Second's Court at Windsor, and from thence to Count Grammont, their gallant and gay historian. We took our favourite passages in turn—one preferring that of Killigrew's country cousin, who, having been resolutely refused by Miss Warminster (one of the Maids of Honour), when he found she had been unexpectedly brought to bed, fell on his knees and thanked God that now she might take compassion on him—another insisting that the Chevalier Hamilton's assignation with Lady Chesterfield, when she kept him all night shivering in an old out-house, was better. Jacob Hall's prowess was not forgotten, nor the story of Miss Stuart's garters. I was getting on in my way with that delicate *endroit* in which Miss Churchill is first introduced at court and is besieged (as a matter of course) by the Duke of York, who was gallant as well as bigoted on system. His assiduities, however, soon slackened, owing (it is said) to her having a pale, thin face: till one day, as they were riding out hunting together, she fell from her horse, and was taken up almost lifeless. The whole assembled court was thrown by this event into admiration that such a body should belong to such a face(4) (so transcendent a pattern was she of the female form), and the Duke was fixed. This, I contended, was striking, affecting, and grand, the sublime of amorous biography, and said I could conceive of nothing finer than the idea of a young person in her situation, who was the object of indifference or scorn from outward appearance, with the proud suppressed consciousness of a Goddess-like symmetry, locked up by 'fear and niceness, the handmaids of all women,' from the wonder and worship of mankind. I said so then, and I think so now: my tongue grew wanton in the praise of this passage, and I believe it bore the bell from its competitors. Wells then spoke of Lucius Apuleius and his Golden Ass, which contains the story of Cupid and Psyche, with other matter rich and rare, and went on to the romance of Heliodorus, Theagenes and Chariclea and in it the presiding deities of Love and Wine appear in all their pristine strength, youth, and grace, crowned and worshipped as of yore. The night waned, but our glasses brightened, enriched with the pearls of Grecian story. Our cup-bearer slept in a corner of the room, like another Endymion, in the pale ray of a half-extinguished lamp, and starting up at a fresh summons for a further supply, he swore it was too late, and was inexorable to entreaty. Mounsey sat with his hat on and with a hectic flush in his face while any hope remained, but as soon as we rose to go, he darted out of the room as quick as lightning, determined not to be the last that went.—I said some time after to the waiter, that 'Mr. Mounsey was no flincher.' 'Oh! sir,' says he, 'you should have known him formerly, when Mr. Hume and Mr. Ayrton used to be here. Now he is quite another man: he seldom stays later than one or two.'—'Why, did they keep it up much then?' 'Oh! yes; and used to sing catches and all sorts.'—'What, did Mr. Mounsey sing catches?' 'He joined chorus, sir, and was as merry as the best of them. He was always a pleasant gentleman!'—This Hume and Ayrton succumbed in the fight. Ayrton was a dry Scotchman, Hume a good-natured, hearty Englishman. I do not mean that the same character applies to all Scotchmen or to all Englishmen. Hume was of the Pipe-Office (not unfitly appointed), and in his cheerfuller cups would delight to speak of a widow and a bowling-green, that ran in his head to the last. 'What is the good of talking of those things now?' said the man of utility. 'I don't know,' replied the other, quaffing another glass of sparkling ale, and with a lambent fire playing in his eye and round his bald forehead—(he had a head that Sir Joshua would have made something bland and genial of)—'I don't know, but they were delightful to me at the time, and are still pleasant to talk and think of.'—*Such a one,* in Touchstone's phrase, *is a natural philosopher;* and in nine cases out of ten that sort of philosophy is the best! I could enlarge this sketch, such as it is; but to prose on to the end of the chapter might prove less profitable than tedious.

I like very well to sit in a room where there are people talking on subjects I know nothing of, if I am only allowed to sit silent and as a spectator; but I do not much like to join in the conversation, except with people and on subjects to my taste. Sympathy is necessary to society. To look on, a variety of faces, humours, and opinions is sufficient; to mix with others, agreement as well as variety is indispensable. What makes good society? I answer, in one word, real fellowship. Without a similitude of tastes, acquirements, and pursuits (whatever may be the difference of tempers and characters) there can be no intimacy or even casual intercourse worth the having. What makes the most agreeable party? A number of people with a number of ideas in common, 'yet so as with a difference'; that is, who can put one or more subjects which they have all studied in the greatest variety of entertaining or useful lights. Or, in other words, a succession of good things said with good-humour, and addressed to the understandings of those who hear them, make the most desirable conversation. Ladies, lovers, beaux, wits, philosophers, the fashionable or the vulgar, are the fittest company for one another. The discourse at Randal's is the best for boxers; that at Long's for lords and loungers. I prefer Hunt's conversation almost to any other person's, because, with a familiar range of subjects, he colours with a totally new and sparkling light, reflected from his own character. Elia, the grave and witty, says things not to be surpassed in essence; but the manner is more painful and less a relief to my own thoughts. Some one conceived he could not be an excellent companion, because he was seen walking down the side of the Thames, *passibus iniquis,* after dining at Richmond. The objection was not valid. I will, however, admit that the said Elia is the worst company in the world in bad company, if it be granted me that in good company he is nearly the best that can be. He is one of those of whom it may be said, Tell me your company, and I'll tell you your manners. He is the creature of sympathy, and makes good whatever opinion you seem to entertain of him. He cannot outgo the apprehensions of the circle, and invariably acts up or down to the point of refinement or vulgarity at which they pitch him. He appears to take a pleasure in exaggerating the prejudice of strangers against him; a pride in confirming the prepossessions of friends. In whatever scale of intellect he is placed, he is as lively or as stupid as the rest can be for their lives. If you think him odd and ridiculous, he becomes more and more so every minute, *a la folie,* till he is a wonder gazed (at) by all—set him against a good wit and a ready apprehension, and he brightens more and more—

```
    Or like a gate of steel
 Fronting the sun, receives and renders back
 Its figure and its heat.
```

We had a pleasant party one evening at Procter's. A young literary bookseller who was present went away delighted with the elegance of the repast, and spoke in raptures of a servant in green livery and a patent lamp. I thought myself that the charm of the evening consisted in some talk about Beaumont and Fletcher and the old poets, in which every one took part or interest, and in a consciousness that we could not pay our host a better compliment than in thus alluding to studies in which he excelled, and in praising authors whom he had imitated with feeling and sweetness!—I should think it may also be laid down as a rule on this subject, that to constitute good company a certain proportion of hearers and speakers is requisite. Coleridge makes good company for this reason. He immediately establishes the principle of the division of labour in this respect wherever he comes. He takes his cue as speaker, and the rest of the party theirs as listeners—a 'Circa herd'—without any previous arrangement having been gone through. I will just add that there can be no good society without perfect freedom from affectation and constraint. If the unreserved communication of feeling or opinion leads to offensive familiarity, it is not well; but it is no better where the absence of offensive remarks arises only from formality and an assumed respectfulness of manner.

I do not think there is anything deserving the name of society to be found out of London; and that for the two following reasons. First, there is *neighbourhood* elsewhere, accidental or unavoidable acquaintance: people are thrown together by chance or grow together like trees; but you can pick your society nowhere but in London. The very persons that of all others you would wish to associate with in almost every line of life (or at least of intellectual pursuit) are to be met with there. It is hard if out of a million of people you cannot find half a dozen to your liking. Individuals may seem lost and hid in the size of the place; but in fact, from this very circumstance, you are within two or three miles' reach of persons that, without it, you would be some hundreds apart from. Secondly, London is the only place in which each individual in company is treated according to his value in company, and to that only. In every other part of the kingdom he carries another character about with him, which supersedes the intellectual or social one. It is known in Manchester or Liverpool what every man in the room is worth in land or money; what are his connections and prospects in life—and this gives a character of servility or arrogance, of mercenaries or impertinence to the whole of provincial intercourse. You laugh not in proportion to a man's wit, but his wealth; you have to consider not what, but whom you contradict. You speak by the pound, and are heard by the rood. In the metropolis there is neither time nor inclination for these remote calculations. Every man depends on the quantity of sense, wit, or good manners he brings into society for the reception he meets with in it. A Member of Parliament soon finds his level as a commoner: the merchant and manufacturer cannot bring his goods to market here: the great landed proprietor shrinks from being the lord of acres into a pleasant companion or a dull fellow. When a visitor enters or leaves a room, it is not inquired whether he is rich or poor, whether he lives in a garret or a palace, or comes in his own or a hackney coach, but whether he has a good expression of countenance, with an unaffected manner, and whether he is a man of understanding or a blockhead. These are the circumstances by which you make a favourable impression on the company, and by which they estimate you in the abstract. In the country, they consider whether you have a vote at the next election or a place in your gift, and measure the capacity of others to instruct or entertain them by the strength of their pockets and their credit with their banker. Personal merit is at a prodigious discount in the provinces. I like the country very well if I want to enjoy my own company; but London is the only place for equal society, or where a man can say a good thing or express an honest opinion without subjecting himself to being insulted, unless he first lays his purse on the table to back his pretensions to talent or independence of spirit. I speak from experience.(5)

FN to ESSAY IV.

(1) It is not very long ago that I saw two Dissenting Ministers (the *Ultima Thud* of the sanguine, visionary temperament in politics) stuffing their pipes with dried currant-leaves, calling it Radical Tobacco, lighting it with a lens in the rays of the sun, and at every puff fancying that they undermined the Boroughmongers, as Trim blew up the army opposed to the Allies! They had *deceived the Senate.* Methinks I see them now, smiling as in scorn of Corruption.

```
    Dream on, blest pair:
 Yet happier if you knew your happiness,
 And knew to know no more!
```

The world of Reform that you dote on, like Berkeley's material world, lives only in your own brain, and long may it live there! Those same Dissenting Ministers throughout the country (I mean the descendants of the old Puritans) are to this hour a sort of Fifth-monarchy men: very turbulent fellows, in my opinion altogether incorrigible, and according to the suggestions of others, should be hanged out of the way without judge or jury for the safety of church and state. Marry, hang them! they may be left to die a natural death: the race is nearly extinct of itself, and can do little more good or harm!

(2) William, our waiter, is dressed neatly in black, takes in the TICKLER (which many of the gentlemen like to look into), wears, I am told, a diamond pin in his shirt-collar, has a music-master to teach him to play on the flageolet two hours before the maids are up, complains of confinement and a delicate constitution, and is a complete Master Stephen in his way.

(3) His account of Dr. Whittle was prodigious-of his occult sagacity, of his eyes prominent and wild like a hare's, fugacious of followers, of the arts by which he had left the City to lure the patients that he wanted after him to the West End, of the ounce of tea that he purchased by stratagem as an unusual treat to his guest, and of the narrow winding staircase, from the height of which he contemplated in security the imaginary approach of duns. He was a large, plain, fair-faced Moravian preacher, turned physician. He was an honest man, but vain of he knew not what. He was once sitting where Sarratt was playing a game at chess without seeing the board; and after remaining for some time

absorbed in silent wonder, he turned suddenly to me and said, 'Do you know, Mr. Hazlitt, that I think there is something I could do?' 'Well, what is that?' 'Why, perhaps you would not guess, but I think I could dance, I'm sure I could; ay, I could dance like Vestris!' Sarratt, who was a man of various accomplishments (among others one of the Fancy), afterwards bared his arm to convince us of his muscular strength, and Mrs. Sarratt going out of the room with another lady said, 'Do you know, Madam, the Doctor is a great jumper!' Moliere could not outdo this. Never shall I forget his pulling off his coat to eat beef-steaks on equal terms with Martin Burney. Life is short, but full of mirth and pastime, did we not so soon forget what we have laughed at, perhaps that we may not remember what we have cried at! Sarratt, the chess-player, was an extraordinary man. He had the same tenacious, epileptic faculty in other things that he had at chess, and could no more get any other ideas out of his mind than he could those of the figures on the board. He was a great reader, but had not the least taste. Indeed the violence of his memory tyrannised over and destroyed all power of selection. He could repeat (all) Ossian by heart, without knowing the best passage from the worst; and did not perceive he was tiring you to death by giving an account of the breed, education, and manners of fighting-dogs for hours together. The sense of reality quite superseded the distinction between the pleasurable and the painful. He was altogether a mechanical philosopher.

(4) Ils ne pouvoient croire qu'un corps de cette beaute fut de quelque chose au visage de Mademoiselle Churchill.'—*Memoires de Grammont,* vol. ii. p. 254.

(5) When I was young I spent a good deal of my time at Manchester and Liverpool; and I confess I give the preference to the former. There you were oppressed only by the aristocracy of wealth; in the latter by the aristocracy of wealth and letters by turns. You could not help feeling that some of their great men were authors among merchants and merchants among authors. Their bread was buttered on both sides, and they had you at a disadvantage either way. The Manchester cotton-spinners, on the contrary, set up no pretensions beyond their looms, were hearty good fellows, and took any information or display of ingenuity on other subjects in good part. I remember well being introduced to a distinguished patron of art and rising merit at a little distance from Liverpool, and was received with every mark of attention and politeness; till, the conversation turning on Italian literature, our host remarked that there was nothing in the English language corresponding to the severity of the Italian ode—except perhaps Dryden's *Alexander's Feast* and Pope's *St. Cecilia!* I could no longer contain my desire to display my smattering in criticism, and began to maintain that Pope's Ode was, as it appeared to me, far from an example of severity in writing. I soon perceived what I had done, but here am I writing *Table-talks* in consequence. Alas! I knew as little of the world then as I do now. I never could understand anything beyond an abstract definition.

ESSAY V. ON THE ARISTOCRACY OF LETTERS

Ha! here's three of us are sophisticated:—off, you lendings.

There is such a thing as an aristocracy or privileged order in letters which has sometimes excited my wonder, and sometimes my spleen. We meet with authors who have never done anything, but who have a vast reputation for what they could have done. Their names stand high, and are in everybody's mouth, but their works are never heard of, or had better remain undiscovered for the sake of their admirers.— *Stat nominis umbra*—their pretensions are lofty and unlimited, as they have nothing to rest upon, or because it is impossible to confront them with the proofs of their deficiency. If you inquire farther, and insist upon some act of authorship to establish the claims of these Epicurean votaries of the Muses, you find that they had a great reputation at Cambridge, that they were senior wranglers or successful prize-essayists, that they visit at Holland House, and, to support that honour, must be supposed, of course, to occupy the first rank in the world of letters.(1) It is possible, however, that they have some manuscript work in hand, which is of too much importance (and the writer has too much at stake in publishing it) hastily to see the light: or perhaps they once had an article in the Edinburgh Review, which was much admired at the time, and is kept by them ever since as a kind of diploma and unquestionable testimonial of merit. They are not like Grub Street authors, who write for bread, and are paid by the sheet. Like misers who hoard their wealth, they are supposed to be masters of all the wit and sense they do not impart to the public. 'Continents have most of what they contain,' says a considerable philosopher; and these persons, it must be confessed, have a prodigious command over themselves in the expenditure of light and learning. The Oriental curse, '0 that mine enemy had written a book!' hangs suspended over them. By never committing themselves, they neither give a handle to the malice of the world, nor excite the jealousy of friends; and keep all the reputation they have got, not by discreetly blotting, but by never writing a line. Some one told Sheridan, who was always busy about some new work and never advancing any farther in it, that he would not write because he was afraid of the author of the *School for Scandal.* So these idle pretenders are afraid of undergoing a comparison with themselves in something they have never done, but have had credit for doing. They do not acquire celebrity, they assume it; and escape detection by never venturing out of their imposing and mysterious incognito. They do not let themselves down by everyday work: for them to appear in print is a work of supererogation as much as in lords and kings; and like gentlemen with a large landed estate, they live on their established character, and do nothing (or as little as possible) to increase or lose it. There is not a more deliberate piece of grave imposture going. I know a person of this description who has been employed many years (by implication) in a translation of Thucydides, of which no one ever saw a word, but it does not answer the purpose of bolstering up a factitious reputation the less on that account. The longer it is delayed and kept sacred from the vulgar gaze, the more it swells into imaginary consequence; the labour and care required for a work of this kind being immense;—and then there are no faults in an unexecuted translation. The only impeccable writers are those that never wrote. Another is an oracle on subjects of taste and classical erudition, because (he says at least) he reads Cicero once a year to keep up the purity of his Latinity. A third makes the indecency pass for the depth of his researches and for a high gusto in *virtu,* till, from his seeing nothing in the finest remains of ancient art, the world by the merest accident find out that there is nothing in him. There is scarcely anything that a grave face with an impenetrable manner will not accomplish, and whoever is weak enough to impose upon himself will have wit enough to impose upon the public—particularly if he can make it their interest to be deceived by shallow boasting, and contrives not to hurt their self-love by sterling acquirements. Do you suppose that the understood translation of Thucydides costs its supposed author nothing? A select party of friends and admirers dine with him once a week at a magnificent town mansion, or a more elegant and picturesque retreat in the country. They broach their Horace and their old hock, and sometimes allude with a considerable degree of candour to the defects of works which are brought out by contemporary writers—the ephemeral offspring of haste and necessity!

Among other things, the learned languages are a ready passport to this sort of unmeaning, unanalysed reputation. They presently lift a man up among the celestial constellations, the signs of the zodiac (as it were) and third heaven of inspiration, from whence he looks down on those who are toiling on in this lower sphere, and earning their bread by the sweat of their brain, at leisure and in scorn. If the graduates in this way condescend to express their thoughts in English, it is understood to be *infra dignitatem*—such light and unaccustomed essays do not fit the ponderous gravity of their pen—they only draw to advantage and with full justice to themselves in the bow of the ancients. Their native tongue is to them strange, inelegant, unapt, and crude. They 'cannot command it to any utterance of harmony. They have not the skill.' This is true enough; but you must not say so, under a heavy penalty—the displeasure of pedants and blockheads. It would be sacrilege against the privileged classes, the Aristocracy of Letters. What! will you affirm that a profound Latin scholar, a perfect Grecian, cannot write a page of common sense or grammar? Is it not to be presumed, by all the charters of the Universities and the foundations of grammar-schools, that he who can speak a dead language must be *a fortiori* conversant with his own? Surely the greater implies the less. He who knows every science and every art cannot be ignorant of the most familiar forms of speech. Or if this plea is found not to hold water, then our scholastic bungler is said to be above this vulgar trial of skill, 'something must be excused to want of practice—but did you not observe the elegance of the Latinity, how well that period would become a classical and studied dress?' Thus defects are 'monster'd' into excellences, and they screen their idol, and require you, at your peril, to pay prescriptive homage to false concords and inconsequential criticisms, because the writer of them has the character of the first or second Greek or Latin scholar in the kingdom. If you do not swear to the truth of these spurious credentials, you are ignorant and malicious, a quack and a scribbler—*flagranti delicto!* Thus the man who can merely read and construe some old author is of a class superior to any living one, and, by parity of reasoning, to those old authors themselves: the poet or prose-writer of true and original genius, by the courtesy of custom, 'ducks to the learned fool'; or, as the author of *Hudibras* has so well stated the same thing—

```
He that is but able to express
No sense at all in several languages,
Will pass for learneder than he that's known
To speak the strongest reason in his own.
```

These preposterous and unfounded claims of mere scholars to precedence in the commonwealth of letters which they set up so formally themselves and which others so readily bow to, are partly owing to traditional prejudice: there was a time when learning was the only distinction from ignorance, and when there was no such thing as popular English literature. Again, there is something more palpable and positive in this kind of acquired knowledge, like acquired wealth, which the vulgar easily recognise. That others know the meaning of signs which they are confessedly and altogether ignorant of is to them both a matter of fact and a subject of endless wonder. The languages are worn like a dress by a man, and distinguish him sooner than his natural figure; and we are, from motives of self-love, inclined to give others credit for the ideas they have borrowed or have come into indirect possession of, rather than for those that originally belong to them and are exclusively their own. The merit in them and the implied inferiority in ourselves is less. Learning is a kind of external appendage or transferable property—

'Twas mine, 'tis his, and may be any man's.

Genius and understanding are a man's self, an integrant part of his personal identity; and the title to these last, as it is the most difficult to be ascertained, is also the most grudgingly acknowledged. Few persons would pretend to deny that Porson had more Greek than they; it was a question of fact which might be put to the immediate proof, and could not be gainsaid; but the meanest frequenter of the Cider Cellar or the Hole in the Wall would be inclined, in his own conceit, to dispute the palm of wit or sense with him, and indemnify his self-complacency for the admiration paid to living learning by significant hints to friends and casual droppers-in, that the greatest men, when you came to know them, were not without their weak sides as well as others. Pedants, I will add here, talk to the vulgar as pedagogues talk to schoolboys, on an understood principle of condescension and superiority, and therefore make little progress in the knowledge of men or things. While they fancy they are accommodating themselves to, or else assuming airs of importance over, inferior capacities, these inferior capacities are really laughing at them. There can be no true superiority but what arises out of the presupposed ground of equality: there can be no improvement but from the free communication and comparing of ideas. Kings and nobles, for this reason, receive little benefit from society—where all is submission on one side, and condescension on the other. The mind strikes out truth by collision, as steel strikes fire from the flint!

There are whole families who are born classical, and are entered in the heralds' college of reputation by the right of consanguinity. Literature, like nobility, runs in the blood. There is the Burney family. There is no end of it or its pretensions. It produces wits, scholars, novelists, musicians, artists in 'numbers numberless.' The name is alone a passport to the Temple of Fame. Those who bear it are free of Parnassus by birthright. The founder of it was himself an historian and a musician, but more of a courtier and man of the world than either. The secret of his success may perhaps be discovered in the following passage, where, in alluding to three eminent performers on different instruments, he says: 'These three illustrious personages were introduced at the Emperor's court,' etc.; speaking of them as if they were foreign ambassadors or princes of the blood, and thus magnifying himself and his profession. This overshadowing manner carries nearly everything before it, and mystifies a great many. There is nothing like putting the best face upon things, and leaving others to find out the difference. He who could call three musicians 'personages' would himself play a personage through life, and succeed in his leading object. Sir Joshua Reynolds, remarking on this passage, said: 'No one had a greater respect than he had for his profession, but that he should never think of applying to it epithets that were appropriated merely to external rank and distinction.' Madame d'Arblay, it must be owned, had cleverness enough to stock a whole family, and to set up her cousin-germans, male and female, for wits and virtuosos to the third and fourth generation. The rest have done nothing, that I know of, but keep up the name.

The most celebrated author in modern times has written without a name, and has been knighted for anonymous productions. Lord Byron complains that Horace Walpole was not properly appreciated, 'first, because he was a gentleman; and secondly, because he was a nobleman.' His Lordship stands in one, at least, of the predicaments here mentioned, and yet he has had justice, or somewhat more, done him. He towers above his fellows by all the height of the peerage. If the poet lends a grace to the nobleman, the nobleman pays it back to the poet with interest. What a fine addition is ten thousand a year and a title to the flaunting pretensions of a modern rhapsodist! His name so accompanied becomes the mouth well: it is repeated thousands of times, instead of hundreds, because the reader in being familiar with the Poet's works seems to claim acquaintance with the Lord.

        Let but a lord once own the happy lines:
        How the wit brightens, and the style refines!

He smiles at the high-flown praise or petty cavils of little men. Does he make a slip in decorum, which Milton declares to be the principal thing? His proud crest and armorial bearings support him: no bend-sinister slurs his poetical escutcheon! Is he dull, or does he put of some trashy production on the public? It is not charged to his account, as a deficiency which he must make good at the peril of his admirers. His Lordship is not answerable for the negligence or extravagances of his Muse. He 'bears a charmed reputation, which must not yield' like one of vulgar birth. The Noble Bard is for this reason scarcely vulnerable to the critics. The double barrier of his pretensions baffles their puny, timid efforts. Strip off some of his tarnished laurels, and the coronet appears glittering beneath: restore them, and it still shines through with keener lustre. In fact, his Lordship's blaze of reputation culminates from his rank and place in society. He sustains two lofty and imposing characters; and in order to simplify the process of our admiration, and 'leave no rubs or botches in the way,' we equalise his pretensions, and take it for granted that he must be as superior to other men in genius as he is in birth. Or, to give a more familiar solution of the enigma, the Poet and the Peer agree to honour each other's acceptances on the bank of Fame, and sometimes cozen the town to some tune between them. Really, however, and with all his privileges, Lord Byron might as well not have written that strange letter about Pope. I could not afford it, poor as I am. Why does he pronounce, *ex cathedra* and robed, that Cowper is no poet? Cowper was a gentleman and of noble family like his critic. He was a teacher of morality as well as a describer of nature, which is more than his Lordship is. His *John Gilpin* will last as long as *Beppo,* and his verses to Mary are not less touching than the *Farewell.* If I had ventured upon such an assertion as this, it would have been worse for me than finding out a borrowed line in the *Pleasures of Hope.*

There is not a more helpless or more despised animal than a mere author, without any extrinsic advantages of birth, breeding, or fortune to set him off. The real ore of talents or learning must be stamped before it will pass current. To be at all looked upon as an author, a man must be something more or less than an author—a rich merchant, a banker, a lord, or a ploughman. He is admired for something foreign to himself, that acts as a bribe to the servility or a set-off to the envy of the community. 'What should such fellows as we do, crawling betwixt heaven and earth';—'coining our hearts for drachmas'; now scorched in the sun, now shivering in the breeze, now coming out in our newest gloss and best attire, like swallows in the spring, now 'sent back like hollowmas or shortest day'? The best wits, like the handsomest faces *upon the town,* lead a harassing, precarious life—are taken up for the bud and promise of talent, which they no sooner fulfil than they are thrown aside like an old fashion—are caressed without reason, and insulted with impunity—are subject to all the caprice, the malice, and fulsome advances of that great keeper, the Public—and in the end come to no good, like all those who lavish their favours on mankind at large, and look to the gratitude of the world for their reward. Instead of this set of Grub Street authors, the mere *canaille* of letters, this corporation of Mendicity, this ragged regiment of genius suing at the corners of streets in *forma pauperis,* give me the gentleman and scholar, with a good house over his head and a handsome table 'with wine of Attic taste' to ask his friends to, and where want and sorrow never come. Fill up the sparkling bowl; heap high the dessert with roses crowned; bring out the hot-pressed poem, the vellum manuscripts, the medals, the portfolios, the intaglios—this is the true model of the life of a man of taste and *virtu*—the possessors, not the inventors of these things, are the true benefactors of mankind and ornaments of letters. Look in, and there, amidst silver services and shining chandeliers, you will see the man of genius at his proper post, picking his teeth and mincing an opinion, sheltered by rank, bowing to wealth—a poet framed, glazed, and hung in a striking light; not a straggling weed, torn and trampled on; not a poor *Kit-run-the-street,* but a powdered beau, a sycophant plant, an exotic reared in a glass case, hermetically sealed,

        Free from the Sirian star and the dread thunder-stroke

whose mealy coat no moth can corrupt nor blight can wither. The poet Keats had not this sort of protection for his person—he lay bare to weather—the serpent stung him, and the poison-tree dropped upon this little western flower: when the mercenary servile crew approached him, he had no pedigree to show them, no rent-roll to hold out in reversion for their praise: he was not in any great man's train, nor the butt and puppet of a lord—he could only offer them 'the fairest flowers of the season, carnations and streaked gilliflowers,'—'rue for remembrance and pansies for thoughts,'—they recked not of his gift, but tore him with hideous shouts and laughter,

        Nor could the Muse protect her son!

Unless an author has all establishment of his own, or is entered on that of some other person, he will hardly be allowed to write English or to spell his own name. To be well spoken of, he must enlist under some standard; he must belong to some *coterie.* He must get the *esprit de corps* on his side: he must have literary bail in readiness. Thus they prop up one another's rickety heads at Murray's shop, and a spurious reputation, like false argument, runs in a circle. Croker affirms that Gifford is sprightly, and Gifford that Croker is genteel; Disraeli that Jacob is wise, and Jacob that Disraeli is good-natured. A Member of Parliament must be answerable that you are not dangerous or dull before you can be of the *entree.* You must commence toad-eater to have your observations attended to; if you are independent, unconnected, you will be regarded as a poor creature. Your opinion is honest, you will say; then ten to one it is not profitable. It is at any rate your own. So much the worse; for then it is not the world's. Tom Hill is a very tolerable barometer in this respect. He knows nothing, hears everything, and repeats just what he hears; so that you may guess pretty well from this round-faced echo what is said by others! Almost everything goes by presumption and appearances. 'Did you not think Mr. B——'s language very elegant?'—I thought he bowed very low. 'Did you not think him remarkably well-behaved?'—He was unexceptionably dressed. 'But were not Mr. C——'s manners quite insinuating?'—He said nothing. "You will at least allow his friend to be a well-informed man."—talked upon all subjects alike. Such would be a pretty faithful interpretation of the tone of what is called *good society*. The surface is everything; we do not pierce to the core. The setting is more valuable than the jewel. Is it not so in other things as well as letters? Is not an R. A. by the supposition a greater man in his profession than any one who is not so blazoned? Compared with that unrivalled list, Raphael had been illegitimate, Claude not classical, and Michael Angelo admitted by special favour. What is a physician without a diploma? An alderman without being knighted? An actor whose name does not appear in great letters? All others are counterfeits—men 'of no mark or likelihood.' This was what made the Jackals of the North so eager to prove that I had been turned out of the *Edinburgh Review*. It was not the merit of the articles which excited their spleen—but their being there. Of the style they knew nothing; for the thought they cared nothing: all that they knew was that I wrote in that powerful journal, and therefore they asserted that I did not!

We find a class of persons who labour under an obvious natural inaptitude for whatever they aspire to. Their manner of setting about it is a virtual disqualification. The simple affirmation, 'What this man has said, I will do,' is not always considered as the proper test of capacity. On the contrary, there are people whose bare pretensions are as good or better than the actual performance of others. What I myself have done, for instance, I never find admitted as proof of what I shall be able to do: whereas I observe others who bring as proof of their competence to any task (and are taken at their word) what they have never done, and who gravely assure those who are inclined to trust them that their talents are exactly fitted for some post because they are just the reverse of what they have ever shown them to be. One man has the air of an Editor as much as another has that of a butler or porter in a gentleman's family. ——- is the model of this character, with a prodigious look of business, an air of suspicion which passes for sagacity, and an air of deliberation which passes for judgment. If his own talents are no ways prominent, it is inferred he will be more impartial and in earnest in making use of those of others. There is Britton, the responsible conductor of several works of taste and erudition, yet (God knows) without an idea in his head relating to any one of them. He is learned by proxy, and successful from sheer imbecility. If he were to get the smallest smattering of the departments which are under his control, he would betray himself from his desire to shine; but as it is, he leaves others to do all the drudgery for him. He signs his name in the title-page or at the bottom of a vignette, and nobody suspects any mistake. This contractor for useful and ornamental literature once offered me two guineas for a *Life and Character of Shakespear,* with an admission to his *converzationi.* I went once. There was a collection of learned lumber, of antiquaries, lexicographers, and other 'illustrious obscure,' and I had given up the day for lost, when in dropped Jack Taylor of the *Sun*—(who would dare to deny that he was 'the Sun of our table'?)—and I had nothing now to do but hear and laugh. Mr. Taylor knows most of the good things that have been said in the metropolis for the last thirty years, and is in particular an excellent retailer of the humours and extravagances of his old friend Peter Pindar. He had recounted a series of them, each rising above the other in a sort of magnificent burlesque and want of literal preciseness, to a medley of laughing and sour faces, when on his proceeding to state a joke of a practical nature by the said Peter, a Mr. ——- (I forget the name) objected to the moral of the story, and to the whole texture of Mr. Taylor's facetiae—upon which our host, who had till now supposed that all was going on swimmingly, thought it time to interfere and give a turn to the conversation by saying, 'Why, yes, gentlemen, what we have hitherto heard fall from the lips of our friend has been no doubt entertaining and highly agreeable in its way; but perhaps we have had enough of what is altogether delightful and pleasant and light and laughable in conduct. Suppose, therefore, we were to shift the subject, and talk of what is serious and moral and industrious and laudable in character—Let us talk of Mr. Tomkins the Penman!'—This staggered the gravest of us, broke up our dinner-party, and we went upstairs to tea. So much for the didactic vein of one of our principal guides in the embellished walks of modern taste, and master manufacturers of letters. He had found that gravity had been a never-failing resource when taken at a pinch—for once the joke miscarried—and Mr. Tomkins the Penman figures to this day nowhere but in Sir Joshua's picture of him!

To complete the natural Aristocracy of Letters, we only want a Royal Society of Authors!

FN to ESSAY V

(1) Lord Holland had made a diary (in the manner of Boswell) of the conversation held at his house, and read it at the end of a week *pro bono publico.* Sir James Mackintosh made a considerable figure in it, and a celebrated poet none at all, merely answering Yes and No. With this result he was by no means satisfied, and talked incessantly from that day forward. At the end of the week he asked, with some anxiety and triumph, If his Lordship had continued his diary, expecting himself to shine in 'the first row of the rubric.' To which his Noble Patron answered in the negative, with an intimation that it had not appeared to him worth while. Our poet was thus thrown again into the background, and Sir James remained master of the field!

ESSAY VI. ON CRITICISM

Criticism is an art that undergoes a great variety of changes, and aims at different objects at different times.

At first, it is generally satisfied to give an opinion whether a work is good or bad, and to quote a passage or two in support of this opinion: afterwards, it is bound to assign the reasons of its decision and to analyse supposed beauties or defects with microscopic minuteness. A critic does nothing nowadays who does not try to torture the most obvious expression into a thousand meanings, and enter into a circuitous explanation of all that can be urged for or against its being in the best or worst style possible. His object indeed is not to do justice to his author, whom he treats with very little ceremony, but to do himself homage, and to show his acquaintance with all the topics and resources of criticism. If he recurs to the stipulated subject in the end, it is not till after he has exhausted his budget of general knowledge; and he establishes his own claims first in an elaborate inaugural dissertation *de omni scibile et quibusdam aliis,* before he deigns to bring forward the pretensions of the original candidate for praise, who is only the second figure in the piece. We may sometimes see articles of this sort, in which no allusion whatever is made to the work under sentence of death, after the first announcement of the title-page; and I apprehend it would be a clear improvement on this species of nominal criticism to give stated periodical accounts of works that had never appeared at all, which would save the hapless author the mortification of writing, and his reviewer the trouble of reading them. If the real author is made of so little account by the modern critic, he is scarcely more an object of regard to the modern reader; and it must be confessed that after a dozen close-packed pages of subtle metaphysical distinction or solemn didactic declamation, in which the disembodied principles of all arts and sciences float before the imagination in undefined profusion, the eye turns with impatience and indifference to the imperfect embryo specimens of them, and the hopeless attempts to realise this splendid jargon in one poor work by one poor author, which is given up to summary execution with as little justice as pity. 'As when a well-graced actor leaves the stage, men's eyes are idly bent on him that enters next'—so it is here. Whether this state of the press is not a serious abuse and a violent encroachment in the republic of letters, is more than I shall pretend to determine. The truth is, that in the quantity of works that issue from the press, it is utterly impossible they should all be read by all sorts of people. There must be *tasters* for the public, who must have a discretionary power vested in them, for which it is difficult to make them properly accountable. Authors in proportion to their numbers become not formidable, but despicable. They would not be heard of or severed from the crowd without the critic's aid, and all complaints of ill-treatment are vain. He considers them as pensioners on his bounty for any pittance or praise, and in general sets them up as butts for his wit and spleen, or uses them as a stalking-horse to convey his own favourite notions and opinions, which he can do by this means without the possibility of censure or appeal. He looks upon his literary *protege* (much as Peter Pounce looked upon Parson Adams) as a kind of humble companion or unnecessary interloper in the vehicle of fame, whom he has taken up purely to oblige him, and whom he may treat with neglect or insult, or set down in the common footpath, whenever it suits his humour or convenience. He naturally grows arbitrary with the exercise of power. He by degrees wants to have a clear stage to himself, and would be thought to have purchased a monopoly of wit, learning, and wisdom—

Assumes the rod, affects the God,

And seems to shake the spheres.

Besides, something of this overbearing manner goes a great way with the public. They cannot exactly tell whether you are right or wrong; and if you state your difficulties or pay much deference to the sentiments of others, they will think you a very silly fellow or a mere pretender. A sweeping, unqualified assertion ends all controversy, and sets opinion at rest. A sharp, sententious, cavalier, dogmatical tone is therefore necessary, even in self-defence, to the office of a reviewer. If you do not deliver your oracles without hesitation, how are the world to receive them on trust and without inquiry? People read to have something to talk about, and 'to seem to know that which they do not.' Consequently, there cannot be too much dialectics and debatable matter, too much pomp and paradox, in a review. *To elevate and surprise* is the great rule for producing a dramatic or critical effect. The more you startle the reader, the more he will be able to startle others with a succession of smart intellectual shocks. The most admired of our Reviews is saturated with this sort of electrical matter, which is regularly played off so as to produce a good deal of astonishment and a strong sensation in the public mind. The intrinsic merits of an author are a question of very subordinate consideration to the keeping up the character of the work and supplying the town with a sufficient number of grave or brilliant topics for the consumption of the next three months!

This decided and paramount tone in criticism is the growth of the present century, and was not at all the fashion in that calm, peaceable period when the *Monthly Review* bore 'sole sovereign sway and masterdom' over all literary productions. Though nothing can be said against the respectability or usefulness of that publication during its long and almost exclusive enjoyment of the public favour, yet the style of criticism adopted in it is such as to appear slight and unsatisfactory to a modern reader. The writers, instead of 'outdoing termagant or out-Heroding Herod,' were somewhat precise and prudish, gentle almost to a fault, full of candour and modesty,

And of their port as meek as is a maid!(1)

There was none of that Drawcansir work going on then that there is now; no scalping of authors, no hacking and hewing of their Lives and Opinions, except that they used those of Tristram Shandy, gent., rather scurvily; which was to be expected. All, however, had a show of courtesy and good manners. The satire was covert and artfully insinuated; the praise was short and sweet. We meet with no oracular theories; no profound analysis of principles; no unsparing exposure of the least discernible deviation from them. It was deemed sufficient to recommend the work in general terms, 'This is an agreeable volume,' or 'This is a work of great learning and research,' to set forth the title and table of contents, and proceed without farther preface to some appropriate extracts, for the most part concurring in opinion with the author's text, but now and then interposing an objection to maintain appearances and assert the jurisdiction of the court. This cursory manner of hinting approbation or dissent would make but a lame figure at present. We must have not only an announcement that 'This is an agreeable or able work'; but we must have it explained at full length, and so as to silence all cavillers, in what the agreeableness or ability of the work consists: the author must be reduced to a class, all the living or defunct examples of which must be characteristically and pointedly *differenced* from one another; the value of this class of writing must be developed and ascertained in comparison with others; the principles of taste, the elements of our sensations, the structure of the human faculties, all must undergo a strict scrutiny and revision. The modern or metaphysical system of criticism, in short, supposes the question, *Why?* to be repeated at the end of every decision; and the answer gives birth to interminable arguments and discussion. The former laconic mode was well adapted to guide those who merely wanted to be informed of the character and subject of a work in order to read it: the present is more useful to those whose object is less to read the work than to dispute upon its merits, and go into company clad in the whole defensive and offensive armour of criticism.

Neither are we less removed at present from the dry and meagre mode of dissecting the skeletons of works, instead of transfusing their living principles, which prevailed in Dryden's Prefaces,(2) and in the criticisms written on the model of the French school about a century ago. A genuine criticism should, as I take it, reflect the colours, the light and shade, the soul and body of a work: here we have nothing but its superficial plan and elevation, as if a poem were a piece of formal architecture. We are told something of the plot or fable, of the moral, and of the observance or violation of the three unities of time, place, and action; and perhaps a word or two is added on the dignity of the persons or the baldness of the style; but we no more know, after reading one of these complacent *tirades*, what the essence of the work is, what passion has been touched, or how skilfully, what tone and movement the author's mind imparts to his subject or receives from it, than if we had been reading a homily or a gazette. That is, we are left quite in the dark as to the feelings of pleasure or pain to be derived from the genius of the performance or the manner in which it appeals to the imagination: we know to a nicety how it squares with the threadbare rules of composition, not in the least how it affects the principles of taste. We know everything about the work, and nothing of it. The critic takes good care not to baulk the reader's fancy by anticipating the effect which the author has aimed at producing. To be sure, the works so handled were often worthy of their commentators; they had the form of imagination without the life or power; and when any one had gone regularly through the number of acts into which they were divided, the measure in which they were written, or the story on which they were founded, there was little else to be said about them. It is curious to observe the effect which the *Paradise Lost* had on this class of critics, like throwing a tub to a whale: they could make nothing of it. 'It was out of all plumb—not one of the angles at the four corners was a right angle!' They did not seek for, nor would they much relish, the marrow of poetry it contained. Like polemics in religion, they had discarded the essentials of fine writing for the outward form and points of controversy. They were at issue with Genius and Nature by what route and in what garb they should enter the Temple of the Muses. Accordingly we find that Dryden had no other way of satisfying himself of the pretensions of Milton in the epic style but by translating his anomalous work into rhyme and dramatic dialogue.(3) So there are connoisseurs who give you the subject, the grouping, the perspective, and all the mechanical circumstances of a picture; but they never say a word about the expression. The reason is, they see the former, but not the latte taking an inventory of works of art (they want a faculty for higher studies), as there are works of art, so called, which seemed to have been composed expressly with an eye to such a class of connoisseurs. In them are to be found no recondite nameless beauties thrown away upon the stupid vulgar gaze; no 'graces snatched beyond the reach of art'; nothing but what the merest pretender may note down in good set terms in his common-place book, just as it is before him. Place one of these half-informed, imperfectly organised spectators before a tall canvas with groups on groups of figures, of the size of life, and engaged in a complicated action, of which they know the name and all the particulars, and there are no bounds to their burst of involuntary enthusiasm. They mount on the stilts of the subject and ascend the highest Heaven of Invention, from whence they see sights and hear revelations which they communicate with all the fervour of plenary explanation to those who may be disposed to attend to their raptures. They float with wings expanded in lofty circles, they stalk over the canvas at large strides, never condescending to pause at anything of less magnitude than a group or a colossal figure. The face forms no part of their collective inquiries; or so that it occupies only a sixth or an eighth proportion to the whole body, all is according to the received rules of composition. Point to a divine portrait of Titian, to an angelic head of Guido, close by—they see and heed it not. What are the 'looks commercing with the skies,' the soul speaking in the face, to them? It asks another and an inner sense to comprehend them; but for the trigonometry of painting, nature has constituted them indifferently well. They take a stand on the distinction between portrait and history, and there they are spell-bound. Tell them that there can be no fine history without portraiture, that the painter must proceed from that ground to the one above it, and that a hundred bad heads cannot make one good historical picture, and they will not believe you, though the thing is obvious to any gross capacity. Their ideas always fly to the circumference, and never fix at the centre. Art must be on a grand scale; according to them, the whole is greater than a part, and the greater necessarily implies the less. The outline is, in this view of the matter, the same thing as the filling-up, and 'the limbs and flourishes of a discourse' the substance. Again, the same persons make an absolute distinction, without knowing why, between high and low subjects. Say that you would as soon have Murillo's Two Beggar Boys at the Dulwich Gallery as almost any picture in the world, that is, that it would be one you would choose out of ten (had you the choice), and they reiterate upon you that surely a low subject cannot be of equal value with a high one. It is in vain that you turn to the picture: they keep to the class. They have eyes, but see not; and, upon their principles of refined taste, would be just as good judges of the merit of the picture without seeing it as with that supposed advantage. They know what the subject is *from the catalogue!*—Yet it is not true, as Lord Byron asserts, that execution is everything, and the class or subject nothing. The highest subjects, equally well executed (which, however, rarely happens), are the best. But the power of execution, the manner of seeing nature, is one thing, and may be so superlative (if you are only able to judge of it) as to countervail every disadvantage of subject. Raphael's storks in the Miraculous Draught of Fishes, exulting in the event, are finer than the head of Christ would have been in almost any other hands. The cant of criticism is on the other side of the question; because execution depends on various degrees of power in the artist, and a knowledge of it on various degrees of feeling and discrimination in you; but to commence artist or connoisseur in the grand style at once, without any distinction of qualifications whatever, it is only necessary for the first to choose his subject and for the last to pin his faith on the sublimity of the performance, for both to look down with ineffable contempt on the painters and admirers of subjects of low life. I remember a young Scotchman once trying to prove to me that Mrs. Dickons was a superior singer to Miss Stephens, because the former excelled in sacred music and the latter did not. At that rate, that is, if it is the singing sacred music that gives the preference, Miss Stephens would only have to sing sacred music to surpass herself and vie with her pretended rival; for this theory implies that all sacred music is equally good, and, therefore, better than any other. I grant that Madame Catalani's singing of sacred music is superior to Miss Stephens's ballad-strains, because her singing is better altogether, and an ocean of sound more wonderful than a simple stream of dulcet harmonies. In singing the last verse of 'God Save the King' not long ago her voice towered above the whole confused noise of the orchestra like an eagle piercing the clouds, and poured 'such sweet thunder' through the ear as excited equal astonishment and rapture!

Some kinds of criticism are as much too insipid as others are too pragmatical. It is not easy to combine point with solidity, spirit with moderation and candour. Many persons see nothing but beauties in a work, others nothing but defects. Those cloy you with sweets, and are 'the very milk of human kindness,' flowing on in a stream of luscious panegyrics; these take delight in poisoning the sources of your satisfaction, and putting you out of conceit with nearly every author that comes in their way. The first are frequently actuated by personal friendship, the last by all the virulence of party spirit. Under the latter head would fall what may be termed *political criticism.* The basis of this style of writing is a *caput mortuum* of impotent spite and dulness, till it is varnished over with the slime of servility, and thrown into a state of unnatural activity by the venom of the most rancorous bigotry. The eminent professors in this grovelling department are at first merely out of sorts with themselves, and vent their spleen in little interjections and contortions of phrase—cry *Pish* at a lucky hit, and *Hem* at a fault, are smart on personal defects, and sneer at 'Beauty out of favour and on crutches'—are thrown into an ague-fit by hearing the name of a rival, start back with horror at any approach to their morbid pretensions, like Justice Woodcock with his gouty limbs—rifle the flowers of the Della Cruscan school, and give you in their stead, as models of a pleasing pastoral style, Verses upon Anna—which you may see in the notes to the *Baviad* and *Maeviad.* All this is like the fable of 'The Kitten and the Leaves.' But when they get their brass collar on and shake their bells of office, they set up their backs like the Great Cat Rodilardus, and pounce upon men and things. Woe to any little heedless reptile of an author that ventures across their path without a safe-conduct from the Board of Control. They snap him up at a mouthful, and sit licking their lips, stroking their whiskers, and rattling their bells over the imaginary fragments of their devoted prey, to the alarm and astonishment of the whole breed of literary, philosophical, and revolutionary vermin that were naturalised in this country by a

Prince of Orange and an Elector of Hanover a hundred years ago.(4) When one of these pampered, sleek, 'demure-looking, spring-nailed, velvet-pawed, green-eyed' critics makes his King and Country parties to this sort of sport literary, you have not much chance of escaping out of his clutches in a whole skin. Treachery becomes a principle with them, and mischief a conscience, that is, a livelihood. They not only *damn* the work in the lump, but vilify and traduce the author, and substitute lying abuse and sheer malignity for sense and satire. To have written a popular work is as much as a man's character is worth, and sometimes his life, if he does not happen to be on the right side of the question. The way in which they set about *stultifying* an adversary is not to accuse you of faults, or to exaggerate those which you may really have, but they deny that you have any merits at all, least of all those that the world have given you credit for; bless themselves from understanding a single sentence in a whole volume; and unless you are ready to subscribe to all their articles of peace, will not allow you to be qualified to write your own name. It is not a question of literary discussion, but of political proscription. It is a mark of loyalty and patriotism to extend no quarter to those of the opposite party. Instead of replying to your arguments, they call you names, put words and opinions into your mouth which you have never uttered, and consider it a species of misprision of treason to admit that a Whig author knows anything of common sense or English. The only chance of putting a stop to this unfair mode of dealing would perhaps be to make a few reprisals by way of example. The Court party boast some writers who have a reputation to lose, and who would not like to have their names dragged through the kennel of dirty abuse and vulgar obloquy. What silenced the masked battery of *Blackwood's Magazine* was the implication of the name of Sir Walter Scott in some remarks upon it—(an honour of which it seems that extraordinary person was not ambitious)—to be 'pilloried on infamy's high stage' was a distinction and an amusement to the other gentlemen concerned in that praiseworthy publication. I was complaining not long ago of this prostitution of literary criticism as peculiar to our own times, when I was told that it was just as bad in the time of Pope and Dryden, and indeed worse, inasmuch as we have no Popes or Drydens now on the obnoxious side to be nicknamed, metamorphosed into scarecrows, and impaled alive by bigots and dunces. I shall not pretend to say how far this remark may be true. The English (it must be owned) are rather a foul-mouthed nation.

Besides temporary or accidental biases of this kind, there seem to be sects and parties in taste and criticism (with a set of appropriate watchwords) coeval with the arts of composition, and that will last as long as the difference with which men's minds are originally constituted. There are some who are all for the elegance of an author's style, and some who are equally delighted with simplicity. The last refer you to Swift as a model of English prose, thinking all other writers sophisticated and naught; the former prefer the more ornamented and sparkling periods of Junius or Gibbon. It is to no purpose to think of bringing about an understanding between these opposite factions. It is a natural difference of temperament and constitution of mind. The one will never relish the antithetical point and perpetual glitter of the artificial prose style; as the plain, unperverted English idiom will always appear trite and insipid to the others. A toleration, not an uniformity of opinion, is as much as can be expected in this case; and both sides may acknowledge, without imputation on their taste or consistency, that these different writers excelled each in their way. I might remark here that the epithet *elegant* is very sparingly used in modern criticism. It has probably gone out of fashion with the appearance of the *Lake School*, who, I apprehend, have no such phrase in their vocabulary. Mr. Rogers was, I think, almost the last poet to whom it was applied as a characteristic compliment. At present it would be considered as a sort of diminutive of the title of poet, like the terms *pretty* or *fanciful*, and is banished from the *haut ton* of letters. It may perhaps come into request at some future period. Again, the dispute between the admirers of Homer and Virgil has never been settled and never will, for there will always be minds to whom the excellences of Virgil will be more congenial, and therefore more objects of admiration and delight than those of Homer, and *vice versa*. Both are right in preferring what suits them best, the delicacy and selectness of the one, or the fulness and majestic flow of the other. There is the same difference in their tastes that there was in the genius of their two favourites. Neither can the disagreement between the French and English school of tragedy ever be reconciled till the French become English or the English French.(5) Both are right in what they admire, both are wrong in condemning the others for what they admire. We see the defects of Racine, they see the faults of Shakespear probably in an exaggerated point of view. But we may be sure of this, that when we see nothing but grossness and barbarism, or insipidity and verbiage, in a writer that is the god of a nation's idolatry, it is we and not they who want true taste and feeling. The controversy about Pope and the opposite school in our own poetry comes to much the same thing. Pope's correctness, smoothness, etc., are very good things and much to be commended in him. But it is not to be expected or even desired that others should have these qualities in the same paramount degree, to the exclusion of everything else. If you like correctness and smoothness of all things in the world, there they are for you in Pope. If you like other things better, such as strength and sublimity, you know where to go for them. Why trouble Pope or any other author for what they have not, and do not profess to give? Those who seem to imply that Pope possessed, besides his own peculiar, exquisite merits, all that is to be found in Shakespear or Milton, are, I should hardly think, in good earnest. But I do not therefore see that, because this was not the case, Pope was no poet. We cannot by a little verbal sophistry confound the qualities of different minds, nor force opposite excellences into a union by all the intolerance in the world. We may pull Pope in pieces as long as we please for not being Shakespear or Milton, as we may carp at them for not being Pope, but this will not make a poet equal to all three. If we have a taste for some one precise style or manner, we may keep it to ourselves and let others have theirs. If we are more catho and beauty, it is spread abroad for us to profusion in the variety of books and in the several growth of men's minds, fettered by no capricious or arbitrary rules. Those who would proscribe whatever falls short of a given standard of imaginary perfection do so, not from a higher capacity of taste or range of intellect than others, but to destroy, to 'crib and cabin in' all enjoyments and opinions but their own.

We find people of a decided and original, and others of a more general and versatile taste. I have sometimes thought that the most acute and original-minded men made bad critics. They see everything too much through a particular medium. What does not fall in with their own bias and mode of composition strikes them as common-place and factitious. What does not come into the direct line of their vision, they regard idly, with vacant, 'lack-lustre eye.' The extreme force of their original impressions, compared with the feebleness of those they receive at second-hand from others, oversets the balance and just proportion of their minds. Men who have fewer native resources, and are obliged to apply oftener to the general stock, acquire by habit a greater aptitude in appreciating what they owe to others. Their taste is not made a sacrifice to their egotism and vanity, and they enrich the soil of their minds with continual accessions of borrowed strength and beauty. I might take this opportunity of observing, that the person of the most refined and least contracted taste I ever knew was the late Joseph Fawcett, the friend of my youth. He was almost the first literary acquaintance I ever made, and I think the most candid and unsophisticated. He had a masterly perception of all styles and of every kind and degree of excellence, sublime or beautiful, from Milton's

Paradise Lost to Shenstone's *Pastoral Ballad,* from Butler's *Analogy* down to *Humphrey Clinker.* If you had a favourite author, he had read him too, and knew all the best morsels, the subtle traits, the capital touches. 'Do you like Sterne?' 'Yes, to be sure,' he would say; 'I should deserve to be hanged if I didn't!' His repeating some parts of *Comus* with his fine, deep, mellow-toned voice, particularly the lines, 'I have heard my mother Circe with the Sirens three,' etc., and the enthusiastic comments he made afterwards, were a feast to the ear and to the soul. He read the poetry of Milton with the same fervour and spirit of devotion that I have since heard others read their own. 'That is the most delicious feeling of all,' I have heard him explain, 'to like what is excellent, no matter whose it is.' In this respect he practised what he preached. He was incapable of harbouring a sinister motive, and judged only from what he felt. There was no flaw or mist in the clear mirror of his mind. He was as open to impressions as he was strenuous in maintaining them. He did not care a rush whether a writer was old or new, in prose or in verse—'What he wanted,' he said, 'was something to make him think.' Most men's minds are to me like musical instruments out of tune. Touch a particular key, and it jars and makes harsh discord with your own. They like *Gil Blas,* but can see nothing to laugh at in *Don Quixote:* they adore Richardson, but are disgusted with Fielding. Fawcett had a taste accommodated to all these. He was not exceptious. He gave a cordial welcome to all sort, provided they were the best in their kind. He was not fond of counterfeits or duplicates. His own style was laboured and artificial to a fault, while his character was frank and ingenuous in the extreme. He was not the only individual whom I have known to counteract their natural disposition in coming before the public, and by avoiding what they perhaps thought an inherent infirmity, debar themselves of their real strength and advantages. A heartier friend or honester critic I never coped withal. He has made me feel (by contrast) the want of genuine sincerity and generous sentiment in some that I have listened to since, and convinced me (if practical proof were wanting) of the truth of that text of Scripture—'That had I all knowledge and could speak with the tongues of angels, yet without charity I were nothing!' I would rather be a man of disinterested taste and liberal feeling, to see and acknowledge truth and beauty wherever I found it, than a man of greater and more original genius, to hate, envy, and deny all excellence but my own—but that poor scanty pittance of it (compared with the whole) which I had myself produced!

There is another race of critics who might be designated as the *Occult School*—*vere adepti.* They discern no beauties but what are concealed from superficial eyes, and overlook all that are obvious to the vulgar part of mankind. Their art is the transmutation of styles. By happy alchemy of mind they convert dross into gold—and gold into tinsel. They see farther into a millstone than most others. If an author is utterly unreadable, they can read him for ever: his intricacies are their delight, his mysteries are their study. They prefer Sir Thomas Browne to the *Rambler* by Dr. Johnson, and Burton's *Anatomy of Melancholy* to all the writers of the Georgian Age. They judge of works of genius as misers do of hid treasure—it is of no value unless they have it all to themselves. They will no more share a book than a mistress with a friend. If they suspected their favourite volumes of delighting any eyes but their own, they would immediately discard them from the list. Theirs are superannuated beauties that every one else has left off intriguing with, bedridden hags, a 'stud of nightmares.' This is not envy or affectation, but a natural proneness to singularity, a love of what is odd and out of the way. They must come at their pleasures with difficulty, and support admiration by an uneasy sense of ridicule and opposition. They despise those qualities in a work which are cheap and obvious. They like a monopoly of taste and are shocked at the prostitution of intellect implied in popular productions. In like manner, they would choose a friend or recommend a mistress for gross defects; and tolerate the sweetness of an actress's voice only for the ugliness of her face. Pure pleasures are in their judgment cloying and insipid—

    An ounce of sour is worth a pound of sweet!

Nothing goes down with them but what is *caviare* to the multitude. They are eaters of olives and readers of black-letter. Yet they smack of genius, and would be worth any money, were it only for the rarity of the thing!

The last sort I shall mention are *verbal critics*—mere word-catchers, fellows that pick out a word in a sentence and a sentence in a volume, and tell you it is wrong.(6) These erudite persons constantly find out by anticipation that you are deficient in the smallest things— that you cannot spell certain words or join the nominative case and the verb together, because to do this is the height of their own ambition, and of course they must set you down lower than their opinion of themselves. They degrade by reducing you to their own standard of merit; for the qualifications they deny you, or the faults they object, are so very insignificant, that to prove yourself possessed of the one or free from the other is to make yourself doubly ridiculous. Littleness is their element, and they give a character of meanness to whatever they touch. They creep, buzz, and fly-blow. It is much easier to crush than to catch these troublesome insects; and when they are in your power your self-respect spares them. The race is almost extinct:—one or two of them are sometimes seen crawling over the pages of the *Quarterly Review!*

FN to ESSAY VI

(1) A Mr. Rose and the Rev. Dr. Kippis were for many years its principal support. Mrs. Rose (I have heard my father say) contributed the Monthly Catalogue. There is sometimes a certain tartness and the woman's tongue in it. It is said of Gray's *Elegy*, 'This little poem, however humble its pretensions, is not without elegance or merit.' The characters of prophet and critic are not always united.

(2) There are some splendid exceptions to this censure. His comparison between Ovid and Virgil and his character of Shakespear are masterpieces of their kind.

(3) We have critics In the present day (1821) who cannot tell what to make of the tragic writers of Queen Elizabeth's age (except Shakespear, who passes by prescriptive right), and are extremely puzzled to reduce the efforts of their 'great and irregular' power to the standard of their own slight and showy common-places. The truth is, they had better give up the attempt to reconcile such contradictions as an artificial taste and natural genius; and repose on the admiration of verses which derive their odour from the scent of rose leaves inserted between the pages, and their polish from the smoothness of the paper on which they are printed. They, and such writers as Decker, and Webster, Beaumont and Fletcher, Ford and Marlowe, move in different orbits of the human intellect, and need never jostle.

(4) The intelligent reader will be pleased to understand that there is here a tacit allusion to Squire Western's significant phrase of *Hanover Rats.*

(5) Of the two the latter alternative is more likely to happen. We abuse and imitate them. They laugh at, but do not imitate us.

(6) The title of *Ultra-Crepidarian critics* has been given to a variety of this species.

ESSAY VII. ON GREAT AND LITTLE THINGS

These little things are great to little man.
—Goldsmith.

The great and the little have, no doubt, a real existence in the nature of things; but they both find pretty much the same level in the mind of man. It is a common measure, which does not always accommodate itself to the size and importance of the objects it represents. It has a certain interest to spare for certain things (and no more) according to its humour and capacity; and neither likes to be stinted in its allowance, nor to muster up an unusual share of sympathy, just as the occasion may require. Perhaps, if we could recollect distinctly, we should discover that the two things that have affected us most in the course of our lives have been, one of them of the greatest, and the other of the smallest possible consequence. To let that pass as too fine a speculation, we know well enough that very trifling circumstances do give us great and daily annoyance, and as often prove too much for our philosophy and forbearance, as matters of the highest moment. A lump of soot spoiling a man's dinner, a plate of toast falling in the ashes, the being disappointed of a ribbon to a cap or a ticket for a ball, have led to serious and almost tragical consequences. Friends not unfrequently fall out and never meet again for some idle misunderstanding, 'some trick not worth an egg,' who have stood the shock of serious differences of opinion and clashing interests in life; and there is an excellent paper in the *Tatler*, to prove that if a married couple do not quarrel about some point in the first instance not worth contesting, they will seldom find an opportunity afterwards to quarrel about a question of real importance. Grave divines, great statesmen, and deep philosophers are put out of their way by very little things: nay, discreet, worthy people, without any pretensions but to good-nature and common sense, readily surrender the happiness of their whole lives sooner than give up an opinion to which they have committed themselves, though in all likelihood it was the mere turn of a feather which side they should take in the argument. It is the being baulked or thwarted in anything that constitutes the grievance, the unpardonable affront, not the value of the thing to which we had made up our minds. Is it that we despise little things; that we are not prepared for them; that they take us in our careless, unguarded moments, and tease us out of our ordinary patience by their petty, incessant, insect warfare, buzzing about us and stinging us like gnats, so that we can neither get rid of nor grapple with them; whereas we collect all our fortitude and resolution to meet evils of greater magnitude? Or is it that there is a certain stream of irritability that is continually fretting upon the wheels of life, which finds sufficient food to play with in straws and feathers, while great objects are too much for it, either choke it up, or divert its course into serious and thoughtful interest? Some attempt might be made to explain this in the following manner.

One is always more vexed at losing a game of any sort by a single hole or ace than if one has never had a chance of winning it. This is no doubt in part or chiefly because the prospect of success irritates the subsequent disappointment. But people have been known to pine and fall sick from holding the next number to the twenty thousand pound prize in the lottery. Now this could only arise from their being so near winning in fancy, from there seeming to be so thin a partition between them and success. When they were within one of the right number, why could they not have taken the next—it was so easy: this haunts their minds and will not let them rest, notwithstanding the absurdity of the reasoning. It is that the will here has a slight imaginary obstacle to surmount to attain its end; it should appear it had only an exceedingly trifling effort to make for this purpose, that it was absolutely in its power (had it known) to seize the envied prize, and it is continually harassing itself by making the obvious transition from one number to the other, when it is too late. That is to say, the will acts in proportion to its fancied power, to its superiority over immediate obstacles. Now in little or indifferent matters there seems no reason why it should not have its own way, and therefore a disappointment vexes it the more. It grows angry according to the insignificance of the occasion, and frets itself to death about an object, merely because from its very futility there can be supposed to be no real difficulty in the way of its attainment, nor anything more required for this purpose than a determination of the will. The being baulked of this throws the mind off its balance, or puts it into what is called *a passion;* and as nothing but an act of voluntary power still seems necessary to get rid of every impediment, we indulge our violence more and more, and heighten our impatience by degrees into a sort of frenzy. The object is the same as it was, but we are no longer as we were. The blood is heated, the muscles are strained. The feelings are wound up to a pitch of agony with the vain strife. The temper is tried to the utmost it will bear. The more contemptible the object or the obstructions in the way to it, the more are we provoked at being hindered by them. It looks like witchcraft. We fancy there is a spell upon us, so that we are hampered by straws and entangled in cobwebs. We believe that there is a fatality about our affairs. It is evidently done on purpose to plague us. A demon is at our elbow to torment and defeat us in everything, even in the smallest things. We see him sitting and mocking us, and we rave and gnash our teeth at him in return. It is particularly hard that we cannot succeed in any one point, however trifling, that we set our hearts on. We are the sport of imbecility and mischance. We make another desperate effort, and fly out into all the extravagance of impotent rage once more. Our anger runs away with our reason, because, as there is little to give it birth, there is nothing to check it or recall us to our senses in the prospect of consequences. We take up and rend in pieces the mere toys of humour, as the gusts of wind take up and whirl about chaff and stubble. Passion plays the tyrant, in a grand tragi-comic style, over the Lilliputian difficulties and petty disappointments it has to encounter, gives way to all the fretfulness of grief and all the turbulence of resentment, makes a fuss about nothing because there is nothing to make a fuss about—when an impending calamity, an irretrievable loss, would instantly bring it to its recollection, and tame it in its preposterous career. A man may be in a great passion and give himself strange airs at so simple a thing as a game at ball, for instance; may rage like a wild beast, and be ready to dash his head against the wall about nothing, or about that which he will laugh at the next minute, and think no more of ten minutes after, at the same time that a good smart blow from the ball, the effects of which he might feel as a serious inconvenience for a month, would calm him directly—

Anon as patient as the female dove,
His silence will sit drooping.

85

The truth is, we pamper little griefs into great ones, and bear great ones as well as we can. We can afford to dally and play tricks with the one, but the others we have enough to do with, without any of the wantonness and bombast of passion—without the swaggering of Pistol or the insolence of King Cambyses' vein. To great evils we submit; we resent little provocations. I have before now been disappointed of a hundred pound job and lost half a crown at rackets on the same day, and been more mortified at the latter than the former. That which is lasting we share with the future, we defer the consideration of till to-morrow: that which belongs to the moment we drink up in all its bitterness, before the spirit evaporates. We probe minute mischiefs to the quick; we lacerate, tear, and mangle our bosoms with misfortune's finest, brittlest point, and wreak our vengeance on ourselves and it for good and all. Small pains are more manageable, ore within our reach; we can fret and worry ourselves about them, can turn them into any shape, can twist and torture them how we please:—a grain of sand in the eye, a thorn in the flesh, only irritates the part, and leaves us strength enough to quarrel and get out of all patience with it: a heavy blow stuns and takes away all power of sense as well as of resistance. The great and mighty reverses of fortune, like the revolutions of nature, may be said to carry their own weight and reason along with them: they seem unavoidable and remediless, and we submit to them without murmuring as to a fatal necessity. The magnitude of the events in which we may happen to be concerned fills the mind, and carries it out of itself, as it were, into the page of history. Our thoughts are expanded with the scene on which we have to act, and lend us strength to disregard our own personal share in it. Some men are indifferent to the stroke of fate, as before and after earthquakes there is a calm in the air. From the commanding situation whence they have been accustomed to view things, they look down at themselves as only a part of the whole, and can abstract their minds from the pressure of misfortune, by the aid of its very violence. They are projected, in the explosion of events, into a different sphere, far from their former thoughts, purposes, and passions. The greatness of the change anticipates the slow effects of time and reflection:—they at once contemplate themselves from an immense distance, and look up with speculative wonder at the height on which they stood. Had the downfall been less complete, it would have been more galling and borne with less resignation, because there might still be a chance of remedying it by farther efforts and farther endurance—but past cure, past hope. It is chiefly this cause (together with something of constitutional character) which has enabled the greatest man in modern history to bear his reverses of fortune with gay magnanimity, and to submit to the loss of the empire of the world with as little discomposure as if he had been playing a game at chess.(1) This does not prove by our theory that he did not use to fly into violent passions with Talleyrand for plaguing him with bad news when things went wrong. He was mad at uncertain forebodings of disaster, but resigned to its consummation. A man may dislike impertinence, yet have no quarrel with necessity!

There is another consideration that may take off our wonder at the firmness with which the principals in great vicissitudes of fortune bear their fate, which is, that they are in the secret of its operations, and know that what to others appears chance-medley was unavoidable. The clearness of their perception of all the circumstances converts the uneasiness of doubt into certainty: they have not the qualms of conscience which their admirers have, who cannot tell how much of the event is to be attributed to the leaders, and how much to unforeseen accidents: they are aware either that the result was not to be helped, or that they did all they could to prevent it.

> Si Pergarna dextra
> Defendi possent, etiam hac defensa fuissent.

It is the mist and obscurity through which we view objects that makes us fancy they might have been or might still be otherwise, The precise knowledge of antecedents and consequents makes men practical as well as philosophical Necessarians.—It is the want of this knowledge which is the principle and soul of gambling, and of all games of chance or partial skill. The supposition is, that the issue is uncertain, and that there is no positive means of ascertaining it. It is dependent on the turn of a die, on the tossing up of a halfpenny: to be fair it must be a lottery; there is no knowing but by the event; and it is this which keeps the interest alive, and works up the passion little short of madness. There is all the agitation of suspense, all the alternation of hope and fear, of good and bad success, all the eagerness of desire, without the possibility of reducing this to calculation, that is, of subjecting the increased action of the will to a known rule, or restraining the excesses of passion within the bounds of reason. We see no cause beforehand why the run of the cards should not be in our favour: we will hear of none afterwards why it should not have been so. As in the absence of all data to judge by, we wantonly fill up the blank with the most extravagant expectations, so, when all is over, we obstinately recur to the chance we had previously. There is nothing to tame us down to the event, nothing to reconcile us to our hard luck, for so we think it. We see no reason why we failed (and there was none, any more than why we should succeed)—we think that, reason apart, our will is the next best thing; we still try to have it our own way, and fret, torment, and harrow ourselves up with vain imaginations to effect impossibilities.(2) We play the game over again: we wonder how it was possible for us to fail. We turn our brain with straining at contradictions, and striving to make things what they are not, or, in other words, to subject the course of nature to our fastastical wishes. *'If it had been so—if we had done such and such a thing'*—we try it in a thousand different ways, and are just as far off the mark as ever. We appealed to chance in the first instance, and yet, when it has decided against us, we will not give in, and sit down contented with our loss, but refuse to submit to anything but reason, which has nothing to do with the matter. In drawing two straws, for example, to see which is the longest, there was no apparent necessity we should fix upon the wrong one, it was so easy to have fixed upon the other, nay, at one time we were going to do it—if we had,—the mind thus runs back to what was so possible and feasible at one time, while the thing was pending, and would fain give a bias to causes so slender and insignificant, as the skittle-player bends his body to give a bias to the bowl he has already delivered from his hand, not considering that what is once determined, be the causes ever so trivial or evanescent, is in the individual instance unalterable. Indeed, to be a great philosopher, in the practical and most important sense of the term, little more seems necessary than to be convinced of the truth of the maxim which the wise man repeated to the daughter of King Cophetua, *That if a thing is, it is,* and there is an end of it!

We often make life unhappy in wishing things to have turned out otherwise than they did, merely because that is possible to the imagination, which is impossible in fact. I remember, when Lamb's farce was damned (for damned it was, that's certain), I used to dream every night for a month after (and then I vowed I would plague myself no more about it) that it was revived at one of the minor or provincial theatres with great success, that such and such retrenchments and alterations had been made in it, and that it was thought *it might do at the other House.* I had heard indeed (this was told in confidence to Lamb) that *Gentleman* Lewis was present on the night of its performance, and said that if he had had it he would have made it, by a few judicious curtailments, 'the most popular little thing that had been brought out for some time.' How often did I conjure up in recollection the full diapason of applause at the end of the *Prologue,* and hear my ingenious friend in the first row of the pit roar with laughter at his own wit! Then I dwelt with forced complacency on some part in which it had been doing well: then we would consider (in concert) whether the long tedious opera of the *Travellers*, which preceded it, had not tired people beforehand, so that they had not spirits left for the quaint and sparkling 'wit skirmishes' of the dialogue; and we all agreed it might have gone down after a tragedy, except Lamb himself, who swore he had no hopes of it from the beginning, and that he knew the name of the hero when it came to be discovered could not be got over. Mr. *H——, thou wert damned! Bright shone the morning on the play-bills that announced thy appearance, and the streets were filled with the buzz of persons asking one another if they would go to see *Mr. H——*, and answering that they would certainly; but before night the gaiety, not of the author, but of his friends and the town was eclipsed, for thou were damned! Hadst thou been anonymous thou haply mightst have lived. But thou didst come to an untimely end for thy tricks, and for want of a better name to pass them off!

In this manner we go back to the critical minutes on which the turn of our fate, or that of any one else in whom we are interested; depended; try them over again with new knowledge and sharpened sensibility; and thus think to alter what is irrevocable, and ease for a moment the pang of lasting regret. So in a game at rackets(3) (to compare small things with great), I think if at such a point I had followed up my success, if I had not been too secure or over-anxious in another part, if I had played for such an opening—in short, if I had done anything but what I did and what has proved unfortunate in the result, the chances were all in my favour. But it is merely because I do not know what would have happened in the other case that I interpret it so readily to my own advantage. I have sometimes lain awake a whole night, trying to serve out the last ball of an interesting game in a particular corner of the court, which I had missed from a nervous feeling. Rackets (I might observe, for the sake of the uninformed reader) is, like any other athletic game, very much a thing of skill and practice; but it is also a thing of opinion, 'subject to all the skyey influences.' If you think you can win, you can win. Faith is necessary to victory. If you hesitate in striking at the ball, it is ten to one but you miss it. If you are apprehensive of committing some particular error (such as striking the ball *foul*) you will be nearly sure to do it. While thinking of that which you are so earnestly bent upon avoiding, your hand mechanically follows the strongest idea, and obeys the imagination rather than the intention of the striker. A run of luck is a forerunner of success, and courage is as much wanted as skill. No one is, however, free from nervous sensations at times. A good player may not be able to strike a single stroke if another comes into the court that he has a particular dread of; and it frequently so happens that a player cannot beat another, even though he can give half the game to an equal player, because he has some associations of jealousy or personal pique against the first which he has not towards the last. *Sed haec hactenus.* Chess is a game I do not understand, and have not comprehension enough to play at. But I believe, though it is so much less a thing of chance than science or skill, eager players pass whole nights in marching and countermarching their men and checkmating a successful adversary, supposing that at a certain point of the game they had determined upon making a particular move instead of the one which they actually did make. I have heard a story of two persons playing at backgammon, one of whom was so enraged at losing his match at a particular point of the game that he took the board and threw it out of the window. It fell upon the head of one of the passengers in the street, who came up to demand instant satisfaction for the affront and injury he had sustained. The losing gamester only asked him if he understood backgammon, and finding that he did, said, that if upon seeing the state of the game he did not excuse the extravagance of his conduct, he would give him any other satisfaction he wished for. The tables were accordingly brought, and the situation of the two contending parties being explained, the gentleman put up his sword and went away perfectly satisfied. To return from this, which to some will seem a digression, and to others will serve as a confirmation of the doctrine I am insisting on.

It is not, then, the value of the object, but the time and pains bestowed upon it, that determines the sense and degree of our loss. Many men set their minds only on trifles, and have not a compass of soul to take an interest in anything truly great and important beyond forms and minutiae. Such persons are really men of little minds, or may be complimented with the title of great children,

    Pleased with a feather, tickled with a straw.

Larger objects elude their grasp, while they fasten eagerly on the light and insignificant. They fidget themselves and others to death with incessant anxiety about nothing. A part of their dress that is awry keeps them in a fever of restlessness and impatience; they sit picking their teeth, or paring their nails, or stirring the fire, or brushing a speck of dirt off their coats, while the house or the world tumbling about their ears would not rouse them from their morbid insensibility. They cannot sit still on their chairs for their lives, though if there were anything for them to do they would become immovable. Their nerves are as irritable as their imaginations are callous and inert. They are addicted to an inveterate habit of littleness and perversity, which rejects every other motive to action or object of contemplation but the daily, teasing, contemptible, familiar, favourite sources of uneasiness and dissatisfaction. When they are of a sanguine instead of a morbid temperament, they become *quid-nuncs* and virtuosos—collectors of caterpillars and odd volumes, makers of fishing-rods and curious in watch-chains. Will Wimble dabbled in this way, to his immortal honour. But many others have been less successful. There are those who build their fame on epigrams or epitaphs, and others who devote their lives to writing the Lord's Prayer in little. Some poets compose and sing their own verses. Which character would they have us think most highly of—the poet or the musician? The Great is One. Some there are who feel more pride in sealing a letter with a head of Homer than ever that old blind bard did in reciting his *Iliad*. These raise a huge opinion of themselves out of nothing, as there are those who shrink from their own merits into the shade of unconquerable humility. I know one person at least, who would rather be the author of an unsuccessful farce than of a successful tragedy. Repeated mortification has produced an inverted ambition in his mind, and made failure the bitter test of desert. He cannot lift his drooping head to gaze on the gaudy crown of popularity placed within his reach, but casts a pensive, riveted look downwards to the modest flowers which the multitude trample under their feet. If he had a piece likely to succeed, coming out under all advantages, he would damn it by some ill-timed, wilful jest, and lose the favour of the public, to preserve the sense of his personal identity. 'Misfortune,' Shakespear says, 'brings a man acquainted with strange bedfellows'; and it makes our thoughts traitors to ourselves.—It is a maxim with many—*'Take care of the pence, and the pounds will take care of themselves.'* Those only put it in practice successfully who think more of the pence than of the pounds. To such, a large sum is less than a small one. Great speculations, great returns are to them extravagant or imaginary: a few hundreds a year are something snug and comfortable. Persons who have been used to a petty, huckstering way of life cannot enlarge their apprehensions to a notion of anything better. Instead of launching out into greater expense and liberality with the tide of fortune, they draw back with the fear of consequences, and think to succeed on a broader scale by dint of meanness and parsimony. My uncle Toby frequently caught Trim standing up behind his chair, when he had told him to be seated. What the corporal did out of respect, others would do out of servility. The menial character does not wear out in three or four generations. You cannot keep some people out of the kitchen, merely because their grandfathers or grandmothers came out of it. A poor man and his wife walking along in the neighbourhood of Portland Place, he said to her peevishly, 'What is the use of walking along these fine streets and squares? Let us turn down some alley!' He felt he should be more at home there. Lamb said of an old acquaintance of his, that when he was young he wanted to be a tailor, but had not spirit! This is the misery of unequal matches. The woman cannot easily forget, or think that others forget, her origin; and, with perhaps superior sense and beauty, keeps painfully in the background. It is worse when she braves this conscious feeling, and displays all the insolence of the upstart and affected fine lady. But shouldst thou ever, my Infelice, grace my home with thy loved presence, as thou hast cheered my hopes with thy smile, thou wilt conquer all hearts with thy prevailing gentleness, and I will show the world what Shakespear's women were!—Some gallants set their hearts on princesses; others descend in imagination to women of quality; others are mad after opera-singers. For my part, I am shy even of actresses, and should not think of leaving my card with Madame Vestris. I am for none of these *bonnes fortunes;* but for a list of humble beauties, servant-maids and shepherd-girls, with their red elbows, hard hands, black stockings and mob-caps, I could furnish out a gallery equal to Cowley's, and paint them half as well. Oh! might I but attempt a description of some of them in poetic prose, Don Juan would forget his Julia, and Mr. Davison might both print and publish this volume. I agree so far with Horace, and differ with Montaigne. I admire the Clementinas and Clarissas at a distance: the Pamelas and Fannys of Richardson and Fielding make my blood tingle. I have written love-letters to such in my time, *d'un pathetique a faire fendre les rochers,* and with about as much effect as if they had been addressed to stone. The simpletons only laughed, and said that 'those were not the sort of things to gain the affections.' I wish I had kept copies in my own justification. What is worse, I have an utter aversion to blue-stockings. I do not care a fig for any woman that knows even what an author means. If I know that she has read anything I have written, I cut her acquaintance immediately. This sort of literary intercourse with me passes for nothing. Her critical and scientific acquirements are *carrying coals to Newcastle.* I do not want to be told that I have published such or such a work. I knew all this before. It makes no addition to my sense of power. I do not wish the affair to be brought about in that way. I would have her read my soul: she should understand the language of the heart: she should know what I am, as if she were another self! She should love me for myself alone. I like myself without any reason: I would have her do so too. This is not very reasonable. I abstract from my temptations to admire all the circumstances of dress, birth, breeding, fortune; and I would not willingly put forward my own pretensions, whatever they may be. The image of some fair creature is engraven on my inmost soul; it is on that I build my claim to her regard, and expect her to see into my heart, as I see her form always before me. Wherever she treads, pale primroses, like her face, vernal hyacinths, like her brow, spring up beneath her feet, and music hangs on every bough; but all is cold, barren, and desolate without her. Thus I feel, and thus I think. But have I over told her so? No. Or if I did, would she understand it? No. I 'hunt the wind, I worship a statue, cry aloud to the desert.' To see beauty is not to be beautiful, to pine in love is not to be loved again—I always was inclined to raise and magnify the power of Love. I thought that his sweet power should only be exerted to join together the loveliest forms and fondest hearts; that none but those in whom his godhead shone outwardly, and was inly felt, should ever partake of his triumphs; and I stood and gazed at a distance, as unworthy to mingle in so bright a throng, and did not (even for a moment) wish to tarnish the glory of so fair a vision by being myself admitted into it. I say this was my notion once, but God knows it was one of the errors of my youth. For coming nearer to look, I saw the maimed, the blind, and the halt enter in, the crooked and the dwarf, the ugly, the old and impotent, the man of pleasure and the man of the world, the dapper and the pert, the vain and shallow boaster, the fool and the pedant, the ignorant and brutal, and all that is farthest removed from earth's fairest-born, and the pride of human life. Seeing all these enter the courts of Love, and thinking that I also might venture in under favour of the crowd, but finding myself rejected, I fancied (I might be wrong) that it was not so much because I was below, as above the common standard. I did feel, but I was ashamed to feel, mortified at my repulse, when I saw the meanest of mankind, the very scum and refuse, all creeping things and every obscene creature, enter in before me. I seemed a species by myself, I took a pride even in my disgrace; and concluded I had elsewhere my inheritance! The only thing I ever piqued myself upon was the writing the *Essay on the Principles of Human Action*—a work that no woman ever read, or would ever comprehend the meaning of. But if I do not build my claim to regard on the pretensions I have, how can I build it on those I am totally without? Or why do I complain and expect to gather grapes of thorns, or figs of thistles? Thought has in me cancelled pleasure; and this dark forehead, bent upon truth, is the rock on which all affection has split. And thus I waste my life in one long sigh; nor ever (till too late) beheld a gentle face turned gently upon mine!... But no! not too late, if that face, pure, modest, downcast, tender, with angel sweetness, not only gladdens the prospect of the future, but sheds its radiance on the past, smiling in tears. A purple light hovers round my head. The air of love is in the room. As I look at my long-neglected copy of the Death of Clorinda, golden gleams play upon the canvas, as they used when I painted it. The flowers of Hope and Joy springing up in my mind, recall the time when they first bloomed there. The years that are fled knock at the door and enter. I am in the Louvre once more. The sun of Austerlitz has not set. It still shines here—in my heart; and he, the son of glory, is not dead, nor ever shall, to me. I am as when my life began. The rainbow is in the sky again. I see the skirts of the departed years. All that I have thought and felt has not been in vain. I am not utterly worthless, unregarded; nor shall I die and wither of pure scorn. Now could I sit on the tomb of Liberty, and write a Hymn to Love. Oh! if I am deceived, let me be deceived still. Let me live in the Elysium of those soft looks; poison me with kisses, kill me with smiles; but still mock me with thy love!(4)

Poets choose mistresses who have the fewest charms, that they may make something out of nothing. They succeed best in fiction, and they apply this rule to love. They make a goddess of any dowdy. As Don Quixote said, in answer to the matter-of-fact remonstrances of Sancho, that Dulcinea del Toboso answered the purpose of signalising his valour just as well as the 'fairest princess under sky,' so any of the fair sex will serve them to write about just as well as another. They take some awkward thing and dress her up in fine words, as children dress up a wooden doll in fine clothes. Perhaps a fine head of hair, a taper waist, or some other circumstance strikes them, and they make the rest out according to their fancies. They have a wonderful knack of supplying deficiencies in the subjects of their idolatry out of the storehouse of their imaginations. They presently translate their favourites to the skies, where they figure with Berenice's locks and Ariadne's crown. This predilection for the unprepossessing and insignificant, I take to arise not merely from a desire in poets to have some subject to exercise their inventive talents upon, but from their jealousy of any pretensions (even those of beauty in the other sex) that might interfere with the continual incense offered to their personal vanity.

Cardinal Mazarine never thought anything of Cardinal de Retz after he told him that he had written for the last thirty years of his life with the same pen. Some Italian poet going to present a copy of verses to the Pope, and finding, as he was looking them over in the coach as he went, a mistake of a single letter in the printing, broke his heart of vexation and chagrin. A still more remarkable case of literary disappointment occurs in the history of a countryman of his, which I cannot refrain from giving here, as I find it related. 'Anthony Codrus Urceus, a most learned and unfortunate Italian, born near Modena, 1446, was a striking instance,' says his biographer, 'of the miseries men bring upon themselves by setting their affections unreasonably on trifles. This learned man lived at Forli, and had an apartment in the palace. His room was so very dark that he was forced to use a candle in the daytime; and one day, going abroad without putting it out, his library was set on fire, and some papers which he had prepared for the press were burned. The instant he was informed of this ill news he was affected even to madness. He ran furiously to the palace, and stopping at the door of his apartment, he cried aloud, "Christ Jesus! what mighty crime have I committed! whom of your followers have I ever injured, that you thus rage with inexpiable hatred against me?" Then turning himself to an image of the Virgin Mary near at hand, "Virgin (says he), hear what I have to say, for I speak in earnest, and with a composed spirit: if I shall happen to address you in my dying moments, I humbly entreat you not to hear me, nor receive me into Heaven, for I am determined to spend all eternity in Hell!" Those who heard these blasphemous expressions endeavoured to comfort him; but all to no purpose: for, the society of mankind being no longer supportable to him, he left the city, and retired, like savage, to the deep solitude of a wood. Some say that he was murdered there by ruffians: others, that he died at Bologna in 1500, after much contrition and penitence.'

Perhaps the censure passed at the outset of the anecdote on this unfortunate person is unfounded and severe, when it is said that he brought his miseries on himself 'by having set his affections unreasonably on trifles.' To others it might appear so; but to himself the labour of a whole life was hardly a trifle. His passion was not a causeless one, though carried to such frantic excess. The story of Sir Isaac Newton presents a strong contrast to the last-mentioned one, who, on going into his study and finding that his dog Tray had thrown down a candle on the table, and burnt some papers of great value, contented himself with exclaiming, 'Ah! Tray, you don't know the mischief you have done!' Many persons would not forgive the overturning a cup of chocolate so soon.

I remember hearing an instance some years ago of a man of character and property, who through unexpected losses had been condemned to a long and heartbreaking imprisonment, which he bore with exemplary fortitude. At the end of four years, by the interest and exertions of friends, he obtained his discharge, with every prospect of beginning the world afresh, and had made his arrangements for leaving his irksome abode, and meeting his wife and family at a distance of two hundred miles by a certain day. Owing to the miscarriage of a letter, some signature necessary to the completion of the business did not arrive in time, and on account of the informality which had thus arisen, he could not set out home till the return of the post, which was four days longer. His spirit could not brook the delay. He had wound himself up to the last pitch of expectation; he had, as it were, calculated his patience to hold out to a certain point, and then to throw down his load for ever, and he could not find resolution to resume it for a few hours beyond this. He put an end to the intolerable conflict of hope and disappointment in a fit of excruciating anguish. Woes that we have time to foresee and leisure to contemplate break their force by being spread over a larger surface and borne at intervals; but those that come upon us suddenly, for however short a time, seem to insult us by their unnecessary and uncalled-for intrusion; and the very prospect of relief, when held out and then withdrawn from us, to however small a distance, only frets impatience into agony by tantalising our hopes and wishes; and to rend asunder the thin partition that separates us from our favourite object, we are ready to burst even the fetters of life itself!

I am not aware that any one has demonstrated how it is that a stronger capacity is required for the conduct of great affairs than of small ones. The organs of the mind, like the pupil of the eye, may be contracted or dilated to view a broader or a narrower surface, and yet find sufficient variety to occupy its attention in each. The material universe is infinitely divisible, and so is the texture of human affairs. We take things in the gross or in the detail, according to the occasion. I think I could as soon get up the budget of Ways and Means for the current year, as be sure of making both ends meet, and paying my rent at quarter-day in a paltry huckster's shop. Great objects move on by their own weight and impulse; great power turns aside petty obstacles; and he who wields it is often but the puppet of circumstances, like the fly on the wheel that said, 'What a dust we raise!' It is easier to ruin a kingdom and aggrandise one's own pride and prejudices than to set up a greengrocer's stall. An idiot or a madman may do this at any time, whose word is law, and whose nod is fate. Nay, he whose look is obedience, and who understands the silent wishes of the great, may easily trample on the necks and tread out the liberties of a mighty nation, deriding their strength, and hating it the more from a consciousness of his own meanness. Power is not wisdom, it is true; but it equally ensures its own objects. It does not exact, but dispenses with talent. When a man creates this power, or new-moulds the state by sage counsels and bold enterprises, it is a different thing from overturning it with the levers that are put into his baby hands. In general, however, it may be argued that great transactions and complicated concerns ask more genius to conduct them than smaller ones, for this reason, viz. that the mind must be able either to embrace a greater variety of details in a more extensive range of objects, or must have a greater faculty of generalising, or a greater depth of insight into ruling principles, and so come at true results in that way. Buonaparte knew everything, even to the names of our cadets in the East India service; but he failed in this, that he did not calculate the resistance which barbarism makes to refinement. He thought that the Russians could not burn Moscow, because the Parisians could not burn Paris. The French think everything must be French. The Cossacks, alas! do not conform to etiquette: the rudeness of the seasons knows no rules of politeness! Some artists think it a test of genius to paint a large picture; and I grant the truth of this position, if the large picture contains more than a small one. It is not the size of the canvas, but the quantity of truth and nature put into it, that settles the point. It is a mistake, common enough on this subject, to suppose that a miniature is more finished than an oil-picture. The miniature is inferior to the oil-picture only because it is less finished, because it cannot follow nature into so many individual and exact particulars. The proof of which is, that the copy of a good portrait will always make a highly finished miniature (see for example Mr. Bone's enamels), whereas the copy of a good miniature, if enlarged to the size of life, will make but a very sorry portrait. Several of our best artists, who are fond of painting large figures, invert this reasoning. They make the whole figure gigantic, not that they may have room for nature, but for the motion of their brush (as if they were painting the side of a house), regarding the extent of canvas they have to cover as an excuse for their slovenly and hasty manner of getting over it; and thus, in fact, leave their pictures nothing at last but overgrown miniatures, but huge caricatures. It is not necessary in any case (either in a larger or a smaller compass) to go into the details, so as to lose sight of the effect, and decompound the face into porous and transparent molecules, in the manner of Denner, who painted what he saw through a magnifying-glass. The painter's eye need not be a microscope, but I contend that it should be a looking-glass, bright, clear, lucid. The *little* in art begins with insignificant parts, with what does not tell in connection with other parts. The true artist will paint not material points, but *moral qualities.* In a word, wherever there is feeling or expression in a muscle or a vein, there is grandeur and refinement too.—I will conclude these remarks with an account of the manner in which the ancient sculptors combined great and little things in such matters. 'That the name of Phidias,' says Pliny, 'is illustrious among all the nations that have heard of the fame of the Olympian Jupiter, no one doubts; but in order that those may know that he is deservedly praised who have not even seen his works, we shall offer a few arguments, and those of his genius only: nor to this purpose shall we insist on the beauty of the Olympian Jupiter, nor on the magnitude of the Minerva at Athens, though it is twenty-six cubits in height (about thirty-five feet), and is made of ivory and gold; but we shall refer to the shield, on which the battle of the Amazons is carved on the outer side; on the inside of the same is the fight of the Gods and Giants; and on the sandals, that between the Centaurs and Lapithae; so well did every part of that work display the powers of the art. Again, the sculptures on the pedestal he called the birth of Pandora: there are to be seen in number thirty gods, the figure of Victory being particularly admirable: the learned also admire the figures of the serpent and the brazen sphinx, writhing under the spear. These things are mentioned, in passing, of an artist never enough to be commended, that it may be seen that he showed the same magnificence even in small things.(5)

FN to ESSAY VII

(1) This Essay was written in January 1821.

(2) Losing gamesters thus become desperate, because the continued and violent irritation of the will against a run of ill luck drives it to extremity, and makes it bid defiance to common sense and every consideration of prudence or self-interest.

(3) Some of the poets in the beginning of the last century would often set out on a simile by observing, 'So in Arabia have I seen a Phoenix!' I confess my illustrations are of a more homely and humble nature.

(4) I beg the reader to consider this passage merely as a specimen of the mock-heroic style, and as having nothing to do with any real facts or feelings.

(5) Pliny's *Natural History,* Book 36.

ESSAY VIII. ON FAMILIAR STYLE

It is not easy to write a familiar style. Many people mistake a familiar for a vulgar style, and suppose that to write without affectation is to write at random. On the contrary, there is nothing that requires more precision, and, if I may so say, purity of expression, than the style I am speaking of. It utterly rejects not only all unmeaning pomp, but all low, cant phrases, and loose, unconnected, *slipshod* allusions. It is not to take the first word that offers, but the best word in common use; it is not to throw words together in any combinations we please, but to follow and avail ourselves of the true idiom of the language. To write a genuine familiar or truly English style is to write as any one would speak in common conversation who had a thorough command and choice of words, or who could discourse with ease, force, and perspicuity, setting aside all pedantic and oratorical flourishes. Or, to give another illustration, to write naturally is the same thing in regard to common conversation as to read naturally is in regard to common speech. It does not follow that it is an easy thing to give the true accent and inflection to the words you utter, because you do not attempt to rise above the level of ordinary life and colloquial speaking. You do not assume, indeed, the solemnity of the pulpit, or the tone of stage-declamation; neither are you at liberty to gabble on at a venture, without emphasis or discretion, or to resort to vulgar dialect or clownish pronunciation. You must steer a middle course. You are tied down to a given and appropriate articulation, which is determined by the habitual associations between sense and sound, and which you can only hit by entering into the author's meaning, as you must find the proper words and style to express yourself by fixing your thoughts on the subject you have to write about. Any one may mouth out a passage with a theatrical cadence, or get upon stilts to tell his thoughts; but to write or speak with propriety and simplicity is a more difficult task. Thus it is easy to affect a pompous style, to use a word twice as big as the thing you want to express: it is not so easy to pitch upon the very word that exactly fits it. Out of eight or ten words equally common, equally intelligible, with nearly equal pretensions, it is a matter of some nicety and discrimination to pick out the very one the preferableness of which is scarcely perceptible, but decisive. The reason why I object to Dr. Johnson's style is that there is no discrimination, no selection, no variety in it. He uses none but 'tall, opaque words,' taken from the 'first row of the rubric'—words with the greatest number of syllables, or Latin phrases with merely English terminations. If a fine style depended on this sort of arbitrary pretension, it would be fair to judge of an author's elegance by the measurement of his words and the substitution of foreign circumlocutions (with no precise associations) for the mother-tongue.(1) How simple is it to be dignified without case, to be pompous without meaning! Surely it is but a mechanical rule for avoiding what is low, to be always pedantic and affected. It is clear you cannot use a vulgar English word if you never use a common English word at all. A fine tact is shown in adhering to those which are perfectly common, and yet never falling into any expressions which are debased by disgusting circumstances, or which owe their signification and point to technical or professional allusions. A truly natural or familiar style can never be quaint or vulgar, for this reason, that it is of universal force and applicability, and that quaintness and vulgarity arise out of the immediate connection of certain words with coarse and disagreeable or with confined ideas. The last form what we understand by *cant* or *slang* phrases.—To give an example of what is not very clear in the general statement, I should say that the phrase *To cut with a knife,* or *To cut a piece of wood,* is perfectly free from vulgarity, because it is perfectly common; but *to cut an acquaintance* is not quite unexceptionable, because it is not perfectly common or intelligible, and has hardly yet escaped out of the limits of slang phraseology. I should hardly, therefore, use the word in this sense without putting it in italics as a license of expression, to be received *cum grano salis.* All provincial or bye-phrases come under the same mark of reprobation—all such as the writer transfers to the page from his fireside or a particular *coterie,* or that he invents for his own sole use and convenience. I conceive that words are like money, not the worse for being common, but that it is the stamp of custom alone that gives them circulation or value. I am fastidious in this respect, and would almost as soon coin the currency of the realm as counterfeit the King's English. I never invented or gave a new and unauthorised meaning to any word but one single one (the term *impersonal* applied to feelings), and that was in an abstruse metaphysical discussion to express a very difficult distinction. I have been (I know) loudly accused of revelling in vulgarisms and broken English. I cannot speak to that point; but so far I plead guilty to the determined use of acknowledged idioms and common elliptical expressions. I am not sure that the critics in question know the one from the other, that is, can distinguish any medium between formal pedantry and the most barbarous solecism. As an author I endeavour to employ plain words and popular modes of construction, as, were I a chapman and dealer, I should common weights and measures.

The proper force of words lies not in the words themselves, but in their application. A word may be a fine-sounding word, of an unusual length, and very imposing from its learning and novelty, and yet in the connection in which it is introduced may be quite pointless and irrelevant. It is not pomp or pretension, but the adaptation of the expression to the idea, that clenches a writer's meaning:—as it is not the size or glossiness of the materials, but their being fitted each to its place, that gives strength to the arch; or as the pegs and nails are as necessary to the support of the building as the larger timbers, and more so than the mere showy, unsubstantial ornaments. I hate anything that occupies more space than it is worth. I hate to see a load of bandboxes go along the street, and I hate to see a parcel of big words without anything in them. A person who does not deliberately dispose of all his thoughts alike in cumbrous draperies and flimsy disguises may strike out twenty varieties of familiar everyday language, each coming somewhat nearer to the feeling he wants to convey, and at last not hit upon that particular and only one which may be said to be identical with the exact impression in his mind. This would seem to show that Mr. Cobbett is hardly right in saying that the first word that occurs is always the best. It may be a very good one; and yet a better may present itself on reflection or from time to time. It should be suggested naturally, however, and spontaneously, from a fresh and lively conception of the subject. We seldom succeed by trying at improvement, or by merely substituting one word for another that we are not satisfied with, as we cannot recollect the name of a place or person by merely plaguing ourselves about it. We wander farther from the point by persisting in a wrong scent; but it starts up accidentally in the memory when we least expected it, by touching some link in the chain of previous association.

There are those who hoard up and make a cautious display of nothing but rich and rare phraseology—ancient medals, obscure coins, and Spanish pieces of eight. They are very curious to inspect, but I myself would neither offer nor take them in the course of exchange. A sprinkling of archaisms is not amiss, but a tissue of obsolete expressions is more fit *for keep than wear.* I do not say I would not use any phrase that had been brought into fashion before the middle or the end of the last century, but I should be shy of using any that had not been employed by any approved author during the whole of that time. Words, like clothes, get old-fashioned, or mean and ridiculous, when they have been for some time laid aside. Mr. Lamb is the only imitator of old English style I can read with pleasure; and he is so thoroughly imbued with the spirit of his authors that the idea of imitation is almost done away. There is an inward unction, a marrowy vein, both in the thought and feeling, an intuition, deep and lively, of his subject, that carries off any quaintness or awkwardness arising from an antiquated style and dress. The matter is completely his own, though the manner is assumed. Perhaps his ideas are altogether so marked and individual as to require their point and pungency to be neutralised by the affectation of a singular but traditional form of conveyance. Tricked out in the prevailing costume, they would probably seem more startling and out of the way. The old English authors, Burton, Fuller, Coryate, Sir Thomas Browne, are a kind of mediators between us and the more eccentric and whimsical modern, reconciling us to his peculiarities. I do not, however, know how far this is the case or not, till he condescends to write like one of us. I must confess that what I like best of his papers under the signature of Elia (still I do not presume, amidst such excellence, to decide what is most excellent) is the account of 'Mrs. Battle's Opinions on Whist,' which is also the most free from obsolete allusions and turns of expression—

A well of native English undefiled.

To those acquainted with his admired prototypes, these *Essays* of the ingenious and highly gifted author have the same sort of charm and relish that Erasmus's *Colloquies* or a fine piece of modern Latin have to the classical scholar. Certainly, I do not know any borrowed pencil that has more power or felicity of execution than the one of which I have here been speaking.

It is as easy to write a gaudy style without ideas as it is to spread a pallet of showy colours or to smear in a flaunting transparency. 'What do you read?' 'Words, words, words.'—'What is the matter?' '*Nothing*,' it might be answered. The florid style is the reverse of the familiar. The last is employed as an unvarnished medium to convey ideas; the first is resorted to as a spangled veil to conceal the want of them. When there is nothing to be set down but words, it costs little to have them fine. Look through the dictionary, and cull out a *florilegium*, rival the *tulippomania*. *Rouge* high enough, and never mind the natural complexion. The vulgar, who are not in the secret, will admire the look of preternatural health and vigour; and the fashionable, who regard only appearances, will be delighted with the imposition. Keep to your sounding generalities, your tinkling phrases, and all will be well. Swell out an unmeaning truism to a perfect tympany of style. A thought, a distinction is the rock on which all this brittle cargo of verbiage splits at once. Such writers have merely *verbal* imaginations, that retain nothing but words. Or their puny thoughts have dragon-wings, all green and gold. They soar far above the vulgar failing of the *Sermo humi obrepens*—their most ordinary speech is never short of an hyperbole, splendid, imposing, vague, incomprehensible, magniloquent, a cento of sounding common-places. If some of us, whose 'ambition is more lowly,' pry a little too narrowly into nooks and corners to pick up a number of 'unconsidered trifles,' they never once direct their eyes or lift their hands to seize on any but the most gorgeous, tarnished, threadbare, patchwork set of phrases, the left-off finery of poetic extravagance, transmitted down through successive generations of barren pretenders. If they criticise actors and actresses, a huddled phantasmagoria of feathers, spangles, floods of light, and oceans of sound float before their morbid sense, which they paint in the style of Ancient Pistol. Not a glimpse can you get of the merits or defects of the performers: they are hidden in a profusion of barbarous epithets and wilful rhodomontade. Our hypercritics are not thinking of these little fantoccini beings—

That strut and fret their hour upon the stage—

but of tall phantoms of words, abstractions, *genera* and *species*, sweeping clauses, periods that unite the Poles, forced alliterations, astounding antitheses—

And on their pens *Fustian* sits plumed.

If they describe kings and queens, it is an Eastern pageant. The Coronation at either House is nothing to it. We get at four repeated images—a curtain, a throne, a sceptre, and a footstool. These are with them the wardrobe of a lofty imagination; and they turn their servile strains to servile uses. Do we read a description of pictures? It is not a reflection of tones and hues which 'nature's own sweet and cunning hand laid on,' but piles of precious stones, rubies, pearls, emeralds, Golconda's mines, and all the blazonry of art. Such persons are in fact besotted with words, and their brains are turned with the glittering but empty and sterile phantoms of things. Personifications, capital letters, seas of sunbeams, visions of glory, shining inscriptions, the figures of a transparency, Britannia with her shield, or Hope leaning on an anchor, make up their stock-in-trade. They may be considered as *hieroglyphical* writers. Images stand out in their minds isolated and important merely in themselves, without any groundwork of feeling—there is no context in their imaginations. Words affect them in the same way, by the mere sound, that is, by their possible, not by their actual application to the subject in hand. They are fascinated by first appearances, and have no sense of consequences. Nothing more is meant by them than meets the ear: they understand or feel nothing more than meets their eye. The web and texture of the universe, and of the heart of man, is a mystery to them: they have no faculty that strikes a chord in unison with it. They cannot get beyond the daubings of fancy, the varnish of sentiment. Objects are not linked to feelings, words to things, but images revolve in splendid mockery, words represent themselves in their strange rhapsodies. The categories of such a mind are pride and ignorance—pride in outside show, to which they sacrifice everything, and ignorance of the true worth and hidden structure both of words and things. With a sovereign contempt for what is familiar and natural, they are the slaves of vulgar affectation—of a routine of high-flown phrases. Scorning to imitate realities, they are unable to invent anything, to strike out one original idea. They are not copyists of nature, it is true; but they are the poorest of all plagiarists, the plagiarists of words. All is far-fetched, dear bought, artificial, oriental in subject and allusion; all is mechanical, conventional, vapid, formal, pedantic in style and execution. They startle and confound the understanding of the reader by the remoteness and obscurity of their illustrations; they soothe the ear by the monotony of the same everlasting round of circuitous metaphors. They are the mock-school in poetry and prose. They flounder about between fustian in expression and bathos in sentiment. They tantalise the fancy, but never reach the head nor touch the heart. Their Temple of Fame is like a shadowy structure raised by Dulness to Vanity, or like Cowper's description of the Empress of Russia's palace of ice, 'as worthless as in show 'twas glittering'—

It smiled, and it was cold!

FN to ESSAY VIII

(1) I have heard of such a thing as an author who makes it a rule never to admit a monosyllable into his vapid verse. Yet the charm and sweetness of Marlowe's lines depended often on their being made up almost entirely of monosyllables.

ESSAY IX. ON EFFEMINACY OF CHARACTER

Effeminacy of character arises from a prevalence of the sensibility over the will; or it consists in a want of fortitude to bear pain or to undergo fatigue, however urgent the occasion. We meet with instances of people who cannot lift up a little finger to save themselves from ruin, nor give up the smallest indulgence for the sake of any other person. They cannot put themselves out of their way on any account. No one makes a greater outcry when the day of reckoning comes, or affects greater compassion for the mischiefs they have occasioned; but till the time comes, they feel nothing, they care for nothing. They live in the present moment, are the creatures of the present impulse (whatever it may be)—and beyond that, the universe is nothing to them. The slightest toy countervails the empire of the world; they will not forego the smallest inclination they feel, for any object that can be proposed to them, or any reasons that can be urged for it. You might as well ask of the gossamer not to wanton in the idle summer air, or of the moth not to play with the flame that scorches it, as ask of these persons to put off any enjoyment for a single instant, or to gird themselves up to any enterprise of pith or moment. They have been so used to a studied succession of agreeable sensations that the shortest pause is a privation which they can by no means endure—it is like tearing them from their very existence—they have been so inured to ease and indolence, that the most trifling effort is like one of the tasks of Hercules, a thing of impossibility, at which they shudder. They lie on beds of roses, and spread their gauze wings to the sun and summer gale, and cannot bear to put their tender feet to the ground, much less to encounter the thorns and briars of the world. Life for them

Rolls o'er Elysian flowers its amber stream,

and they have no fancy for fishing in troubled waters. The ordinary state of existence they regard as something importunate and vain, and out of nature. What must they think of its trials and sharp vicissitudes? Instead of voluntarily embracing pain, or labour, or danger, or death, every sensation must be wound up to the highest pitch of voluptuous refinement, every motion must be grace and elegance; they live in a luxurious, endless dream, or

Die of a rose in aromatic pain!

Siren sounds must float around them; smiling forms must everywhere meet their sight; they must tread a soft measure on painted carpets or smooth-shaven lawns; books, arts, jests, laughter occupy every thought and hour—what have they to do with the drudgery, the struggles, the poverty, the disease or anguish which are the common lot of humanity? These things are intolerable to them, even in imagination. They disturb the enchantment in which they are lapt. They cause a wrinkle in the clear and polished surface of their existence. They exclaim with impatience and in agony, 'Oh, leave me to my repose!' How 'they shall discourse the freezing hours away, when wind and rain beat dark December down,' or 'bide the pelting of the pitiless storm,' gives them no concern, it never once enters their heads. They close the shutters, draw the curtains, and enjoy or shut out the whistling of the approaching tempest 'They take no thought for the morrow,' not they. They do not anticipate evils. Let them come when they will come, they will not run to meet them. Nay more, they will not move one step to prevent them, nor let any one else. The mention of such things is shocking; the very supposition is a nuisance that must not be tolerated. The idea of the obviate disagreeable consequences oppresses them to death, is an exertion too great for their enervated imaginations. They are not like Master Barnardine in *Measure for Measure*, who would not 'get up to be hanged'—they would not get up to avoid being hanged. They are completely wrapped up in themselves; but then all their self-love is concentrated in the present minute. They have worked up their effeminate and fastidious appetite of enjoyment to such a pitch that the whole of their existence, every moment of it, must be made up of these exquisite indulgences; or they will fling it all away, with indifference and scorn. They stake their entire welfare on the gratification of the passing instant. Their senses, their vanity, their thoughtless gaiety have been pampered till they ache at the smallest suspension of their perpetual dose of excitement, and they will purchase the hollow happiness of the next five minutes by a mortgage on the independence and comfort of years. They must have their will in everything, or they grow sullen and peevish like spoiled children. Whatever they set their eyes on, or make up their minds to, they must have that instant. They may pay for it hereafter. But that is no matter. They snatch a joy beyond the reach of fate, and consider the present time sacred, inviolable, unaccountable to that hard, churlish, niggard, inexorable taskmaster, the future. *Now or never* is their motto. They are madly devoted to the plaything, the ruling passion of the moment. What is to happen to them a week hence is as if it were to happen to them a thousand years hence. They put off the consideration for another day, and their heedless unconcern laughs at it as a fable. Their life is 'a cell of ignorance, travelling a-bed'; their existence is ephemeral; their thoughts are insect-winged; their identity expires with the whim, the folly, the passion of the hour.

Nothing but a miracle can rouse such people from their lethargy. It is not to be expected, nor is it even possible in the natural course of things. Pope's striking exclamation,

    Oh! blindness to the future kindly given,
    That each may fill the circuit mark'd by Heaven!

hardly applies here; namely, to evils that stare us in the face, and that might be averted with the least prudence or resolution. But nothing can be done. How should it? A slight evil, a distant danger, will not move them; and a more imminent one only makes them turn away from it in greater precipitation and alarm. The more desperate their affairs grow, the more averse they are to look into them; and the greater the effort required to retrieve them, the more incapable they are of it. At first, they will not do anything; and afterwards, it is too late. The very motives that imperiously urge them to self-reflection and amendment, combine with their natural disposition to prevent it. This amounts pretty nearly to a mathematical demonstration. Ease, vanity, pleasure are the ruling passions in such cases. How will you conquer these, or wean their infatuated votaries from them? By the dread of hardship, disgrace, pain? They turn from them, and you who point them out as the alternative, with sickly disgust; and instead of a stronger effort of courage or self-denial to avert the crisis, hasten it by a wilful determination to pamper the disease in every way, and arm themselves, not with fortitude to bear or to repel the consequences, but with judicial blindness to their approach. Will you rouse the indolent procrastinator to an irksome but necessary effort, by showing him how much he has to do? He will only draw back the more for all your entreaties and representations. If of a sanguine turn, he will make a slight attempt at a new plan of life, be satisfied with the first appearance of reform, and relapse into indolence again. If timid and undecided, the hopelessness of the undertaking will put him out of heart with it, and he will stand still in despair. Will you save a vain man from ruin, by pointing out the obloquy and ridicule that await him in his present career? He smiles at your forebodings as fantastical; or the more they are realised around him, the more he is impelled to keep out the galling conviction, and the more fondly he clings to flattery and death. He will not make a bold and resolute attempt to recover his reputation, because that would imply that it was capable of being soiled or injured; or he no sooner meditates some desultory project, than he takes credit to himself for the execution, and is delighted to wear his unearned laurels while the thing is barely talked of. The chance of success relieves the uneasiness of his apprehensions; so that he makes use of the interval only to flatter his favourite infirmity again. Would you wean a man from sensual excesses by the inevitable consequences to which they lead?—What holds more antipathy to pleasure than pain? The mind given up to self-indulgence revolts at suffering, and throws it from it as an unaccountable anomaly, as a piece of injustice when it comes. Much less will it acknowledge any affinity with or subjection to it as a mere threat. If the prediction does not immediately come true, we laugh at the prophet of ill: if it is verified, we hate our adviser proportionably, hug our vices the closer, and hold them dearer and more precious the more they cost us. We resent wholesome counsel as an impertinence, and consider those who warn us of impending mischief as if they had brought it on our heads. We cry out with the poetical enthusiast—

    And let us nurse the fond deceit;
    And what if we must die in sorrow?
    Who would not cherish dreams so sweet,
    Though grief and pain should come to-morrow?

But oh thou! who didst lend me speech when I was dumb, to whom I owe it that I have not crept on my belly all the days of my life like the serpent, but sometimes lift my forked crest or tread the empyrean, wake thou out of thy mid-day slumbers! Shake off the heavy honeydew of thy soul, no longer lulled with that Circean cup, drinking thy own thoughts with thy own ears, but start up in thy promised likeness, and shake the pillared rottenness of the world! Leave not thy sounding words in air, write them in marble, and teach the coming age heroic truths! Up, and wake the echoes of Time! Rich in deepest lore, die not the bed-rid churl of knowledge, leaving the survivors unblest! Set, set as thou didst rise in pomp and gladness! Dart like the sunflower one broad, golden flash of light; and ere thou ascendest thy native sky, show us the steps by which thou didst scale the Heaven of philosophy, with Truth and Fancy for thy equal guides, that we may catch thy mantle, rainbow-dipped, and still read thy words dear to Memory, dearer to Fame!

There is another branch of this character, which is the trifling or dilatory character. Such persons are always creating difficulties, and unable or unwilling to remove them. They cannot brush aside a cobweb, and are stopped by an insect's wing. Their character is imbecility, rather than effeminacy. The want of energy and resolution in the persons last described arises from the habitual and inveterate predominance of other feelings and motives; in these it is a mere want of energy and resolution, that is, an inherent natural defect of vigour of nerve and voluntary power. There is a specific levity about such persons, so that you cannot propel them to any object, or give them a decided *momentum* in any direction or pursuit. They turn back, as it were, on the occasion that should project them forward with manly force and vehemence. They shrink from intrepidity of purpose, and are alarmed at the idea of attaining their end too soon. They will not act with steadiness or spirit, either for themselves or you. If you chalk out a line of conduct for them, or commission them to execute a certain task, they are sure to conjure up some insignificant objection or fanciful impediment in the way, and are withheld from striking an effectual blow by mere feebleness of character. They may be officious, good-natured, friendly, generous in disposition, but they are of no use to any one. They will put themselves to twice the trouble you desire, not to carry your point, but to defeat it; and in obviating needless objections, neglect the main business. If they do what you want, it is neither at the time nor in the manner that you wish. This timidity amounts to treachery; for by always anticipating some misfortune or disgrace, they realise their unmeaning apprehensions. The little bears sway in their minds over the great: a small inconvenience outweighs a solid and indispensable advantage; and their strongest bias is uniformly derived from the weakest motive. They hesitate about the best way of beginning a thing till the opportunity for action is lost, and are less anxious about its being done than the precise manner of doing it. They will destroy a passage sooner than let an objectionable word pass; and are much less concerned about the truth or the beauty of an image than about the reception it will meet with from the critics. They alter what they write, not because it is, but because it may possibly be wrong; and in their tremulous solicitude to avoid imaginary blunders, run into real ones. What is curious enough is, that with all this caution and delicacy, they are continually liable to extraordinary oversights. They are, in fact, so full of all sorts of idle apprehensions, that they do not know how to distinguish real from imaginary grounds of apprehension; and they often give some unaccountable offence, either from assuming a sudden boldness half in sport, or while they are secretly pluming themselves on their dexterity in avoiding everything exceptionable; and the same distraction of motive and shortsightedness which gets them into scrapes hinders them from seeing their way out of them. Such persons (often of ingenious and susceptible minds) are constantly at cross-purposes with themselves and others; will neither do things nor let others do them; and whether they succeed or fail, never feel confident or at their case. They spoil the freshness and originality of their own thoughts by asking contradictory advice; and in befriending others, while they are *about it and about it,* you might have done the thing yourself a dozen times over.

There is nothing more to be esteemed than a manly firmness and decision of character. I like a person who knows his own mind and sticks to it; who sees at once what is to be done in given circumstances and does it. He does not beat about the bush for difficulties or excuses, but goes the shortest and most effectual way to work to attain his own ends or to accomplish a useful object. If he can serve you, he will do so; if he cannot, he will say so without keeping you in needless suspense, or laying you under pretended obligations. The applying to him in any laudable undertaking is not like stirring 'a dish of skimmed milk.' There is stuff in him, and it is of the right practicable sort. He is not all his life at hawk-and-buzzard whether he shall be a Whig or a Tory, a friend or a foe, a knave or a fool; but thinks that life is short, and that there is no time to play fantastic tricks in it, to tamper with principles, or trifle with individual feelings. If he gives you a character, he does not add a damning clause to it: he does not pick holes in you lest others should, or anticipate objections lest he should be thought to be blinded by a childish partiality. His object is to serve you; and not to play the game into your enemies' hands.

    A generous friendship no cold medium knows,
    Burns with one love, with one resentment glows.

I should be sorry for any one to say what he did not think of me; but I should not be pleased to see him slink out of his acknowledged opinion, lest it should not be confirmed by malice or stupidity. He who is well acquainted and well inclined to you ought to give the tone, not to receive it from others, and may set it to what key he pleases in certain cases.

There are those of whom it has been said, that to them an obligation is a reason for not doing anything, and there are others who are invariably led to do the reverse of what they should. The last are perverse, the first impracticable people. Opposed to the effeminate in disposition and manners are the coarse and brutal. As those were all softness and smoothness, these affect or are naturally attracted to whatever is vulgar and violent, harsh and repulsive in tone, in modes of speech, in forms of address, in gesture and behaviour. Thus there are some who ape the lisping of the fine lady, the drawling of the fine gentleman, and others who all their life delight in and catch the uncouth dialect, the manners and expressions of clowns and hoydens. The last are governed by an instinct of the disagreeable, by an appetite and headlong rage for violating decorum and hurting other people's feelings, their own being excited and enlivened by the shock. They deal in home truths, unpleasant reflections, and unwelcome matters of fact; as the others are all compliment and complaisance, insincerity and insipidity.

We may observe an effeminacy of style, in some degree corresponding to effeminacy of character. Writers of this stamp are great interliners of what they indite, alterers of indifferent phrases, and the plague of printers' devils. By an effeminate style I would be understood to mean one that is all florid, all fine; that cloys by its sweetness, and tires by its sameness. Such are what Dryden calls 'calm, peaceable writers.' They only aim to please, and never offend by truth or disturb by singularity. Every thought must be beautiful *per se,* every expression equally fine. They do not delight in vulgarisms, but in common-places, and dress out unmeaning forms in all the colours of the rainbow. They do not go out of their way to think—that would startle the indolence of the reader: they cannot express a trite thought in common words—that would be a sacrifice of their own vanity. They are not sparing of tinsel, for it costs nothing. Their works should be printed, as they generally are, on hot-pressed paper, with vignette margins. The Della Cruscan school comes under this description, which is now nearly exploded. Lord Byron is a pampered and aristocratic writer, but he is not effeminate, or we should not have his works with only the printer's name to them! I cannot help thinking that the fault of Mr. Keats's poems was a deficiency in masculine energy of style. He had beauty, tenderness, delicacy, in an uncommon degree, but there was a want of strength and substance. His *Endymion* is a very delightful description of the illusions of a youthful imagination given up to airy dreams—we have flowers, clouds, rainbows, moonlight, all sweet sounds and smells, and Oreads and Dryads flitting by—but there is nothing tangible in it, nothing marked or palpable—we have none of the hardy spirit or rigid forms of antiquity. He painted his own thoughts and character, and did not transport himself into the fabulous and heroic ages. There is a want of action, of character, and so far of imagination, but there is exquisite fancy. All is soft and fleshy, without bone or muscle. We see in him the youth without the manhood of poetry. His genius breathed 'vernal delight and joy.' 'Like Maia's son he stood and shook his plumes,' with fragrance filled. His mind was redolent of spring. He had not the fierceness of summer, nor the richness of autumn, and winter he seemed not to have known till he felt the icy hand of death!

FN to ESSAY IX

ESSAY X. WHY DISTANT OBJECTS PLEASE

Distant objects please, because, in the first place, they imply an idea of space and magnitude, and because, not being obtruded too close upon the eye, we clothe them with the indistinct and airy colours of fancy. In looking at the misty mountain-tops that bound the horizon, the mind is as it were conscious of all the conceivable objects and interests that lie between; we imagine all sorts of adventures in the interim; strain our hopes and wishes to reach the air-drawn circle, or to 'descry new lands, rivers, and mountains,' stretching far beyond it: our feelings, carried out of themselves, lose their grossness and their husk, are rarefied, expanded, melt into softness and brighten into beauty, turning to ethereal mould, sky-tinctured. We drink the air before us, and borrow a more refined existence from objects that hover on the brink of nothing. Where the landscape fades from the dull sight, we fill the thin, viewless space with shapes of unknown good, and tinge the hazy prospect with hopes and wishes and more charming fears.

> But thou, oh Hope! with eyes so fair,
> What was thy delighted measure?
> Still it whisper'd promised pleasure,
> And bade the lovely scenes at distance hail!

Whatever is placed beyond the reach of sense and knowledge, whatever is imperfectly discerned, the fancy pieces out at its leisure; and all but the present moment, but the present spot, passion claims for its own, and brooding over it with wings outspread, stamps it with an image of itself. Passion is lord of infinite space, and distant objects please because they border on its confines and are moulded by its touch. When I was a boy, I lived within sight of a range of lofty hills, whose blue tops blending with the setting sun had often tempted my longing eyes and wandering feet. At last I put my project in execution, and on a nearer approach, instead of glimmering air woven into fantastic shapes, found them huge lumpish heaps of discoloured earth. I learnt from this (in part) to leave 'Yarrow unvisited,' and not idly to disturb a dream of good!

Distance of time has much the same effect as distance of place. It is not surprising that fancy colours the prospect of the future as it thinks good, when it even effaces the forms of memory. Time takes out the sting of pain; our sorrows after a certain period have been so often steeped in a medium of thought and passion that they 'unmould their essence'; and all that remains of our original impressions is what we would wish them to have been. Not only the untried steep ascent before us, but the rude, unsightly masses of our past experience presently resume their power of deception over the eye: the golden cloud soon rests upon their heads, and the purple light of fancy clothes their barren sides! Thus we pass on, while both ends of our existence touch upon Heaven! There is (so to speak) 'a mighty stream of tendency' to good in the human mind, upon which all objects float and are imperceptibly borne along; and though in the voyage of life we meet with strong rebuffs, with rocks and quicksands, yet there is 'a tide in the affairs of men,' a heaving and a restless aspiration of the soul, by means of which, 'with sails and tackle torn,' the wreck and scattered fragments of our entire being drift into the port and haven of our desires! In all that relates to the affections, we put the will for the deed; so that the instant the pressure of unwelcome circumstances is removed, the mind recoils from their hold, recovers its elasticity, and reunites itself to that image of good which is but a reflection and configuration of its own nature. Seen in the distance, in the long perspective of waning years, the meanest incidents, enlarged and enriched by countless recollections, become interesting; the most painful, broken and softened by time, soothe. How any object that unexpectedly brings back to us old scenes and associations startles the mind! What a yearning it creates within us; what a longing to leap the intermediate space! How fondly we cling to, and try to revive the impression of all that we then were!

> Such tricks hath strong imagination!

In truth we impose upon ourselves, and know not what we wish. It is a cunning artifice, a quaint delusion, by which, in pretending to be what we were at a particular moment of time, we would fain be all that we have since been, and have our lives to come over again. It is not the little, glimmering, almost annihilated speck in the distance that rivets our attention and 'hangs upon the beatings of our hearts': it is the interval that separates us from it, and of which it is the trembling boundary, that excites all this coil and mighty pudder in the breast. Into that great gap in our being 'come thronging soft desires' and infinite regrets. It is the contrast, the change from what we then were, that arms the half-extinguished recollection with its giant strength, and lifts the fabric of the affections from its shadowy base. In contemplating its utmost verge, we overlook the map of our existence, and re-tread, in apprehension, the journey of life. So it is that in early youth we strain our eager sight after the pursuits of manhood; and, as we are sliding off the stage, strive to gather up the toys and flowers that pleased our thoughtless childhood.

When I was quite a boy my father used to take me to the Montpelier Tea Gardens at Walworth. Do I go there now? No; the place is deserted, and its borders and its beds o'erturned. Is there, then, nothing that can

> Bring back the hour
> Of glory in the grass, of splendour in the flower?

Oh! yes. I unlock the casket of memory, and draw back the warders of the brain; and there this scene of my infant wanderings still lives unfaded, or with fresher dyes. A new sense comes upon me, as in a dream; a richer perfume, brighter colours start out; my eyes dazzle; my heart heaves with its new load of bliss, and I am a child again. My sensations are all glossy, spruce, voluptuous, and fine: they wear a candied coat, and are in holiday trim. I see the beds of larkspur with purple eyes; tall hollyhocks, red or yellow; the broad sunflowers, caked in gold, with bees buzzing round them; wildernesses of pinks, and hot glowing peonies; poppies run to seed; the sugared lily, and faint mignonette, all ranged in order, and as thick as they can grow; the box-tree borders, the gravel-walks, the painted alcove, the confectionery, the clotted cream:—I think I see them now with sparkling looks; or have they vanished while I have been writing this description of them? No matter; they will return again when I least think of them. All that I have observed since, of flowers and plants, and grass-plots, and of suburb delights, seems to me borrowed from 'that first garden of my innocence'—to be slips and scions stolen from that bed of memory. In this manner the darlings of our childhood burnish out in the eye of after years, and derive their sweetest perfume from the first heartfelt sigh of pleasure breathed upon them,

> Like the sweet south,
>
> That breathes upon a bank of violets,
>
> Stealing and giving odour!

If I have pleasure in a flower-garden, I have in a kitchen-garden too, and for the same reason. If I see a row of cabbage-plants, or of peas or beans coming up, I immediately think of those which I used so carefully to water of an evening at Wem, when my day's tasks were done, and of the pain with which I saw them droop and hang down their leaves in the morning's sun. Again, I never see a child's kite in the air but it seems to pull at my heart. It is to me 'a thing of life.' I feel the twinge at my elbow, the flutter and palpitation, with which I used to let go the string of my own, as it rose in the air, and towered among the clouds. My little cargo of hopes and fears ascended with it; and as it made a part of my own consciousness then, it does so still, and appears 'like some gay creature of the element,' my playmate when life was young, and twin-born with my earliest recollections. I could enlarge on this subject of childish amusements, but Mr. Leigh Hunt has treated it so well, in a paper in the *Indicator,* on the productions of the toy-shops of the metropolis, that if I were to insist more on it I should only pass for an imitator of that ingenious and agreeable writer, *and for an indifferent one into the bargain.*

Sounds, smells, and sometimes tastes, are remembered longer than visible objects, and serve, perhaps, better for links in the chain of association. The reason seems to be this: they are in their nature intermittent, and comparatively rare; whereas objects of sight are always before us, and, by their continuous succession, drive one another out. The eye is always open; and between any given impression and its recurrence a second time, fifty thousand other impressions have, in all likelihood, been stamped upon the sense and on the brain. The other senses are not so active or vigilant. They are but seldom called into play. The ear, for example, is oftener courted by silence than noise; and the sounds that break that silence sink deeper and more durably into the mind. I have a more present and lively recollection of certain scents, tastes, and sounds, for this reason, than I have of mere visible images, because they are more original, and less worn by frequent repetition. Where there is nothing interposed between any two impressions, whatever the distance of time that parts them, they naturally seem to touch; and the renewed impression recalls the former one in full force, without distraction or competitor. The taste of barberries, which have hung out in the snow during the severity of a North American winter, I have in my mouth still, after an interval of thirty years; for I have met with no other taste in all that time at all like it. It remains by itself, almost like the impression of a sixth sense. But the colour is mixed up indiscriminately with the colours of many other berries, nor should I be able to distinguish it among them. The smell of a brick-kiln carries the evidence of its own identity with it: neither is it to me (from peculiar associations) unpleasant. The colour of brickdust, on the contrary, is more common, and easily confounded with other colours. Raphael did not keep it quite distinct from his flesh colour. I will not say that we have a more perfect recollection of the human voice than of that complex picture the human face, but I think the sudden hearing of a well-known voice has something in it more affecting and striking than the sudden meeting with the face: perhaps, indeed, this may be because we have a more familiar remembrance of the one than the other, and the voice takes us more by surprise on that account. I am by no means certain (generally speaking) that we have the ideas of the other senses so accurate and well made out as those of visible form: what I chiefly mean is, that the feelings belonging to the sensations of our other organs, when accidentally recalled, are kept more separate and pure. Musical sounds, probably, owe a good deal of their interest and romantic effect to the principle here spoken of. Were they constant, they would become indifferent, as we may find with respect to disagreeable noises, which we do not hear after a time. I know no situation more pitiable than that of a blind fiddler who has but one sense left (if we except the sense of snuff-taking(1)) and who has that stunned or deafened by his own villainous noises. Shakespear says.

> How silver-sweet sound lovers' tongues by night!

It has been observed in explanation of this passage, that it is because in the day-time lovers are occupied with one another's faces, but that at night they can only distinguish the sound of each other's voices. I know not how this may be; but I have, ere now, heard a voice break so upon the silence,

> To angels' 'twas most like,

and charm the moonlight air with its balmy essence, that the budding leaves trembled to its accents. Would I might have heard it once more whisper peace and hope (as erst when it was mingled with the breath of spring), and with its soft pulsations lift winged fancy to heaven. But it has ceased, or turned where I no more shall hear it!—Hence, also, we see what is the charm of the shepherd's pastoral reed; and why we hear him, as it were, piping to his flock, even in a picture. Our ears are fancy stung! I remember once strolling along the margin of a stream, skirted with willows and plashy sedges, in one of those low sheltered valleys on Salisbury Plain, where the monks of former ages had planted chapels and built hermits' cells. There was a little parish church near, but tall elms and quivering alders hid it from my sight, when, all of a sudden, I was startled by the sound of the full organ pealing on the ear, accompanied by rustic voices and the willing choir of village maids and children. It rose, indeed, 'like an exhalation of rich distilled perfumes.' The dew from a thousand pastures was gathered in its softness; the silence of a thousand years spoke in it. It came upon the heart like the calm beauty of death; fancy caught the sound, and faith mounted on it to the skies. It filled the valley like a mist, and still poured out its endless chant, and still it swells upon the ear, and wraps me in a golden trance, drowning the noisy tumult of the world!

There is a curious and interesting discussion on the comparative distinctness of our visual and other external impressions, in Mr. Fearn's *Essay on Consciousness*, with which I shall try to descend from this rhapsody to the ground of common sense and plain reasoning again. After observing, a little before, that 'nothing is more untrue than that sensations of vision do necessarily leave more vivid and durable ideas than those of grosser senses,' he proceeds to give a number of illustrations in support of this position. 'Notwithstanding,' he says, 'the advantages here enumerated in favour of sight, I think there is no doubt that a man will come to forget acquaintance, and many other visible objects, noticed in mature age, before he will in the least forget taste and smells, of only moderate interest, encountered either in his childhood or at any time since.

'In the course of voyaging to various distant regions, it has several times happened that I have eaten once or twice of different things that never came in my way before nor since. Some of these have been pleasant, and some scarce better than insipid; but I have no reason to think I have forgot, or much altered the ideas left by those single impulses of taste; though here the memory of them certainly has not been preserved by repetition. It is clear I must have seen as well as tasted those things; and I am decided that I remember the tastes with more precision than I do the visual sensations.

'I remember having once, and only once, eat Kangaroo in New Holland; and having once smelled a baker's shop having a peculiar odour in the city of Bassorah. Now both these gross ideas remain with me quite as vivid as any visual ideas of those places; and this could not be from repetition, but really from interest in the sensation.

'Twenty-eight years ago, in the island of Jamaica, I partook (perhaps twice) of a certain fruit, of the taste of which I have now a very fresh idea; and I could add other instances of that period.

'I have had repeated proofs of having lost retention of visual objects, at various distances of time, though they had once been familiar. I have not, during thirty years, forgot the delicate, and in itself most trifling sensation that the palm of my hand used to convey, when I was a boy, trying the different effects of what boys call *light* and *heavy* tops; but I cannot remember within several shades of the brown coat which I left off a week ago. If any man thinks he can do better, let him take an ideal survey of his wardrobe, and then actually refer to it for proof.

'After retention of such ideas, it certainly would be very difficult to persuade me that feeling, taste, and smell can scarce be said to leave ideas, unless indistinct and obscure ones....

'Show a Londoner correct models of twenty London churches, and, at the same time, a model of each, which differs, in several considerable features, from the truth, and I venture to say he shall not tell you, in any instance, which is the correct one, except by mere chance.

'If he is an architect he may be much more correct than any ordinary person: and this obviously is because he has felt an interest in viewing these structures, which an ordinary person does not feel: and here interest is the sole reason of his remembering more correctly than his neighbour.

'I once heard a person quaintly ask another, How many trees there are in St. Paul's churchyard? The question itself indicates that many cannot answer it; and this is found to be the case with those who have passed the church a hundred times: whilst the cause is, that every individual in the busy stream which glides past St. Paul's is engrossed in various other interests.

'How often does it happen that we enter a well-known apartment, or meet a well-known friend, and receive some vague idea of visible difference, but cannot possibly find out *what* it is; until at length we come to perceive (or perhaps must be told) that some ornament or furniture is removed, altered, or added in the apartment; or that our friend has cut his hair, taken a wig, or has made any of twenty considerable alterations in his appearance. At other times we have no perception of alteration whatever, though the like has taken place.

'It is, however, certain that sight, apposited with interest, can retain tolerably exact copies of sensations, especially if not too complex, such as of the human countenance and figure: yet the voice will convince us when the countenance will not; and he is reckoned an excellent painter, and no ordinary genius, who can make a tolerable likeness from memory. Nay, more, it is a conspicuous proof of the inaccuracy of visual ideas, that it is an effort of consummate art, attained by many years' practice, to take a strict likeness of the human countenance, even when the object is present; and among those cases where the wilful cheat of flattery has been avoided, we still find in how very few instances the best painters produce a likeness up to the life, though practice and interest join in the attempt.

'I imagine an ordinary person would find it very difficult, supposing he had some knowledge of drawing, to afford from memory a tolerable sketch of such a familiar object as his curtain, his carpet, or his dressing-gown, if the pattern of either be at all various or irregular; yet he will instantly tell, with precision, either if his snuff or his wine has not the same character it had yesterday, though both these are compounds.

'Beyond all this I may observe, that a draper who is in the daily habit of such comparisons cannot carry in his mind the particular shade of a colour during a second of time; and has no certainty of tolerably matching two simple colours, except by placing the patterns in contact.'(2)

I will conclude the subject of this Essay with observing that (as it appears to me) a nearer and more familiar acquaintance with persons has a different and more favourable effect than that with places or things. The latter improve (as an almost universal rule) by being removed to a distance: the former, generally at least, gain by being brought nearer and more home to us. Report or imagination seldom raises any individual so high in our estimation as to disappoint us greatly when we are introduced to him: prejudice and malice constantly exaggerate defects beyond the reality. Ignorance alone makes monsters or bugbears: our actual acquaintances are all very commonplace people. The thing is, that as a matter of hearsay or conjecture, we make abstractions of particular vices, and irritate ourselves against some particular quality or action of the person we dislike: whereas individuals are concrete existences, not arbitrary denominations or nicknames; and have innumerable other qualities, good, bad, and indifferent, besides the damning feature with which we fill up the portrait or caricature in our previous fancies. We can scarcely hate any one that we know. An acute observer complained, that if there was any one to whom he had a particular spite, and a wish to let him see it, the moment he came to sit down with him his enmity was disarmed by some unforeseen circumstance. If it was a Quarterly Reviewer, he was in other respects like any other man. Suppose, again, your adversary turns out a very ugly man, or wants an eye, you are baulked in that way: he is not what you expected, the object of your abstract hatred and implacable disgust. He may be a very disagreeable person, but he is no longer the same. If you come into a room where a man is, you find, in general, that he has a nose upon his face. 'There's sympathy!' This alone is a diversion to your unqualified contempt. He is stupid, and says nothing, but he seems to have something in him when he laughs. You had conceived of him as a rank Whig or Tory—yet he talks upon other subjects. You knew that he was a virulent party-writer; but you find that the man himself is a tame sort of animal enough. He does not bite. That's something. In short, you can make nothing of it. Even opposite vices balance one another. A man may be pert in company, but he is also dull; so that you cannot, though you try, hate him cordially, merely for the wish to be offensive. He i did not know before—that he is a fool as well; so you forgive him. On the other hand, he may be a profligate public character, and may make no secret of it; but he gives you a hearty shake by the hand, speaks kindly to servants, and supports an aged father and mother. Politics apart, he is a very honest fellow. You are told that a person has carbuncles on his face; but you have ocular proofs that he is sallow, and pale as a ghost. This does not much mend the matter; but it blunts the edge of the ridicule, and turns your indignation against the inventor of the lie; but he is ——-, the editor of a Scotch magazine; so you are just where you were. I am not very fond of anonymous criticism; I want to know who the author can be: but the moment I learn this, I am satisfied. Even ——- would do well to come out of his disguise. It is the mask only that we dread and hate: the man may have something human about hi from partial representations, or from guess-work, are simple uncompounded ideas, which answer to nothing in reality: those which we derive from experience are mixed modes, the only true, and, in general, the most favourable ones. Instead of naked deformity, or abstract perfection—

        Those faultless monsters which the world ne'er saw—

'the web of our lives is of mingled yarn, good and ill together: our virtues would be proud, if our faults whipt them not; and our vices would despair, if they were not encouraged by our virtues.' This was truly and finely said long ago, by one who knew the strong and weak points of human nature; but it is what sects, and parties, and those philosophers whose pride and boast it is to classify by nicknames, have yet to know the meaning of!

FN to ESSAY X

(1) See Wilkie's Blind Fiddler.

(2) *Essay on Consciousness*, p. 303.

ESSAY XI. ON CORPORATE BODIES

        Corporate bodies have no soul.

Corporate bodies are more corrupt and profligate than individuals, because they have more power to do mischief, and are less amenable to disgrace or punishment. They feel neither shame, remorse, gratitude, nor goodwill. The principle of private or natural conscience is extinguished in each individual (we have no moral sense in the breasts of others), and nothing is considered but how the united efforts of the whole (released from idle scruples) may be best directed to the obtaining of political advantages and privileges to be shared as common spoil. Each member reaps the benefit, and lays the blame, if there is any, upon the rest. The *esprit de corps* becomes the ruling passion of every corporate body, compared with which the motives of delicacy or decorum towards others are looked upon as being both impertinent and improper. If any person sets up a plea of this sort in opposition to the rest, he is overruled, he gets ill-blood, and does no good: he is regarded as an interloper, a *black sheep* in the flock, and is either *sent to Coventry* or obliged to acquiesce in the notions and wishes of those he associates and is expected to co-operate with. The refinements of private judgment are referred to and negatived in a committee of the whole body, while the projects and interests of the Corporation meet with a secret but powerful support in the self-love of the different members. Remonstrance, opposition, is fruitless, troublesome, invidious; it answers no one end; and a conformity to the sense of the company is found to be no less necessary to a reputation for good-fellowship than to a quiet life. Self-love and social here look like the same; and in consulting the interests of a particular class, which are also your own, there is even a show of public virtue. He who is a captious, impracticable, dissatisfied member of his little club or *coterie* is immediately set down as a bad member of the community in general, as no friend to regularity and order, as 'a pestilent fellow,' and one who is incapable of sympathy, attachment, or cordial co-operation in any department or undertaking. Thus the most refractory novice in such matters becomes weaned from his obligations to the larger society, which only breed him inconvenience without any adequate recompense, and wedded to a nearer and dearer one, where he finds every kind of comfort and consolation. He contracts the vague and unmeaning character of Man into the more emphatic title of Freeman and Alderman. The claims of an undefined humanity sit looser and looser upon him, at the same time that he draws the bands of his new engagements closer and tighter about him. He loses sight, by degrees, of all common sense and feeling in the petty squabbles, intrigues, feuds, and airs of affected importance to which he has made himself an accessory. He is quite an altered man. 'Really the society were under considerable obligations to him in that last business'; that is to say, in some paltry job or underhand attempt to encroach upon the rights or dictate to the understandings of the neighbourhood. In the meantime they eat, drink, and carouse together. They wash down all minor animosities and unavoidable differences of opinion in pint bumpers; and the complaints of the multitude are lost in the clatter of plates and the roaring of loyal catches at every quarter's meeting or mayor's feast. The town-hall reels with an unwieldy sense of self-importance; 'the very stones prate' of processions; the common pump creaks in concert with the uncorking of bottles and tapping of beer-barrels: the market-cross looks big with authority. Everything has an ambiguous, upstart, repulsive air. Circle within circle is formed, an *imperium in imperio*: and the business is to exclude from the first circle all the notions, opinions, ideas, interests, and pretensions of the second. Hence there arises not only an antipathy to common sense and decency in those things where there is a real opposition of interest or clashing of prejudice, but it becomes a habit and a favourite amusement in those who are 'dressed in a little brief authority,' to thwart, annoy, insult, and harass others on all occasions where the least opportunity or pretext for it occurs. Spite, bickerings, back-biting, insinuations, lies, jealousies, nicknames are the order of the day, and nobody knows what it's all about. One would think that the mayor, aldermen, and liverymen were a higher and more select species of animals than their townsmen; though there is no difference whatever but in their gowns and staff of office! This is the essence of the *esprit de corps*. It is certainly not a very delectable source of contemplation or subject to treat of.

Public bodies are so far worse than the individuals composing them, because the *official* takes place of the *moral sense.* The nerves that in themselves were soft and pliable enough, and responded naturally to the touch of pity, when fastened into a machine of that sort become callous and rigid, and throw off every extraneous application that can be made to them with perfect apathy. An appeal is made to the ties of individual friendship: the body in general know nothing of them. A case has occurred which strongly called forth the compassion of the person who was witness of it; but the body (or any special deputation of them) were not present when it happened. These little weaknesses and 'compunctious visitings of nature' are effectually guarded against, indeed, by the very rules and regulations of the society, as well as by its spirit. The individual is the creature of his feelings of all sorts, the sport of his vices and his virtues—like the fool in Shakespear, 'motley's his proper wear':—corporate bodies are dressed in a moral uniform; mixed motives do not operate there, frailty is made into a system, 'diseases are turned into commodities.' Only so much of any one's natural or genuine impulses can influence him in his artificial capacity as formally comes home to the aggregate conscience of those with whom he acts, or bears upon the interests (real or pretended), the importance, respectability, and professed objects of the society. Beyond that point the nerve is bound up, the conscience is seared, and the torpedo-touch of so much inert matter operates to deaden the best feelings and harden the heart. Laughter and tears are said to be the characteristic signs of humanity. Laughter is common enough in such places as a set-off to the mock-gravity; but who ever saw a public body in tears? Nothing but a job or some knavery can keep them serious for ten minutes together.(1)

Such are the qualifications and the apprenticeship necessary to make a man tolerated, to enable him to pass as a cypher, or be admitted as a mere numerical unit, in any corporate body: to be a leader and dictator he must be diplomatic in impertinence, and officious in every dirty work. He must not merely conform to established prejudices; he must flatter them. He must not merely be insensible to the demands of moderation and equity; he must be loud against them. He must not simply fall in with all sorts of contemptible cabals and intrigues; he must be indefatigable in fomenting them, and setting everybody together by the ears. He must not only repeat, but invent lies. He must make speeches and write handbills; he must be devoted to the wishes and objects of the society, its creature, its jackal, its busybody, its mouthpiece, its prompter; he must deal in law cases, in demurrers, in charters, in traditions, in common-places, in logic and rhetoric—in everything but common sense and honesty. He must (in Mr. Burke's phrase) 'disembowel himself of his natural entrails, and be stuffed with paltry, blurred sheets of parchment about the rights' of the privileged few. He must be a concentrated essence, a varnished, powdered representative of the vices, absurdities, hypocrisy, jealousy, pride, and pragmaticalness of his party. Such a one, by bustle and self-importance and puffing, by flattering one to his face and abusing another behind his back, by lending himself to the weaknesses of some, and pampering the mischievous propensities of others, will pass for a great man in a little society.

Age does not improve the morality of public bodies. They grow more and more tenacious of their idle privileges and senseless self-consequence. They get weak and obstinate at the same time. Those who belong to them have all the upstart pride and pettifogging spirit of their present character ingrafted on the venerableness and superstitious sanctity of ancient institutions. They are naturally at issue, first with their neighbours, and next with their contemporaries, on all matters of common propriety and judgment. They become more attached to forms, the more obsolete they are; and the defence of every absurd and invidious distinction is a debt which (by implication) they owe to the dead as well as the living. What might once have been of serious practical utility they turn to farce, by retaining the letter when the spirit is gone: and they do this the more, the more glaring the inconsistency and want of sound reasoning; for they think they thus give proof of their zeal and attachment to the abstract principle on which old establishments exist, the ground of prescription and authority. *The greater the wrong, the greater the right,* in all such cases. The *esprit de corps* does not take much merit to itself for upholding what is justifiable in any system, or the proceedings of any party, but for adhering to what is palpably injurious. You may exact the first from an enemy: the last is the province of a friend. It has been made a subject of complaint, that the champions of the Church, for example, who are advanced to dignities and honours, are hardly ever those who defend the common principles of Christianity, but those who volunteer to man the out-works, and set up ingenious excuses for the questionable points, the ticklish places in the established form of worship, that is, for those which are attacked from without, and are supposed in danger of being undermined by stratagem, or carried by assault!

The great resorts and seats of learning often outlive in this way the intention of the founders as the world outgrows them. They may be said to resemble antiquated coquettes of the last age, who think everything ridiculous and intolerable but what was in fashion when they were young, and yet are standing proofs of the progress of taste and the vanity of human pretensions. Our universities are, in a great measure, become cisterns to hold, not conduits to disperse knowledge. The age has the start of them; that is, other sources of knowledge have been opened since their formation, to which the world have had access, and have drunk plentifully at those living fountains, but from which they are debarred by the tenor of their charter, and as a matter of dignity and privilege. They have grown poor, like the old grandees in some countries, by subsisting on the inheritance of learning, while the people have grown rich by trade. They are too much in the nature of *fixtures* in intellect: they stop the way in the road to truth; or at any rate (for they do not themselves advance) they can only be of service as a check-weight on the too hasty and rapid career of innovation. All that has been invented or thought in the last two hundred years they take no cognizance of, or as little as possible; they are above it; they stand upon the ancient landmarks, and will not budge; whatever was not known when they were first endowed, they are still in profound and lofty ignorance of. Yet in that period how much has been done in literature, arts, and science, of which (with the exception of mathematical knowledge, the hardest to gainsay or subject to the trammels of prejudice and barbarous *ipse dixits*) scarce any trace is to be found in the authentic modes of study and legitimate inquiry which prevail at either of our Universities! The unavoidable aim of all corporate bodies of learning is not to grow wise, or teach others wisdom, but to prevent any one else from being or seeming wiser than themselves; in other words, their infallible tendency is in the end to suppress inquiry and darken knowledge, by setting limits to the mind of man, and saying to his proud spirit, *Hitherto shalt thou come, and no farther!* It would not be an unedifying experiment to make a collection of the titles of works published in the course of the year by Members of the Universities. If any attempt is to be made to patch up an idle system in policy or legislation, or church government, it is by a member of the University: if any hashed-up speculation on an old exploded argument is to be brought forward 'in spite of *shame,* in erring reason's spite,' it is by a Member of the University: if a paltry project is ushered into the world for combining ancient prejudices with modern time-serving, it is by a Member of the University. Thus we get at a stated supply of the annual Defences of the Sinking Fund, Thoughts on the Evils of Education, Treatises on Predestination, and Eulogies on Mr. Malthus, all from the same source, and through the same vent. If they came from any other quarter nobody would look at them; but they have an *Imprimatur* from dulness and authority: we know that there is no offence in them; and they are stuck in the shop windows, and read (in the intervals of Lord Byron's works, or the Scotch novels) in cathedral towns and close boroughs!

It is, I understand and believe, pretty much the same in more modern institutions for the encouragement of the Fine Arts. The end is lost in the means: rules take place of nature and genius; cabal and bustle, and struggle for rank and precedence, supersede the study and the love of art. A Royal Academy is a kind of hospital and infirmary for the obliquities of taste and ingenuity—a receptacle where enthusiasm and originality stop and stagnate, and spread their influence no farther, instead of being a school founded for genius, or a temple built to fame. The generality of those who wriggle, or fawn, or beg their way to a seat there, live on their certificate of merit to a good old age, and are seldom heard of afterwards. If a man of sterling capacity gets among them, and minds his own business he is nobody; he makes no figure in council, in voting, in resolutions or speeches. If he comes forward with plans and views for the good of the Academy and the advancement of art, he is immediately set upon as a visionary, a fanatic, with notions hostile to the interest and credit of the existing members of the society. If he directs the ambition of the scholars to the study of History, this strikes at once at the emoluments of the profession, who are most of them (by God's will) portrait painters. If he eulogises the Antique, and speaks highly of the Old Masters, he is supposed to be actuated by envy to living painters and native talent. If, again, he insists on a knowledge of anatomy as essential to correct drawing, this would seem to imply a want of it in our most eminent designers. Every plan, suggestion, argument, that has the general purposes and principles of art for its object, is thwarted, scouted, ridiculed, slandered, as having a malignant aspect towards the profits and pretensions of the great mass of flourishing and respectable artists in the country. This leads to irritation and ill-will on all sides. The obstinacy of the constituted authorities keeps pace with the violence and extravagance opposed to it; and they lay all the blame on the folly and mistakes they have themselves occasioned or increased. It is considered as a personal quarrel, not a public question; by which means the dignity of the body is implicated in resenting the slips and inadvertencies of its members, not in promoting their common and declared objects. In this sort of wretched *tracasserie* the Barrys and H——s stand no chance with the Catons, the Tubbs, and F——s. Sir Joshua even was obliged to hold himself aloof from them, and Fuseli passes as a kind of nondescript, or one of his own grotesques. The air of an academy, in short, is not the air of genius and immortality; it is too close and heated, and impregnated with the notions of the common sort. A man steeped in a corrupt atmosphere of this description is no longer open to the genial impulses of nature and truth, nor sees visions of ideal beauty, nor dreams of antique grace and grandeur, nor has the finest works of art continually hovering and floating through his uplifted fancy; but the images that haunt it are rules of the academy, charters, inaugural speeches, resolutions passed or rescinded, cards of invitation to a council-meeting, or the annual dinner, prize medals, and the king's diploma, constituting him a gentleman and esquire. He 'wipes out all trivial, fond records'; all romantic aspirations; 'the Raphael grace, the Guido air'; and the commands of the academy alone 'must live within the book and volume of his brain, unmixed with baser matter.' It may be doubted whether any work of lasting reputation and universal interest can spring up in this soil, or ever has done in that of any academy. The last question is a matter of fact and history, not of mere opinion or prejudice; and may be ascertained as such accordingly. The mighty names of former times rose before the existence of academies; and the three greatest painters, undoubtedly, that this country has produced, Reynolds, Wilson, and Hogarth, were not 'dandled and swaddled' into artists in any institution for the fine arts. I do not apprehend that the names of Chantrey or Wilkie (great as one, and considerable as the other of them is) can be made use of in any way to impugn the jet of this argument. We may find a considerable improvement in some of our artists, when they get out of the vortex for a time. Sir Thomas Lawrence is all the better for having been abstracted for a year or two from Somerset House; and Mr. Dawe, they say, has been doing wonders in the North. When will he return, and once more 'bid Britannia rival Greece'?

Mr. Canning somewhere lays it down as a rule, that corporate bodies are necessarily correct and pure in their conduct, from the knowledge which the individuals composing them have of one another, and the jealous vigilance they exercise over each other's motives and characters; whereas people collected into mobs are disorderly and unprincipled from being utterly unknown and unaccountable to each other. This is a curious *pass* of wit. I differ with him in both parts of the dilemma. To begin with the first, and to handle it somewhat cavalierly, according to the model before us; we know, for instance, there is said to be honour among thieves, but very little honesty towards others. Their honour consists in the division of the booty, not in the mode of acquiring it: they do not (often) betray one another, but they will waylay a stranger, or knock out a traveller's brains: they may be depended on in giving the alarm when any of their posts are in danger of being surprised; and they will stand together for their ill-gotten gains to the last drop of their blood. Yet they form a distinct society, and are strictly responsible for their behaviour to one another and to their leader. They are not a mob, but a *gang,* completely in one another's power and secrets. Their familiarity, however, with the proceedings of the *corps* does not lead them to expect or to exact from it a very high standard of moral honesty; that is out of the question; but they are sure to gain the good opinion of their fellows by committing all sorts of depredations, fraud, and violence against the community at large. So (not to speak it profanely) some of Mr. Croker's friends may be very respectable people in their way—'all honourable men'—but their respectability is confined within party limits; every one does not sympathise in the integrity of their views; the understanding between them and the public is not well defined or reciprocal. Or, suppose a gang of pickpockets hustle a passenger in the street, and the mob set upon them, and proceed to execute summary justice upon such as they can lay hands on, am I to conclude that the rogues are in the right, because theirs is a system of well-organised knavery, which they settled in the morning, with their eyes one upon the other, and which they regularly review at night, with a due estimate of each other's motives, character, and conduct in the business; and that the honest men are in the wrong, because they are a casual collection of unprejudiced, disinterested individuals, taken at a venture from the mass of the people, acting without concert or responsibility, on the spur of the occasion, and giving way to their instantaneous impulses and honest anger? Mobs, in fact, then, are almost always right in their feelings, and often in their judgments, on this very account—that being utterly unknown to and disconnected with each other, they have no point of union or principle of co-operation between them, but the natural sense of justice recognised by all persons in common. They appeal, at the first meeting, not to certain symbols and watchwords privately agreed upon, like Freemasons, but to the maxims and instincts proper to all the world. They have no other clue to guide them to their object but either the dictates of the heart or the universally understood sentiments of society, neither of which are likely to be in the wrong. The flame which bursts out and blazes from popular sympathy is made of honest but homely materials. It is not kindled by sparks of wit or sophistry, nor damped by the cold calculations of self-interest. The multitude may be wantonly set on by others, as is too often the case, or be carried too far in the impulse of rage and disappointment; but their resentment, when they are left to themselves, is almost uniformly, in the first instance, excited by some evident abuse and wrong; and the excesses into which they run arise from that very want of foresight and regular system which is a pledge of the uprightness and heartiness of their intentions. In short, the only class of persons to sinister and corrupt motives is not applicable is that body of individuals which usually goes by the name of the *People!*

FN to ESSAY XI

(1) We sometimes see a whole playhouse in tears. But the audience at a theatre, though a public assembly, are not a public body. They are not Incorporated into a framework of exclusive, narrow-minded interests of their own. Each individual looks out of his own insignificance at a scene, *ideal* perhaps, and foreign to himself, but true to nature; friends, strangers, meet on the common ground of humanity, and the tears that spring from their breasts are those which 'sacred pity has engendered.' They are a mixed multitude melted Into sympathy by remote, imaginary events, not a combination cemented by petty views, and sordid, selfish prejudices.

ESSAY XII. WHETHER ACTORS OUGHT TO SIT IN THE BOXES?

I think not; and that for the following reasons, as well as I can give them:—

Actors belong to the public: their persons are not their own property. They exhibit themselves on the stage: that is enough, without displaying themselves in the boxes of the theatre. I conceive that an actor, on account of the very circumstances of his profession, ought to keep himself as much incognito as possible. He plays a number of parts disguised, transformed into them as much as he can 'by his so potent art,' and he should not disturb this borrowed impression by unmasking before company more than he can help. Let him go into the pit, if he pleases, to see—not into the first circle, to be seen. He is seen enough without that: he is the centre of an illusion that he is bound to support, both, as it appears to me, by a certain self-respect which should repel idle curiosity, and by a certain deference to the public, in whom he has inspired certain prejudices which he is covenanted not to break. He represents the majesty of successive kings; he takes the responsibility of heroes and lovers on himself; the mantle of genius and nature falls on his shoulders; we 'pile millions' of associations on him, under which he should be 'buried quick,' and not perk out an inauspicious face upon us, with a plain-cut coat, to say, 'What fools you all were!—I am not Hamlet the Dane!'

It is very well and in strict propriety for Mr. Mathews, in his AT HOME, after he has been imitating his inimitable Scotchwoman, to slip out as quick as lightning, and appear in the side-box shaking hands with our old friend Jack Bannister. It adds to our surprise at the versatility of his changes of place and appearance, and he had been before us in his own person during a great part of the evening. There was no harm done—no imaginary spell broken—no discontinuity of thought or sentiment. Mr. Mathews is himself (without offence be it spoken) both a cleverer and more respectable man than many of the characters he represents. Not so when

    O'er the stage the Ghost of Hamlet stalks,
    Othello rages, Desdemona mourns,
    And poor Monimia pours her soul in love.

A different feeling then prevails:—close, close the scene upon them, and never break that fine phantasmagoria of the brain. Or if it must be done at all, let us choose some other time and place for it: let no one wantonly dash the Circean cup from our lips, or dissolve the spirit of enchantment in the very palace of enchantment. Go, Mr. ——, and sit somewhere else! What a thing it is, for instance, for any part of an actor's dress to come off unexpectedly while he is playing! What a *cut* it is upon himself and the audience! What an effort he has to recover himself, and struggle through this exposure of the naked truth! It has been considered as one of the triumphs of Garrick's tragic power, that once, when he was playing Lear, his crown of straw came off, and nobody laughed or took the least notice, so much had he identified himself with the character. Was he, after this, to pay so little respect to the feelings he had inspired, as to tear off his tattered robes, and take the old crazed king with him to play the fool in the boxes?

    No; let him pass. Vex not his parting spirit,
    Nor on the rack of this rough world
    Stretch him out farther!

Some lady is said to have fallen in love with Garrick from being present when he played the part of Romeo, on which he observed, that he would undertake to cure her of her folly if she would only come and see him in Abel Drugger. So the modern tragedian and fine gentleman, by appearing to advantage, and conspicuously, *in propria persona,* may easily cure us of our predilection for all the principal characters he shines in. 'Sir! do you think Alexander looked o' this fashion in his lifetime, or was perfumed so? Had Julius Caesar such a nose? or wore his frill as you do? You have slain I don't know how many heroes "with a bare bodkin," the gold pin in your shirt, and spoiled all the fine love speeches you will ever make by picking your teeth with that inimitable air!'

An actor, after having performed his part well, instead of courting farther distinction, should affect obscurity, and 'steal most guilty-like away,' conscious of admiration that he can support nowhere but in his proper sphere, and jealous of his own and others' good opinion of him, in proportion as he is a darling in the public eye. He cannot avoid attracting disproportionate attention: why should he wish to fix it on himself in a perfectly flat and insignificant part, viz. his own character? It was a bad custom to bring authors on the stage to crown them. *Omne Ignotum pro magnifico est.* Even professed critics, I think, should be shy of putting themselves forward to applaud loudly: any one in a crowd has 'a voice potential' as the press: it is either committing their pretensions a little indiscreetly, or confirming their own judgment by a clapping of hands. If you only go and give the cue lustily, the house seems in wonderful accord with your opinions. An actor, like a king, should only appear on state occasions. He loses popularity by too much publicity; or, according to the proverb, *familiarity breeds contempt.* Both characters personate a certain abstract idea, are seen in a fictitious costume, and when they have 'shuffled off this more than mortal coil,' they had better keep out of the way—the acts and sentiments emanating from themselves will not carry on the illusion of our prepossessions. Ordinary transactions do not give scope to grace and dignity like romantic situations or prepared pageants, and the *little* is apt to prevail over the *great,* if we come to count the instances.

The motto of a great actor should be *aut Caesar aut nihil.* I do not see how with his crown, or plume of feathers, he can get through those little box-doors without stooping and squeezing his artificial importance to tatters. The entrance of the stage is arched so high 'that *players* may get through, and keep their gorgeous turbans on, without good-morrow to the gods!'

The top-tragedian of the day has too large and splendid a train following him to have room for them in one of the dress-boxes. When he appears there, it should be enlarged expressly for the occasion; for at his heels march the figures, in full costume, of Cato, and Brutus, and Cassius, and of him with the falcon eye, and Othello, and Lear, and crook-backed Richard, and Hamlet, Prince of Denmark, and numbers more, and demand entrance along with him, shadows to which he alone lends bodily substance! 'The graves yawn and render up their dead to push us from our stools.' There is a mighty bustle at the door, a gibbering and squeaking in the lobbies. An actor's retinue is imperial, it presses upon the imagination too much, and he should therefore slide unnoticed into the pit. Authors, who are in a manner his makers and masters, sit there contented—why should not he? 'He is used to show himself.' That, then, is the very reason he should conceal his person at other times. A habit of ostentation should not be reduced to a principle. If I had seen the late Gentleman Lewis fluttering in a prominent situation in the boxes, I should have been puzzled whether to think of him as the Copper Captain, or as Bobadil, or Ranger, or Young Rapid, or Lord Foppington, or fifty other whimsical characters; then I should have got Munden and Quick and a parcel more of them in my head, till 'my brain would have been like a smoke-jack': I should not have known what to make of it; but if I had seen him in the pit, I should merely have eyed him with respectful curiosity, and have told every one that that was Gentleman Lewis. We should have concluded from the circumstance that he was a modest, sensible man: we all knew beforehand that he could show off whenever he pleased!

There is one class of performers that I think is quite exempt from the foregoing reasoning, I mean *retired actors.* Come when they will and where they will, they are welcome to their old friends. They have as good a right to sit in the boxes as children at the holidays. But they do not, somehow, come often. It is but a melancholy recollection with them:—

> Then sweet,
> Now sad to think on!

Mrs. Garrick still goes often, and hears the applause of her husband over again in the shouts of the pit. Had Mrs. Pritchard or Mrs. Clive been living, I am afraid we should have seen little of them-it would have been too *home* a feeling with them. Mrs. Siddons seldom if ever goes, and yet she is almost the only thing left worth seeing there. She need not stay away on account of any theory that I can form. She is out of the pale of all theories, and annihilates all rules. Wherever she sits there is grace and grandeur, there is tragedy personified. Her seat is the undivided throne of the Tragic Muse. She had no need of the robes, the sweeping train, the ornaments of the stage; in herself she is as great as any being she ever represented in the ripeness and plenitude of her power! I should not, I confess, have had the same paramount abstracted feeling at seeing John Kemble there, whom I venerate at a distance, and should not have known whether he was playing off the great man or the great actor:—

> A little more than kin, and less than kind.

I know it may be said in answer to all this pretext of keeping the character of the player inviolate, 'What is there more common, in fact, than for the hero of a tragedy to speak the prologue, or than for the heroine, who has been stabbed or poisoned, to revive, and come forward laughing in the epilogue?' As to the epilogue, it is spoken to get rid of the idea of the tragedy altogether, and to ward off the fury of the pit, who may be bent on its damnation. The greatest incongruity you can hit upon is, therefore, the most proper for this purpose. But I deny that the hero of a tragedy, or the principal character in it, is ever pitched upon to deliver the prologue. It is always, by prescription, some walking shadow, some poor player, who cannot even spoil a part of any consequence. Is there not Mr. Claremont always at hand for this purpose, whom the late king pronounced three times to be 'a bad actor'?(1) What is there in common between that accustomed wave of the hand and the cocked hat under the arm, and any passion or person that can be brought forward on the stage? It is not that we can be said to acquire a prejudice against so harmless an actor as Mr. Claremont: we are born with a prejudice against a speaker of prologues. It is an innate idea: a natural instinct: there is a particular organ in the brain provided for it. Do we not all hate a manager? It is not because he is insolent or impertinent, or fond of making ridiculous speeches, or a notorious puffer, or ignorant, or mean, or vain, but it is because we see him in a coat, waistcoat, and breeches. The stage is the world of fantasy: it is Queen Mab that has invited us to her revels there, and all that have to do with it should wear motley!

Lastly, there are some actors by profession whose faces we like to see in the boxes or anywhere else; but it is because they are no actors, but rather gentlemen and scholars, and in their proper places in the boxes, or wherever they are. Does not an actor himself, I would ask, feel conscious and awkward in the boxes if he thinks that he is known? And does he not sit there in spite of this uneasy feeling, and run the gauntlet of impertinent looks and whispers, only to get a little by-admiration, as he thinks? It is hardly to be supposed that he comes to see the play—the show. He must have enough of plays and finery. But he wants to see a favourite (perhaps a rival) actor in a striking part. Then the place for him to do this is the pit. Painters, I know, always get as close up to a picture they want to copy as they can; and I should imagine actors would want to do the same, in order to look into the texture and mechanism of their art. Even theatrical critics can make nothing of a part that they see from the boxes. If you sit in the stage-box, your attention is drawn off by the company and other circumstances. If you get to a distance (so as to be out of the reach of notice) you can neither hear nor see well. For myself, I would as soon take a seat on the top of the Monument to give an account of a first appearance, as go into the second or third tier of boxes to do it. I went, but the other day, with a box-ticket to see Miss Fanny Brunton come out in Juliet, and Mr. Macready make a first appearance in Romeo; and though I was told (by a tolerable judge) that the new Juliet was the most elegant figure on the stage, and that Mr. Macready's Romeo was quite beautiful, I vow to God I knew nothing of it. So little could I tell of the matter that at one time I mistook Mr. Horrebow for Mr.

Abbott. I have seen Mr. Kean play Sir Giles Overreach one night from the front of the pit, and a few nights after from the front boxes facing the stage. It was another thing altogether. That which had been so lately nothing but flesh and blood, a living fibre, 'instinct with fire' and spirit, was no better than a little fantoccini figure, darting backwards and forwards on the stage, starting, screaming, and playing a number of fantastic tricks before the audience. I could account, in the latter instance, for the little approbation of the performance manifested around me, and also for the general scepticism with respect to Mr. Kean's acting, which has been said to prevail among those who cannot condescend to go into the pit, and have not interest in the orchestra—to see him act. They may, then, stay away altogether. His face is the running comment on his acting, which reconciles the audience to it. Without that index to his mind, you are not prepared for the vehemence and suddenness of his gestures; his pauses are long, abrupt, and unaccountable, if not filled up by the expression; it is in the working of his face that you see the writhing and coiling up of the passions before they make their serpent-spring; the lightning of his eye precedes the hoarse burst of thunder from his voice.

One may go into the boxes, indeed, and criticise acting and actors with Sterne's stop-watch, but not otherwise—'"And between the nominative case and the verb (which, as your lordship knows, should agree together in number, person, etc.) there was a full pause of a second and two-thirds."—"But was the eye silent—did the look say nothing?" "I looked only at the stop-watch, my lord."—"Excellent critic!"'—If any other actor, indeed, goes to see Mr. Kean act, with a view *to avoid imitation,* this may be the place, or rather it is the way to run into it, for you see only his extravagances and defects, which are the most easily carried away. Mr. Mathews may translate him into an AT HOME even from the *slips!*—Distinguished actors, then, ought, I conceive, to set the example of going into the pit, were it only for their own sakes. I remember a trifling circumstance, which I worked up at the time into a confirmation of this theory of mine, engrafted on old prejudice and tradition.(2) I had got into the middle of the pit, at considerable risk of broken bones, to see Mr. Kean in one of his early parts, when I perceived two young men seated a little behind me, with a certain space left round them. They were dressed in the height of the fashion, in light drab-coloured greatcoats, and with their shirt-sleeves drawn down over their hands, at a time when this was not so common as it has since become. I took them for younger sons of some old family at least. One of them, that was very good-looking, I thought might be Lord Byron, and his companion might be Mr. Hobhouse. They seemed to have wandered from another sphere of this our planet to witness a masterly performance to the utmost advantage. This stamped the thing. They were, undoubtedly, young men of rank and fashion; but their taste was greater than their regard for appearances. The pit was, after all, the true resort of thoroughbred critics and amateurs. When there was anything worth seeing, this was the place; and I began to feel a sort of reflected importance in the consciousness that I also was a critic. Nobody sat near them—it would have seemed like an intrusion. Not a syllable was uttered.—They were two clerks in the Victualling Office!

What I would insist on, then, is this—that for Mr. Kean, or Mr. Young, or Mr. Macready, or any of those that are 'cried out upon in the top of the compass' to obtrude themselves voluntarily or ostentatiously upon our notice, when they are out of character, is a solecism in theatricals. For them to thrust themselves forward before the scenes, is to drag us behind them against our will, than which nothing can be more fatal to a true passion for the stage, and which is a privilege that should be kept sacred for impertinent curiosity. Oh! while I live, let me not be admitted (under special favour) to an actor's dressing-room. Let me not see how Cato painted, or how Caesar combed! Let me not meet the prompt-boys in the passage, nor see the half-lighted candles stuck against the bare walls, nor hear the creaking of machines, or the fiddlers laughing; nor see a Columbine practising a pirouette in sober sadness, nor Mr. Grimaldi's face drop from mirth to sudden melancholy as he passes the side-scene, as if a shadow crossed it, nor witness the long-chinned generation of the pantomime sit twirling their thumbs, nor overlook the fellow who holds the candle for the moon in the scene between Lorenzo and Jessica! Spare me this insight into secrets I am not bound to know. The stage is not a mistress that we are sworn to undress. Why should we look behind the glass of fashion? Why should we prick the bubble that reflects the world, and turn it to a little soap and water? Trust a little to first appearances—leave something to fancy. I observe that the great puppets of the real stage, who themselves play a grand part, like to get into the boxes over the stage; where they see nothing from the proper point of view, but peep and pry into what is going on like a magpie looking into a marrow-bone. This is just like them. So they look down upon human life, of which they are ignorant. They see the exits and entrances of the players, something that they suspect is meant to be kept from them (for they think they are always liable to be imposed upon): the petty pageant of an hour ends with each scene long before the catastrophe, and the tragedy of life is turned to farce under their eyes. These people laugh loud at a pantomime, and are delighted with clowns and pantaloons. They pay no attention to anything else. The stage-boxes exist in contempt of the stage and common sense. The private boxes, on the contrary, should be reserved as the receptacle for the officers of state and great diplomatic characters, who wish to avoid, rather than court popular notice!

FN to ESSAY XII

(1) Mr. Munden and Mr. Claremont went one Sunday to Windsor to see the king. They passed with other spectators once or twice: at last, his late majesty distinguished Munden in the crowd and called him to him. After treating him with much cordial familiarity, the king said, 'And, pray, who is that with you?' Munden, with many congees, and contortions of face, replied, 'An please your majesty, it's Mr. Claremont of the Theatre Royal Drury Lane.' 'Oh! yes,' said the king, 'I know him well—a bad actor, a bad actor, a bad actor!' Why kings should repeat what they say three times is odd: their saying it once is quite enough. I have always liked Mr. Claremont's face since I heard this anecdote, and perhaps the telling it may have the same effect on other people.

(2) The trunk-maker, I grant, in the *Spectator's* time, sat in the two-shilling gallery. But that was in the *Spectator's* time, and not in the days of Mr. Smirke and Mr. Wyatt.

ESSAY XIII. ON THE DISADVANTAGES OF INTELLECTUAL SUPERIORITY

The chief disadvantage of knowing more and seeing farther than others, is not to be generally understood. A man is, in consequence of this, liable to start paradoxes, which immediately transport him beyond the reach of the common-place reader. A person speaking once in a slighting manner of a very original-minded man, received for answer, "He strides on so far before you that he dwindles in the distance!"

Petrarch complains that 'Nature had made him different from other people'—*singular' d' altri genti.* The great happiness of life is, to be neither better nor worse than the general run of those you meet with, you soon find a mortifying level in their difference to what you particularly pique yourself upon. What is the use of being moral in a night-cellar, or wise in Bedlam? 'To be honest, as this world goes, is to be one man picked out of ten thousand.' So says Shakespear; and the commentators have not added that, under these circumstances, a man is more likely to become the butt of slander than the mark of admiration for being so. 'How now, thou particular fellow?'(1) is the common answer to all such out-of-the-way pretensions. By not doing as those at Rome do, we cut ourselves off from good-fellowship and society. We speak another language, have notions of our own, and are treated as of a different species. Nothing can be more awkward than to intrude with any such far-fetched ideas among the common herd, who will be sure to

> Stand all astonished, like a sort of steers,
> 'Mongst whom some beast of strange and foreign race
> Unwares is chanced, far straying from his peers:
> So will their ghastly gaze betray their hidden fears.

Ignorance of another's meaning is a sufficient cause of fear, and fear produces hatred: hence the suspicion and rancour entertained against all those who set up for greater refinement and wisdom than their neighbours. It is in vain to think of softening down this spirit of hostility by simplicity of manners, or by condescending to persons of low estate. The more you condescend, the more they will presume upon it; they will fear you less, but hate you more; and will be the more determined to take their revenge on you for a superiority as to which they are entirely in the dark, and of which you yourself seem to entertain considerable doubt. All the humility in the world will only pass for weakness and folly. They have no notion of such a thing. They always put their best foot forward; and argue that you would do the same if you had any such wonderful talents as people say. You had better, therefore, play off the great man at once—hector, swagger, talk big, and ride the high horse over them: you may by this means extort outward respect or common civility; but you will get nothing (with low people) by forbearance and good-nature but open insult or silent contempt. Coleridge always talks to people about what they don't understand: I, for one, endeavour to talk to them about what they do understand, and find I only get the more ill-will by it. They conceive I do not think them capable of anything better; that I do not think it worth while, as the vulgar saying is, to *throw a word to a dog.* I once complained of this to Coleridge, thinking it hard I should be sent to Coventry for not making a prodigious display. He said: 'As you assume a certain character, you ought to produce your credentials. It is a tax upon people's good-nature to admit superiority of any kind, even where there is the most evident proof of it; but it is too hard a task for the imagination to admit it without any apparent ground at all.'

There is not a greater error than to suppose that you avoid the envy, malice, and uncharitableness, so common in the world, by going among people without pretensions. There are no people who have no pretensions; or the fewer their pretensions, the less they can afford to acknowledge yours without some sort of value received. The more information individuals possess, or the more they have refined upon any subject, the more readily can they conceive and admit the same kind of superiority to themselves that they feel over others. But from the low, dull, level sink of ignorance and vulgarity, no idea or love of excellence can arise. You think you are doing mighty well with them; that you are laying aside the buckram of pedantry and pretence, and getting the character of a plain, unassuming, good sort of fellow. It will not do. All the while that you are making these familiar advances, and wanting to be at your ease, they are trying to recover the wind of you. You may forget that you are an author, an artist, or what not—they do not forget that they are nothing, nor bate one jot of their desire to prove you in the same predicament. They take hold of some circumstance in your dress; your manner of entering a room is different from that of other people; you do not eat vegetables—that's odd; you have a particular phrase, which they repeat, and this becomes a sort of standing joke; you look grave, or ill; you talk, or are more silent than usual; you are in or out of pocket: all these petty, inconsiderable circumstances, in which you resemble, or are unlike other people, form so many counts in the indictment which is going on in their imaginations against you, and are so many contradictions in your character. In any one else they would pass unnoticed, but in a person of whom they had heard so much they cannot make them out at all. Meanwhile, those things in which you may really excel go for nothing, because they cannot judge of them. They speak highly of some book which you do not like, and therefore you make no answer. You recommend them to go and see some Picture in which they do not find much to admire. How are you to convince them that you are right? Can you make them perceive that the fault is in them, and not in the picture, unless you could give them your knowledge? They hardly distinguish the difference between a Correggio and a common daub. Does this bring you any nearer to an understanding? The more you know of the difference, the more deeply you feel it, or the more earnestly you wish to convey it, the farther do you find yourself removed to an immeasurable distance from the possibility of making them enter into views and feelings of which they have not even the first rudiments. You cannot make them see with your eyes, and they must judge for themselves.

Intellectual is not like bodily strength. You have no hold of the understanding of others but by their sympathy. Your knowing, in fact, so much more about a subject does not give you a superiority, that is, a power over them, but only renders it the more impossible for you to make the least impression on them. Is it, then, an advantage to you? It may be, as it relates to your own private satisfaction, but it places a greater gulf between you and society. It throws stumbling-blocks in your way at every turn. All that you take most pride and pleasure in is lost upon the vulgar eye. What they are pleased with is a matter of indifference or of distaste to you. In seeing a number of persons turn over a portfolio of prints from different masters, what a trial it is to the patience, how it jars the nerves to hear them fall into raptures at some common-place flimsy thing, and pass over some divine expression of countenance without notice, or with a remark that it is very singular-looking? How useless it is in such cases to fret or argue, or remonstrate? Is it not quite as well to be without all this hypercritical, fastidious knowledge, and to be pleased or displeased as it happens, or struck with the first fault or beauty that is pointed out by others? I would be glad almost to change my acquaintance with pictures, with books, and, certainly, what I know of mankind, for anybody's ignorance of them!

It is recorded in the life of some worthy (whose name I forget) that he was one of those 'who loved hospitality and respect': and I profess to belong to the same classification of mankind. Civility is with me a jewel. I like a little comfortable cheer, and careless, indolent chat, I hate to be always wise, or aiming at wisdom. I have enough to do with literary cabals, questions, critics, actors, essay-writing, without taking them out with me for recreation, and into all companies. I wish at these times to pass for a good-humoured fellow; and good-will is all I ask in return to make good company. I do not desire to be always posing myself or others with the questions of fate, free-will, foreknowledge absolute, etc. I must unbend sometimes. I must occasionally lie fallow. The kind of conversation that I affect most is what sort of a day it is, and whether it is likely to rain or hold up fine for to-morrow. This I consider as enjoying the *otium cum dignitate,* as the end and privilege of a life of study. I would resign myself to this state of easy indifference, but I find I cannot. I must maintain a certain pretension, which is far enough from my wish. I must be put on my defence, I must take up the gauntlet continually, or I find I lose ground. 'I am nothing, if not critical.' While I am thinking what o'clock it is, or how I came to blunder in quoting a well-known passage, as if I had done it on purpose, others are thinking whether I am not really as dull a fellow as I am sometimes said to be. If a drizzling shower patters against the windows, it puts me in mind of a mild spring rain, from which I retired twenty years ago, into a little public-house near Wem in Shropshire, and while I saw the plants and shrubs before the door imbibe the dewy moisture, quaffed a glass of sparkling ale, and walked home in the dusk of evening, brighter to me than noonday suns at present are! Would I indulge this feeling? In vain. They ask me what news there is, and stare if I say I don't know. If a new actress has come out, why must I have seen her? If a new novel has appeared, why must I have read it? I, at one time, used to go and take a hand at cribbage with a friend, and afterwards discuss a cold sirloin of beef, and throw out a few lackadaisical remarks, in a way to please myself, but it would not do long. I set up little pretension, and therefore the little that I did set up was taken from me. As I said nothing on that subject myself, it was continually thrown in my teeth that I was an author. From having me at this disadvantage, my friend wanted to peg on a hole or two in the game, and was displeased if I would not let him. If I won off him, it was hard he should be beat by an author. If he won, it would be strange if he did not understand the game better than I did. If I mentioned my favourite game of rackets, there was a general silence, as if this was my weak point. If I complained of being ill, it was asked why I made myself so. If I said such an actor had played a part well, the answer was, there was a different account in one of the newspapers. If any allusion was made to men of letters, there was a suppressed smile. If I told a humorous story, it was difficult to say whether the laugh was at me or at the narrative. The wife hated me for my ugly face; the servants, because I could not always get them tickets for the play, and because they could not tell exactly what an author meant. If a paragraph appeared against anything I had written, I found it was ready there before me, and I was to undergo a regular *roasting.* I submitted to all this till I was tired, and then I gave it up.

One of the miseries of intellectual pretensions is, that nine-tenths of those you come in contact with do not know whether you are an impostor or not. I dread that certain anonymous criticisms should get into the hands of servants where I go, or that my hatter or shoemaker should happen to read them, who cannot possibly tell whether they are well or ill founded. The ignorance of the world leaves one at the mercy of its malice. There are people whose good opinion or good-will you want, setting aside all literary pretensions; and it is hard to lose by an ill report (which you have no means of rectifying) what you cannot gain by a good one. After a *diatribe* in the *Quarterly* (which is taken in by a gentleman who occupies my old apartments on the first floor), my landlord brings me up his bill (of some standing), and on my offering to give him so much in money and a note of hand for the rest, shakes his head, and says he is afraid he could make no use of it. Soon after, the daughter comes in, and, on my mentioning the circumstance carelessly to her, replies gravely, 'that indeed her father has been almost ruined by bills.' *This is the unkindest cut of all.* It is in vain for me to endeavour to explain that the publication in which I am abused is a mere government engine—an organ of a political faction. They know nothing about that. They only know such and such imputations are thrown out; and the more I try to remove them, the more they think there is some truth in them. Perhaps the people of the house are strong Tories—government agents of some sort. Is it for me to enlighten their ignorance? If I say, I once wrote a thing called *Prince Maurice's Parrot,* and an *Essay on the Regal Character,* in the former of which allusion is made to a noble marquis, and in the latter to a great personage (so at least, I am told, it has been construed), and that Mr. Croker has peremptory instructions to retaliate, they cannot conceive what connection there can be between me and such distinguished characters. I can get no farther. Such is the misery of pretensions beyond your situation, and which are not backed by any external symbols of wealth or rank, intelligible to all mankind!

The impertinence of admiration is scarcely more tolerable than the demonstrations of contempt. I have known a person whom I had never seen before besiege me all dinner-time with asking what articles I had written in the *Edinburgh Review?* I was at last ashamed to answer to my splendid sins in that way. Others will pick out something not yours, and say they are sure no one else could write it. By the first sentence they can always tell your style. Now I hate my style to be known, as I hate all *idiosyncrasy.* These obsequious flatterers could not pay me a worse compliment. Then there are those who make a point of reading everything you write (which is fulsome); while others, more provoking, regularly lend your works to a friend as soon as they receive them. They pretty well know your notions on the different subjects, from having heard you talk about them. Besides, they have a greater value for your personal character than they have for your writings. You explain things better in a common way, when you are not aiming at effect. Others tell you of the faults they have heard found with your last book, and that they defend your style in general from a charge of obscurity. A friend once told me of a quarrel he had had with a near relation, who denied that I knew how to spell the commonest words. These are comfortable confidential communications to which authors who have their friends and excusers are subject. A gentleman told me that a lady had objected to my use of the word *learneder* as bad grammar. He said he thought it a pity that I did not take more care, but that the lady was perhaps prejudiced, as her husband held a government office. I looked for the word, and found it in a motto from Butler. I was piqued, and desired him to tell the fair critic that the fault was not in me, but in one who had far more wit, more learning, and loyalty than I could pretend to. Then, again, some will pick out the flattest thing of yours they can find to load it with panegyrics; and others tell you (by way of letting you see how high they rank your capacity) that your best passages are failures. Lamb has a knack of tasting (or as he would say, *palating*) the insipid. Leigh Hunt has a trick of turning away from the relishing morsels you put on his plate. There is no getting the start of some people. Do what you will, they can do it better; meet with what success you may, their own good opinion stands them in better stead, and runs before the applause of the world. I once showed a person of this overweening turn (with no small triumph, I confess) a letter of a very flattering description I had received from the celebrated Count Stendhal, dated Rome. He returned it with a smile of indifference, and said, he had had a letter from Rome himself the day before, from his friend S——! I did not think this 'germane to the matter.' Godwin pretends I never wrote anything worth a farthing but my 'Answers to Vetus,' and that I fail altogether when I attempt to write an essay, or anything in a short compass.

What can one do in such cases? Shall I confess a weakness? The only set-off I know to these rebuffs and mortifications is sometimes in an accidental notice or involuntary mark of distinction from a stranger. I feel the force of Horace's *digito monstrari*—I like to be pointed out in the street, or to hear people ask in Mr. Powell's court, *Which is Mr. Hazlitt?* This is to me a pleasing extension of one's personal identity. Your name so repeated leaves an echo like music on the ear: it stirs the blood like the sound of a trumpet. It shows that other people are curious to see you; that they think of you, and feel an interest in you without your knowing it. This is a bolster to lean upon; a lining to your poor, shivering, threadbare opinion of yourself. You want some such cordial to exhausted spirits, and relief to the dreariness of abstract speculation. You are something; and, from occupying a place in the thoughts of others, think less contemptuously of yourself. You are the better able to run the gauntlet of prejudice and vulgar abuse. It is pleasant in this way to have your opinion quoted against yourself, and your own sayings repeated to you as good things. I was once talking to an intelligent man in the pit, and criticising Mr. Knight's performance of Filch. 'Ah!' he said, 'little Simmons was the fellow to play that character.' He added, 'There was a most excellent remark made upon his acting it in the *Examiner* (I think it was)—*That he looked as if he had the gallows in one eye and a pretty girl in the other.*' I said nothing, but was in remarkably good humour the rest of the evening. I have seldom been in a company where fives-playing has been talked of but some one has asked in the course of it, 'Pray, did any one ever see an account of one Cavanagh that appeared some time back in most of the papers? Is it known who wrote it?' These are trying moments. I had a triumph over a person, whose name I will not mention, on the following occasion. I happened to be saying something about Burke, and was expressing my opinion of his talents in no measured terms, when this gentleman interrupted me by saying he thought, for his part, that Burke had been greatly overrated, and then added, in a careless way, 'Pray, did you read a character of him in the last number of the ——?' 'I wrote it!'—I could not resist the antithesis, but was afterwards ashamed of my momentary petulance. Yet no one that I find ever spares me.

Some persons seek out and obtrude themselves on public characters in order, as it might seem, to pick out their failings, and afterwards betray them. Appearances are for it, but truth and a better knowledge of nature are against this interpretation of the matter. Sycophants and flatterers are undesignedly treacherous and fickle. They are prone to admire inordinately at first, and not finding a constant supply of food for this kind of sickly appetite, take a distaste to the object of their idolatry. To be even with themselves for their credulity, they sharpen their wits to spy out faults, and are delighted to find that this answers better than their first employment. It is a course of study, 'lively, audible, and full of vent.' They have the organ of wonder and the organ of fear in a prominent degree. The first requires new objects of admiration to satisfy its uneasy cravings: the second makes them crouch to power wherever its shifting standard appears, and willing to curry favour with all parties, and ready to betray any out of sheer weakness and servility. I do not think they mean any harm: at least, I can look at this obliquity with indifference in my own particular case. I have been more disposed to resent it as I have seen it practised upon others, where I have been better able to judge of the extent of the mischief, and the heartlessness and idiot folly it discovered.

I do not think great intellectual attainments are any recommendation to the women. They puzzle them, and are a diversion to the main question. If scholars talk to ladies of what they understand, their hearers are none the wiser: if they talk of other things, they prove themselves fools. The conversation between Angelica and Foresight in *Love for Love* is a receipt in full for all such overstrained nonsense: while he is wandering among the signs of the zodiac, she is standing a-tiptoe on the earth. It has been remarked that poets do not choose mistresses very wisely. I believe it is not choice, but necessity. If they could throw the handkerchief like the Grand Turk, I imagine we should see scarce mortals, but rather goddesses, surrounding their steps, and each exclaiming, with Lord Byron's own Ionian maid—

> So shalt thou find me ever at thy side,
>
> Here and hereafter, if the last may be!

Ah! no, these are bespoke, carried of by men of mortal, not of ethereal mould, and thenceforth the poet from whose mind the ideas of love and beauty are inseparable as dreams from sleep, goes on the forlorn hope of the passion, and dresses up the first Dulcinea that will take compassion on him in all the colours of fancy. What boots it to complain if the delusion lasts for life, and the rainbow still paints its form in the cloud?

There is one mistake I would wish, if possible, to correct. Men of letters, artists, and others not succeeding with women in a certain rank of life, think the objection is to their want of fortune, and that they shall stand a better chance by descending lower, where only their good qualities or talents will be thought of. Oh! worse and worse. The objection is to themselves, not to their fortune—to their abstraction, to their absence of mind, to their unintelligible and romantic notions. Women of education may have a glimpse of their meaning, may get a clue to their character, but to all others they are thick darkness. If the mistress smiles at their ideal advances, the maid will laugh outright; she will throw water over you, get her sister to listen, send her sweetheart to ask you what you mean, will set the village or the house upon your back; it will be a farce, a comedy, a standing jest for a year, and then the murder will out. Scholars should be sworn at Highgate. They are no match for chambermaids, or wenches at lodging-houses. They had better try their hands on heiresses or ladies of quality. These last have high notions of themselves that may fit some of your epithets! They are above mortality; so are your thoughts! But with low life, trick, ignorance, and cunning, you have nothing in common. Whoever you are, that think you can make a compromise or a conquest there by good nature or good sense, be warned b a friendly voice, and retreat in time from the unequal contest.

If, as I have said above, scholars are no match for chambermaids, on the other hand gentlemen are no match for blackguards. The former are on their honour, act on the square; the latter take all advantages, and have no idea of any other principle. It is astonishing how soon a fellow without education will learn to cheat. He is impervious to any ray of liberal knowledge; his understanding is

> Not pierceable by power of any star—

but it is porous to all sorts of tricks, chicanery, stratagems, and knavery, by which anything is to be got. Mrs. Peachum, indeed, says, that to succeed at the gaming-table, the candidate should have the education of a nobleman. I do not know how far this example contradicts my theory. I think it is a rule that men in business should not be taught other things. Any one will be almost sure to make money who has no other idea in his head. A college education, or intense study of abstract truth, will not enable a man to drive a bargain, to overreach another, or even to guard himself from being overreached. As Shakespear says, that 'to have a good face is the effect of study, but reading and writing come by nature'; so it might be argued, that to be a knave is the gift of fortune, but to play the fool to advantage it is necessary to be a learned man. The best politicians are not those who are deeply grounded in mathematical or in ethical science. Rules stand in the way of expediency. Many a man has been hindered from pushing his fortune in the world by an early cultivation of his moral sense, and has repented of it at leisure during the rest of his life. A shrewd man said of my father, that he would not send a son of his to school to him on any account, for that by teaching him to speak the truth he would disqualify him from getting his living in the world!

It is hardly necessary to add any illustration to prove that the most original and profound thinkers are not always the most successful or popular writers. This is not merely a temporary disadvantage; but many great philosophers have not only been scouted while they were living, but forgotten as soon as they were dead. The name of Hobbes is perhaps sufficient to explain this assertion. But I do not wish to go farther into this part of the subject, which is obvious in itself. I have said, I believe, enough to take off the air of paradox which hangs over the title of this Essay.

FN to ESSAY XIII

(1) Jack Cade's salutation to one who tries to recommend himself by saying he can write and read—see *Henry VI*. Part Second.

ESSAY XIV. ON PATRONAGE AND PUFFING

    A gentle usher, Vanity by name. —Spenser.

A lady was complaining to a friend of mine of the credulity of people in attending to quack advertisements, and wondering who could be taken in by them—"for that she had never bought but one half-guinea bottle of Dr. ——'s Elixir of Life, and it had done her no sort of good!" This anecdote seemed to explain pretty well what made it worth the doctor's while to advertise his wares in every newspaper in the kingdom. He would no doubt be satisfied if every delicate, sceptical invalid in his majesty's dominions gave his Elixir one trial, merely to show the absurdity of the thing. We affect to laugh at the folly of those who put faith in nostrums, but are willing to see ourselves whether there is any truth in them.

There is a strong tendency in the human mind to flatter itself with secret hopes, with some lucky reservation in our own favour, though reason may point out the grossness of the trick in general; and, besides, there is a wonderful power in words, formed into regular propositions, and printed in capital letters, to draw the assent after them, till we have proof of their fallacy. The ignorant and idle believe what they read, as Scotch philosophers demonstrate the existence of a material world, and other learned propositions, from the evidence of their senses. The ocular proof is all that is wanting in either case. As hypocrisy is said to be the highest compliment to virtue, the art of lying is the strongest acknowledgment of the force of truth. We can hardly *believe* a thing to be a lie, though we *know* it to be so. The 'puff direct,' even as it stands in the columns of the *Times* newspaper, branded with the title of Advertisement before it, claims some sort of attention and respect for the merits that it discloses, though we think the candidate for public favour and support has hit upon (perhaps) an injudicious way of laying them before the world. Still there may be something in them; and even the outrageous improbability and extravagance of the statement on the very face of it stagger us, and leave a hankering to inquire farther into it, because we think the advertiser would hardly have the impudence to hazard such barefaced absurdities without some foundation. Such is the strength of the association between words and things in the mind—so much oftener must our credulity have been justified by the event than imposed upon. If every second story we heard was an invention, we should lose our mechanical disposition to trust to the meaning of sounds, just as when we have met with a number of counterfeit pieces of coin, we suspect good ones; but our implicit assent to what we hear is a proof how much more sincerity and good faith there is in the sum total of our dealings with one another than artifice and imposture.

'To elevate and surprise' is the great art of quackery and puffing; to raise a lively and exaggerated image in the mind, and take it by surprise before it can recover breath, as it were; so that by having been caught in the trap, it is unwilling to retract entirely—has a secret desire to find itself in the right, and a determination to see whether it is or not. Describe a picture as *lofty, imposing,* and *grand,* these words excite certain ideas in the mind like the sound of a trumpet, which are not to be quelled, except by seeing the picture itself, nor even then, if it is viewed by the help of a catalogue, written expressly for the occasion by the artist himself. It is not to be supposed that *he* would say such things of his picture unless they were allowed by all the world; and he repeats them, on this gentle understanding, till all the world allows them.(1) So Reputation runs in a vicious circle, and Merit limps behind it, mortified and abashed at its own insignificance. It has been said that the test of fame or popularity is to consider the number of times your name is repeated by others, or is brought to their recollection in the course of a year. At this rate, a man has his reputation in his own hands, and, by the help of puffing and the press, may forestall the voice of posterity, and stun the 'groundling' ear of his contemporaries. A name let off in your hearing continually, with some bouncing epithet affixed to it, startles you like the report of a pistol close at your ear: you cannot help the effect upon the imagination, though you know it is perfectly harmless—*vox et praeterea nihil.* So, if you see the same name staring you in the face in great letters at the corner of every street, you involuntarily think the owner of it must be a great man to occupy so large a space in the eye of the town. The appeal is made, in the first instance, to the senses, but it sinks below the surface into the mind. There are some, indeed, who publish their own disgrace, and make their names a common by-word and nuisance, notoriety being all that they wa though you may laugh in his face, it pays expenses. Parolles and his drum typify many a modern adventurer and court-candidate for unearned laurels and unblushing honours. Of all puffs, lottery puffs are the most ingenious and most innocent. A collection of them would make an amusing *Vade mecum.* They are still various and the same, with that infinite ruse with which they lull the reader at the outset out of all suspicion. the insinuating turn in the middle, the home-thrust at the ruling passion at last, by which your spare cash is conjured clean out of the pocket in spite of resolution, by the same stale, well-known, thousandth-time repeated artifice of *All prizes* and *No blanks*—a self-evident imposition! Nothing, however, can be a stronger proof of the power of fascinating the public judgment through the eye alone. I know a gentleman who amassed a considerable fortune (so as to be able to keep his carriage) by printing nothing but lottery placards and handbills of a colossal size. Another friend of mine (of no mean talents) was applied to (as a snug thing in the way of business) to write regular lottery puffs for a large house in the city, and on having a parcel of samples returned on his hands as done in too severe and terse a style, complained quaintly enough, *'That modest merit never could succeed!'* Even Lord Byron, as he tells us, has been accused of writing lottery-puffs. There are various ways of playing one's-self off before the public, and keeping one's name alive. The newspapers, the lamp-posts, the walls of empty houses, the shutters of windows, the blank covers of magazines and reviews, are open to every one. I have heard of a man of literary celebrity sitting in his study writing letters of remonstrance to himself, on the gross defects of a plan of education he had just published, and which remained unsold on the bookseller's counter. Another feigned himself dead in order to see what would be said of him in the newspapers, and to excite a sensation in this way. A flashy pamphlet has been run to a five-and-thirtieth edition, and thus ensured the writer a 'deathless date' among political charlatans, by regularly striking off a new title-page to every fifty or a hundred copies that were sold. This is a vile practice. It is an erroneous idea got abroad (and which I will contradict here) that paragraphs are paid for in the leading journals. It is quite out of the question. A favourable notice of an author, an actress, etc., may be inserted through interest, or to oblige a friend, but it must invariably be done for *love,* not *money!*

When I formerly had to do with these sort of critical verdicts, I was generally sent out of the way when any *debutant* had a friend at court, and was to be tenderly handled. For the rest, or those of robust constitutions, I had *carte blanche* given me. Sometimes I ran out of the course, to be sure. Poor Perry! what bitter complaints he used to make, that by *running-a-muck* at lords and Scotchmen I should not leave him a place to dine out at! The expression of his face at these moments, as if he should shortly be without a friend in the world, was truly pitiable. What squabbles we used to have about Kean and Miss Stephens, the only theatrical favourites I ever had! Mrs. Billington had got some notion that Miss Stephens would never make a singer, and it was the torment of Perry's life (as he told me in confidence) that he could not get any two people to be of the same opinion on any one point. I shall appearance in the *Beggar's Opera.* I have reason to remember that article: it was almost the last I ever wrote with any pleasure to myself. I had been down on a visit to my friends near Chertsey, and on my return had stopped at an inn near Kingston-upon-Thames, where I had got the *Beggar's Opera,* and had read it over-night. The next day I walked cheerfully to town. It was a fine sunny morning, in the end of autumn, and as I repeated the beautiful song, 'Life knows no return of Spring,' I meditated my next day's criticism, trying to do all the justice I could to so inviting a subject. I was not a little proud of it by anticipation. I had just then begun to stammer out my sentiments on paper, and was in a kind of honeymoon of authorship. But soon after, my final hopes of happiness and of human liberty were blighted nearly at the same time; and since then I have had no pleasure in anything—

And Love himself can flatter me no more.

It was not so ten years since (ten short years since.—Ah! how fast those years run that hurry us away from our last fond dream of bliss!) when I loitered along thy green retreats, O Twickenham! and conned over (with enthusiastic delight) the chequered view which one of thy favourites drew of human life! I deposited my account of the play at the Morning Chronicle office in the afternoon, and went to see Miss Stephens as Polly. Those were happy times, in which she first came out in this character, in Mandane, where she sang the delicious air, 'If o'er the cruel tyrant, Love' (so as it can never be sung again), in *Love in a Village,* where the scene opened with her and Miss Matthews in a painted garden of roses and honeysuckles, and 'Hope, thou nurse of young Desire' thrilled from two sweet voices in turn. Oh! may my ears sometimes still drink the same sweet sounds, embalmed with the spirit of youth, of health, and joy, but in the thoughts of an instant, but in a dream of fancy, and I shall hardly need to complain! When I got back, after the play, Perry called out, with his cordial, grating voice, 'Well, how did she do?' and on my speaking in high terms, answered, that 'he had been to dine with his friend the Duke, that some conversation had passed on the subject, he was afraid it was not the thing, it was not the true *sostenuto* style; but as I had written the article' (holding my peroration on the *Beggar's Opera* carelessly in his hand), 'it might pass!' I could perceive that the rogue licked his lips at it, and had already in imagination 'bought golden opinions of all sorts of people' by this very criticism, and I had the satisfaction the next day to meet Miss Stephens coming out of the editor's room, who had been to thank him for his very flattering account of her.

I was sent to see Kean the first night of his performance in Shylock, when there were about a hundred people in the pit; but from his masterly and spirited delivery of the first striking speech, 'On such a day you called me a dog,' etc., I perceived it was a hollow thing. So it was given out in the *Chronicle;* but Perry was continually at me as other people were at him, and was afraid it would not last. It was to no purpose I said *it would last:* yet I am in the right hitherto. It has been said, ridiculously, that Mr. Kean was written up in the *Chronicle.* I beg leave to state my opinion that no actor can be written up or down by a paper. An author may be puffed into notice, or damned by criticism, because his book may not have been read. An artist may be overrated, or undeservedly decried, because the public is not much accustomed to see or judge of pictures. But an actor is judged by his peers, the play-going public, and must stand or fall by his own merits or defects. The critic may give the tone or have a casting voice where popular opinion is divided; but he can no more *force* that opinion either way, or wrest it from its base in common sense and feeling, than he can move Stonehenge. Mr. Kean had, however, physical disadvantages and strong prejudices to encounter, and so far the *liberal* and *independent* part of the press might have been of service in helping him to his seat in the public favour. May he long keep it with dignity and firmness!(2)

It was pretended by the Covent Garden people, and some others at the time, that Mr. Kean's popularity was a mere effect of love of novelty, a nine days' wonder, like the rage after Master Betty's acting, and would be as soon over. The comparison did not hold. Master Betty's acting was so far wonderful, and drew crowds to see it as a mere singularity, because he was a boy. Mr. Kean was a grown man, and there was no rule or precedent established in the ordinary course of nature why some other man should not appear in tragedy as great as John Kemble. Farther, Master Betty's acting was a singular phenomenon, but it was also as beautiful as it was singular. I saw him in the part of Douglas, and he seemed almost like 'some gay creature of the element,' moving about gracefully, with all the flexibility of youth, and murmuring AEolian sounds with plaintive tenderness. I shall never forget the way in which he repeated the line in which young Norval says, speaking of the fate of two brothers:

And in my mind happy was he that died!

The tones fell and seemed to linger prophetic on my ear. Perhaps the wonder was made greater than it was. Boys at that age can often read remarkably well, and certainly are not without natural grace and sweetness of voice. The Westminster schoolboys are a better company of comedians than we find at most of our theatres. As to the understanding a part like Douglas, at least, I see no difficulty on that score. I myself used to recite the speech in Enfield's *Speaker* with good emphasis and discretion when at school, and entered, about the same age, into the wild sweetness of the sentiments in Mrs. Radcliffe's *Romance of the Forest*, I am sure, quite as much as I should do now; yet the same experiment has been often tried since and has uniformly failed.(3)

It was soon after this that Coleridge returned from Italy, and he got one day into a long tirade to explain what a ridiculous farce the whole was, and how all the people abroad were shocked at the *gullibility* of the English nation, who on this and every other occasion were open to the artifices of all sorts of quacks, wondering how any persons with the smallest pretensions to common sense could for a moment suppose that a boy could act the characters of men without any of their knowledge, their experience, or their passions. We made some faint resistance, but in vain. The discourse then took a turn, and Coleridge began a laboured eulogy on some promising youth, the son of an English artist, whom he had met in Italy, and who had wandered all over the Campagna with him, whose talents, he assured us, were the admiration of all Rome, and whose early designs had almost all the grace and purity of Raphael's. At last, some one interrupted the endless theme by saying a little impatiently, 'Why just now you would not let us believe our own eyes and ears about young Betty, because you have a theory against premature talents, and now you start a boy phenomenon that nobody knows anything about but yourself—a young artist that, you tell us, is to rival Raphael!' The truth is, we like to have something to admire ourselves, as well as to make other people gape and stare at; but then it must be a discovery of our own, an idol of our own making and setting up:—if others stumble on the discovery before us, or join in crying it up to the skies, we then set to work to prove that this is a vulgar delusion, and show our sagacity and freedom from prejudice by pulling it in pieces with all the coolness imaginable. Whether we blow the bubble or crush it in our hands, vanity and the desire of empty distinction are equally at the bottom of our sanguine credulity or fastidious scepticism. There are some who always fall in with the fashionable prejudice as others affect singularity of opinion on all such points, according as they think they have more or less wit to judge for themselves.

If a little varnishing and daubing, a little puffing and quacking, and giving yourself a good name, and getting a friend to speak a word for you, is excusable in any profession, it is, I think, in that of painting. Painting is an occult science, and requires a little ostentation and mock-gravity in the professor. A man may here rival Katterfelto, 'with his hair on end at his own wonders, wondering for his bread'; for, if he does not, he may in the end go without it. He may ride on a high-trotting horse, in green spectacles, and attract notice to his person anyhow he can, if he only works hard at his profession. If 'it only is when he is *out* he is acting,' let him make the fools stare, but give others something worth looking at. Good Mr. Carver and Gilder, good Mr. Printer's Devil, good Mr. Billsticker, 'do me your offices' unmolested! Painting is a plain ground, and requires a great many heraldic quarterings and facings to set it off. Lay on, and do not spare. No man's merit can be fairly judged of if he is not known; and how can he be known if he keeps entirely in the background?(4) A great name in art goes but a little way, is chilled as it creeps along the surface of the world without something to revive and make it blaze up with fresh splendour. Fame is here almost obscurity. It is long before your name affixed to a sterling design will be spelt out by an undiscerning regardless public. Have it proclaimed, therefore, as a necessary precaution, by sound of trumpet at the corners of the street, let it be stuck as a label in your mouth, carry it on a placard at your back. Otherwise, the world will never trouble themselves about you, or will very soon forget you. A celebrated artist of the present day, whose name is engraved at the bottom of some of the most touching specimens of English art, once had a frame-maker call on him, who, on entering his room, exclaimed with some surprise, 'What, are you a painter, sir?' The other made answer, a little startled in his turn, 'Why, didn't you know that? Did you never see my name at the bottom of prints?' He could not recollect that he had. 'And yet you sell picture-frames and prints?'—'Yes.'—'What painter's names, then, did he recollect: did he know West's?' 'Oh! yes.'—'And Opie's?' 'Yes.'—'And Fuseli's?' 'Oh! yes.—'But you never heard of me?' 'I cannot say that I ever did!' It was plain from this conversation that Mr. Northcote had not kept company enough with picture-dealers and newspaper critics. On another occasion, a country gentleman, who was sitting to him for his portrait, asked him if he had any pictures in the Exhibition at Somerset House, and on his replying in the affirmative, desired to know what they were. He mentioned, among others, The Marriage of Two Children; on which the gentleman expressed great surprise, and said that was the very picture his wife was always teasing him to go and have another look at, though he had never noticed the painter's name. When the public are so eager to be amused, and care so little who it is that amuses them, it is not amiss to remind them of it now and then; or even to have a starling taught to repeat the name, to which they owe such misprised obligations, in their drowsy ears. On any other principle I cannot conceive how painters (not without genius or industry) can fling themselves at the head of the public in the manner they do, having lives written of themselves, busts made of themselves, prints stuck in the shop-windows of themselves, and their names placed in 'the first row of the rubric,' with those of Rubens, Raphael, and Michael Angelo, swearing by themselves or their proxies that these glorified spirits would do well to leave the abodes of the blest in order to stand in mute wonder and with uplifted hands before some production of theirs which is yet hardly dry! Oh! whatever you do, leave that string untouched. It will jar the rash and unhallowed hand that meddles with it. Profane not the mighty dead by mixing them up with the uncanonised living. Leave yourself a reversion in immortality, beyond the noisy clamour of the day. Do not quite lose your respect for public opinion by making it in all cases a palpable cheat, the echo of your own lungs that are hoarse with calling on the world to admire. Do not think to bully posterity, or to cozen your contemporaries. Be not always anticipating the effect of your picture on the town—think more about deserving success than commanding it. In issuing so many promissory notes upon the bank of fame, do not forget you have to pay in sterling gold. Believe that there is something in the pursuit of high art, beyond the manufacture of a paragraph or the collection of receipts at the door of an exhibition. Venerate art as art. Study the works of others, and inquire into those of nature. Gaze at beauty. Become great by great efforts, and not by pompous pretensions. Do not think the world was blind to merit before your time, nor make the reputation of great geniuses the stalking-horse to your vanity. You have done enough to insure yourself attention: you have now only to do something to deserve it, and to make good all that you have aspired to do.

There is a silent and systematic assumption of superiority which is as barefaced and unprincipled an imposture as the most impudent puffing. You may, by a tacit or avowed censure on all other arts, on all works of art, on all other pretensions, tastes, talents, but your own,

109

produce a complete ostracism in the world of intellect, and leave yourself and your own performances alone standing, a mighty monument in an universal waste and wreck of genius. By cutting away the rude block and removing the rubbish from around it, the idol may be effectually exposed to view, placed on its pedestal of pride, without any other assistance. This method is more inexcusable than the other. For there is no egotism or vanity so hateful as that which strikes at our satisfaction in everything else, and derives its nourishment from preying, like the vampire, on the carcase of others' reputation. I would rather, in a word, that a man should talk for ever of himself with vapid, senseless assurance, than preserve a malignant, heartless silence when the merit of a rival is mentioned. I have seen instances of both, and can judge pretty well between them.

There is no great harm in putting forward one's own pretensions (of whatever kind) if this does not bear a sour, malignant aspect towards others. Every one sets himself off to the best advantage he can, and tries to steal a march upon public opinion. In this sense, too, 'all the world's a stage, and all the men and women merely players.' Life itself is a piece of harmless quackery. A great house over your head is of no use but to announce the great man within. Dress, equipage, title, livery-servants are only so many quack advertisements and assumptions of the question of merit. The star that glitters at the breast would be worth nothing but as a badge of personal distinction; and the crown itself is but a symbol of the virtues which the possessor inherits from a long line of illustrious ancestors! How much honour and honesty have been forfeited to be graced with a title or a ribbon; how much genius and worth have sunk to the grave without an escutcheon and without an epitaph!

As men of rank and fortune keep lackeys to reinforce their claims to self-respect, so men of genius sometimes surround themselves with a coterie of admirers to increase their reputation with the public. These *proneurs,* or satellites, repeat all their good things, laugh loud at all their jokes, and remember all their oracular decrees. They are their shadows and echoes. They talk of them in all companies, and bring back word of all that has been said about them. They hawk the good qualities of their patrons as shopmen and *barkers* tease you to buy goods. I have no notion of this vanity at second-hand; nor can I see how this servile testimony from inferiors ('some followers of mine own') can be a proof of merit. It may soothe the ear, but that it should impose on the understanding, I own, surprises me; yet there are persons who cannot exist without a *cortege* of this kind about them, in which they smiling read the opinion of the world, in the midst of all sorts of rancorous abuse and hostility, as Otho called for his mirror in the Illyrian field. One good thing is, that this evil, in some degree, cures itself; and when a man has been nearly ruined by a herd of these sycophants, he finds them leaving him, like thriftless dependants, for some more eligible situation, carrying away with them all the tattle they can pick up, and some left-off suit of finery. The same proneness to adulation which made them lick the dust before one idol makes them bow as low to the rising Sun; they are as lavish of detraction as they were prurient with praise; and the *protege* and admirer of the editor of the ——- figures in Blackwood's train. The man is a lackey, and it is of little consequence whose livery he wears!

I would advise those who volunteer the office of puffing to go the whole length of it. No half-measures will do. Lay it on thick and threefold, or not at all. If you are once harnessed into that vehicle, it will be in vain for you to think of stopping. You must drive to the devil at once. The mighty Tamburlane, to whose car you are yoked, cries out:

> Holloa, you pamper'd jades of Asia,
> Can you not drive but twenty miles a day?

He has you on the hip, for you have pledged your taste and judgment to his genius. Never fear but he will drive this wedge. If you are once screwed into such a machine, you must extricate yourself by main force. No hyperboles are too much: any drawback, any admiration on this side idolatry, is high treason. It is an unpardonable offence to say that the last production of your patron is not so good as the one before it, or that a performer shines more in one character than another. I remember once hearing a player declare that he never looked into any newspapers or magazines on account of the abuse that was always levelled at himself in them, though there were not less than three persons in company who made it their business through these conduit pipes of fame to 'cry him up to the top of the compass.' This sort of expectation is a little *exigeante!*

One fashionable mode of acquiring reputation is by patronising it. This may be from various motives—real good nature, good taste, vanity, or pride. I shall only speak of the spurious ones in this place. The quack and the *would-be* patron are well met. The house of the latter is a sort of curiosity shop or *menagerie,* where all sorts of intellectual pretenders and grotesques, musical children, arithmetical prodigies, occult philosophers, lecturers, *accoucheurs,* apes, chemists, fiddlers, and buffoons are to be seen for the asking, and are shown to the company for nothing. The folding doors are thrown open, and display a collection that the world cannot parallel again. There may be a few persons of common sense and established reputation, *rari nantes in gurgite vasto,* otherwise it is a mere scramble or lottery. The professed encourager of *virtu* and letters, being disappointed of the great names, sends out into the highways for the halt, the lame, and the blind, for all who pretend to distinction, defects, and obliquities, for all the disposable vanity or affectation floating on the town, in hopes that, among so many oddities, chance may bring some jewel or treasure to his door, which he may have the good fortune to appropriate in some way to his own use, or the credit of displaying to others. The art is to encourage rising genius—to bring forward doubtful and unnoticed merit. You thus get a set of novices and raw pretenders about you, whose actual productions do not interfere with your self-love, and whose future efforts may reflect credit on your singular sagacity and faculty for finding out talent in the germ; and in the next place, by having them completely in your power, you are at liberty to dismiss them whenever you will, and to supply the deficiency by a new set of wondering, unwashed faces in a rapid succession; an 'aiery of children,' embryo actors, artists, poets, or philosophers. Like unfledged birds, they are hatched, nursed, and fed by hand: this gives room for a vast deal of management, meddling, care, and condescending solicitude; but the instant the callow brood are fledged, they are driven from the nest, and forced to shift for themselves in the wide world. One sterling production decides the question between them and their patrons, and from that time they become the property of the public. Thus a succession of importunate, hungry, idle, overweening candidates for fame are encouraged by these fickle keepers, only to be betrayed, and left to starve or beg, or pine in obscurity, while the man of merit and respectability is neglected, discountenanced, and stigmatised, because he will not lend himself as a tool to this system of splendid imposition, or pamper the luxury and weaknesses of the Vulgar Great. When a young artist is too independent to subscribe to the dogmas of his superiors, or fulfils their predictions and prognostics of wonderful contingent talent too soon, so as to get out of leading-strings, and lean on public opinion for partial support, exceptions are taken to his dress, dialect, or manners, and he is expelled the circle with a character for ingratitude and treachery. None can procure toleration long but those who do not contradict the opinions or excite the jealousy of their betters. One independent step is an appeal from them to the public, their natural and hated rivals, and annuls the contract between them, which implies ostentatious countenance on the one part and servile submission on the other. But enough of this.

The patronage of men of talent, even when it proceeds from vanity, is often carried on with a spirit of generosity and magnificence, as long as these are in difficulties and a state of dependence; but as the principle of action in this case is a love of power, the complacency in the object of friendly regard ceases with the opportunity or necessity for the same manifest display of power; and when the unfortunate *protege* is just coming to land, and expects a last helping hand, he is, to his surprise, pushed back, in order that he may be saved from drowning once more. You are not hailed ashore, as you had supposed, by these kind friends, as a mutual triumph after all your struggles and their exertions in your behalf. It is a piece of presumption in you to be seen walking on *terra firma*: you are required, at the risk of their friendship, to be always swimming in troubled waters, that they may have the credit of throwing out ropes, and sending out lifeboats to you, without ever bringing you ashore. Your successes, your reputation, which you think would please them, as justifying their good opinion, are coldly received, and looked at askance, because they remove your dependence on them: if you are under a cloud, they do all they can to keep you there by their goodwill: they are so sensible of your gratitude that they wish your obligations never to cease, and take care you shall owe no one else a good turn; and provided you are compelled or contented to remain always in poverty, obscurity, and disgrace, they will continue your very good friends and humble servants to command, to the end of the chapter. The tenure of these indentures is hard. Such persons will wilfully forfeit the gratitude created by years of friendship, by refusing to perform the last act of kindness that is likely ever to be demanded of them: will lend you money, if you have no chance of repaying them: will give you their good word, if nobody will believe it; and the only thing they do not forgive is an attempt or probability on your part of being able to repay your obligations. There is something disinterested in all this: at least, it does not show a cowardly or mercenary disposition, but it savours too much of arrogance and arbitrary pretension. It throws a damning light on this question, to consider who are mostly the subjects of the patronage of the great, and in the habit of receiving cards of invitation to splendid dinners. I confess, for one, I am not on the list; at which I do not grieve much, nor wonder at all. Authors, in general, are not in much request. Dr. Johnson was asked why he was not more frequently invited out; and he said, 'Because great lords and ladies do not like to have their mouths stopped.' Garrick was not in this predicament: he could amuse the company in the drawing-room by imitating the great moralist and lexicographer, and make the negro-boy in the courtyard die with laughing to see him take off the swelling airs and strut of the turkey-cock. This was clever and amusing, but it did not involve an opinion, it did not lead to a difference of sentiment, in which the owner of the house might be found in the wrong. Players, singers, dancers, are hand and glove with the great. They embellish, and have an *eclat* in their names, but do not come into collision. Eminent portrait-painters, again, are tolerated, because they come into personal contact with the great; and sculptors hold equality with lords when they have a certain quantity of solid marble in their workshops to answer for the solidity of their pretensions. People of fashion and property must have something to show for their patronage, something visible or tangible. A sentiment is a visionary thing; an argument may lead to dangerous consequences, and those who are likely to broach either one or the other ate not, therefore, fit for good company in general. Poets and men of genius who find their way there, soon find their way out. They are not of that ilk, with some exceptions. Painters who come in contact with majesty get on by servility or buffoonery, by letting themselves down in some way. Sir Joshua was never a favourite at court. He kept too much at a distance. Beechey gained a vast deal of favour by familiarity, and lost it by taking too great freedoms.(5) West ingratiated himself in the same quarter by means of practices as little creditable to himself as his august employer, namely, by playing the hypocrite, and professing sentiments the reverse of those he naturally felt. Kings (I know not how justly) have been said to be lovers of low company and low conversation. They are also said to be fond of dirty practical jokes. If the fact is so, the reason is as follows. From the elevation of their rank, aided by pride and flattery, they look down on the rest of mankind, and would not be thought to have all their advantages for nothing. They wish to maintain the same precedence in private life that belongs to them as a matter of outward ceremony. This pretension they cannot keep up by fair means; for in wit or argument they are not superior to the common run of men. They therefore answer a repartee by a practical joke, which turns the laugh against others, and cannot be retaliated with safety. That is, they avail themselves of the privilege of their situation to take liberties, and degrade those about them, as they can only keep up the idea of their own dignity by proportionably lowering their company.

FN to ESSAY XIV

(1) It is calculated that West cleared some hundred pounds by the catalogues that were sold of his great picture of Death riding on the Pale Horse.

(2) I cannot say how in this respect it might have fared if a Mr. Mudford, a fat gentleman, who might not have 'liked yon lean and hungry Roscius,' had continued in the theatrical department of Mr. Perry's paper at the time of this actor's first appearance; but I had been put upon this duty just before, and afterwards Mr. Mudford's *spare* talents were not in much request. This, I believe, is the reason why he takes pains every now and then to inform the readers of the *Courier* that it is impossible for any one to understand a word that I write.

(3) I (not very long ago) had the pleasure of spending an evening with Mr. Betty, when we had some 'good talk' about the good old times of acting. I wanted to insinuate that I had been a sneaking admirer, but could not bring it in. As, however, we were putting on our greatcoats downstairs I ventured to break the ice by saying, 'There is one actor of that period of whom we have not made honourable mention, I mean Master Betty.' 'Oh!' he said, 'I have forgot all that.' I replied, that he might, but that I could not forget the pleasure I had had in seeing him. On which he turned off, and, shaking his sides heartily, and with no measured demand upon his lungs, called out, 'Oh, memory! memory!' in a way that showed he felt the full force of the allusion. I found afterwards that the subject did not offend, and we were to have drunk some Burton ale together the following evening, but were prevented. I hope he will consider that the engagement still stands good.

(4) Sir Joshua, who was not a vain man, purchased a tawdry sheriff's carriage, soon after he took his house in Leicester Fields, and desired his sister to ride about in it, in order that people might ask, 'Whose it was?' and the answer would be, 'It belongs to the great painter!'

(5) Sharp became a great favourite of the king on the following occasion. It was the custom, when the king went through the lobbies of the palace, for those who preceded him to cry out, 'Sharp, sharp, look sharp!' in order to clear the way. Mr. Sharp, who was waiting in a

room just by (preparing some colours), hearing his name repeated so urgently, ran out in great haste, and came up with all his force against the king, who was passing the door at the time. The young artist was knocked down in the encounter, and the attendants were in the greatest consternation; but the king laughed heartily at the adventure, and took great notice of the unfortunate subject of it from that time forward.

ESSAY XV. ON THE KNOWLEDGE OF CHARACTER

It is astonishing, with all our opportunities and practice, how little we know of this subject. For myself, I feel that the more I learn, the less I understand it.

I remember, several years ago, a conversation in the diligence coming from Paris, in which, on its being mentioned that a man had married his wife after thirteen years' courtship, a fellow-countryman of mine observed, that 'then, at least, he would be acquainted with her character'; when a Monsieur P——, inventor and proprietor of the *Invisible Girl,* made answer, 'No, not at all; for that the very next day she might turn out the very reverse of the character that she had appeared in during all the preceding time.'(1) I could not help admiring the superior sagacity of the French juggler, and it struck me then that we could never be sure when we had got at the bottom of this riddle.

There are various ways of getting at a knowledge of character—by looks, words, actions. The first of these, which seems the most superficial, is perhaps the safest, and least liable to deceive: nay, it is that which mankind, in spite of their pretending to the contrary, most generally go by. Professions pass for nothing, and actions may be counterfeited; but a man cannot help his looks. 'Speech,' said a celebrated wit, 'was given to man to conceal his thoughts.' Yet I do not know that the greatest hypocrites are the least silent. The mouth of Cromwell is pursed up in the portraits of him, as if he was afraid to trust himself with words. Lord Chesterfield advises us, if we wish to know the real sentiments of the person we are conversing with, to look in his face, for he can more easily command his words than his features. A man's whole life may be picture painted of him by a great artist would probably stamp his true character on the canvas, and betray the secret to posterity. Men's opinions were divided, in their lifetimes, about such prominent personages as Charles V. and Ignatius Loyola, partly, no doubt, from passion and interest, but partly from contradictory evidence in their ostensible conduct: the spectator, who has ever seen their pictures by Titian, judges of them at once, and truly. I had rather leave a good portrait of myself behind me than have a fine epitaph. The face, for the most part, tells what we have thought and felt—the rest is nothing. I prefixed to his poems than from anything he ever wrote. Caesar's *Commentaries* would not have redeemed him in my opinion, if the bust of him had resembled the Duke of Wellington. My old friend Fawcett used to say, that if Sir Isaac Newton himself had lisped, he could not have thought anything of him. So I cannot persuade myself that any one is a great man who looks like a fool. In this I may be wrong.

First impressions are often the truest, as we find (not unfrequently) to our cost when we have been wheedled out of them by plausible professions or actions. A man's look is the work of years, it is stamped on his countenance by the events of his whole life, nay, more, by the hand of nature, and it is not to be got rid of easily. There is, as it has been remarked repeatedly, something in a person's appearance at first sight which we do not like, and that gives us an odd twinge, but which is overlooked in a multiplicity of other circumstances, till the mask is taken off, and we see this lurking character verified in the plainest manner in the sequel. We are struck at first, and by chance, with what is peculiar and characteristic; also with permanent *traits* and general effect: this afterwards goes off in a set of unmeaning, common-place details. This sort of *prima facie* evidence, then, shows what a man is better than what he says or does; for it shows us the habit of his mind, which is the same under all circumstances and disguises. You will say, on the other hand, that there is no judging by appearances, as a general rule. No one, for instance, would take such a person for a very clever man without knowing who he was. Then, ten to one, he is not: he may have got the reputation, but it is a mistake. You say, there is Mr. ——, undoubtedly a person of great genius; yet, except when excited by something extraordinary, he seems half dead. He has wit at will, yet wants life and spirit. He is capable of the most generous acts, yet meanness seems to cling to every motion. He looks like a poor creature—and in truth he is one! The first impression he gives you of him answers nearly to the feeling he has of his personal identity; and this image of himself, rising from his thoughts, and shrouding his faculties, is that which sits with him in the house, walks out with him into the street, and haunts his bedside. The best part of his existence is dull, cloudy, leaden: the flashes of light that proceed from it, or streak it here and there, may dazzle others, but do not deceive himse deficiency it indicates. He who undervalues himself is justly undervalued by others. Whatever good properties he may possess are, in fact, neutralised by a 'cold rheum' running through his veins, and taking away the zest of his pretensions, the pith and marrow of his performances. What is it to me that I can write these TABLE-TALKS? It is true I can, by a reluctant effort, rake up a parcel of half-forgotten observations, but they do not float on the surface of my mind, nor stir it with any sense of pleasure, nor even of pride. Others have more property in them than I have: they may reap the benefit, I have only had the pain. Otherwise, they are to me as if they had never existed; nor should I know that I had ever thought at all, but that I am reminded of it by the strangeness of my appearance, and my unfitness for everything else. Look in Coleridge's face while he is talking. His words are such as might 'create a soul under the ribs of death.' His face is a blank. Which are we to consider as the true index of his mind? Pain, languor, shadowy remembrances, are the uneasy inmates there: his lips move mechanically!

There are people that we do not like, though we may have known them long, and have no fault to find with them, 'their appearance, as we say, is so much against them.' That is not all, if we could find it out. There is, generally, a reason for this prejudice; for nature is true to itself. They may be very good sort of people too, in their way, but still something is the matter. There is a coldness, a selfishness, a levity, an insincerity, which we cannot fix upon any particular phrase or action, but we see it in their whole persons and deportment. One reason that we do not see it in any other way may be, that they are all the time trying to conceal this defect by every means in their power. There is, luckily, a sort of *second sight* in morals: we discern the lurking indications of temper and habit a long while before their palpable effects appear. I once used to meet with a person at an ordinary, a very civil, good-looking man in other respects, but with an odd look about his eyes, which I could not explain, as if he saw you under their fringed lids, and you could not see him again: this man was a common sharper. The greatest hypocrite I ever knew was a little, demure, pretty, modest-looking girl, with eyes timidly cast upon the ground, and an air soft as enchantment; the only circumstance that could lead to a suspicion of her true character was a cold, sullen, watery, glazed look about the eyes, which she bent on vacancy, as if determined to avoid all explanation with yours. I might have spied in their glittering, motionless surface the rocks and quicksands that awaited me below! We do not feel quite at ease in the company or friendship of those who have any natural obliquity or imperfection of person. The reason is, they are not on the best terms with themselves, and are sometimes apt to play off on others the tricks that nature has played them. This, however, is a remark that, perhaps, ought not to have been made. I know a person to whom it has been objected as a disqualification for friendship, that he never shakes you cordially by the hand. I own this is a damper to sanguine and florid temperaments, who abound in these practical demonstrations and 'compliments extern.' The same person who testifies the least pleasure at meeting you, is the last to quit his seat in your company, grapples with a subject in conversation right earnestly, and is, I take it, backward to give up a cause or a friend. Cold and distant in appearance, he piques himself on being the king of *good haters,* and a no less zealous partisan. The most phlegmatic constitutions often contain the most inflammable spirits—a fire is struck from the hardest flints.

And this is another reason that makes it difficult to judge of character. Extremes meet; and qualities display themselves by the most contradictory appearances. Any inclination, in consequence of being generally suppressed, vents itself the more violently when an opportunity presents itself: the greatest grossness sometimes accompanies the greatest refinement, as a natural relief, one to the other; and we find the most reserved and indifferent tempers at the beginning of an entertainment, or an acquaintance, turn out the most communicative and cordial at the end of it. Some spirits exhaust themselves at first: others gain strength by progression. Some minds have a greater facility of throwing off impressions—are, as it were, more transparent or porous than others. Thus the French present a marked contrast to the English in this respect. A Frenchman addresses you at once with a sort of lively indifference: an Englishman is more on his guard, feels his way, and is either exceedingly reserved, or lets you into his whole confidence, which he cannot so well impart to an entire stranger. Again, a Frenchman is naturally humane: an Englishman is, I should say, only friendly by habit. His virtues and his vices cost him more than they do his more gay and volatile neighbours. An Englishman is said to speak his mind more plainly than others,—yes, if it will give you pain to hear it. He does not care whom he offends by his discourse: a foreigner generally strives to oblige in what he says. The French are accused of promising more than they perform. That may be, and yet they may perform as many good-natured acts as the English, if the latter are as averse to perform as they are to promise. Even the professions of the French may be sincere at the time, or arise out of the impulse of the moment; though their desire to serve you may be neither very violent nor very lasting. I cannot think, notwithstanding, that the French are not a serious people; nay, that they are not a more reflecting people than the common run of the English. Let those who think them merely light and mercurial explain that enigma, their everlasting prosing tragedy. The English are considered as comparatively a slow, plodding people. If the French are quicker, they are also more plodding. See, for example, how highly finished and elaborate their works of art are! How systematic and correct they aim at being in all their productions of a graver cast! 'If the French have a fault,' as Yorick said, 'it is that they are too grave.' With wit, sense, cheerfulness, patience, good-nature, and refinement of manners, all they want is imagination and sturdiness of moral principle! Such are some of the contradictions in the character of the two nations, and so little does the character of either appear to have been understood! Nothing can be more ridiculous indeed than the way in which we exaggerate each other's vices and extenuate our own. The whole is an affair of prejudice on one side of the question, and of partiality on the other. Travellers who set out to carry back a true report of the case appear to lose not only the use of their understandings, but of their senses, the instant they set foot in a foreign land. The commonest facts and appearances are distorted and discoloured. They go abroad with certain preconceived notions on the subject, and they make everything answer, in reason's spite, to their favourite theory. In addition to the difficulty of explaining customs and manners foreign to our own, there are all the obstacles of wilful prepossession thrown in the way. It is not, therefore, much to be wondered at that nations have arrived at so little knowledge of one another's characters; and that, where the object has been to widen the breach between them, any slight differences that occur are easily blown into a blaze of fury by repeated misrepresentations, and all the exaggerations that malice or folly can invent!

This ignorance of character is not confined to foreign nations: we are ignorant of that of our own countrymen in a class a little below or above ourselves. We shall hardly pretend to pronounce magisterially on the good or bad qualities of strangers; and, at the same time, we are ignorant of those of our friends, of our kindred, and of our own. We are in all these cases either too near or too far off the object to judge of it properly.

Persons, for instance, in a higher or middle rank of life know little or nothing of the characters of those below them, as servants, country people, etc. I would lay it down in the first place as a general rule on this subject, that all uneducated people are hypocrites. Their sole business is to deceive. They conceive themselves in a state of hostility with others, and stratagems are fair in war. The inmates of the kitchen and the parlour are always (as far as respects their feelings and intentions towards each other) in Hobbes's; 'state of nature.' Servants and others in that line of life have nothing to exercise their spare talents for invention upon but those about them. Their superfluous electrical particles of wit and fancy are not carried off by those established and fashionable conductors, novels and romances. Their faculties are not buried in books, but all alive and stirring, erect and bristling like a cat's back. Their coarse conversation sparkles with 'wild wit, invention ever new.' Their betters try all they can to set themselves up above them, and they try all they can to pull them down to their own level. They do this by getting up a little comic interlude, a daily, domestic, homely drama out of the odds and ends of the family failings, of which there is in general a pretty plentiful supply, or make up the deficiency of materials out of their own heads. They turn the qualities of their masters and mistresses inside out, and any real kindness or condescension only sets them the more against you. They are not to be taken in that way—they will not be baulked in the spite they have to you. They only set to work with redoubled alacrity, to lessen the favour or to blacken your character. They feel themselves like a degraded *caste,* and cannot understand how the obligations can be all on one side, and the advantages all on the other. You cannot come to equal terms with them—they reject all such overtures as insidious and hollow—nor can you ever calculate upon their gratitude or goodwill, any more than if they were so many strolling Gipsies or wild Indians. They have no fellow-feeling, they keep no faith with the more privileged classes. They are in your power, and they endeavour to be even with you by trick and cunning, by lying and chicanery. In this they have nothing to restrain them. Their whole life is a succession of shifts, excuses, and expedients. The love of truth is a principle with those only who have made it their study, who have applied themselves to the pursuit of some art or science, where the intellect is severely tasked, and learns by habit to take a pride in, and to set a just value on, the correctness of its conclusions. To have a disinterested regard to truth, the mind must have contemplated it in abstract and remote questions; whereas the ignorant and vulgar are only conversant with those things in which their own interest is concerned. All their notions are local, personal, and consequently gross and selfish. They say whatever comes uppermost—turn whatever happens to their own account—and invent any story, or give any answer that suits their purposes. Instead of being bigoted to general principles, they trump up any lie for the occasion, and the more of a *thumper* it is, the better they like it; the more unlooked-for it is, why, so much the more of a *God-send!* They have no conscience about the matter; and if you find them out in any of their manoeuvres, are not ashamed of themselves, but angry with you. If you remonstrate with them, they laugh in your face. The only hold you have of them is their interest—you can but dismiss them from your employment; and *service is no inheritance.* If they effect anything like decent remorse, and hope you will pass it over, all the while they are probably trying to recover the wind of you. Persons of liberal knowledge or sentiments have no kind of chance in this sort of mixed intercourse with these barbarians in civilised life. You cannot tell, by any signs or principles, what is passing in their minds. There is no common point of view between you. You have not the same topics to refer to, the same language to express yourself. Your interests, your feelings are quite distinct. You take certain things for granted as rules of action: they take nothing for granted but their own ends, pick up all their knowledge out of their own occasions, are on the watch only for what they can catch—are

Subtle as the fox for prey:

Like warlike as the wolf, for what they eat.

They have indeed a regard to their character, as this last may affect their livelihood or advancement, none as it is connected with a sense of propriety; and this sets their mother-wit and native talents at work upon a double file of expedients, to bilk their consciences, and salve their reputation. In short, you never know where to have them, any more than if they were of a different species of animals; and in trusting to them, you are sure to be betrayed and overreached. You have other things to mind; they are thinking only of you, and how to turn you to advantage. *Give and take* is no maxim here. You can build nothing on your own moderation or on their false delicacy. After a familiar conversation with a waiter at a tavern, you overhear him calling you by some provoking nickname. If you make a present to the daughter of the house where you lodge, the mother is sure to recollect some addition to her bill. It is a running fight. In fact, there is a principle in human nature not willingly to endure the idea of a superior, a sour, jacobinical disposition to wipe out the score of obligation, or efface the tinsel of external advantages—and where others have the opportunity of coming in contact with us, they generally find the means to establish a sufficiently marked degree of degrading equality. No man is a hero to his valet-de-chambre, is an old maxim. A new illustration of this principle occurred the other day. While Mrs. Siddons was giving her readings of Shakespear to a brilliant and admiring drawing-room, one of the servants in the hall below was saying, 'What, I find the old lady is making as much noise as ever!' So little is there in common between the different classes of society, and so impossible is it ever to unite the diversities of custom and knowledge which separate them.

Women, according to Mrs. Peachum, are 'bitter bad judges' of the characters of men; and men are not much better of theirs, if we can form any guess from their choice in marriage. Love is proverbially blind. The whole is an affair of whim and fancy. Certain it is that the greatest favourites with the other sex are not those who are most liked or respected among their own. I never knew but one clever man who was what is called a *lady's man;* and he (unfortunately for the argument) happened to be a considerable coxcomb. It was by this irresistible quality, and not by the force of his genius, that he vanquished. Women seem to doubt their own judgments in love, and to take the opinion which a man entertains of his own prowess and accomplishments for granted. The wives of poets are (for the most part) mere pieces of furniture in the room. If you speak to them of their husbands' talents or reputation in the world, it is as if you made mention of some office that they held. It can hardly be otherwise, when the instant any subject is started or conversation arises, in which men are interested, or try one another's strength, the women leave the room, or attend to something else. The qualities, then, in which men are ambitious to excel, and which ensure the applause of the world,—eloquence, genius, learning, integrity,—are not those which gain the favour of the fair. I must not deny, however, that wit and courage have this effect. Neither is youth or beauty the sole passport to their affections.

The way of woman's will is hard to find,

Harder to hit.

Yet there is some clue to this mystery, some determining cause; for we find that the same men are universal favourites with women, as others are uniformly disliked by them. Is not the loadstone that attracts so powerfully, and in all circumstances, a strong and undisguised bias towards them, a marked attention, a conscious preference of them to every other passing object or topic? I am not sure, but I incline to think so. The successful lover is the *cavalier servente* of all nations. The man of gallantry behaves as if he had made an assignation with every woman he addresses. An argument immediately draws off my attention from the prettiest woman in the room. I accordingly succeed better in argument—than in love!—I do not think that what is called *Love at first sight* is so great an absurdity as it is sometimes imagined to be. We generally make up our minds beforehand to the sort of person we should like,—grave or gay, black, brown, or fair; with golden tresses or with raven locks;—and when we meet with a complete example of the qualities we admire, the bargain is soon struck. We have never seen anything to come up to our newly-discovered goddess before, but she is what we have been all our lives looking for. The idol we fall down and worship is an image familiar to our minds. It has been present to our waking thoughts, it has haunted us in our dreams, like some fairy vision. Oh! thou who, the first time I over beheld thee, didst draw my soul into the circle of thy heavenly looks, and wave enchantment round me, do not think thy conquest less complete because it was instantaneous; for in that gentle form (as if another Imogen had entered) I saw all that I had ever loved of female grace, modesty, and sweetness!

I shall not say much of friendship as giving an insight into character, because it is often founded on mutual infirmities and prejudices. Friendships are frequently taken up on some sudden sympathy, and we see only as much as we please of one another's characters afterwards. Intimate friends are not fair witnesses to character, any more than professed enemies. They cool, indeed, in time, part, and retain only a rankling grudge of past errors and oversights. Their testimony in the latter case is not quite free from suspicion.

One would think that near relations, who live constantly together, and always have done so, must be pretty well acquainted with one another's characters. They are nearly in the dark about it. Familiarity confounds all traits of distinction: interest and prejudice take away the power of judging. We have no opinion on the subject, any more than of one another's faces. The Penates, the household gods, are veiled. We do not see the features of those we love, nor do we clearly distinguish their virtues or their vices. We take them as they are found in the lump,—by weight, and not by measure. We know all about the individuals, their sentiments, history, manners, words, actions, everything; but we know all these too much as facts, as inveterate, habitual impressions, as clothed with too many associations, as sanctified with too many affections, as woven too much into the web of our hearts, to be able to pick out the different threads, to cast up the items of the debtor and creditor account, or to refer them to any general standard of right and wrong. Our impressions with respect to them are too strong, too real, too much *sui generis,* to be capable of a comparison with anything but themselves. We hardly inquire whether those for whom we are thus interested, and to whom we are thus knit, are *better* or *worse* than others—the question is a kind of profanation—all we know is, they are *more* to us than any one else can be. Our sentiments of this kind are rooted and grow in us, and we cannot eradicate them by voluntary means. Besides, our judgments are bespoke, our interests take part with our blood. If any doubt arises, if the veil of our implicit confidence is drawn aside by any accident for a moment, the shock is too great, like that of a dislocated limb, and we recoil on our habitual impressions again. Let not that veil ever be rent entirely asunder, so that those images may be left bare of reverential awe, and lose their religion; for nothing can ever support the desolation of the heart afterwards.

The greatest misfortune that can happen among relations is a different way of bringing up, so as to set one another's opinions and characters in an entirely new point of view. This often lets in an unwelcome daylight on the subject, and breeds schisms, coldness, and incurable heart-burnings in families. I have sometimes thought whether the progress of society and march of knowledge does not do more harm in this respect, by loosening the ties of domestic attachment, and preventing those who are most interested in and anxious to think well of one another from feeling a cordial sympathy and approbation of each other's sentiments, manners, views, etc., than it does good by any real advantage to the community at large. The son, for instance, is brought up to the Church, and nothing can exceed the pride and pleasure the father takes in him while all goes on well in this favourite direction. His notions change, and he imbibes a taste for the Fine Arts. From this moment there is an end of anything like the same unreserved communication between them. The young man may talk with enthusiasm of his 'Rembrandts, Correggios, and stuff': it is all *Hebrew* to the elder; and whatever satisfaction he may feel in the hearing of his son's progress, or good wishes for his success, he is never reconciled to the new pursuit, he still hankers after the first object that he had set his mind upon. Again, the grandfather is a Calvinist, who never gets the better of his disappointment at his son's going over to the Unitarian side of the question. The matter rests here till the grandson, some years after, in the fashion of the day and 'infinite agitation of men's wit,' comes to doubt certain points in the creed in which he has been brought up, and the affair is all abroad again. Here are three generations made uncomfortable and in a manner set at variance by a veering point of theology, and the officious, meddling biblical critics! Nothing, on the other hand, can be more wretched or common than that upstart pride and insolent good fortune which is ashamed of its origin; nor are there many things more awkward than the situation of rich and poor relations. Happy, much happier, are those tribes and people who are confined to the same *caste* and way of life from sire to son, where prejudices are transmitted like instincts, and where the same unvarying standard of opinion and refinement blends countless generations in its improgressive, everlasting mould!

Not only is there a wilful and habitual blindness in near kindred to each other's defects, but an incapacity to judge from the quantity of materials, from the contradictoriness of the evidence. The chain of particulars is too long and massy for us to lift it or put it into the most approved ethical scales. The concrete result does not answer to any abstract theory, to any logical definition. There is black, and white, and grey, square and round—there are too many anomalies, too many redeeming points, in poor human nature, such as it actually is, for us to arrive at a smart, summary decision on it. We know too much to come to any hasty or partial conclusion. We do not pronounce upon the present act, because a hundred others rise up to contradict it. We suspend our judgments altogether, because in effect one thing unconsciously balances another; and perhaps this obstinate, pertinacious indecision would be the truest philosophy in other cases, where we dispose of the question of character easily, because we have only the smallest part of the evidence to decide upon. Real character is not one thing, but a thousand things; actual qualities do not conform to any factitious standard in the mind, but rest upon their own truth and nature. The dull stupor under which we labour in respect of those whom we have the greatest opportunities of inspecting nearly, we should do well to imitate before we give extreme and uncharitable verdicts against those whom we only see in passing or at a distance. If we knew them better, we should be disposed to say less about them.

In the truth of things, there are none utterly worthless, none without some drawback on their pretensions or some alloy of imperfection. It has been observed that a familiarity with the worst characters lessens our abhorrence of them; and a wonder is often expressed that the greatest criminals look like other men. The reason is that *they are like other men in many respects.* If a particular individual was merely the wretch we read of, or conceive in the abstract, that is, if he was the mere personified idea of the criminal brought to the bar, he would not disappoint the spectator, but would look like what he would be—a monster! But he has other qualities, ideas, feelings, nay, probably virtues, mixed up with the most profligate habits or desperate acts. This need not lessen our abhorrence of the crime, though it does of the criminal; for it has the latter effect only by showing him to us in different points of view, in which he appears a common mortal, and not the caricature of vice we took him for, or spotted all over with infamy. I do not, at the same time, think this is a lax or dangerous, though it is a charitable view of the subject. In my opinion, no man ever answered in his own mind (except in the agonies of conscience or of repentance, in which latter case he throws the imputation from himself in another way) to the abstract idea of a *murderer.* He may have killed a man in self-defence, or 'in the trade of war,' or to save himself from starving, or in revenge for an injury, but always 'so as with a difference,' or from mixed and questionable motives. The individual, in reckoning with himself, always takes into the account the considerations of time, place, and circumstance, and never makes out a case of unmitigated, unprovoked villainy, of 'pure defecated evil' against himself. There are degrees in real crimes: we reason and moralise only by names and in classes. I should be loth, indeed, to say that 'whatever is, is right'; but almost every actual choice inclines to it, with some sort of imperfect, unconscious bias. This is the reason, besides the ends of secrecy, of the invention of *slang* terms for different acts of profligacy committed by thieves, pickpockets, etc. The common names suggest associations of disgust in the minds of others, which those who live by them do not willingly recognise, and which they wish to sink in a technical phraseology. So there is a story of a fellow who, as he was writing down his confession of a murder, stopped to ask how the word *murder* was spelt; this, if true, was partly because his imagination was staggered by the recollection of the thing, and partly because he shrunk from the verbal admission of it. '*Amen* stuck in his throat'! The defence made by Eugene Aram of himself against a charge of murder, some years before, shows that he in imagination completely flung from himself the *nominal* crime imputed to him: he might, indeed, have staggered an old man with a blow, and buried his body in a cave, and lived ever since upon the money he found upon him, but there was 'no malice in the case, none at all,' as Peachum says. The very coolness, subtlety, and circumspection of his defence (as masterly a legal document as there is upon record) prove that he was guilty of the act, as much as they prove that he was unconscious of the *crime*.(2) In the same spirit, and I conceive with great metaphysical truth, Mr. Coleridge, in his tragedy of *Remorse,* makes Ordonio (his chief character) wave the acknowledgment of his meditated guilt to his own mind, by putting into his mouth that striking soliloquy:

```
Say, I had lay'd a body in the sun!
Well! in a month there swarm forth from the corse
A thousand, nay, ten thousand sentient beings
In place of that one man.  Say I had kill'd him!
Yet who shall tell me, that each one and all
Of these ten thousand lives Is not as happy
As that one life, which being push'd aside,
Made room for these unnumber'd.—Act ii. Sc. 2.
```

I am not sure, indeed, that I have not got this whole train of speculation from him; but I should not think the worse of it on that account. That gentleman, I recollect, once asked me whether I thought that the different members of a family really liked one another so well, or had so much attachment, as was generally supposed; and I said that I conceived the regard they had towards each other was expressed by the word *interest* rather than by any other, which he said was the true answer. I do not know that I could mend it now. Natural affection is not pleasure in one another's company, nor admiration of one another's qualities; but it is an intimate and deep knowledge of the things that affect those to whom we are bound by the nearest ties, with pleasure or pain; it is an anxious, uneasy fellow-feeling with them, a jealous watchfulness over their good name, a tender and unconquerable yearning for their good. The love, in short, we bear them is the nearest to that we bear ourselves. *Home,* according to the old saying, *is home, be it never so homely.* We love ourselves, not according to our deserts, but our cravings after good: so we love our immediate relations in the next degree (if not, even sometimes a higher one), because we know best what they have suffered and what sits nearest to their hearts. We are implicated, in fact, in their welfare by habit and sympathy, as we are in our own.

```
If our devotion to our own interests is much the same as to theirs, we
are ignorant of our own characters for the same reason. We are parties
too much concerned to return a fair verdict, and are too much in
the secret of our own motives or situation not to be able to give a
favourable turn to our actions. We exercise a liberal criticism upon
ourselves, and put off the final decision to a late day. The field is
large and open. Hamlet exclaims, with a noble magnanimity, 'I count
myself indifferent honest, and yet I could accuse me of such things!'
If you could prove to a man that he is a knave, it would not make much
difference in his opinion, his self-love is stronger than his love of
virtue. Hypocrisy is generally used as a mask to deceive the world, not
to impose on ourselves: for once detect the delinquent in his knavery,
and he laughs in your face or glories in his iniquity. This at least
happens except where there is a contradiction in the character, and our
vices are involuntary and at variance with our convictions. One
great difficulty is to distinguish ostensible motives, or such as we
acknowledge to ourselves, from tacit or secret springs of action. A man
changes his opinion readily, he thinks it candour: it is levity of min
 We are callous by custom to our defects or excellences, unless where
vanity steps in to exaggerate or extenuate them. I cannot conceive how
it is that people are in love with their own persons, or astonished at
their own performances, which are but a nine days' wonder to every one
else. In general it may be laid down that we are liable to this twofold
mistake in judging of our own talents: we, in the first place, nurse the
rickety bantling, we think much of that which has cost us much pains
and labour, and comes against the grain; and we also set little store by
what we do with most ease to ourselves, and therefore best. The works of
the greatest genius are produced almost unconsciously, with an ignorance
on the part of the persons themselves that they have done anything
extraordinary. Nature has done it for them. How little Shakespear seems
```

to have thought of himself or of his fame! Yet, if 'to know another
well were to know one's self,' he must have been acquainted with his
own pretensions and character, 'who knew all qualities with a learned
spirit.' His eye seems never to have been bent upon himself, but
outwards upon nature. A man who thinks highly of himself may almost set
it down that it is without reason. Milton, notwithstanding, appears to
have had a high opinion of himself, and to have made it good. He was
conscious of his powers, and great by design. Perhaps his tenaciousness,
on the score of his own merit, might arise from an early habit of
polemical writing, in which his pretensions were continually called to
the bar of prejudice and party-spirit, and he had to plead not guilty to
the indictment. Some men have died unconscious of immortality, as others
have almost exhausted the sense of it in their lifetimes. Correggio
might be mentioned as an instance of the one, Voltaire of the other.

There is nothing that helps a man in his conduct through life more than a knowledge of his own characteristic weaknesses (which, guarded against, become his strength), as there is nothing that tends more to the success of a man's talents than his knowing the limits of his faculties, which are thus concentrated on some practicable object. One man can do but one thing. Universal pretensions end in nothing. Or, as Butler has it, too much wit requires

As much again to govern it.

There are those who have gone, for want of this self-knowledge, strangely out of their way, and others who have never found it. We find many who succeed in certain departments, and are yet melancholy and dissatisfied, because they failed in the one to which they first devoted themselves, like discarded lovers who pine after their scornful mistress. I will conclude with observing that authors in general overrate the extent and value of posthumous fame: for what (as it has been asked) is the amount even of Shakespear's fame? That in that very country which boasts his genius and his birth, perhaps, scarce one person in ten has ever heard of his name or read a syllable of his writings!

FN to ESSAY XV

(1) 'It is not a year or two shows us a man.'—AEmilia, in *Othello.*

(2) The bones of the murdered man were dug up in an old hermitage. On this, as one instance of the acuteness which he displayed all through the occasion, Aram remarks, 'Where would you expect to find the bones of a man sooner than in a hermit's cell, except you were to look for them in a cemetery?'—See *Newgate Calendar* for the year 1758 or 1759.

ESSAY XVI. ON THE PICTURESQUE AND IDEAL

(A Fragment)

The natural in visible objects is whatever is ordinarily presented to the senses: the picturesque is that which stands out and catches the attention by some striking peculiarity: the *ideal* is that which answers to the preconceived imagination and appetite in the mind for love and beauty. The picturesque depends chiefly on the principle of discrimination or contrast; the *ideal* on harmony and continuity of effect: the one surprises, the other satisfies the mind; the one starts off from a given point, the other reposes on itself; the one is determined by an excess of form, the other by a concentration of feeling.

The picturesque may be considered as something like an excrescence on the face of nature. It runs imperceptibly into the fantastical and grotesque. Fairies and satyrs are picturesque; but they are scarcely *ideal.* They are an extreme and unique conception of a certain thing, but not of what the mind delights in or broods fondly over. The image created by the artist's hand is not moulded and fashioned by the love of good and yearning after grace and beauty, but rather the contrary: that is they are ideal deformity, not ideal beauty. Rubens was perhaps the most picturesque of painters; but he was almost the least *ideal.* So Rembrandt was (out of sight) the most picturesque of colourists; as Correggio was the most *ideal.* In other words, his composition of light and shade is more a whole, more in unison, more blended into the same harmonious feeling than Rembrandt's, who staggers by contrast, but does not soothe by gradation. Correggio's forms, indeed, had a picturesque air; for they often incline (even when most beautiful) to the quaintness of caricature. Vandyke, I think, was at once the least picturesque and least *ideal* of all the great painters. He was purely natural, and neither selected from outward forms nor added anything from his own mind. He owes everything to perfect truth, clearness, and transparency; and though his productions certainly arrest the eye, and strike in a room full of pictures, it is from the contrast they present to other pictures, and from being stripped quite naked of all artificial advantages. They strike almost as a piece of white paper would, hung up in the same situation—I began with saying that whatever stands out from a given line, and as it were projects upon the eye, is picturesque; and this holds true (comparatively) in form and colour. A rough terrier dog, with the hair bristled and matted together, is picturesque. As we say, there is a decided character in it, a marked determination to an extreme point. A shock-dog is odd and disagreeable, but there is nothing picturesque in its appearance; it is a mere mass of flimsy confusion. A goat with projecting horns and pendent beard is a picturesque animal; a sheep is not. A horse is only picturesque from

117

opposition of colour; as in Mr. Northcote's study of Gadshill, where the white horse's head coming against the dark, scowling face of the man makes as fine a contrast as can be imagined. An old stump of a tree with rugged bark, and one or two straggling branches, a little stunted hedge-row line, marking the boundary of the horizon, a stubble-field, a winding path, a rock seen against the sky, are picturesque, because they have all of them prominence and a distinctive character of their own. They are not objects (to borrow Shakespear's phrase) 'of no mark or likelihood.' A country may be beautiful, romantic, or sublime, without being picturesque. The Lakes in the North of England are not picturesque, though certainly the most interesting sight in this country. To be a subject for painting, a prospect must present sharp, striking points of view or singular forms, or one object must relieve and set off another. There must be distinct stages and salient points for the eye to rest upon or start from in its progress over the expanse before it. The distance of a landscape will oftentimes look flat or heavy, that the trunk of a tree or a ruin in the foreground would immediately throw into perspective and turn to air. Rembrandt's landscapes are the least picturesque in the world, except from the straight lines and sharp angles, the deep incision and dragging of his pencil, like a harrow over the ground, and the broad contrast of earth and sky. Earth, in his copies, is rough and hairy; and Pan has struck his hoof against it!—A camel is a picturesque ornament in a landscape or history-piece. This is not merely from its romantic and oriental character; for an elephant has not the same effect, and if introduced as a necessary appendage, is also an unwieldy incumbrance. A negro's head in a group is picturesque from contrast; so are the spots on a panther's hide. This was the principle that Paul Veronese went upon, who said the rule for composition was *black upon white, and while upon black.* He was a pretty good judge. His celebrated picture of the Marriage of Cana is in all likelihood the completest piece of workmanship extant in the art. When I saw it, it nearly covered one side of a large room in the Louvre (being itself forty feet by twenty)—and it seemed as if that side of the apartment was thrown open, and you looked out at the open sky, at buildings, marble pillars, galleries with people in them, emperors, female slaves, Turks, negroes, musicians, all the famous painters of the time, the tables loaded with viands, goblets, and dogs under them—a sparkling, overwhelming confusion, a bright, unexpected reality—the only fault you could find was that no miracle was going on in the faces of the spectators: the only miracle there was the picture itself! A French gentleman, who showed me this 'triumph of painting' (as it has been called), perceiving I was struck with it, observed, 'My wife admires it exceedingly for the facility of the execution.' I took this proof of sympathy for a compliment. It is said that when Humboldt, the celebrated traveller and naturalist, was introduced to Buonaparte, the Emperor addressed him in these words—*'Vous aimez la botanique, Monsieur';* and on the other's replying in the affirmative, added, *'Et ma femme aussi!'* This has been found fault with as a piece of brutality and insolence in the great man by bigoted critics, who do not know what a thing it is to get a Frenchwoman to agree with them in any point. For my part, I took the observation as it was meant, and it did not put me out of conceit with myself or the picture that Madame M——liked it as well as *Monsieur l'Anglois.* Certainly, there could be no harm in that. By the side of it happened to be hung two allegorical pictures of Rubens (and in such matters he too was 'no baby'(1))—I don't remember what the figures were, but the texture seemed of wool or cotton. The texture of the Paul Veronese was not wool or cotton, but stuff, jewels, flesh, marble, air, whatever composed the essence of the varied subjects, in endless relief and truth of handling. If the Fleming had seen his two allegories hanging where they did, he would, without a question, have wished them far enough.

I imagine that Rubens's landscapes are picturesque: Claude's are *ideal*. Rubens is always in extremes; Claude in the middle. Rubens carries some one peculiar quality or feature of nature to the utmost verge of probability: Claude balances and harmonises different forms and masses with laboured delicacy, so that nothing falls short, no one thing overpowers another. Rainbows, showers, partial gleams of sunshine, moonlight, are the means with which Rubens produces his most gorgeous and enchanting effects: there are neither rainbows, nor showers, nor sudden bursts of sunshine, nor glittering moonbeams in Claude. He is all softness and proportion: the other is all spirit and brilliant excess. The two sides (for example) of one of Claude's landscapes balance one another, as in a scale of beauty: in Rubens the several objects are grouped and thrown together with capricious wantonness. Claude has more repose: Rubens more gaiety and extravagance. And here it might be asked, Is a rainbow a picturesque or an *ideal* object? It seems to me to be both. It is an accident in nature; but it is an inmate of the fancy. It startles and surprises the sense, but it soothes and tranquillises the spirit. It makes the eye glisten to behold it, but the mind turns to it long after it has faded from its place in the sky. It has both properties, then, of giving an extraordinary impulse to the mind by the singularity of its appearance, and of riveting the imagination by its intense beauty. I may just notice here in passing, that I think the effect of moonlight is treated in an *ideal* manner in the well-known line in Shakespear—

See how the moonlight *sleeps* upon yon bank.

The image is heightened by the exquisiteness of the expression beyond its natural beauty, and it seems as if there could be no end to the delight taken in it.—A number of sheep coming to a pool of water to drink, with shady trees in the background, the rest of the flock following them, and the shepherd and his dog left carelessly behind, is surely the *ideal* in landscape-composition, if the *ideal* has its source in the interest excited by a subject, in its power of drawing the affections after it linked in a golden chain, and in the desire of the mind to dwell on it for ever. The *ideal*, in a word, is the height of the pleasing, that which satisfies and accords with the inmost longing of the soul: the picturesque is merely a sharper and bolder impression of reality. A morning mist drawing a slender veil over all objects is at once picturesque and *ideal*; for it in the first place excites immediate surprise and admiration, and in the next a wish for it to continue, and a fear lest it should be too soon dissipated. Is the Cupid riding on a lion in the ceiling at Whitehall, and urging him with a spear over a precipice, with only clouds and sky beyond, most picturesque or *ideal*? It has every effect of startling contrast and situation, and yet inspires breathless expectation and wonder for the event. Rembrandt's Jacob's Dream, again, is both fearful to the eye, but realising that loftiest vision of the soul. Take two faces in Leonardo da Vinci's Last Supper, the Judas and the St John: the one is all strength, repulsive character; the other is all divine grace and mild sensibility. The individual, the characteristic in painting, is that *which is* in a marked manner—the *ideal* is that which we wish anything to be, and to contemplate without measure and without end. The first is truth, the last is good. The one appeals to the sense and understanding, the other to the will and the affections. The truly beautiful and grand attracts the mind to it by instinctive harmony, is absorbed in it, and nothing can ever part them afterwards. Look at a Madonna of Raphael's: what gives the *ideal* character to the expression,—the insatiable purpose of the soul, or its measureless content in the object of its contemplation? A portrait of Vandyke's is mere indifference and still-life in the comparison: it has not in it the principle of growing and still unsatisfied desire. In the *ideal* there is no fixed stint or limit but the limit of possibility: it is the infinite with respect to human capacities and wishes. Love is for this reason an *ideal* passion. We give to it our all of hope, of fear, of present enjoyment, and stake our last chance of happiness wilfully and desperately upon it. A good authority puts into the mouth of one of his heroines—

```
My bounty is as boundless as the sea,
My love as deep!
```

How many fair catechumens will there be found in all ages to repeat as much after Shakespear's Juliet!

FN to ESSAY XVI

(1) And surely Mandricardo was no baby. —HARRINGTON's *Ariosto.*

ESSAY XVII. ON THE FEAR OF DEATH

```
And our little life is rounded with a sleep.
```

Perhaps the best cure for the fear of death is to reflect that life has a beginning as well as an end. There was a time when we were not: this gives us no concern—why, then, should it trouble us that a time will come when we shall cease to be? I have no wish to have been alive a hundred years ago, or in the reign of Queen Anne: why should I regret and lay it so much to heart that I shall not be alive a hundred years hence, in the reign of I cannot tell whom?

When Bickerstaff wrote his Essays I knew nothing of the subjects of them; nay, much later, and but the other day, as it were, in the beginning of the reign of George III., when Goldsmith, Johnson, Burke, used to meet at the Globe, when Garrick was in his glory, and Reynolds was over head and ears with his portraits, and Sterne brought out the volumes of *Tristram Shandy* year by year, it was without consulting me: I had not the slightest intimation of what was going on: the debates in the House of Commons on the American War, or the firing at Bunker's Hill, disturbed not me: yet I thought this no evil—I neither ate, drank, nor was merry, yet I did not complain: I had not then looked out into this breathing world, yet I was well; and the world did quite as well without me as I did without it! Why, then, should I make all this outcry about parting with it, and being no worse off than I was before? There is nothing in the recollection that at a certain time we were not come into the world that 'the gorge rises at'—why should we revolt at the idea that we must one day go out of it? To die is only to be as we were before we were born; yet no one feels any remorse, or regret, or repugnance, in contemplating this last idea. It is rather a relief and disburthening of the mind: it seems to have been holiday-time with us then: we were not called to appear upon the stage of life, to wear robes or tatters, to laugh or cry, be hooted or applauded; we had lain *perdus* all this while, snug, out of harm's way; and had slept out our thousands of centuries without wanting to be waked up; at peace and free from care, in a long nonage, in a sleep deeper and calmer than that of infancy, wrapped in the softest and finest dust. And the worst that we dread is, after a short, fretful, feverish being, after vain hopes and idle fears, to sink to final repose again, and forget the troubled dream of life!... Ye armed men, knights templars, that sleep in the stone aisles of that old Temple church, where all is silent above, and where a deeper silence reigns below (not broken by the pealing organ), are ye not contented where ye lie? Or would you come out of your long homes to go to the Holy War? Or do ye complain that pain no longer visits you, that sickness has done its worst, that you have paid the last debt to nature, that you hear no more of the thickening phalanx of the foe, or your lady's waning love; and that while this ball of earth rolls its eternal round, no sound shall ever pierce through to disturb your lasting repose, fixed as the marble over your tombs, breathless as the grave that holds you! And thou, oh! thou, to whom my heart turns, and will turn while it has feeling left, who didst love in vain, and whose first was thy last sigh, wilt not thou too rest in peace (or wilt thou cry to me complaining from thy clay-cold bed) when that sad heart is no longer sad, and that sorrow is dead which thou wert only called into the world to feel!

It is certain that there is nothing in the idea of a pre-existent state that excites our longing like the prospect of a posthumous existence. We are satisfied to have begun life when we did; we have no ambition to have set out on our journey sooner; and feel that we have had quite enough to do to battle our way through since. We cannot say,

```
The wars we well remember of King Nine,
Of old Assaracus and Inachus divine.
```

Neither have we any wish: we are contented to read of them in story, and to stand and gaze at the vast sea of time that separates us from them. It was early days then: the world was not *well-aired* enough for us: we have no inclination to have been up and stirring. We do not consider the six thousand years of the world before we were born as so much time lost to us: we are perfectly indifferent about the matter. We do not grieve and lament that we did not happen to be in time to see the grand mask and pageant of human life going on in all that period; though we are mortified at being obliged to quit our stand before the rest of the procession passes.

It may be suggested in explanation of this difference, that we know from various records and traditions what happened in the time of Queen Anne, or even in the reigns of the Assyrian monarchs, but that we have no means of ascertaining what is to happen hereafter but by awaiting the event, and that our eagerness and curiosity are sharpened in proportion as we are in the dark about it. This is not at all the case; for at that rate we should be constantly wishing to make a voyage of discovery to Greenland or to the Moon, neither of which we have, in general, the least desire to do. Neither, in truth, have we any particular solicitude to pry into the secrets of futurity, but as a pretext for prolonging our own existence. It is not so much that we care to be alive a hundred or a thousand years hence, any more than to have been alive a hundred or a thousand years ago: but the thing lies here, that we would all of us wish the present moment to last for ever. We would be as we are, and would have the world remain just as it is, to please us.

```
The present eye catches the present object—
```

to have and to hold while it may; and abhors, on any terms, to have it torn from us, and nothing left in its room. It is the pang of parting, the unloosing our grasp, the breaking asunder some strong tie, the leaving some cherished purpose unfulfilled, that creates the repugnance to go, and 'makes calamity of so long life,' as it often is.

    O! thou strong heart!
    There's such a covenant 'twixt the world and thee
    They're loth to break!

The love of life, then, is an habitual attachment, not an abstract principle. Simply *to be* does not 'content man's natural desire': we long to be in a certain time, place, and circumstance. We would much rather be now, 'on this bank and shoal of time,' than have our choice of any future period, than take a slice of fifty or sixty years out of the Millennium, for instance. This shows that our attachment is not confined either to *being* or to *well-being*; but that we have an inveterate prejudice in favour of our immediate existence, such as it is. The mountaineer will not leave his rock, nor the savage his hut; neither are we willing to give up our present mode of life, with all its advantages and disadvantages, for any other that could be substituted for it. No man would, I think, exchange his existence with any other man, however fortunate. We had as lief *not be*, as *not be ourselves*. There are some persons of that reach of soul that they would like to live two hundred and fifty years hence, to see to what height of empire America will have grown up in that period, or whether the English constitution will last so long. These are points beyond me. But I confess I should like to live to see the downfall of the Bourbons. That is a vital question with me; and I shall like it the better, the sooner it happens!

No young man ever thinks he shall die. He may believe that others will, or assent to the doctrine that 'all men are mortal' as an abstract proposition, but he is far enough from bringing it home to himself individually.(1) Youth, buoyant activity, and animal spirits, hold absolute antipathy with old age as well as with death; nor have we, in the hey-day of life, any more than in the thoughtlessness of childhood, the remotest conception how

    This sensible warm motion can become
    A kneaded clod—

nor how sanguine, florid health and vigour, shall 'turn to withered, weak, and grey.' Or if in a moment of idle speculation we indulge in this notion of the close of life as a theory, it is amazing at what a distance it seems; what a long, leisurely interval there is between; what a contrast its slow and solemn approach affords to our present gay dreams of existence! We eye the farthest verge of the horizon, and think what a way we shall have to look back upon, ere we arrive at our journey's end; and without our in the least suspecting it, the mists are at our feet, and the shadows of age encompass us. The two divisions of our lives have melted into each other: the extreme points close and meet with none of that romantic interval stretching out between them that we had reckoned upon; and for the rich, melancholy, solemn hues of age, 'the sear, the yellow leaf,' the deepening shadows of an autumnal evening, we only feel a dank, cold mist, encircling all objects, after the spirit of youth is fled. There is no inducement to look forward; and what is worse, little interest in looking back to what has become so trite and common. The pleasures of our existence have worn themselves out, are 'gone into the wastes of time,' or have turned their indifferent side to us: the pains by their repeated blows have worn us out, and have left us neither spirit nor inclination to encounter them again in retrospect. We do not want to rip up old grievances, nor to renew our youth like the phoenix, nor to live our lives twice over. Once is enough. As the tree falls, so let it lie. Shut up the book and close the account once for all!

It has been thought by some that life is like the exploring of a passage that grows narrower and darker the farther we advance, without a possibility of ever turning back, and where we are stifled for want of breath at last. For myself, I do not complain of the greater thickness of the atmosphere as I approach the narrow house. I felt it more formerly,(2) when the idea alone seemed to suppress a thousand rising hopes, and weighed upon the pulses of the blood. At present I rather feel a thinness and want of support, I stretch out my hand to some object and find none, I am too much in a world of abstraction; the naked map of life is spread out before me, and in the emptiness and desolation I see Death coming to meet me. In my youth I could not behold him for the crowd of objects and feelings, and Hope stood always between us, saying, 'Never mind that old fellow!' If I had lived indeed, I should not care to die. But I do not like a contract of pleasure broken off unfulfilled, a marriage with joy unconsummated, a promise of happiness rescinded. My public and private hopes have been left a ruin, or remain only to mock me. I would wish them to be re-edified. I should like to see some prospect of good to mankind, such as my life began with. I should like to leave some sterling work behind me. I should like to have some friendly hand to consign me to the grave. On these conditions I am ready, if not willing, to depart. I shall then write on my tomb—GRATEFUL AND CONTENTED! But I have thought and suffered too much to be willing to have thought and suffered in vain.—In looking back, it sometimes appears to me as if I had in a manner slept out my life in a dream or shadow on the side of the hill of knowledge, where I have fed on books, on thoughts, on pictures, and only heard in half-murmurs the trampling of busy feet, or the noises of the throng below. Waked out of this dim, twilight existence, and startled with the passing scene, I have felt a wish to descend to the world of realities, and join in the chase. But I fear too late, and that I had better return to my bookish chimeras and indolence once more! *Zanetto, lascia le donne, et studia la matematica.* I will think of it.

It is not wonderful that the contemplation and fear of death become more familiar to us as we approach nearer to it: that life seems to ebb with the decay of blood and youthful spirits; and that as we find everything about us subject to chance and change, as our strength and beauty die, as our hopes and passions, our friends and our affections leave us, we begin by degrees to feel ourselves mortal!

I have never seen death but once, and that was in an infant. It is years ago. The look was calm and placid, and the face was fair and firm. It was as if a waxen image had been laid out in the coffin, and strewed with innocent flowers. It was not like death, but more like an image of life! No breath moved the lips, no pulse stirred, no sight or sound would enter those eyes or ears more. While I looked at it, I saw no pain was there; it seemed to smile at the short pang of life which was over: but I could not bear the coffin-lid to be closed—it seemed to stifle me; and still as the nettles wave in a corner of the churchyard over his little grave, the welcome breeze helps to refresh me, and ease the tightness at my breast!

An ivory or marble image, like Chantry's monument of the two children, is contemplated with pure delight. Why do we not grieve and fret that the marble is not alive, or fancy that it has a shortness of breath? It never was alive; and it is the difficulty of making the transition from life to death, the struggle between the two in our imagination, that confounds their properties painfully together, and makes us conceive that the infant that is but just dead, still wants to breathe, to enjoy, and look about it, and is prevented by the icy hand of death, locking up its faculties and benumbing its senses; so that, if it could, it would complain of its own hard state. Perhaps religious considerations reconcile the mind to this change sooner than any others, by representing the spirit as fled to another sphere, and leaving the body behind it. So in reflecting on death generally, we mix up the idea of life with it, and thus make it the ghastly monster it is. We think, how we should feel, not how the dead feel.

> Still from the tomb the voice of nature cries;
> Even in our ashes live their wonted fires!

There is an admirable passage on this subject in Tucker's *Light of Nature Pursued*, which I shall transcribe, as by much the best illustration I can offer of it.

'The melancholy appearance of a lifeless body, the mansion provided for it to inhabit, dark, cold, close and solitary, are shocking to the imagination; but it is to the imagination only, not the understanding; for whoever consults this faculty will see at first glance, that there is nothing dismal in all these circumstances; if the corpse were kept wrapped up in a warm bed, with a roasting fire in the chamber, it would feel no comfortable warmth therefrom; were store of tapers lighted up as soon as day shuts in, it would see no objects to divert it; were it left at large it would have no liberty, nor if surrounded with company would be cheered thereby; neither are the distorted features expressions of pain, uneasiness, or distress. This every one knows, and will readily allow upon being suggested, yet still cannot behold, nor even cast a thought upon those objects without shuddering; for knowing that a living person must suffer grievously under such appearances, they become habitually formidable to the mind, and strike a mechanical horror, which is increased by the customs of the world around us.'

There is usually one pang added voluntarily and unnecessarily to the fear of death, by our affecting to compassionate the loss which others will have in us. If that were all, we might reasonably set our minds at rest. The pathetic exhortation on country tombstones, 'Grieve not for me, my wife and children dear,' etc., is for the most part speedily followed to the letter. We do not leave so great a void in society as we are inclined to imagine, partly to magnify our own importance, and partly to console ourselves by sympathy. Even in the same family the gap is not so great; the wound closes up sooner than we should expect. Nay, *our room* is not unfrequently thought better than *our company*. People walk along the streets the day after our deaths just as they did before, and the crowd is not diminished. While we were living, the world seemed in a manner to exist only for us, for our delight and amusement, because it contributed to them. But our hearts cease to beat, and it goes on as usual, and thinks no more about us than it did in our lifetime. The million are devoid of sentiment, and care as little for you or me as if we belonged to the moon. We live the week over in the Sunday's paper, or are decently interred in some obituary at the month's end! It is not surprising that we are forgotten so soon after we quit this mortal stage; we are scarcely noticed while we are on it. It is not merely that our names are not known in China—they have hardly been heard of in the next street. We are hand and glove with the universe, and think the obligation is mutual. This is an evident fallacy. If this, however, does not trouble us now, it will not hereafter. A handful of dust can have no quarrel to pick with its neighbours, or complaint to make against Providence, and might well exclaim, if it had but an understanding and a tongue, 'Go thy ways, old world, swing round in blue ether, voluble to every age, you and I shall no more jostle!'

It is amazing how soon the rich and titled, and even some of those who have wielded great political power, are forgotten.

> A little rule, a little sway,
> Is all the great and mighty have
> Betwixt the cradle and the grave—

and, after its short date, they hardly leave a name behind them. 'A great man's memory may, at the common rate, survive him half a year.' His heirs and successors take his titles, his power, and his wealth—all that made him considerable or courted by others; and he has left nothing else behind him either to delight or benefit the world. Posterity are not by any means so disinterested as they are supposed to be. They give their gratitude and admiration only in return for benefits conferred. They cherish the memory of those to whom they are indebted for instruction and delight; and they cherish it just in proportion to the instruction and delight they are conscious they receive. The sentiment of admiration springs immediately from this ground, and cannot be otherwise than well founded.(3)

The effeminate clinging to life as such, as a general or abstract idea, is the effect of a highly civilised and artificial state of society. Men formerly plunged into all the vicissitudes and dangers of war, or staked their all upon a single die, or some one passion, which if they could not have gratified, life became a burden to them—now our strongest passion is to think, our chief amusement is to read new plays, new poems, new novels, and this we may do at our leisure, in perfect security, *ad infinitum*. If we look into the old histories and romances, before the *belles-lettres* neutralised human affairs and reduced passion to a state of mental equivocation, we find the heroes and heroines not setting their lives 'at a pin's fee,' but rather courting opportunities of throwing them away in very wantonness of spirit. They raise their fondness for some favourite pursuit to its height, to a pitch of madness, and think no price too dear to pay for its full gratification. Everything else is dross. They go to death as to a bridal bed, and sacrifice themselves or others without remorse at the shrine of love, of honour, of religion, or any other prevailing feeling. Romeo runs his 'sea-sick, weary bark upon the rocks' of death the instant he finds himself deprived of his Juliet; and she clasps his neck in their last agonies, and follows him to the same fatal shore. One strong idea takes possession of the mind and overrules every other; and even life itself, joyless without that, becomes an object of indifference or loathing. There is at least more of imagination in such a state of things, more vigour of feeling and promptitude to act, than in our lingering, languid, protracted attachment to life for its own poor sake. It is, perhaps, also better, as well as more heroical, to strike at some daring or darling object, and if we fail in that, to take the consequences manfully, than to renew the lease of a tedious, spiritless, charmless existence, merely (as Pierre says) 'to lose it afterwards in some vile brawl' for some worthless object. Was there not a spirit of martyrdom as well as a spice of the reckless energy of barbarism in this bold defiance of death? Had not religion something to do with it: the implicit belief in a future life, which rendered this of less value, and embodied something beyond it to the imagination; so that the rough soldier, the infatuated lover, the valorous knight, etc., could afford to throw away the present venture, and take a leap into the arms of futurity, which the modern sceptic shrinks back from, with all his boasted reason and vain philosophy, weaker than a woman! I cannot help thinking so myself; but I have endeavoured to explain this point before, and will not enlarge farther on it here.

A life of action and danger moderates the dread of death. It not only gives us fortitude to bear pain, but teaches us at every step the precarious tenure on which we hold our present being. Sedentary and studious men are the most apprehensive on this score. Dr. Johnson was an instance in point. A few years seemed to him soon over, compared with those sweeping contemplations on time and infinity with which he had been used to pose himself. In the *still-life* of a man of letters there was no obvious reason for a change. He might sit in an arm-chair and pour out cups of tea to all eternity. Would it had been possible for him to do so! The most rational cure after all for the inordinate fear of death is to set a just value on life. If we merely wish to continue on the scene to indulge our headstrong humours and tormenting passions, we had better begone at once; and if we only cherish a fondness for existence according to the good we derive from it, the pang we feel at parting with it will not be very severe!

FN to ESSAY XVII

(1) All men think all men mortal but themselves.

 —YOUNG.

(2) I remember once, In particular, having this feeling in reading Schiller's *Don Carlos*, where there is a description of death, in a degree that almost stifled me.

(3) It has been usual to raise a very unjust clamour against the enormous salaries of public singers, actors, and so on. This matter seems reducible to a moral equation. They are paid out of money raised by voluntary contributions in the strictest sense; and if they did not bring certain sums into the treasury, the managers would not engage them. These sums are exactly in proportion to the number of Individuals to whom their performance gives an extraordinary degree of pleasure. The talents of a singer, actor, etc., are therefore worth just as much as they will fetch.

Made in the USA
Coppell, TX
11 January 2024

27598631R00070